THE PERFECT BROTHER

CHRIS PATCHELL

Chris Patchell Ink
ISBN: 978-1-7335452-4-2
Salem, OR
Library of Congress Control Number: 2022905918

To my brother, Jeff, our family's golden boy, whose love and support have seen me through some of the best and worst days. Though you're pretty close to perfect, I'm willing to bet that I can still beat you at backgammon.

PROLOGUE

KATIE LORD KNEW HER FIANCÉ TIM COULDN'T POSSIBLY MEAN WHAT he'd said when he'd stormed out of her apartment last night. They weren't over. It was just a stupid argument. But for the hundredth time that morning, she picked up her phone, hoping to see a message. *Nothing.* Despite the dozens of texts she'd sent him, she hadn't received a single response. She checked her reception. It wouldn't be the first time she missed a message because the cellular network was crap.

Four bars.

Dammit.

Katie slammed down the phone, no longer able to deny the ugly truth. He was ignoring her, treating her as if everything was her fault.

Hell yes, she'd been angry. Any girl in her situation with a brain in her head would be. They were engaged, and yet he was getting text messages from a girl at work—a girl he claimed was "just a friend."

Just a friend, her ass. That damned girl was always sniffing around him. Whenever a group from work went out for beers, she was eager to join; and when the guys had planned an overnight camping trip, guess who wanted to tag along? Then when everyone else had dropped out... Well, it should have been obvious to Tim that the right thing to do would have been to cancel the trip. But no. They'd had to fight about it instead.

"Don't you trust me?" Tim had snapped, hands on his hips, glaring at Katie as if she was in the wrong.

"This isn't about you. It's about *her*."

"If you trusted me, we wouldn't be arguing about this."

Tim was dead wrong. If he wanted to act naïve and treat Katie like she was a jealous lunatic, then so be it, but Katie wasn't fooled. She knew how girls operated and this one didn't give a damn that Tim was engaged. She was trying to drive a wedge between Katie and Tim, and it was working.

Katie wrenched the engagement ring off her finger and stared at the ugly white tan line left behind. She tried to imagine what her life would be like without him, but she couldn't. Just the thought of it made her ache as if half of her soul had been stripped away. Shoving the ring back into place, Katie shook off her fears.

She was being ridiculous. Dramatic. Didn't Tim always say so? Once he'd had time to cool off, he'd call her, and they'd make up, the same way they always did.

Until then, she'd lose her mind if she spent another minute obsessing. Grabbing her phone, Katie plugged in her earbuds and headed outside. A run would be just the thing to get Tim off her mind and quiet the drumbeat of panic steadily building inside her.

The morning had started out rainy, but now the sun had pierced a hole in the angry clouds and set the maple leaves ablaze. Stunning shades of crimson and gold adorned the trees that bordered the twisty trail through the woods to the park.

Katie didn't bother stretching. Surely the steep uphill walk from her apartment to the trail would be enough of a warm-up. Jamming her favorite playlist, she broke into a lumbering jog, losing herself in Meghan Trainor's rendition of "Me Too." It was just the right song to shake off her dour mood.

A quarter mile into her run, Katie was already panting. With her chest heaving and heart pounding, she slowed. *Damn, this is hard.* It had been months since her last run. She didn't expect to feel winded quite so soon. Katie promised herself she would only walk long enough to catch her breath, then she'd hit it again. If she needed more motivation to get back into shape, her pathetic lack of cardio would be enough.

Besides, just last week Tim made a crack about the five pounds she'd gained since they'd gotten engaged. Five lousy pounds.

He was the one who insisted they swing by the coffee shop every morning before he dropped her off at school instead of going for a run. She would have suggested he go alone, but Katie didn't like the way the barista at the coffee shop flirted with him. Tim didn't seem to notice, and when she'd finally worked up the nerve to mention it, he'd accused her of being paranoid.

Easy for him to say. He wouldn't much like it if some strange guy was hitting on her. And why wouldn't someone hit on her? Despite the extra weight she was carrying, she still looked cute.

A burst of anger at Tim's thoughtlessness spurred her into another sprint. She'd get back into shape and then she'd be the one going on hiking trips with her friends instead of wasting hours waiting for a message that might never come. The thought of Tim waiting on her for a change cheered Katie.

By the time she made it to the center of the park, her heart rate crested one hundred fifty beats per minute. Half a mile. Not bad for her first run.

Katie flattened her palm against her chest and waited for her breath to slow, and that's when she felt it. The first pea-sized pellet of hail streaked down from an angry sky. Charcoal clouds gathered overhead and choked out the sun. The first strike was quickly followed by a second, and then...

Katie uttered an indignant squeal. Desperately scanning the trail, she searched for a place to take shelter and spied a white gazebo. She hurtled across the slippery grass as fast as her neon green Nikes would carry her and pounded up the steps. Katie slid to a sudden halt when she realized that she wasn't the only runner seeking shelter from the storm.

Tim.

Just the sight of him standing in the gazebo with his back turned sent an electric pulse of relief surging through her. Her hungry gaze devoured his broad shoulders and lean waist. She yanked out her earbuds and rushed toward him when he turned.

Tim's name died on her lips. Katie's hopes plummeted as she took in the man's face. It wasn't Tim, but there was something familiar about the handsome stranger. She studied his bronze complexion and ebony eyes, trying to place him. She'd seen him before, she was sure of it, but where? As if sensing her confusion, his mouth curved into a grin that made Katie's heart stop.

"Hell of a storm," he said.

Katie's breath sped up, forming dewy clouds in the cooling air. He had a killer smile.

"Sure is."

"You were running too?" he asked.

With a self-conscious grin, Katie glanced down at her bare legs, which she hadn't shaved in a few days, and shrugged.

"If you could call it that. I used to run every day, but it's been a while."

She was lying. Even back when she did run, she'd be lucky to make it out twice a week, but that sounded pathetic. From the way his rain-streaked hoodie clung to his well-toned torso, he looked in shape. His buff frame showed no hint of the slight paunch that Tim's belly was starting to form.

"Nice shoes," he said.

A glimmer of admiration flashed in his dark eyes as his gaze swept over her, from her flushed cheeks, all the way down to her size nine Nikes. She warmed under his lingering appraisal, wondering how long it had been since Tim had looked at her that way.

"The trail over by the reservoir is my favorite," he said. "What's yours?"

"I like the one through the woods."

God, could she sound any more lame? Hailstones struck the gazebo's tin roof in an atonal symphony that filled the silence between them.

"You're Katie, right?"

An unexpected thrill raced through her.

"Do I know you?"

He flashed an amused grin. "From school. Business ethics class."

Something clicked inside Katie's mind and her mouth dropped open.

"Oh my god, of course. You know how it is when you see someone out of context."

"Yeah."

He gave a quick laugh and shifted his gaze beyond her, watching the ice pellets bounce off the tin roof onto the grass. Goosebumps rippled across Katie's arms and she shivered, wishing she'd brought a jacket. As if reading her mind, he stripped off his sweatshirt and draped it around her shoulders. The soft fabric still held the warmth from his body. Katie hugged it close.

"Thank you."

"Seeing as how my run's pretty much shot for the day, want to grab some coffee? I know a place close by…"

Her pulse leapt at the unexpected question. It was dangerous. She was engaged. What would Tim say?

Nestled in the armband strapped around her bicep, Katie's phone buzzed. In that moment, a sudden realization struck her. She didn't give a damn what Tim thought. He was the one who had walked out on her. He was the one who saw no harm in flirting with the girl from work. And the barista. And god only knew who else.

It was just coffee. Nothing more.

Besides, a little harmless flirtation never killed anyone, right?

1

ONE HUNDRED SEVENTY-TWO DAYS UNTIL GRADUATION, AND THEN she'd get a real job. One that didn't start so damned early. Even god wasn't up yet, Mallory Riggins thought as she eased out of the apartment, locking the door behind her. The wind hissed through the towering pines, sending a damp chill racing through her. Deep shadows fell across the lawn, and not for the first time, she wished the security light mounted to the edge of the house still worked.

It was spooky out here alone. Normally, she parked her car in the garage, one of the few luxuries the small apartment carved out of the sprawling duplex offered, but the landlord's son had arrived home last night for an unexpected visit and had parked in her spot, which meant that she had to park her rust bucket on the side of the road.

The sound of the closing door triggered the landlord's dog. From somewhere up above, JoJo erupted into a barking fit. Mallory cringed.

"Hush, JoJo," she muttered, hoping the dog wouldn't rouse her roommate. Shelby was already annoyed that after two years, the dog still greeted them as if they were armed intruders.

The barking dog had jarred her awake last night too. Mallory hadn't bothered to see what was causing all the racket. Between her heavy class load, late-night study sessions, and her new boyfriend, she needed all the sleep she could get. As much as she would have preferred calling in sick and getting some extra rest, the meager funds in her bank account were already dangerously low, and somehow, she still had to make it through the end of the school year.

Then all she had to do was find a job that paid more than minimum wage to cover the rent, the utilities, and still have enough money left over to buy food. In a city as expensive as Vancouver, how hard could that be?

Mallory scrambled up the steep hill toward the roadside, her feet sliding in the wet earth. It had stormed overnight. Pine cones and downed branches lay scattered across the narrow road, shaken free from the fierce wind.

By the time she reached her car, Mallory was shivering, and her day, which already wasn't winning any awards, got a whole lot worse.

Pebbles of glass crunched beneath her feet. She stared at her car in dismay. The driver's side window was shattered.

The universe was definitely sending her a message, and if she had an ounce of common sense, she'd crawl back beneath the covers and start over. But that wasn't an option. With a broken window to fix, she needed the money from her job even more. Sheathing her hand with the sleeve of her coat, she swept the chunks of glass from the seat and climbed inside the car.

Rain had blown in through the broken window. The wet seat soaked through her jeans and Mallory groaned. She cranked the key and the sputtering engine coughed to life. Lights from the neighboring houses flickered on. The sleepy residential neighborhood was just beginning to stir to life as Mallory drove off.

The Daily Grind, with its brick walls, metal stools, and wooden tables, had a homey feel. The earthy scent of freshly roasted beans welcomed her as she pushed through the doors. For the next three hours, this place would be the first stop for every caffeine junkie in a five-mile radius starting out on their morning commute.

No sooner had she entered the shop when she locked gazes with her boss. There was no denying the fact that she was late. Rather than belabor the point, Mallory muttered an apology, strapped on her apron, and went to work.

Nothing about the morning had gone smoothly so far, so it should have come as no surprise when Mallory fumbled a hot cup of tea. It struck the edge of the countertop, spun around in a cartwheel, and sent a plume of hot water flying. Mallory jumped back, avoiding the worst of the spill, but a few stray drops scalded her forearm. She breathed in a painful hiss and grabbed a rag.

Meanwhile, the line tripled in size.

Ignoring the painful burn, she pinned on a frozen smile and greeted the next customer. *Mr. Quad Grande Breve.* He was cute with dark hair and kind eyes.

"The usual?" she asked.

"You always remember," he said with a grin. "Toss in an extra shot this morning, please. God knows, I could use it."

Puffy bags shadowed his dark eyes, and Mallory noticed that the poor guy looked as tired as she felt.

"A quad grande breve with an extra shot of love for Tim," she called to her boss, Jenn, who was working the machines. "That will be four dollars and ten cents."

Uncapping a black Sharpie, Mallory jotted down the drink order, and winced at the sting of the red welt forming on her arm.

"Are you okay?" Tim asked, gesturing toward the angry burn. "You really should get that under some cold water."

If it wasn't so damned busy, she would do just that, but with the lineup curving out the door, she didn't have time.

"'Tis but a flesh wound," Mallory quipped, making light of the pain.

"Kind of early for Monty Python, don't you think?"

Mallory grinned in surprise at his quick pick-up on the line. "Well, what can I say? So far, it's been a shitty day. My car was broken into last night."

"The Toyota?"

Mallory nodded. "They smashed the window."

"That sucks. What did they steal?"

She shrugged. "Not sure. I might need to sacrifice a chicken, or an eggplant, or whatever the universe deems necessary to get back into karma's good graces."

Tim chuckled, handing her a stack of one-dollar coins. Loonies. Mallory made change, which Tim dropped into the tip jar. The coins rang against the glass and she thanked him with a smile. The next customer in line uttered an impatient sigh. Mallory took the hint.

"Have a good one," she said to Tim.

"Hope your day gets better. If you need someone to fix your glass, or find a live chicken, I know a guy. He does good work."

"With the window or the chicken?" Mallory smirked.

"Both."

With a friendly wave, Tim was gone, and Mallory took the next order. Dozens of customers later, when the line finally began to subside, something he'd said stuck inside Mallory's mind.

"Wait. How does he know I drive a Toyota?"

She'd muttered the question under her breath. Both Tim and his drink were long gone.

"Who? Mr. Quad Grande Breve?" Jenn asked. "Any fool with eyes could see he's got a thing for you."

"Nah, he's got a girlfriend."

Jenn snorted. "That bitter pill? She wasn't with him this morning. Besides, you know how men are. My ex was onto his third girlfriend before I found out."

A single mother with two exes, Jenn never had a nice word to say about anyone.

"Maybe he's a stalker," Joe the dishwasher said.

Joe was an acting student. He was always mimicking someone, and this morning, it was Arnold Schwarzenegger, adapting a line from the movie *Kindergarten Cop*.

"Not you too," she groaned.

Joe chuckled and slid behind the counter, carrying a tray of freshly washed mugs. Mallory shook her head and took the next order. They were both paranoid. Mr. Quad Grande Breve...Tim... was a nice guy. He always asked how her day was going, and unlike most people she met, he seemed to care about the answer. And he always bought his girlfriend's drinks. Few guys she met at the shop were that considerate.

By ten o'clock the rush had slowed to a trickle. Mallory tallied her tips and grabbed her purse.

"Leaving?"

"Gotta run. Class awaits."

"Do it. Do it now," Joe called after her, still using the ridiculous Schwarzenegger voice.

Mallory rolled her eyes. "Hate to break it to you, Joe, but you're a foot and a half too short to make a convincing Arnie."

Even with his chest puffed out and stretched to his full height, Joe was still an inch or two shorter than she was.

"If Tom Cruise can play Jack Reacher, why can't I be the Terminator?"

"Point taken," she said with a laugh.

By the time Mallory left the shop, she'd forgotten all about the burn on her arm and Tim, and pretty much everything but school. Sheets of rain blew across the busy street. Mallory pulled her hood up and waited for a break in traffic. Why couldn't her car have been broken into on a day when it wasn't so blustery? By now, with the rain blowing through the busted window, the driver's seat would feel like a wet sponge.

The stream of traffic slowed, and Mallory dashed across the street. She didn't see the car that streaked around the corner until its headlights hit her square in the eyes. A burst of panic exploded inside her chest as she dodged out of the way. Tripping over a storm drain, she crashed to the ground beside her car, landing on all fours.

And that was when Mallory's phone broke.

2

FROM HIS VANTAGE POINT IN THE GAZEBO, DETECTIVE RAY Bradford surveyed the clearing while a dozen uniformed cops fanned out, searching the bushes for any sign of Katie Lord. The massive rhododendrons grew in thick stands, plugging the gaps between the towering cedar trees. While this time of year they lay dormant, in the spring they would burst into a riot of color that would breathe new life into the park.

His mother loved rhododendrons. She looked at them and saw hearty plants that were every gardener's dream. He looked at them and saw their massive sprawl as the perfect place for a would-be perpetrator to hide.

Just last month, they'd tracked down a rapist responsible for attacking a couple of women in Stanley Park. Young women who, like Katie Lord, insisted on jogging alone. You'd think after all the publicity that case had garnered that people would wise up and start jogging with friends. Barely more than a kid herself, Katie was like the majority of young women who believed wholeheartedly that nothing bad would ever happen to them. They were invincible. He dearly hoped that bravado hadn't cost Katie her life.

"Anything yet?" Detective Wes Moreland asked.

Cast-off droplets of rain clung to Moreland's jacket, shed by the evergreens swaying in the blustery November wind.

Bradford shook his head. "The Lord girl was gone for over twenty-four hours before anyone called it in."

With a slow shake of his head, Moreland said, "My kid's a freshman at U-Vic. She doesn't text me back within the hour, and I'm ready to deploy."

Bradford chuckled. "Our kids aren't like most kids. Safety protocols are hammered into the neuropathways of every cop's child from birth. The parents say that Katie was prone to drama. Said it wasn't unusual for her to go days without responding to her parents' texts."

Not only did Bradford consider this kind of behavior juvenile, he also knew that in situations like this, it could prove deadly.

"She was probably running with her headphones in, music cranked. No inkling whatsoever about what was going on around her."

"You think he watched?"

Moreland shrugged. "Maybe. Could have been a creeper. Could also have been a crime of opportunity—just another perv waiting for a girl running alone. Do you know how many sex offenders live within spitting distance of the park?"

Bradford blew out a breath. Steam billowed in the cold morning air. He swept his gaze across the interior of the gazebo, searching each centimeter of the gray plank floor for any signs of a struggle. Hair fibers caught in a nail. Brownish-red streaks of blood pooled into the grooves between the floorboards. But there was nothing. Nothing but rust-colored pine needles and decaying leaves.

Bradford descended the steps and headed across the mulch-covered path toward the rhododendrons. The beat cops had already searched the area, but Bradford couldn't resist looking around himself. He approached the thick tangle of brush where two paths met and parted the shrubbery, scouring the rich black earth for footprints, drag marks, some indication that Katie had been here.

With each minute that passed, another section of the park surrounding the gazebo was examined, and Bradford's hopes of finding anything of interest dimmed. Too much time had passed. Too many people were in and out of this park every day. He'd all but given up when he swept a thatch of ferns with his foot and caught a glint of an object half-buried in the dirt.

The object was shiny. *Plastic.*

"Got something," he called over his shoulder to Moreland.

His knees cracked in protest as he hunkered down to retrieve the object. Moreland's footsteps thundered across the grass. He stopped on the path behind Bradford.

Pulling on a fresh set of gloves, Bradford reached beneath the ferns and withdrew the object. A cell phone. He turned it over in his hands. He stared at the image rendered on the back and felt the same hitch in his chest he always did when the case involved a kid.

"Didn't Katie's parents say something about a cartoon character on her phone?"

Moreland gave a grim nod. "Yeah. That's it. Akko. She's an anime character from the *Little Witch Academia* series, a Harry Potter sort of thing."

"How do you know that?"

"My kid was into anime for a time."

"Well, shit."

Bradford blew out a breath and bagged the evidence. Slowly

rising from the ground, he brushed the dirt from the cuffs of his pants. Back at the station, he'd make the kind of call he always dreaded in cases like this. He'd call the parents. Tell them what he'd found. The evidence indicated that Katie hadn't disappeared on her own.

She was taken.

3

Indira Saraf tried not to squirm as she listened to the presentation about the new product direction. For years they had been harvesting data from consumer cell phones and spinning it into marketing gold—everything from what brand of toothpaste you bought, to the songs on your Spotify playlist, to where you liked to walk your dog.

It was downright freaky all the data they collected for their marketing application, and until now, she'd been able to hold her nose and ignore the slow accumulation of disdain she felt about what they were doing. Harvesting data was one thing, but using AI and machine learning to predict customer patterns and create individual profiles... It was so invasive, going well beyond general patterns into the specifics of an individual's daily life. It didn't matter how much incomprehensible gobbledygook they crammed into the terms of use agreements. There were certain ethical lines relating to privacy that she had no wish to cross.

Selling people more of what they didn't need wasn't why she'd gotten into software development in the first place. They were supposed to be making people's lives better instead of kowtowing to the Instant Gratification Monkey, driving hapless souls with a tragic lack of impulse control into the poorhouse. And for what? So they could listen to the latest Miley Cyrus aberration through headphones that cost more than a week's worth of groceries?

Seriously. She needed to look for another job at a company that was interested in making the world a better place. Maybe the Gates Foundation had some openings. Maybe a local non-profit.

In the back of her mind, Indira heard her father scoff. *A non-profit? I didn't move to this country so you could throw away your education and work for the same kind of wages you'd make serving Frappuccinos at Starbucks.*

Of the six software engineers sitting around the conference room table, she was the only one who looked like she wanted to vomit. Preet Chopra, their charismatic senior director of engineering, was broadcasting the product strategy from a boardroom in San Jose to the Vancouver team watching on video. Some of her colleagues were bobbing their heads with enthusiastic grins, while others jotted down notes.

"Using replay technology, we can play back customers' cell phone usage data to predict consumer patterns, like our test user Sunny, who meets her girlfriends every Sunday morning for brunch at Medina Café. Now based on her cell phone data..." Preet paused and touched the screen, which showed three digital ads that Sunny had clicked on in the past week. "We know that she's been looking for the perfect sandals to take on her trip to Cabo next month."

The image on the display changed to show a pair of orange strappy sandals with three-inch wedge heels that Indira wouldn't be caught dead in. She preferred her well-worn Converse, although the thought of adding another three inches to her five-foot frame was appealing. The display also showed the resort where Sunny would be staying, as well as her arrival and departure dates. Creepy.

"Because we know the path Sunny usually takes to the restaurant, we know she'll pass by at least three stores selling similar shoes. Real-time coupons will be sent via text message to Sunny's phone," Dylan Marsh, the project lead said, picking up on Preet's train of thought. "We can also send her a daily deal for a glass bottom boat tour she can take from the resort."

"Exactly, and each time one of our coupons is clicked, we get a slice of the transaction," Preet said with a bright smile.

Of course Dylan was quick to jump in. He was such a kiss ass. Such a shame that a brain like his was wasted on building a shopping algorithm instead of working on a cause that held more social value, like building programs to feed the hungry, or helping doctors diagnose and treat cancer, or securing the power grid from terrorist attacks.

God, she needed out of here.

"You've been unusually quiet today, Indira. What are your thoughts?"

Preet's curious look stretched through the video screen and rested on her. Typically by now, she and Dylan would be sparring over competing opinions on whose technical approach was best. But not today. Indira leaned forward and swept her gaze around the table, regarding the team.

"Am I the only one who thinks this is a bad idea?"

She glanced over at her friend Sabina, who was the in-house counsel for the company. Surely Sabina of all people understood the legal perils they faced, but Sabina's expression remained inscrutable, and she avoided Indira's gaze. In the awkward silence that followed, no one was looking her way. No one except Preet, and Dylan.

"Maybe we should just let Sunny drink mimosas with her

friends while we find something more worthwhile to focus our efforts on."

"Such as what?" Dylan asked.

Indira refused to be intimidated by Dylan's imperious tone. She met his direct gaze with a steely one of her own.

"Something less stalkery."

"The data tells a story." Dylan shrugged, as if this absolved them of responsibility.

Surely she wasn't the only one who had taken classes in business ethics, but not one of her fellow engineers spoke up. As usual. *Cowards.* She had become the mechanism through which they voiced their concerns. Not Dylan. Not Preet. Which meant that she was the only one squandering her precious political capital doing what she felt was right.

Indira threw her hands up in an exasperated gesture as she surveyed the team. "What happened to privacy? We shouldn't know where Sunny has brunch, let alone where she's heading on vacation. It's bad enough that we know where she likes to shop..."

She gestured toward the whiteboard at the stereotyped user profile they had concocted of Sunny the shopaholic. Angry. Frustrated. No one was listening.

"People have a right to privacy."

"A right they signed away when they agreed to the terms of use on their phones," Dylan cut in without missing a beat.

Indira's hackles rose.

"You mean the twenty pages of fine print they never read? Have you read them?"

"Of course. Have you?"

Indira ignored Dylan's pointed question. As if struck by a genius notion, she stabbed her finger into the air.

"I know. Maybe we could construct a meme directing people to post their porn star name by combining the name of their first pet with their mother's maiden name. Surely that's the kind of data we could use to gain direct access to their social insurance numbers, their bank accounts. If we could tap into those directly, it would save us a lot of time and effort, don't you think?"

Sabina glanced up from her laptop and gave her head a subtle shake. Indira knew she should stop now, but she just couldn't. Dylan's infuriating smirk sent her blazing toward the edge of oblivion. Or unemployment. Whichever came first.

"Does anyone else have questions or comments?" Preet asked, knowing full well that if no one had spoken up before Indira's rant, they weren't about to now. "You all have your assignments. Two weeks from now, I want to be able to demo the workflow for the execs. Now let's get to work."

A low rumble of chairs filled the meeting room as the team pushed away from the table. Indira followed Sabina toward the door.

"Did you sign off on this?"

Sabina shrugged. "As long as we update our terms of use, from a legal standpoint, we're covered."

"Forget legal. I'm talking about ethical—"

Her statement was cut short by Dylan's summons. As the team filtered out of the conference room, he stood in the doorway waiting for her. Indira wanted to ignore him, but knew it would only make matters worse.

Wordlessly, Indira turned to meet his gaze and waited for him to speak. If there was one lesson she'd learned from her father, it was the power of a protracted silence.

"What was that?" Dylan crossed his arms and stared at her like she was the dumbest human being on the planet.

"What?"

"Let's start with your attitude."

She'd expected a stronger opening. There was no denying that Dylan's technical skills were top-notch, but his management skills were another matter.

"My attitude?" Indira arched her eyebrows. "I thought you valued dissenting opinions. I didn't realize you wanted a code monkey."

Indira's barb hit its mark. Dylan flinched.

"The direction has been set. I expect you to get on board. If you can't..."

Dylan's sentence trailed off, but Indira got the point. Argue all you want, but once a decision was made, it was everyone's job to make it successful. Did Dylan get all his leadership lessons directly from Jean Luc Picard? God, he was such a dork.

"I was simply voicing my opinion. I'm still allowed to do that, or is that against company policy too?"

"I didn't hear you offer anything constructive, any alternatives to what was proposed."

How was she supposed to come up with alternatives when everything about the idea was so wrong? Indira shook her head and headed for the door, knowing full well that nothing she said would make a damned bit of difference. They'd already made up their minds.

"Doesn't it bother you?" she asked, stopping at the door and craning her head around to meet Dylan's gaze.

"What?"

"It's like George Orwell's book, *1984*. Only we're Big Brother. It's not right. You know that, don't you?"

Dylan tipped his head back and heaved a sigh, as if drained by the herculean task of dealing with her.

"It's just business, Indira. If we don't make this product, someone else will."

Indira offered a bitter smile. "Well thank god for that. Because of us, Sunny will save five bucks on a pair of shoes she doesn't need and probably can't afford."

"Good thing she won't have to pay full price then."

Indira turned away in disgust. Why had she even bothered?

Dylan was a company man. He'd never had an altruistic thought in his whole entitled life.

"I can talk to Preet about reassigning you to another team if you'd like," he said.

And how would that look? She already had a reputation of being hard to work with. If she wasn't the best engineer on the team, they'd probably fire her for insubordination.

"Don't bother," she snapped. "I'm fine."

Or she would be, just as soon as she updated her résumé.

4

MALLORY USED DUCT TAPE AND A SHOPPING BAG TO SEAL THE BROKEN window. The rattling noise of the thin plastic rippling in the wind drove her nuts, but at least it kept the rain out. She had just left Best Buy, where she had squandered her meager savings on a new cell phone instead of fixing the car. Hell, she could deal with the annoyance of a broken window for a few weeks but living without a cell phone was inhuman.

The unexpected errand had made her late for the one class she didn't want to be late for. *Business ethics.*

When it came to tardy students, Dr. Amar Saraf was merciless. Breaking every speed limit between Best Buy and campus, Mallory parked in the lot closest to the lecture hall and hustled across the quad. It didn't matter. The empty hallways signaled that class was already in session.

Mallory tried to slip through the back entrance of the lecture hall unnoticed, but the heavy clang of the steel door resonated through the classroom, turning all eyes on her. Dr. Saraf, who half the girls on campus called Dr. Hottie, shot her a withering gaze as she scurried to the first empty seat closest to the door.

It was just her luck that she landed beside Brock Sinclair—an insufferable class know-it-all who hit on her every chance he got.

"You're late," he whispered with a grin as she slid her laptop onto the desk.

"Thank you, Captain Obvious," she sniped back, irritation rippling across her already raw nerves.

The professor's laser gaze cut her way, and Mallory fell silent. This afternoon's lecture was on online privacy. Not exactly riveting stuff. While she waited for her laptop to boot, she pulled the new phone from her pocket and thumbed the power button. The screen lit up, and for the first time all day, Mallory caught a break. They really did make the setup process easy. Within a few minutes, she'd connected to her cloud account and started downloading apps while the professor moderated a class discussion on the moral dilemma surrounding the use of biometric scans as a form of identification.

Mallory barely heard a word of the lecture. The terms and conditions page for the application she was installing flashed across her screen. Mallory pressed the accept button without reading a word.

"Yeah, yeah," she muttered, speeding through the setup.

"You really should read that," Brock said.

Mallory tilted the phone away from his prying eyes. "Bugger off and mind your own business."

"What were your thoughts on the topic, Ms. Riggins?"

Dr. Hottie was glaring directly at her. Inwardly, she groaned.

"I—I'm sorry?" Mallory stammered.

"Perhaps you could share your views on FIP and consent with the class."

A scalding blush spread across Mallory's face. She scoured her memory for any recollection of the acronym but came up empty.

"FIP?" she asked in an unsteady voice.

Dr. Saraf rolled his eyes and heaved an exaggerated sigh.

"Really, Ms. Riggins, if you can't pay attention in class, at least do the reading. Mr. Sinclair," he said, calling on Brock instead. "Could you please enlighten your esteemed colleague?"

"FIP stands for fair information principles—a set of issues surrounding internet privacy; things like notice, consent, access, security, and collection limitations that could be codified into law. They're the sorts of things you really want to pay attention to if you're setting up a new phone, for instance."

Mallory wanted to slap the self-satisfied smirk off Brock's face.

"Thank you, Mr. Sinclair. Good to know someone up there is paying attention."

A low rumble of laughter rolled through the lecture hall. Mallory felt the slow burn of shame in the blush that crept across her cheeks.

"Those are laws that protect your privacy, Ms. Riggins. On that little phone-thingy you have so cleverly hidden beneath your leg."

More laughter followed the remark, and Mallory slid the phone from its hiding spot and placed it face-down on the desk. From over the rim of his tortoiseshell glasses, Dr. Saraf stared at her. She notched her chin up a fraction and met his gaze head-on. With a curt nod, he continued the lecture.

"Dr. Hottie's in a mood," Brock mumbled.

Ignoring him, Mallory propped her chin on her fist and focused on the lecture. By seven o'clock in the evening, class was over. It had been a long day. Cold and exhausted, Mallory fired her laptop into her backpack and zipped it closed. Her thoughts were filled with visions of a hot shower and bed. She rose from her seat and headed to the door. Brock stood in the middle of the aisle blocking her way.

"A few of us are heading to the Library for drinks. Want to come?"

The Library was a popular off-campus bar. Even if she was in the mood to go out, she wouldn't be caught dead going anywhere with him.

"Can't. I've got an early class in the morning. And apparently, I need to read up on e-commerce privacy laws."

Brock snorted. "Tomorrow night then?"

"Hate to burst your bubble, Brock, but I have a boyfriend."

She tried to slide around him, but he extended his arm and propped it against the wall, barring her path.

"Who?"

"None of your business."

Brock cocked his head, looking smug. "A mystery boyfriend? So either he's fictional, married, or gay. Which is it?"

"Seriously?"

He was a pig. As much as Mallory longed to shove him aside, he outweighed her by more than fifty pounds. Just then, her new phone pinged with a notification. Brock's phone chimed at the same time. He checked his screen and his expression fell. Without another word, he spun on his heel and left the lecture hall.

Surprised by the sudden shift in his demeanor, Mallory read the news.

Search for missing college student, Katie Lord, begins...

5

KATIE LORD? MALLORY CLICKED ON THE LINK TO THE ARTICLE TO find out more. The photo of the missing woman had a chilling effect. She knew this girl, had seen this girl. They were in a few classes together and...and wasn't she the girlfriend of the guy who came into the shop every day? Tim. *Mr. Quad Grande Breve?*

The final few students still lingering in the hallway dispersed. Mallory left the building, anxious to get home and scour the internet for news about Katie's disappearance. It was cold outside. The damp night enveloped her as she cut down a narrow path between two towering limestone buildings. Not for the first time, she noticed how poorly lit this part of campus was. She slid into a gully of shadows, accelerating her pace to a brisk walk.

Reaching the halfway point, the light from the streetlamps fell away, and the river of darkness deepened. She heard something. Like footsteps behind her. The hairs on the back of Mallory's neck stood on end. She whirled and searched the shadows for the Bogeyman, Sasquatch, and other things that went bump in the night.

But there was no one. The path was empty.

As she started walking again, she remembered watching one of those creepy true crime shows on serial killers that her roommate, Shelby, loved. They'd shown a haunting photograph of an alleyway on the University of Washington campus, where one of Ted Bundy's victims had last been seen. That picture could have been taken on any campus in North America, including this one. One minute the young woman was there, the next, she was gone, never to be seen or heard from again.

How long had it taken her friends and family to realize that she was missing? She was probably dead before anyone had thought to look. A shiver ran through Mallory and she forced a laugh.

Ted freaking Bundy? Seriously, Mallory. Get a grip.

There wasn't a killer lurking in the shadows just waiting for a single woman to happen by. A plausible explanation for what might have happened to Katie must exist. Still, Mallory quickened her pace. Fallen leaves whispered across the path between the buildings. The sound of a car door slamming in the distance almost made her jump out of her skin.

A hundred yards off, the silvery glow of the parking lot lights cut through the misty rain. Mallory breathed a sigh of relief as she neared the end of the building. And that's when it happened.

Her heart seized as she felt a hand grab her shoulder. She spun around, off balance, too startled to scream.

Then she saw his face. Inches from hers. Mallory let out a breath.

"Asshole," she said, slamming her open palm against her boyfriend's shoulder hard enough to sting.

"Sorry," he said. "I didn't mean to scare you. I thought you heard me coming."

"Seriously?"

Her racing heart began to slow. He chuckled softly and pulled her into a hug. He felt so good.

"Are you okay?"

"You shouldn't sneak up on people like that. Especially after..."

"After what?"

"Didn't you hear? There's a student missing. Katie Lord."

A flicker of a shadow crossed his face.

"You know her?" Mallory asked.

Rain misted across the lenses of his tortoiseshell glasses and glistened like drops of silver in his dark hair. He looked away.

"She's in one of my classes. She's missing? You're sure?"

"Yeah, scanned the news and it seems legit..." Mallory shook her head and took a deep breath as the adrenaline rush subsided. "Scaring the hell out of me isn't the only reason I'm mad at you, *Dr. Saraf*."

Mallory gazed into his handsome face. Even in the low light, she could see the amused grin that tugged at the corners of his full lips. It took all her self-control not to smile back at him.

"Is that so?"

"You made me look like an idiot in class."

He tilted her face upward until she was staring directly into his dark eyes.

"Oh no, Ms. Riggins, that was fully your own doing. You didn't do your homework and you weren't paying attention during class. Besides, I can't very well make it look like I'm playing favorites, can I? Need I remind you that I don't yet have tenure?"

"Still, you didn't have to be so nasty about it."

"You're smart and capable. You owe it to yourself to do the work."

His mouth descended in a lingering kiss. His tongue brushed hers and she felt a tug in her gut. A pulsing heat spread through her, and once more, her breath quickened. He was utterly addictive.

"I know how you can make it up to me," she murmured.

Mallory's upturned gaze was designed to melt even the hardest of hearts. She buried her hands in his dark curls and pulled him closer, hungry for him. It had been days since they'd been together. His long fingers dug into her hips and pressed her close. She could feel his need pressing against her, as hot and urgent as her own. Mallory pulled in a ragged breath as they broke apart.

"Your place?" he breathed.

"Can't. My roommate's home. Yours?"

Amar shook his head. Mallory tensed. Whenever the topic of his place was raised, Amar dismissed it. The first few times, it hadn't bothered her, but Brock's words came back in a rush. Amar certainly wasn't fictional, or gay.

"You're married, aren't you?" she asked.

She'd just assumed he wasn't, but what if she'd been wrong? In the few weeks since the affair began, she'd never asked. And as the weeks went by, he'd never invited her to his place. He'd never mentioned his family. It was as if he'd built a wall around his private life that she couldn't penetrate, and it scared her.

"My sister's visiting," he said.

"So?" Wasn't she good enough to meet his sister?

"I can't very well tell her that I'm seeing one of my students."

He gave her a beseeching look and she sighed. Mallory planted a palm firmly on his chest and eased him away.

"Tell me you're not married."

He cupped his hand around the back of her neck. Staring down into her eyes he said, "I'm not married."

"You promise?"

"I promise."

He seemed sincere, and she wanted to believe him, but what if he was lying? How would she know? The Google search she'd done on him when they'd first started to flirt hadn't turned up much that she hadn't already known from reading his bio. He was thirty-two. Born in Vancouver. He'd earned his degree at York University in Toronto and then done his post-graduate work at McGill. There had been no mention of his family, or a wife, but that didn't mean anything.

Amar eased toward her and whispered, "I know a place we could go…"

He nuzzled her neck. The bristles of his stubble tickled, setting her blood on fire. He nipped playfully at her earlobe and Mallory groaned. No one she'd met had ever had this kind of effect on her. He was like a drug and she couldn't get enough.

"Okay," Mallory said. "But afterwards you have to tell me everything you know about fair information principles."

"I'm your teacher, not your tutor."

She slid her hand beneath his shirt. Her cold fingers brushed against his hot skin and he gasped.

"There's no reason you can't be both."

6

INDIRA COULDN'T RESIST A PUZZLE, AND WHILE SHE STILL FOUND THE privacy issues relating to the new product direction disturbing, she'd fallen down the rabbit hole, doing what she loved to do best —writing code. Exploring new ideas. Her ability to find unconventional ways to solve complex problems was her superpower, according to her team, and honestly, that's what kept her glued to her laptop long after everyone else had gone home.

She sat at her desk, fully absorbed in her work. The noise-canceling headphones she wore blocked out everything except her own inner thoughts. Apparently, they worked a little too well. Indira had completely lost track of time when the bouncing icon of her messaging app demanded her attention. She read the message.

AMAR: Are you still at work?

Still? What did he mean, still? Indira checked the time. Could it really be almost nine? She glanced around the office, a converted warehouse in the Yaletown district, surprised to find herself alone. Night had fallen outside her window, and she gazed across the glimmering city lights. High-rise residential towers crowded the skyline from Yaletown to the edge of False Creek.

INDIRA: Yeah. Where are you?
AMAR: Across the street at the brewery. Want to grab a bite?

Now that he mentioned it, she was kind of hungry, and it had been weeks since she'd last seen her brother.

INDIRA: On my way.

Shutting down the laptop, she gathered her things and left the building. The rain had stopped. A damp wind ruffled her hair. Tucking her hands inside her pockets, Indira slid between two cars jockeying for parking spots in front of the brewery and crossed the street.

Bypassing the hostess stand, Indira threaded her way through the densely packed tables toward Amar, who was sitting near the back. Radiohead's version of "Creep" blasted through the speakers. Her stomach grumbled at the mouthwatering scent of seared duck. She slid into the seat across from her brother. He assessed her with a smirk.

"Nice tattoo."

Indira tugged up the sleeve of her leather jacket, revealing the intricate mandala tattoo etched on the inside of her wrist.

"I knew you'd like it," she said.

"Mom's going to love it too. So, are you planning to wear long sleeves the rest of your life?"

Fully anticipating his reaction, Indira returned his smirk. As much as Amar liked to think of himself as progressive, he was still a product of his upbringing.

"Maybe, but I'm sure you didn't come here to talk about my tattoo. How's school?"

"Good."

"Good. That's all?"

"Yeah, the beginning of the year is always hectic, but things are settling into a rhythm. What about you? Do you always work so late?"

"New project. I lost track of time."

"Still like it there?"

It was unusual for Amar to waste so much time on small talk. She guessed there was more than work on his mind.

"So, out with it," Indira prodded him.

"Since when do I need a reason to have dinner with my favorite sister?"

"Only sister, and who has dinner past eight o'clock on a school night?"

"Apparently us."

"All right. You've got me there. For the record, I already know what you're going to say."

"Really?" Amar cocked a cynical eyebrow and gestured for her to continue. "Are you suddenly clairvoyant?"

"Comes with the tattoo. And for the record, the answer is no."

Irritation rippled across his face, and he gave an impatient sigh.

"I haven't even asked, and already you—"

"You think I've forgotten Mom's birthday? Work is really crazy, and besides, I don't want to go."

"This is family, Indira. Since when does *want* have anything to do with it?"

"Come on, Amar. You know what's going to happen. As soon as

I arrive, I'll be grilled about my relationship status." Indira grimaced and raked a hand through her long hair.

Just then, her phone dinged. Indira peeked at the screen and uttered a noise, part sigh, part growl.

Indira held up her phone, showing Amar the photo their mother had sent. Predictably, the guy in the photo was in his early thirties, an engineer like her. Good-looking enough, she supposed, and he had all the credentials her mother thought mattered. Good family. Good job. Decent earning potential. She had no idea what Indira actually wanted, and worse, she didn't care.

"Did you have to put up with this?"

Amar gave a snort of amusement. "What do you think?"

But Indira wasn't amused. She dismissed the message notification and placed her phone face-down on the table.

"Just ignore it," he said.

Ignore it? If only it was *that* easy.

"Every day Mom sends me the profile of some guy she found on the matrimony site. Do you know how many filters I've had to create to deal with that nonsense? She's absolutely obsessed with the idea of marriage and she doesn't listen when I say that I'm not the least bit interested in her matchmaking skills. You want to do something for me? Make an excuse. Tell her I've come down with the flu, or smallpox, or use that big brain of yours to dream up some other viable reason why I can't possibly attend."

He grasped her hand. "You can't call in sick to your mother's birthday party."

"Why not? Is there some rule I'm unaware of?"

The look Amar gave her required no interpretation. Indira uttered a bark of frustration and tried to pull away, but Amar's grasp tightened. He made it sound so simple, but there was nothing simple about it. She spent her whole life trying to please parents whose views on gender roles were formed by their traditional Indian roots while she longed for freedom. Equality. The right to choose her own path, rights that most of her peers took for granted and put her at odds with the people who were supposed to love her best.

"You're coming," he said, as if it was a fact already agreed to, when she had done no such thing.

The timely appearance of the waitress broke their stony silence. Indira tugged her hand again. Amar reluctantly let go.

"I'll have a burger. Rare. And fries. Oh, and a beer. An IPA."

Raised on a strict vegetarian diet, her mother would faint if she saw what Indira was eating. Amar's eyebrows rose in faint amusement at her defiance as she handed the menu back to the waitress.

"I'll have the black bean chili," he said.

"Anything to drink?"

"Just water, thanks," Amar answered.

The waitress smiled at her handsome brother and left the table. Indira shook her head in mock wonder.

"Vegetarian. No alcohol. You really are the perfect son, aren't you?"

The barb hit its mark and the look of amusement faded from Amar's face.

"Stop wallowing. You're not the only one who has to deal with family expectations."

"How is Rani?"

Amar heaved a sigh and raised his hands in a dismissive gesture. "She's fine."

"How are the wedding plans coming along?"

Though Amar tried to hide it, she saw him flinch. The last time her parents had tried to foist a fiancé on her, she'd shown up to meet her intended with a boyfriend in tow. *A white boyfriend*. It had taken her parents months to get over the scandal it had caused, not that it had put an end to her mother's plans.

Amar had finally caved into the pressure and accepted that there would be no peace until he agreed to get married to "a suitable woman from a good family." The whole process of searching for a mate who matched a defined set of criteria sickened Indira. She wasn't picking out a couch, or a china pattern, or some other "object" to complete her life. And while even she had to agree that Amar's fiancée, Rani, was beautiful, she had about as much personality as a throw pillow.

"You don't have to go through with it, you know."

"You say that like there's an actual choice," Amar said, staring at his hands.

Indira snorted in disgust. "Tell me you're not going to spend the rest of your life married to someone you hate."

"I don't hate her."

"But you don't love her either."

They both knew couples in arranged marriages, some of whom were miserable, while others seemed to come to terms with their mates. She had no intention of settling, but as the only son, the expectation was that Amar would eventually fulfill her father's role as head of the family. So far, his biggest rebellion was enrolling in business school instead of medicine, but somehow, he'd made that an acceptable compromise by earning his doctorate.

Indira worried that her brother was going to sit passively by while their family planned this wedding for him. But even as the thought slipped through her mind, she spied something that made her reconsider her position. There was a mark on the side of Amar's neck. Purple. Almost a bruise.

A hickey? A smile flitted across Indira's face and she shot him a smug look. Surely that wasn't Rani's handiwork. She hadn't so much as seen them hold hands.

"So, tell me something, brother dear. Does your girlfriend know about your fiancée?"

A small jolt of satisfaction passed through Indira at the look of shock that crossed Amar's face.

"I don't know what you're talking about."

"You're such a bad liar. Who is she?"

"Whatever," Amar said, refusing to meet her gaze. "So, you're coming to Mom's party, right?"

The waitress set a pint glass in front of Indira. She sighed and took a sip.

"If I must."

7

BY THE TIME SHE MADE IT BACK TO HER APARTMENT, MALLORY WAS chilled to the bone. While the plastic bag taped to her car window kept out the rain, the ancient heater was no match for the damp cold that seeped through the paper-thin barrier. Her roommate, Shelby, sat cross-legged on the couch with a laptop balanced on her knees and a notebook poised beside her. She looked up in surprise as Mallory unlocked the patio door.

"Why didn't you park in the garage?" Shelby asked.

"I can't find the remote control."

Earlier in the day, she'd texted Shelby about the car break-in. She still held out a glimmer of hope that the remote control was hiding somewhere beneath the piles of crap haphazardly tossed across the back seat. Her cursory search had turned up nothing so far. But it was dark. She could have missed it. She'd do a more thorough search in the morning.

"You think it was stolen?" Shelby asked, nervously.

"Maybe."

Mallory shrugged and Shelby cast a wary glance toward the

garage door that opened off the tiny kitchen. Mallory picked up on her train of thought. If someone did steal the remote control, there wasn't much stopping them from entering the apartment.

"Maybe we should let James and Iris know."

Fat lot of good that would do. In the two years that Mallory lived there, the landlords had been slow to respond to any of her requests. It had taken a week to get a plumber to fix the leaking toilet. What a mess that had been. They would be annoyed when she told them about the lost remote control. They may even decide to take away access to the garage, and she'd be forced to spend the winter parking out front. She was in no rush to trigger that alarm. Maybe, for once, luck would be on her side, and the remote control would magically reappear. She could hope.

"I'll text them later."

Though how much later, Mallory didn't say. Right now, all she wanted was a hot shower and her pajamas. It had been a long day and she still had hours of homework to slog through before she called it a night.

"Did you get your window fixed?"

Mallory shook her head and flopped into a nearby chair. "I replaced my phone instead."

"So you're driving around with a busted window, eh?"

"Unless you've got a couple hundred bucks I could borrow..."

"I wish," Shelby said. "Seriously, if I had it, I'd give it to you."

They weren't just empty words, she knew. Shelby had helped her out before when her bank account was overdrawn and she'd needed money for groceries. As it was, Shelby was already paying for the utilities. She couldn't very well ask for more.

"Have you called your parents? Maybe they could help."

"Maybe," Mallory said half-heartedly.

Shelby was right. The rainy season had barely begun and driving around with a broken window was already miserable. All that water leaking into the car wouldn't be good for it either. She supposed she should call her mom, but what good would that do? She would find a way to blame Mallory for the situation, the same way she always did. Besides, her mother lived in Ontario. With the time difference, it would be after midnight there. Too late to call.

Though the lukewarm shower fell short of the piping hot temperature she'd fantasized about, it was enough to fight off the chill. Donning fleecy pajama bottoms and a T-shirt, she retired to her room for the night.

As a kid, when she'd needed lunch money, or when she'd needed a permission form signed, she had always gone to her father first. He was the one who took care of her, who took her to the doctor when she was sick. Whatever the problem, he understood.

After the divorce, he'd moved in with his girlfriend and her two little kids. There were times when she missed him so much it felt like an ache inside her chest, and tonight, she could use some cheering up. Unlike her mother, he stayed up late.

"There's my little college girl. How are you, baby?"

The pleasure she felt at hearing his voice was blunted by the slight slurring of his words. He'd been drinking.

"I'm okay, Daddy. How are you?"

"Fine. Just fine. Work's crazy. They have me on the road every second week."

"That must get tiring."

"Yeah, but you didn't call to hear me bellyache. What's going on with you? How's school?"

"School's good, Daddy, but..."

"But?"

"My car got broken into."

"Ah, sweetie. I'm sorry to hear that. Are you okay?"

"Yeah, but I can't afford to get my window fixed. I was hoping—"

Mallory stopped when she heard her father's sigh. Her heart sank.

"You know I would help if I could, pumpkin, but back-to-school shopping for the twins has cleaned me out."

"I know," Mallory said, doing her best to mask her disappointment. In the background, she heard the soft clink of ice cubes in his glass.

"You remember what it was like when you were their age? How you sprouted up over the summer and needed everything—"

Tears filled Mallory's eyes as she thought about how close they'd once been. She remembered how he used to swing her in his arms, holding onto her so tightly, it felt as if he'd never let go.

"It's okay, Daddy. It's just a broken window. No big deal. It's not supposed to rain tomorrow anyway."

Her father heaved another sigh. "Let me talk to your mother. Maybe we can work something out."

"Thanks, Daddy."

"Goodnight, pumpkin."

Mallory hung up. It was an empty promise. She couldn't remember the last time her parents had worked anything out without the help of lawyers. And to make matters worse, Amar wasn't answering his phone. Was it too much to ask to have someone she could count on?

On days like today, adulting really sucked.

8

"INDIRA! WHERE HAVE YOU BEEN HIDING? IT HAS BEEN TOO LONG since I have seen you."

The shopkeeper rounded the counter, enveloping Indira in a hug. Indira remembered visiting the shop with her mother when she was a little girl barely tall enough to peek over the countertop. Her mother came here before every family celebration. The scent of cinnamon and cardamom permeating the shop brought back so many happy memories. Coconut sweets for Indira, and gulab jamun for Amar.

"Look at you, so grown up, so beautiful." The shopkeeper twirled a lock of Indira's hair around a finger and tucked it behind her ear. "I keep wondering when you and your mother are going to show up with an order for your wedding."

Not her too. Was marriage all anyone thought of? Indira faked a smile but didn't respond as she peered through the glass showcase at the tasty treats.

"How is your mother?"

"She's fine, thank you. It's her birthday. I was hoping to get some coconut barfi."

"Of course. I remember you're partial to modak. Would you like some?"

The coconut dumplings laced with nutmeg and saffron were one of her favorites. Though she was tempted, Indira shook her head. "Not today, but I would love some chai."

"Of course."

The coconut barfi she had ordered was being boxed as she waited for Sabina to arrive. The chai tea set before her was piping hot.

"Give my best to your mother and don't make it so long before you come in again. I miss seeing your beautiful face. I have a nephew..."

Before she could finish, Indira thrust a twenty-dollar bill over the counter. "Thank you. I'll tell Mom you send your best."

She scooped the goods off the countertop and hurried away, settling on a high-backed stool by the window. She didn't want to hear about a nephew, or a neighbor, or any other guy who would make a suitable bookend. She was just fine the way she was. *Seriously.*

Indira watched the steady flow of foot traffic streaming past. One of the things she loved most about Vancouver was the city's diversity. Citizens from all over the world called Vancouver home —she had spent so much time exploring the ethnically unique neighborhoods, from Chinatown, to the Punjabi Market, to Greektown. Her parents had been drawn to the city because of its former British roots, and for the daughter of an immigrant, she easily blended into the welcoming social fabric of this place she called home. Here, it didn't matter what color her skin was.

The prospect of leaving Vancouver was one of the reasons why she was dragging her feet when it came to her job search. She could have easily found another position in Toronto or Ottawa, but she would miss walking the seawall along English Bay, looking out across the water to the cargo ships anchored offshore. She would miss the beauty of the mountains that were close enough to touch, not to mention the temperate climate. So what if it rained more than half a year? It beat freezing her ass off in the snow.

Indira's phone beeped, interrupting her thoughts. No sooner had she checked her notifications when she looked up, catching sight of Sabina, who swung into the doorway.

Spotting Indira perched by the window, Sabina shifted sideways and made her way through the crowded aisles. Both hands were loaded down with shopping bags. Though she tried to be careful, Sabina still managed to bump into a guy sitting at one of the tables.

"Excuse me," Sabina said, flashing a flirty grin.

One look at Sabina melted the irritated expression from the guy's face. There wasn't a straight guy in the world immune to her friend's charms.

Sabina maneuvered through the remaining tables without incident and arrived at Indira's side. She set the bags down and climbed onto a stool. Indira nudged the chai tea toward her. Sabina raised it in a toast before taking a sip.

"Looks like the test run was a success," Indira said, eyeing the shopping bags with a bemused shake of her head. "You were supposed to acknowledge the notifications, not act on them."

Sabina beamed. "The application is nothing short of genius. It knew exactly where I liked to shop, and the way the coupons magically appeared on my phone was a thing of beauty."

"The data doesn't lie," Indira said, mimicking another of Dylan's mantras.

"I was able to buy these faux snakeskin boots for half price, and I got this sweater for thirty bucks. Thirty bucks. And it's designer."

Indira flashed a patient smile and silently hoped that Sabina wouldn't bore her with the fashion pedigree of everything she bought. She was more interested in how the algorithm she'd designed had functioned.

"Any glitches?"

Sabina shrugged. "One of the coupons I received had expired. Too bad. I had my eyes on a pair of earrings at the Swarovski outlet, but hey, maybe next time. Aside from that, it worked like a charm. How did you get it working so fast?"

"It wasn't rocket science. Besides, I already have your data. That allowed me to skip the part where I had to build a data map of your location patterns and your shopping preferences. For instance, according to the algorithm, you'll be working out at your favorite gym tonight. You'll probably stop for pho at that place you like on Davie Street before heading home. You know, all the info I might need if I was stalking you, or something."

"Are you still on that?" Sabina asked. Indira hitched a shoulder in a grudging shrug. "Let it go, Indira. We're not breaking any privacy laws. Dylan's going to lose his mind when he sees how far you've come."

No one was taking her concerns seriously. Especially not Dylan. Eventually, she'd have to show him how much progress she'd made, but not yet. She was holding back, still hoping he'd come to his senses.

Yeah. Like that would happen.

Her half-hearted job search on LinkedIn hadn't yielded much. There were some interesting public domain projects—engineers who were collaborating virtually on cool technology to help the planet—but those were unpaid positions, and as much as she would like to pitch in, she needed a paycheck. So, instead of doing something worthwhile for humanity, she was stuck designing shopping apps.

Sabina opened a Neiman Marcus bag and rustled through the tissue paper. She pulled out a black top and tossed it to Indira.

"What's this?"

"It's for you," Sabina said.

The shirt was made of a soft, semi-transparent fabric. It had a V-neck collar and rolled up sleeves.

"Nice, but isn't this more your speed?"

"Not my size. Besides, you need to start upping your game. A girl can only own so many camo T-shirts."

"Thanks," Indira said.

She folded the shirt and stowed it inside her messenger's bag.

"Promise me you'll wear it," Sabina said.

"Yeah, for all those dates I'm going on."

"About that..." Sabina started, only to be stopped cold by Indira's raised palm.

"My dating life is not open for discussion."

Sabina heaved a longsuffering sigh and let the subject drop. She switched her focus to the pink pastry box sitting on the counter in front of Indira. "What's this?"

Sabina pulled the box toward her and pried open the lid. The smell of coconut and cardamom wafted out.

"Oh, my auntie used to make these."

Sabina closed her eyes and breathed in the scent of her childhood. She reached inside, but before she could grab one of the treats, Indira snatched it away.

"They're not for me."

Sabina arched her eyebrows in a curious look. "Do you have an Indian boyfriend I don't know about?"

Indira snorted. "As if."

Just then, her phone dinged with another text from her mother. The daily bachelor alert.

"Oh, he's not bad," Sabina purred, peering over Indira's shoulder.

Indira's jaw clenched. "You marry him then."

She typed in a quick message.

INDIRA: I'm already in love.

Sabina's eyes widened in surprise at the cheeky response. Indira scoured her photo collection until she found what she was looking for. She clicked on the photo and hit send.

Sabina gasped. "Wait. Was that...?"

A second later, Indira's mother responded.

MOM: Albert Einstein?

Indira smirked in satisfaction as she pocketed her phone. Sabina laughed and shook her head.

"So, if these aren't for a boyfriend, is it your brother's birthday?"

"God, you're so nosy."

"And you're so mysterious."

"If you must know, it's my mother's birthday." Indira shook her head and glanced out the window at the sea of pedestrians passing by. "Dylan's going to have a stroke if we're not back soon."

"You meant to say if *you're* not back soon. Unlike you, I don't report to him and have already finished my meetings for the day. I'm heading to the gym. The new Pilates instructor is to die for."

"I swear the only exercise you get is flirting."

"That's not the only exercise I get," Sabina winked. "You should try it sometime."

"Yeah, yeah. Thanks for helping me test, and for the shirt."

"My pleasure, darling."

Sabina dropped air kisses in the vicinity of Indira's cheek. Then, somehow, she managed to haul the shopping bags and the chai tea outside without spilling a drop. Indira slung her bag over her shoulder and picked up the box of sweets.

She would go back to work and troubleshoot the problem with the coupon misfire. And then...

And then she'd brave the gauntlet of public transit to White Rock, a suburb south of the city where her parents lived.

Indira left the shop and crossed the street heading toward the office. Immersing herself in the flow of pedestrians moving along Cambie Street, she paused at the lights. The box she held reminded her of the evening ahead. What her family would say.

Marriage. How scandalous it was to be a young woman living alone in the city. Her tattoo. And that was just the beginning.

Her head throbbed.

The light up ahead turned red, and Indira gazed down the street at the store fronts. She caught sight of her reflection in a nearby window of a hair salon. Her dark hair fell in thick waves halfway down her back. The light turned green, but Indira didn't follow the flow of traffic across the street. Instead, she ducked into the hair salon and closed the door behind her.

Maybe it was time she updated her look. Who needed all this hair anyway?

9

FROM THE LINE OF CARS ALREADY CLOGGING THE STREET, AMAR knew he was among the last to arrive. His chest tightened as he saw the late model Mercedes parked in the driveway. It belonged to Rani's mother, which meant that his fiancée was here. He hadn't invited her. His mother, or one of his aunties, must have. Amar blew out a long breath and trudged toward the door. He entered the house without knocking.

"You. Always late," his auntie called from the kitchen.

Amar smiled.

"I'm not late," he protested, shedding his wool coat and cashmere scarf.

"Everyone else was here half an hour ago, which makes you late."

Amar laughed and slung an arm around his auntie. "I can't help it if everyone else is early. Smells great."

Korma, with its gingerroot and subtle spice, was one of his favorites. His auntie laughed at his rumbling belly.

"At least you brought your appetite. Now go. Your mother is waiting."

She gave him a gentle shove toward the living room where his family had gathered. Shouted greetings were exchanged with the uncles and cousins he passed. His mother was sitting in her favorite seat, a plush, plum-colored wingback chair Amar jokingly referred to as her throne. Dressed in a flowing red sari imprinted with gold flowers and a gold and purple trim, she looked like a queen receiving her guests.

"Amar," she said.

The gold bangles around her wrist clanged as she reached for him.

"Mom." He bent, brushing his lips across her cheek, and handed her the wrapped present he'd brought. "You look beautiful."

"And you, you look so skinny."

He laughed and shook his head. She wouldn't be satisfied until he was an old married man with a thick beard and potbelly.

"Where have you been? It's been weeks since you visited."

"Work. We just finished mid-terms, and I have a mountain of papers to grade."

"Work, always work," she grumbled good-naturedly.

Amar took the chair beside her. The loud, cheerful voices of his family filled the house. A deep feeling of contentment settled over him. For the first time in weeks, his mind was at peace.

"What have you brought me?" she asked.

"Open it."

Running a careful finger beneath the seam of the wrapping paper, his mother opened the present. The silk shawl was red with gold thread running through it in an intricate pattern. Knotting her hands in the soft fabric, she raised it to her face and ran it across her lined cheek.

"Something to warm these old bones. Thank you."

She squeezed his hand.

"Not so old, I think. Indira helped me pick it out. She says it's your favorite color."

"Speaking of your sister, where is she?"

A note of irritation crept into his mother's voice and who could blame her? Just a few days ago he'd told Indira to show up, so why wasn't she here? She should be helping the aunties prepare the meal.

"I'm sure she'll be along soon."

His mother placed the scarf on the small mountain of unopened gifts beside her chair.

"You should have given her a ride."

"She lives downtown, Mom. You know what traffic is like this time of day."

"She could have taken the SkyTrain to Burnaby and the two of you could have driven together. You know how I feel about her living in the city."

"Indira's job is there, Mom. You can't expect her to spend three hours a day commuting."

The reproach in his voice did nothing to soften his mother's hard expression.

"She should live with you then. It's not right for a young woman of her age to live alone. I've told her that, but your sister, she is so headstrong."

"I wonder where she gets that from?" Amar shot his mother an affectionate gaze, and the lines of irritation etched into her face softened.

"Amar!"

The sharp summons came from Rani's mother, Falguni. His future mother-in-law. Amar repressed a groan. Both women had entered the living room and were standing behind him, waiting to be acknowledged. Rani was dressed in a light orange sari, the color perfectly accenting her flawless caramel skin. She looked beautiful with her long hair falling to her waist. Dark makeup emphasized her large, almond-shaped eyes. She bore little resemblance to her mother. Where Rani's features were soft, Falguni's looked as if they were hewn from stone. Her eyes, small specks of obsidian, locked on him.

"Why didn't you tell us it was your mother's birthday? We heard it from your auntie."

"It's good to see you both," he lied.

"We brought you some tea," Rani said and handed his mother a box.

"Thank you, my dear," his mother said, grasping Rani's hand affectionately. "I'm so glad you were able to come."

"The tea. It's Nilgiri," Falguni said. "The very best. My brother sends it."

"Thank you," his mother said graciously.

Amar vacated his chair, anxious to put some distance between him and his future mother-in-law. Rani's gaze followed him.

"And how are you?" he asked, addressing her at last.

"Glad to finally be seeing you. You've been ignoring me."

A petulant look crossed her face, and he felt a slight pang of guilt. He wasn't in love with her. If he was being completely honest with himself, he wasn't sure he even liked her that much. They had nothing in common. She had no intellectual curiosity that he could discern. She wanted a husband, not *him*. Someone to look after her. Care for her. Support her. That was all. And he fit the bill. He came from a good family. Had a good job.

"Don't they look lovely together," his mother breathed, and Falguni nodded.

"They're a fine match, but when are we going to start planning the wedding? I've been asking Rani, but she says that Amar hasn't been available to meet. Work, she says."

"He's a professor and the start of the school year is busy," his mother said, parroting Amar's favorite excuse.

Falguni snorted in disgust. "If he's that busy, maybe we should take over the planning. We could call the hall right now and find out when they have their next opening."

"Yes, we've already waited long enough, haven't we, Amar?" Rani asked, peering through her lashes at him.

A knot of resentment formed inside his chest. He recognized the tactic. Their attempt to pressure him in front of his family was as obvious as it was pathetic. Did they really consider him so weak-minded that he could be bullied into doing their bidding? Indira was right. He had to call off the engagement.

Rani wasn't the only woman he was lying to. If Mallory found out about Rani, she would never understand, just like his parents would never understand his choice to break off the engagement. To them, Mallory would always be an outsider, a betrayal of his family's values.

"Amar?" his mother said.

"What's the rush? I've just started a new semester and—"

Not only did the providential chime of the doorbell bring an end to the current conversation, but it gave Amar an excuse to leave the room. His relief was short-lived. Amar's mouth dropped open in shock as he stared at his sister.

"Nice hair," he said.

Indira skimmed her hand over the two-centimeter stubble that graced the left side of her skull. She had shaved the area from her temple back behind her left ear while leaving the other side of it long enough to brush her shoulders. He supposed he should have been grateful that she hadn't shaved both sides in a faux mohawk, like so many other students he saw on campus, but still... His mouth twitched in amusement as he met his sister's defiant stare.

"You like it?"

"Wow." It was all he could say without laughing, and Indira's eyes narrowed.

"So, are you going to let me in, or are you just going to stand there?"

"It's your funeral."

Amar hung back, content to watch the drama from the safe haven of the hallway.

"Indira!" his mother beckoned.

Head held high, Indira strode into the living room.

"Happy birthday, Mom."

Ignoring her mother's frozen expression, Indira held out the pastry box and a wrapped gift. Her mother was too shocked to respond.

"What have you done to your hair?"

"I cut it. Do you like it?"

Indira set the boxes down on the mountain of gifts and ran a hand beneath the back of her hair. She swept it across her shoulders and flashed her mother a reckless grin. Falguni eyed his sister with contempt. At least Rani tried to hide her surprise.

"I most certainly do not like it. What were you thinking? How could you do this to yourself? What man is going to want to marry a woman whose hair looks like that?"

"So, I'm ugly now, is that it?"

"You are certainly doing your best to look that way. What were you thinking, Indira? Amar, maybe you can talk some sense into your sister."

Amar raised his hands in mock surrender and ducked into the kitchen where his aunties had begun to serve. The familiar buzz of activity surfaced fond memories of his childhood. Playing with his cousins while his aunties cooked. *Family.* He could live a thousand years and still not imagine a world in which Mallory would fit into this scene.

Amar was caught between two worlds—the past he remembered and the future he wanted. He wished he was the kind of man who could marry Rani and be happy, but he knew that any contentment he might find would be short-lived.

His auntie put a dish of shahi paneer on the table and Amar dipped his finger inside. A rich dish with a hint of turmeric, he tasted the subtle tang of red chili powder. Amar licked it off his finger and his auntie gave him a good-natured swat.

"You, out of the kitchen. We'll call you when it's ready."

He wandered toward the back of the house where the men congregated. His father was sitting with his uncles. They turned as he entered.

"You're a lucky man," his father said. "Rani will be a good wife."

"I'm sure she will be."

The ambivalent response earned him a piercing look and his father leaned close. "Never forget where you came from, Amar."

The familiar refrain reminded him of the many talks he'd had with his father over the years. A reminder to be thankful for all he had, laced with the expectation of what it meant to be a man in this family.

"She is a great beauty, like your mother."

Amar acknowledged his father's remark with a nod. He understood that he was viewed as an extension of his family, not an individual. The thought that they might want different things in a partner was unfathomable. Amar wanted so much more than someone who cooked and cleaned. He wanted a woman with a curious mind, who thirsted for knowledge. Someone who challenged him and made him feel alive. Rani was not that woman, but how could he admit to his family that the life they wanted was not enough? Like many families of their generation, his parents' marriage had been arranged. They had barely met before the wedding. How could he begin to make them understand, let alone accept, that he was different?

"You need to come home more often," his father said. "Your mother—"

The serious expression on his father's face drove a sudden spike of fear into Amar's heart. "What about her?"

"She is not well. Her headaches have gotten worse and she's tired. Not herself. She says it is nothing, but I am not so sure. You know how stubborn she can be."

"I'll talk to her," Amar promised.

Soon, they were summoned to the table and the meal was served. Amar sat among his boisterous cousins. Dishes were passed. The lighthearted celebration was punctuated by raucous bouts of laughter. His mother presided at the head of the table, all smiles for her favorites. Indira sat quietly to one side, picking at her food. Beside her sat Rani and Falguni, who barely spoke. Amar tried to catch his sister's eyes, but Indira refused to look up.

As the meal progressed, Amar studied his mother through new eyes. She looked tired. There was a hollowness to her cheeks he hadn't seen before.

Worry robbed him of his appetite, and like Indira, he picked at the remainder of his meal. Once the dishes were whisked away, he guided his mother back to her armchair in the living room. Indira's present still sat on the top of the pile, unopened.

"How are you feeling?"

A wary look invaded his mother's gaze. "Fine."

"Dad said that you're not feeling well."

"He worries too much."

"He said you have headaches."

His mother scowled and straightened in her chair. "When you get to be my age, you will have headaches too."

"Is it your blood pressure?"

His mother gave a dismissive snort and waved her hand. "I'm taking the pills."

"Pills?" Falguni asked, insinuating herself into the conversation. Amar's jaw tightened. "Pills are no good. Western medicine relies too heavily on pharmaceutical companies who are just there to make money. I have some herbs..."

"She doesn't need herbs," Amar snapped. "She needs to set up an appointment with her doctor. Isn't that right, Mom?"

He understood his mother well enough to read her stiff nod as a dismissal. His father was right to worry, but Amar knew better than to push. In a day or two, he'd call her and cajole her into seeing the doctor, for his father's peace of mind if nothing else. The guilt she so often wielded as a weapon cut both ways.

"Amar." He ignored Falguni's summons, refusing to turn and meet her gaze. Undaunted, she plowed ahead. "Your mother and I have agreed to meet for dinner Saturday evening at my house to discuss the wedding. You're expected to arrive at six."

His phone buzzed with a text message. Sliding it from his pocket, he checked the notification. The flirty message was from Mallory. Amar froze, aware that Rani was standing beside him, peering over his shoulder at the screen.

"Who is that from?" she asked.

Amar thumbed the power button, and the phone went dark.

"Just a student," he said, wondering how much of the text she'd seen.

"Indira, get your brother some more of the coconut barfi. He's gotten so thin."

"He's a grown man. Let him get his own sweets."

"Indira, do not talk to your mother so," her father growled, fixing her with a fierce look of disapproval she knew all too well.

Indira rolled her eyes and left the living room. She could be starving, and yet her mother would put Amar's needs first. The women of her family were chatting amicably as they cleaned the dishes. Rani and Falguni followed her from the room. They seated themselves at the table. Indira picked up a small plate and surveyed the sweets.

"I've made an appointment to see the new houses they're building near Metrotown," Indira overheard Rani say.

"The ones with the fountains in front? Oh yes, they'll be plenty big enough."

"Big enough for what?" Indira asked, turning toward Rani and her mother.

"Big enough for all of us. After the wedding. And then when the babies come."

"What? You're planning to move in after the wedding?"

"Of course," Falguni said, as if this should be obvious. "When the little ones start coming, Rani will need my help."

They already had him married off and fathering a brood of children. Imagine living with the pair of them. She wouldn't last fifteen minutes without losing her mind.

"What does Amar have to say about this?"

Falguni laughed.

"Men. Bah. What would a man care as long as he has a beautiful wife in his bed, a clean house, and food on the table?"

"Quite a lot, I imagine."

"Your mother may not care how you've turned out," Falguni said, eyeing Indira with disdain, "but it's time your brother took his rightful place as the head of his family."

"And just where do you think the money for this big new house is coming from? He may be a professor, but he's at the beginning of his career. Untenured. The kind of house you're talking about would cost—"

"He's the only son of a successful businessman. Money is not an issue."

Indira bit back a retort, marveling at the woman's gall. Not only had she settled Amar's future, but she had plans for her father's business too. Unbelievable. The thought that if Amar didn't grow a backbone soon, this woman was going to become part of her family turned Indira's stomach. She shook her head and exited the kitchen, slipping into the crowded living room.

Amar sat next to his cousin on the couch. The two were carrying on a loud and colorful conversation, blissfully unaware that his fiancée and future mother-in-law had already named his children.

Tipping her head close to her brother's ear, Indira said in a low voice, "Would you mind driving me home?"

"No, Indira, stay," her mother implored. "You can sleep in your old room."

Indira grasped her mother's outstretched hand, the bones easily discernible through her mother's thinning flesh. "I can't, Mom. I've got work in the morning."

"You work too hard. You should quit. Find a job closer to home."

"I like my job," Indira said, releasing her grip.

It wasn't a lie. Disagreements about the product direction aside, she loved writing code and solving complex puzzles. And she was not about to give up her freedom by moving home again.

"We could find you a good husband. Once your hair grows out—"

Nothing ever changed. *Find a husband. Get married. Give up your life.* Indira rolled her eyes.

"But, Mom, what man would ever want me looking like this?"

Her mother's eyes narrowed at Indira's mocking tone, but she was too angry to care.

"Amar, are you going to drive me, or should I catch a bus?"

Her brother heaved a deep sigh and rose from the couch. Stooping low, he kissed his mother's cheek.

"Call the doctor in the morning," he ordered.

"All right. If I must."

"You must."

Planting a hand between Indira's shoulder blades, he gave her a small shove toward the hallway. Indira pushed back. Ignoring her silent protest, Amar steered her toward the door, and they left the house together.

The fresh scent of cedar and rain carried on the night breeze. Indira pulled in a cleansing breath. She would have much rather spent the evening in the condo with Hazel, or out with Sabina having a drink. Instead, the night had gone just as she'd expected. Her mother was irritated. She was mad. And for what? Because she refused to play along?

Wordlessly, Indira slid into the BMW beside Amar. They barely made it out of the driveway when he lit into her.

"Why must you make everything so hard, Indira? You should show her more respect."

"Maybe if she stopped picking on me, I would."

"It's her birthday and you show up with that ridiculous haircut knowing it will upset her."

"It's not ridiculous," Indira muttered, skimming a hand across the shaved side.

"Would it kill you to at least pretend to go along with her wishes?"

"Oh, I should be more like you? I should pretend to be someone I'm not? Lie?" Indira gave a bitter laugh. "You know what? Never mind, golden boy. You deserve what you get. Before you know it, you'll be married to *that* woman. Miserable. When are you going to stop hiding, Amar? When are you going to stand up for yourself?"

Amar didn't answer. Indira fell silent. Crossing her arms, she slouched low in the seat. She'd left the party with every intention of telling him about Rani and Falguni's grandiose plans for his life but decided against it.

Since he was so smart, he could damned well figure it out for himself. When it all came crashing down around him, she wouldn't be the one to save him.

10

IT WILL ALL BE OVER SOON.

It was this thought, and this thought alone, that brought a modicum of relief, a scrap of sanity into a world that had been upended by the sudden appearance of the girl sprawled across the bed. The roommate slept on the other side of the apartment. Neither girl had stirred.

Mallory's dark hair fanned across the pristine pillowcase. She was beautiful. Yes. A jewel on display, dreaming her blissful dreams. Unaware that she was no longer alone.

All things in life had a cycle—a beginning and an end.

This girl—her life would come to an end. Soon.

The figure stood beside the bed, breathing hard. A remote control was clenched in one hand. A knife was clutched in the other.

A drumbeat of rage built inside the watcher, slowly rising from the pit of the stomach, amplifying through the chest, until the pounding beat through the base of the skull. Until the thundering rage became a roar too deafening to ignore.

The girl. The girl. The girl.

Fingers spasmed around the hilt, tightening the grip.

It will all be over soon.

The floorboards creaked as the intruder stepped closer. Then a noise cut through the silence. It was coming from somewhere above.

A dog. *Barking.*

The girl on the bed stirred.

The intruder's breath caught.

11

WINGS. A RUSH OF WINGS BEAT AGAINST THE BEDROOM WINDOW. A steady thump, thump, thump rattled the glass as they tried to fight their way inside. Two black birds. No. Three. The birds stared through the glass at Mallory, their hollow eyes as dark as night.

Fear clawed its way up the back of Mallory's throat, filling her mouth with a metallic tang. Black birds were bad luck, her grandmother used to say.

Then the three birds became five. Ten. *More.*

The birds crowded the fence outside her window, their ebony feathers choking out the blue sky.

Then the birds took flight. Wings thrashed as they drove toward her window. Beaks and claws scraped against the glass. Mallory's fear expanded, filling her. Consuming her. Overflowing until she cried out in terror.

She waved her arms, as heavy as lead, trying to scare them off. But the birds...they refused to go. They just kept coming. Everywhere she looked, there were more. Hundreds of them.

All coming. Pounding the glass. Desperate to claw their way inside.

The window finally broke. Panic exploded like a bomb inside Mallory's chest. Her heart thundered as they drove toward the hole in the glass. Screaming. Scrabbling their way inside. She collapsed as the birds came at her. Curled on her side. Knees to her chest. Arms pulled tight, protecting her face. The flock descended. Sharp beaks. Razor claws. Pecking her. Scratching. Shredding her skin.

The pounding torrent of wings drowned out Mallory's screams.

"Mallory!"

The pounding grew louder, jarring her from sleep. Shelby cracked the bedroom door open.

"If you're going to leave your phone lying around, Mal, at least have the decency to mute the stupid thing."

Cold sweat clung to Mallory's skin like dew. She pulled the comforter close around her and sat up.

"My phone?" *Not possible.* Confused, she stared at the object grasped in Shelby's hand. "I always plug it in here."

The charging cable dangled uselessly over the edge of her night table. Shelby tossed the phone onto her bed. It landed on the comforter with a thud.

"Apparently not. It's been ringing for the last fifteen minutes."

"Sorry," Mallory said.

She remembered plugging it in before she'd gone to sleep, just like she had every other night. She was still trying to sort it out as Shelby groused.

"Oh, and I've just about had it with that dog."

"JoJo?"

"Who else?" Shelby ran her hands through her hair, smoothing down the sleep-disheveled spikes. "Two a.m. and that damned dog was barking loud enough to wake the dead. Didn't you hear him?"

"I must have died."

"Lucky you. I'm tempted to pick up some antifreeze. That will shut the mutt up."

"Shelby!"

Mallory knew it was an empty threat. As tough as Shelby liked to talk, she would never hurt an animal. JoJo wasn't to blame for his owners' negligence.

"I'll text Iris and James," Mallory promised.

"Whatever," Shelby grumbled and left the room.

Mallory powered up the phone to check her messages, but as the time flashed across the screen, she realized that if she didn't get a move on, she'd be late. She hopped out of bed and dressed in a hurry. Skimming her hair into a ponytail, she emerged from the bedroom and went in search of the keys. Table. Bookshelf. Countertop. *Nothing.* Shelby stood in the kitchen, spooning coffee into a filter as Mallory threw her hands up in disgust.

"My keys. Have you seen them?"

Shelby rolled her eyes. "Seriously, Mal."

"I know, but I'm going to be late."

Shelby heaved a sigh. Setting the coffee tin aside, she checked the countertop while Mallory dumped the contents of her purse.

"Here."

Shelby pitched the keys to Mallory, who caught them mid-air.

"Thanks. You're a lifesaver."

"Hey," Shelby called from the kitchen. "I thought you said the remote control for the garage was missing."

"Yeah."

Shelby lobbed another object at her. It landed like a hot coal in Mallory's cupped palms.

The remote control.

What the fuck? Was she losing her mind?

"Where...?"

"Beside the coffee pot with your keys."

It was impossible. It wasn't there—hadn't been there—and yet... And yet, it appeared out of nowhere, as if the Universe had somehow spat it out. She couldn't explain it. Nothing about this morning made sense, and Mallory couldn't shake the eerie feeling that swept over her. The nightmare. The phone. Her keys. Now the remote control. It was as if someone was trying to mess with her. But who? Why?

There were no answers as the cold rain leaked through the broken car window on her frantic drive to work. This time of morning, with the commute well underway, parking was a nightmare. Mallory tucked her car into the first open spot and hurried toward the shop.

By the time she arrived, it looked as if a bomb had gone off behind the counter. The lineup extended well past the door. Between customers, Mallory did her best to clean up the mess. Looping her finger through a few of the used ceramic coffee mugs haphazardly dumped on the counter by customers on their way out the door, Mallory heard the order.

"Quad grande breve, please."

She fumbled one of the cups she was carrying and sent it tumbling to the floor. Bits of glass flew everywhere as she spun to face Tim.

"Oh, shit," she said, staring down at the mess.

His face flushed a deep scarlet. "Are you okay?" he asked.

"What? Oh, yeah." She caught her breath and forced a smile. "Just galactically clumsy, that's all."

For a fraction of a second, Mallory's gaze strayed away from Tim's face long enough to catch a glimpse of Katie on the missing persons flyer. Long enough for him to know, without a doubt, that Mallory was lying.

"What's wrong with you? You're off your game."

Jenn's comment was cut short when she caught sight of Tim.

"Quad grande breve," Mallory said, her traitorous voice quavering.

Jenn nodded dully and got to work as Mallory stepped over the glass. The sound of the shattering mug had drawn Joe out of the back. Armed with a dustpan and broom, he slid behind the counter.

"So, uh, how are you? I haven't seen you for a while," Mallory asked, grasping for small talk to help ease the awkward moment.

Tim's face colored. "I've been sort of busy."

"Yeah, I imagine so."

Of all the stupid things to say. Mallory chided herself and punched the order in.

"That'll be four-ten."

Tim reached into his pocket and dug out a wad of change. He dropped two toonies and a loonie into Mallory's upturned palm and tossed another loonie in the tip jar.

"Thanks."

The espresso machine roared to life, filling the tense silence. Mallory crouched to clean up the mess, acutely aware of Tim's presence, but Joe shooed her away.

"I've got this," he said.

Mallory stood up, replaying what she'd said in her head, looking anywhere but at Tim. How are you? Seriously? What was the poor guy supposed to say?

Oh, you know, things have been super weird since my girlfriend went missing and everyone started looking at me as if I'm a serial killer, but hey, a quad grande breve should fix things right up. Idiot.

By the time Joe finished sweeping up the broken glass and depositing it into the trash, Tim's drink was ready. Jenn set it on the counter and Tim grabbed it, looking every bit as relieved to be out of the shop as they were at seeing him go.

With her gaze fixed on the missing persons flyer, Jenn shook her head. "Christ, the balls on the guy, showing up here."

"He has every right to be here. I mean, he needs to get his coffee somewhere, right?"

"Let him go to Timmy's. We'll survive without his business."

There was a Tim Horton's off Lougheed, but it was a pain to get to. Besides, she still wasn't convinced that Tim would actually hurt his girlfriend, but there was no denying that Katie's disappearance was disturbing.

Joe craned his head in Mallory's direction. "You kind of look like her, you know."

"Who?"

His gaze cut to the missing persons flyer.

"Joe!" Mallory swatted him.

"I didn't realize it before, but you're right," Jenn said, piling on and making the whole situation worse.

"You're both being paranoid."

Mallory turned away from the bulletin board and tried to shake off the thought.

Her phone dinged. Mallory pulled it out of her pocket and checked the notification. Snapchat. Mallory thumbed the application and a photo flashed across the screen. The bolt of fear that pierced her chest set her pulse racing.

It was her. And Amar. Outside the school. Locked in an embrace.

Though the photo was dark, there was no mistaking their identities. She remembered walking in the darkness between the two buildings. The creepy sense that swept over her, as if she was being followed.

"Mallory, are you okay? You look like you've seen my dead grandmother's ghost."

Mallory was shaking. Before she could even think to take a

screenshot, the photo disappeared. She forced her gaze away from the phone and drew in a shaky breath.

"Yeah."

But she wasn't okay. She was anything but. She needed to tell somebody about what was happening to her.

Not Joe. Not Jenn.

Amar.

12

THE DAY STARTED LIKE ANY OTHER. A KID FROM HIS SECOND-YEAR class sauntered in looking like he'd just rolled out of bed. The skunky smell of pot wafted off him, explaining the student's bloodshot eyes. The kid dropped a creased copy of the last essay onto Amar's desk. The edges of the paper were curled and frayed, as if it had been crumpled by an angry fist.

"What can I do for you today, Mr. Davis?"

"We need to talk about this."

He gestured toward the red F slashed in the upper right-hand corner of the paper, too large to ignore. Amar suppressed a smirk.

"You do realize that you're enrolled in a class on business ethics, do you not?"

Davis scratched at the scruffy beard on his pockmarked face and shot Amar a withering look.

"Obviously."

This time, Amar couldn't stop the amused grin from sliding across his face. He normally didn't think of his students as dumb, but this kid was something special.

"Tell me, Mr. Davis, are you familiar with the term plagiarism?"

Picking at the frayed fabric of his shredded jeans, the kid gave a lethargic nod.

"It's when you copy something off Wikipedia."

"Mmmm," Amar said, and Davis brightened like he'd just received a gold star. "But you do know that plagiarism doesn't just apply to Wikipedia, right?"

Davis's bloodshot eyes narrowed. "I worked my ass off on this paper. I spent hours poring over source materials. My girlfriend read it and she was impressed. This is my work, Dr. Saraf. I'd swear it on a stack of Bibles."

Davis was a liar. Worse, he was an idiot who thought he was a *good* liar. Amar maintained eye contact but said nothing. The longer the silence dragged on, the more fidgety Davis became. He snatched his paper off the desk and flipped to the back page.

"Okay, I may have forgotten to cite a source or two... It's easy to miss when you get so much stuff off the internet."

"Oh, yes, it must have been very hard," Amar agreed in a mocking tone. "But when you copy an essay word-for-word, you do have to admit that it cuts down on the amount of source material you are required to cite. Wouldn't you agree?"

The kid jerked back in his chair with an indignant look. Amar touched a key on his laptop and his screen sprang to life. He'd preloaded an article published three years ago in *The Harvard Business Review*.

"Indulge me, Mr. Davis. Please read the first paragraph out loud."

He tilted the monitor toward Davis, whose face turned an unhealthy shade of scarlet.

"I didn't copy it. I may have borrowed a few sentences but—"

"It's a word-for-word copy of an article I wrote for *The Harvard Business Journal*," Amar said.

The kid's Adam's apple bobbed once. Twice. His mouth worked soundlessly as if trying to generate an excuse.

"That...that was yours?"

Amar nodded. He knew some lazy students, but this kind of negligence was inexcusable. Davis hadn't even checked the article's byline. Faced with irrefutable evidence of his cheating, Davis was rendered speechless. He stared down at his paper for a long moment. Amar waited to see if he'd try to argue or somehow justify his poor choices. When the kid finally looked up, he wore a faint but hopeful grin.

"Well, seeing as how it's a pretty good paper, and you're a smart guy, Dr. Saraf, I've gotta ask how you justify giving it an F."

Amar emitted a bark of laughter. The kid laughed too, and Amar slowly shook his head.

"I may deserve an A, but you definitely deserve an F."

The smile faded and Davis's chin dropped. "My father will freak if I fail—"

"As fathers frequently do. Furthermore, Simon Fraser University follows a fundamental policy forbidding this type of far-flung folly, which I'm confident that you yourself signed."

The flurry of F words left Davis dazed and blinking, to which his only response was, "Fuck."

"Well said, Mr. Davis."

The student fell silent and ground a thumb and forefinger into his bloodshot eyes. And damned if Amar didn't feel a twinge of pity for the kid. After all, he could write his own master's thesis on family expectations.

"Plagiarism is a serious breach of ethics, Mr. Davis. According to the school's policy, it constitutes immediate expulsion. I will spend some time considering how best to proceed."

A soft knock sounded at the door. It was almost time for his next appointment. Amar looked up, expecting to see another student in the doorway, but the person standing there had no business being in his office, let alone the school.

"Hope I'm not interrupting," Rani said in a softly accented voice.

Amar's shoulders stiffened at the sight of her. She had never been to his office before, and this morning, his calendar was filled with back-to-back appointments. He had no time for this.

"That's all, Mr. Davis," Amar said.

Davis rose, a man defeated, and picked the paper up off the desk. He skulked from the office, the smell of pot in his wake. Rani moved aside to let him pass. Amar went to the window and opened it a crack, allowing the fresh scent of rain to clear the air. He turned to face his fiancée.

"Dr. Saraf sounds so formal," Rani said. "I hope you don't mind my dropping by. I've never seen your office before, and I thought if you were free, we could have lunch."

Her gaze took in the room, from the bookshelves crammed with carefully cultivated tomes, to the stacks of papers neatly piled on his desk. Though some professors littered their offices with family photographs and other trinkets that provided insight into their lives, there were few personal touches inside his.

"There's not much to see," he said, gesturing to the four walls where he spent the majority of his time hunched over his laptop, working.

Rani nodded. "It could use a woman's touch. Maybe some photographs. We never did have a proper engagement photo done."

Wordlessly, Amar shook his head. She wanted her picture on display. An engagement photo, soon to be followed by wedding portraits, and family snapshots of children. A lifetime summed up in silver frames.

"I'm busy," Amar said, a little more sharply than he intended.

Rani's expression fell. Anger flared in her eyes. "I texted you this morning asking if I could stop by, but you never answered. I came all the way here to see you, and now you treat me as if I'm unwelcome."

If Rani thought that pouting would make him feel guilty, she had no clue what he put up with on a daily basis. Before he could say another word, he sensed someone else lingering in his doorway.

Amar looked up. The ground beneath his feet seemed to shift at the sight of Mallory staring at them. The two women he intended never to meet were now within fifteen feet of each other, and it took every ounce of his self-control to hide the sudden storm of emotions he felt. Rani shifted her stance, as if somehow, intuitively, she'd picked up on the significance of the moment. Her dark eyes turned flinty as she returned Mallory's stare.

It didn't help that Mallory was so damned beautiful. He was afraid to look at her—to look at either of them.

"Ms. Riggins. I wasn't aware we had an appointment," Amar said.

"I...I didn't mean to interrupt."

A tremor of uncertainty shook Mallory's voice, as if she too realized that she'd walked in on something she wasn't meant to see.

Rani flashed a hard smile. "Amar, this must be one of your students. I'm Rani, Amar's fiancée."

"Fiancée?" Mallory said.

"I was just leaving."

Rani pressed up on her toes and planted a searing kiss on Amar's lips. She had never kissed him so boldly before, and he knew damned well the kiss wasn't meant for him. She was making a point. Branding him.

Amar ran the back of his hand across his mouth as if he could wipe away the stain of what had just happened. When he finally looked at Mallory, her face was ashen.

In that moment, Amar realized that he was every bit as weak and duplicitous as Davis, the cheating student who had just fled his office. His lies had finally caught up with him.

"Look, Mallory..."

His pulse throbbed. He felt it all the way from his temples to his fingertips. Mallory spun away, but not before he saw her tears. His heart cracked open at the pain he'd caused. He had never felt more ashamed.

"You've been lying all along."

"No—"

Amar stopped himself. Why couldn't he speak the truth? For once? She deserved to know what a coward he was. The easy, and maybe the right, thing to do would be to make a clean break. Ending the relationship would solve so many problems with his job, with Rani and his family, but standing here staring down into her face, the thought of ending things made his chest ache. She was a bright spot, a glimmer of light and happiness in his life, and he didn't want to let her slip away.

His mind was still reeling with what to do when he heard a knock.

Surely to god, he could have ten minutes without another student barging in.

"Dr. Saraf."

Amar closed his eyes and heaved a heavy sigh. He turned his gaze toward the door where two men stood waiting. The shorter man was fit, with gray strands threaded through the temples of his brown hair. The taller of the two had a paunch and a blond brush cut. They were both dressed in suits.

Without a word, Mallory wiped her cheeks and fled the office. Amar watched her go. Gathering his composure, he met the curious stares of the men.

"Dr. Saraf, I'm Detective Wes Moreland, and this is Detective

Ray Bradford," the taller man said. "We need a few minutes of your time."

Police?

"What's this about?"

"It's about your student, Katie Lord."

13
_____

"WHO WAS THAT?" DETECTIVE BRADFORD ASKED, SHOOTING A curious gaze after Mallory, who had just fled.

The detective's timing couldn't be worse. Amar needed a moment to think. To compose himself. To sort through the storm of emotions that raged inside him. But there was no time.

He took a breath and forced himself to focus on the immediate problem at hand.

"A student," he said.

"She looked upset."

"This may shock you, detective, but I deal with dozens of students every day who are dissatisfied with their grades, who are failing their courses because they can't be bothered to hand in their assignments and blame me for their failings. They come in droves to my office so they can rail against the injustice of it all. In fact, another student is due to arrive at any moment. I suggest we schedule an appointment to meet at a more convenient time."

The two detectives exchanged a look that indicated they had no intention of being dismissed.

"This will only take a few minutes, Dr. Saraf."

Nettled, Amar rounded his desk and took a seat. He fiddled with his monitor, repositioning the display, then set the contents of his desk back to rights. Pens were stowed. Papers stacked. Several seconds passed in silence. Amar looked up.

"What about Ms. Lord?" he prompted, anxious for this to be over.

"You're aware she is missing?"

"Suffice it to say that every student and faculty member on campus is aware. You'd have to live under a rock not to be."

"She is one of your students?"

Amar nodded. "Among hundreds of others."

"According to her calendar, she had a meeting with you the morning she disappeared."

Amar shrugged in a palms-up gesture. "If it's on my calendar, then it must be so."

"You don't remember?"

"Have you spoken to all of Ms. Lord's other professors?"

"Not yet," the tall one with the paunch said.

Amar arched an eyebrow. "Only those of a non-Caucasian variety?"

The insinuation was clear, and the detective's face flushed. "Can you tell us about your meeting with—?"

"I'm sorry," Amar interrupted. "I didn't catch your name."

"Detective Moreland. So, about Ms. Lord—"

"Ms. Lord recently failed an assignment and arranged a meeting with me to discuss ways in which she could earn extra credit."

"Extra credit?" Moreland cocked his eyebrow suggestively and Amar shot him a withering look.

"I'm sure Wikipedia has defined the term 'extra credit.' I can look it up for you if you like."

The cutting tone hit its mark and the detective scowled.

"Did you see Ms. Lord on the day she disappeared?"

Amar heaved a sigh. He checked the appointment on his calendar and clicked on his daily notes file. It took less than twenty characters to sum up the results of the meeting.

"She never showed."

The two detectives exchanged a skeptical look. "Did you call her?"

"Of course I didn't call her," Amar scoffed. "Why would I? I'm not her parent. I didn't see her. I didn't speak with her. I don't know where she is, now if that's everything…"

Amar made a show of checking his watch. The policemen rose from their chairs.

"Thank you for your time, Professor."

Amar nodded, glad to be rid of the pair. The student who was supposed to arrive next was a no-show.

The unexpected break in his schedule came as a relief. He texted Rani, asking if she was still free for lunch. After everything that had happened that morning, they needed to talk. Her response was almost immediate.

Amar chose a restaurant close to campus. By the time he arrived, Rani was already seated at a table by the window. Her placid gaze stretched beyond the lush gardens to a graceful wooden bridge arched over a koi pond. Amar studied her as he approached,

expecting to see at least a fraction of the fury and betrayal in her face that he'd seen in Mallory's eyes.

Her welcoming smile held no trace of bitterness as he took the seat across from her.

"I'm sorry, Amar. I shouldn't have stopped by your office without calling."

He expected her to yell, to call him out for being a lying, cheating sonofabitch. But instead, she sat across the table, smiling at him as if this was a date.

It didn't make sense. The moment Mallory had entered his office, Amar had felt the tension in the room spike, and he knew that Rani perceived Mallory's presence as a threat. It was the whole reason she'd kissed him the way she had, and now she was acting as if none of that had ever occurred. Instead of feeling relieved, the incongruity of her response left him deeply unsettled.

"Rani, it's time we talked—"

"I agree," she said, cutting him off. "We've waited too long to have this conversation."

A wave of relief crashed over Amar, draining the tension from his shoulders. Could it really be this simple? Had she come to the same conclusion that he had, that their relationship wasn't going to work and it was time to move on?

"I'm glad you agree. I've been trying to—"

A bright smile broke across her face and she reached for his hand. "I've found the perfect place for the wedding."

In the stunned silence that followed Rani's proclamation, Amar blinked. Extricating his hand from hers, he picked up his water glass and took a sip, carefully composing his thoughts.

"I think you've misunderstood, Rani. I don't want to marry you."

Rani recoiled. Her hands flew to her mouth. Tears filled her eyes and Amar shrank back. The guilt that had been hardwired in him since birth left him feeling like the most loathsome creature in the world.

"What do you mean?" Rani's shrill voice trembled, drawing attention from a pair of women sitting nearby.

Amar leaned across the table toward her, softening his tone.

"You know things aren't right between us."

"Not right?" Rani blinked, sending tears streaking down her face. "What do you mean not right? We're engaged. We're going to get married—"

Just then, at the worst possible moment, the waiter appeared.

Amar shook his head, waving him off. He drew in a steadying breath and forced the words out.

"We're not. I can't. I...I don't love you."

They were direct. Brutal. Undeniably true. Rani's face crumpled in response.

"What...what will my mother say? What will she think?"

"She doesn't matter. This is about us. Rani, please—"

"This is because we—" With a quick shake of her head, Rani bit the words off. Averting her gaze, she looked out the window toward the gardens, where the rain began to fall. "Am I not enough?"

He'd never meant to make her feel this way and the fact that he had strung her along filled him with shame.

"I'm sorry, Rani."

She jerked back from the table and abruptly stood. All eyes were on them as Rani forced an agonized smile and fled.

14

Indira emerged from her apartment and quickly walked Hazel three blocks to the postage-stamp park closest to her house. Fog wafted in off English Bay, making the morning feel a full ten degrees colder than it was. Indira shivered in her leather jacket, wishing she'd grabbed something warmer.

The dog's gray snout nuzzled the ground as she searched the damp grass, the tree roots, and traversed along the dormant flower beds looking for just the right place to do her business.

Indira's thoughts were on work and not the dog. She didn't see the older lady walking the small puffball of fur at the end of a sparkly pink leash until it was too late. Hazel spied the Yorkie first and took off like a rocket. The torque of the pit bull's sudden lunge to the end of her leash almost ripped Indira's arm from her socket. She emitted a yelp of pain as the leash was ripped from her grasp. But Indira's cry was nothing compared to the terrified yelp from the Yorkie.

The Yorkie took off and Hazel gave chase. Indira sprinted after them. Indira was shouting for her dog to stop, but Hazel didn't hear her—her brain was locked onto the Yorkie, whose keen survival instincts kept it one step ahead. Half a dozen blocks passed in a furious blur of startled pedestrians scrambling to get out of the path of the running pit bull, and the blare of car horns as the two dogs darted out into traffic.

Indira lagged a block behind, still screaming at Hazel to stop, arms pumping, heart hammering. Sweat dripped down her scalp and stung Indira's eyes. She was running as fast as she could, but the dogs were still a block and a half away when she saw Hazel cut into an alley.

Indira burst into the alley and found Hazel stopped in front of a dumpster. Her snout was shoved in the narrow space between it and the ground. From six feet away, she could hear Hazel sniff. Then, throwing her head back, great, thunderous barks shook the dog's chest.

From beneath the dumpster, Indira heard the terrified Yorkie screech. Indira stumbled forward and grabbed Hazel's leash. Using every ounce of strength she had left, she dragged Hazel away from the dumpster and the small dog.

"Hazel, no."

She had barely managed to regain control of the dog when the Yorkie's owner came blazing into the alley with a young police officer in tow. Mascara tracks smeared down the woman's face as she lit into Indira.

"That dog is a menace. What were you thinking, bringing him to the park? Vicious dogs like that ought to be destroyed."

"She's not vicious."

"He would have shredded my poor baby to pieces. I should sue you. I should..."

"Ma'am," the police officer said, trying to inject reason into the conversation. "I know you're upset, but if you could calm down."

"Charge her, officer. My taxes pay your salary and I demand that you charge her and that killer dog."

The cop turned toward Indira while the Yorkie's owner dropped to her knees and tried to coax the terrified animal from its hiding spot.

"I'm sorry, officer. This has never happened before. She's usually such a good girl."

The officer nodded and checked the dog's license. Hazel was sitting by her side with a look of such pure innocence, it was impossible to fathom that she was the source of such chaos. Indira ran her fingers along the ragged edge of Hazel's ear. The lady at the shelter told her that the injury had occurred when Hazel was just a pup. Indira hadn't gone looking for a pit bull, but one look into the dog's soulful eyes and she knew she couldn't leave her there to be destroyed.

"Are you okay, ma'am?"

Indira nodded. "Just winded."

"I can't believe that you brought that beast to the park. There should be a city-wide ban on dogs like that."

Indira bit her tongue to stop herself from defending Hazel. The police officer held up a hand, bringing the older woman's tirade to a merciful halt.

"I understand that you're upset, ma'am," he said, "but your dog is fine."

"Fine? Fine?" the woman asked, burying her nose into the Yorkie's matted blonde coat. "She's terrified. Just feel her. She's shaking all over."

The cop met Indira's eyes and gave his head a small jerk toward the sidewalk, where passersby had gathered to watch. He followed.

"Because no one was hurt, I'm going to let you off with a warning."

"Thank you," Indira said, relieved that both dogs were safe.

Binding the leash around her arm, Indira strode down the alley. The crowd parted, giving the dog a wide berth.

"Oh, Hazel," she muttered under her breath. Hazel trotted alongside, oblivious to all the drama she had caused.

Indira arrived to work far later than she'd intended, emotionally and physically spent from the drama of the chase. The team was gathered around the conference room table as Dylan walked through the demo on the screen. Indira took a seat in the back.

"Based on a number of factors, including location, browsing history, and keyword recognition, we have constructed a profile that allows us to predict Sunny's buying patterns—what she's likely to buy, what price she's willing to pay, even where she's likely to buy it."

"Very impressive, Dylan," Troy Goff, the vice president of engineering, said with an approving nod. "Your team has made significant progress in a short time. Great work."

"Thank you, Troy. We couldn't have done it without Indira. Her work on the predictive algorithm has put us weeks ahead of schedule."

A ripple of applause broke out across the conference room, and Indira felt the heat rise in her cheeks. Troy and Preet both smiled at her and she acknowledged them with a nod. It was good of Dylan to recognize her contributions, but she preferred her praise in private.

"Any team who has worked this hard deserves a celebration," Preet said.

The team filed out of the conference room. A few stopped to congratulate Indira as they left the building, reconvening for a team offsite across the street at the Yaletown Brewery.

On her way out of the office, Sabina stopped by Indira's desk.

"There she is—the woman of the hour. Ready to go?"

"God no, I've had a day."

"Oh, no you don't." Sabina shook her head and tugged Indira from her chair. "You don't get to hide here while the team celebrates your success."

"It's not just my success," Indira protested.

"Suddenly you're modest?"

"Fine. Let's go."

Just past noon, the brewery was quiet, with only a handful of patrons populating the bar. They followed the sound of laughter and loud conversation to a room near the back where the team had reassembled.

Sabina sized up the group in an instant, focusing her attention on a handsome guy in marketing. He'd travelled from the San Jose office with Troy and Preet for the demo.

"Well hello," Sabina purred. "Let's go meet him."

"Not me. You're on your own," Indira said.

"What? I thought you were supposed to be my wingman."

"You're perfectly capable of flirting without me."

Sabina shot her a smirk. "Well, if you insist."

Indira watched Sabina with a touch of admiration. When Sabina saw something she wanted, she went after it. Indira drifted toward the back of the room and took a seat with the engineering group. A waitress passed by, carrying a tray of foam-capped beer pitchers. Indira grabbed an empty glass and filled it up.

Her gaze drifted to where Dylan sat, deep in conversation with a group of fellow engineers. They were talking over each other, verbally sparring, the way they always did when they were talking shop. For a moment, Indira was tempted to jump in, but held back. She wasn't intimidated by their technical knowledge; she knew she could more than hold her own. Indira contented herself to sip her beer and watch the team dynamics play out.

They looked up to Dylan and he'd slid into his new role as team lead with apparent ease. The way he'd highlighted her contributions in front of the executives surprised Indira, and she wasn't sure quite what to make of it. They'd spent years trying to outdo each other on the technical front. It was a dynamic she was comfortable with. And this...this was something new.

For some inexplicable reason, she was still watching Dylan when Preet interrupted her thoughts.

"I never did develop a taste for beer," Preet said, pulling up a chair beside Indira.

"You couldn't pay me to drink a lager, but this..." She held up the glass to the light, admiring the amber hue. "This is good."

"I'll drink to that 'cause you know what they say, it's five o'clock somewhere."

Preet summoned the waitress and ordered a glass of sauvignon blanc. Indira looked around, hoping to catch Sabina's gaze, but no luck. Indira was comfortable with the engineers, but Preet was a different animal. Smart. Political. Right about now she would welcome anyone willing to join their group. Even Dylan.

"You've been doing great work, and believe me when I say, it's being noticed," Preet said. "Troy is definitely looking at you as one of the up-and-comers on the team."

"Despite what Dylan said, it's been a team effort."

"Spoken like a true leader." Preet eyed Indira with a curious look and sipped her wine. "So, speaking of leadership, how's Dylan doing in his new role?"

"He's fine."

"Fine," Preet mimicked with a laugh. "Do tell."

"I meant to say he's good. He's doing well." Dammit. Why was she so nervous?

"Funny, I got the distinct impression the two of you didn't get along."

Indira shrugged. "We have different styles, that's all."

Preet's expression turned thoughtful as she took another sip of wine. "You know, we're opening a role for an architect in the San Jose office. I was thinking you might be a perfect fit. You've definitely got the skill set and it would be good to have more women in leadership roles, especially on the technical side."

The last thing that Indira expected from Preet was a promotion, especially considering the project's rocky start where she'd basically accused them of being morally bankrupt based on their cavalier treatment of privacy.

A promotion like this could really be great for her career. Great for her life. Her parents would stop nagging her about moving home. She would finally get the independence she craved. A smile broke across Indira's face.

Beer in hand, Dylan approached the two of them.

"This looks serious. I'm not interrupting, am I?"

Without missing a beat, Preet turned away from Indira and offered Dylan a brilliant smile.

"Interrupting? Of course not. We were just having a little girl talk."

Dylan reached across the table for the pitcher of beer. Suddenly in the mood to celebrate, Indira stopped him.

"Forget the beer. Let's order some shots."

She raised her hand to flag down the waiter. Just then, her phone pinged. She ignored it, refusing to let the daily bachelor update interrupt the team celebration. Two seconds later it rang.

Her mother.

Indira heaved a heavy sigh. Excusing herself, she stepped away from Dylan and Preet and answered the phone.

"Mom, I'm at work. This isn't a good time."

"Did you know?" her mother demanded.

Indira rubbed her forehead, confounded, feeling as if she had walked into a conversation that was already underway. "Know what?"

"What your brother has done?"

"Amar? What are you—?"

"He's made a mess of everything. I want you to call him. You both need to come home. Tonight. Your father is very upset."

"Look, I'm sure if you just called him—"

"No. He won't answer my calls. You need to call him, Indira. Now."

What the hell had Amar done to upset her parents? Before she could protest, or find out more, her mother hung up. Indira pocketed the phone.

Over the rim of his beer glass, Dylan studied her. "Is everything okay?"

Indira grimaced. "Family drama. I've got to go."

"What about the shots?"

"Next time."

15

AMAR ARRIVED AT THE LECTURE HALL AS HIS STUDENTS WERE FILING in. On a normal day, he would have already set up for his lesson. But nothing about today had been normal. The toll this morning's events had taken on him left him feeling shaky. He needed to focus. Forget his problems and get through this class. Then he'd talk to Mallory.

Amar removed the laptop from his bag and hooked it up to the video system. Even as he fired up the slides he'd prepared for tonight's lecture, he knew that he just couldn't do it—stay focused while he drilled through the dry material laid out in the syllabus. He scanned the auditorium, hoping for a glimpse of Mallory. An electric jolt of adrenaline coursed through him as he spotted her, and his breath quickened.

"Today we were going to talk about Acting Out Ethics, but tonight, I thought we could have a more personal discussion about something we all face as students, workers, and, dare I say it, human beings in all our flawed glory."

Amar paused and glanced toward the back of the auditorium

where Mallory sat, only to find that she was staring at her phone. On any other night, and if she were any other student, he'd call her out for being on her phone, but tonight he didn't dare. It was enough that she was here. That had to mean something. Amar cleared his throat.

"Tonight, we're going to talk about lying," he said.

Dozens of students looked up, their curiosity piqued. Even Mallory met his eyes, though her expression remained guarded. Not that he could blame her, after what he'd put her through.

"As children we are taught that we shouldn't lie to our parents, to our friends, our teachers. Our caregivers tell us cautionary tales about what happens to naughty little children who lie. We grow long noses like Pinocchio, or we place ourselves in physical peril like the boy who cried wolf one time too many. Tell me, is there anyone sitting in this class who hasn't told a lie?"

A ripple of chuckles passed through the students, and as expected, not a single one raised their hand. Amar's racing pulse slowed as he started to find his rhythm.

"Thank you for being honest," Amar said amid the students' trailing laughter. "So, if we're all taught that lying is wrong, let me ask you this. Is it ever right to tell a lie?"

A low murmur rumbled across the auditorium as the students contemplated the question.

"Do these jeans make my ass look fat?" one student called out.

"No, your ass does it for you," another student answered.

A hearty round of laughter followed the tired joke. Amar let it play out for a few seconds before raising his hands, instructing the class to settle.

"Yes, if asked that question by your mate, every man with an intellect bigger than a frozen pea knows that this probably isn't the moment for brutal honesty. So, from this we can infer that lying could potentially be the right choice if your goal is to spare the feelings of someone you care about. Are there other circumstances in which lying might be appropriate?"

"No, Mom, I'm totally getting A's across the board."

"Consider this, it's moments before your boss goes on stage to give a high-stakes presentation, and she asks you about her outfit. Frankly, you think it's a very unflattering choice, the color's wrong, or the fit. Whatever the issue, at this critical juncture, she's asked for your opinion. What would you tell her?"

A student raised her hand. Amar gestured for her to speak.

"I would tell her the truth. I mean, she wouldn't have asked if she didn't want to know."

"Really?" Amar said, injecting a note of skepticism into his voice. "If you had a speck of spinach lodged in your teeth, I would surely tell you, but would you pick this exact moment to tell the brutal truth, knowing that if she's worried about how she looks, it is likely to have a detrimental effect on her self-confidence and she could fall flat on her face?"

"Still, she asked. How could she trust your opinion if you lie?" the girl persisted.

"Let me change the scenario slightly. What if your boss asked you that same question a few hours before the meeting? She has enough time to go home and change. Would you do it then? Would your answer differ if time weren't a factor?"

Teaching was all about making students think, and he relished the quiet that settled over the classroom as his students contemplated the subtle shift in the scenario, more fully appreciating the nuance of the ethical dilemma.

"Break up into groups of four. I want you to discuss your own personal code of ethics when it comes to lying. What's acceptable? What isn't? Where do you draw the line?"

A spike of energy followed his directions as the class began their discussions. Amar allowed his gaze to drift toward Mallory again, hoping for a glimpse into what she was feeling. Of course, she was sitting beside that idiot, Sinclair. Somehow, he always managed to find a way to position himself next to her. Whatever the idiot had said made Mallory smile. Amar looked away.

The bastard was flirting with her, and there wasn't a damned thing he could do about it.

"What's the biggest thing you've ever lied about, Mr. Sinclair?" Amar called out, hoping to catch the idiot off guard and break up their little tête-à-tête.

"Uh, my parents found pot in my room once. I said I was holding it for my buddy."

"Inventive. So your own personal ethic is to protect yourself at all costs? Did any of you find motivations other than the need for self-preservation highlighted in Mr. Sinclair's example that demonstrated a more complex code of ethics?"

Sinclair deflated before Amar's eyes and sank into a petulant state. A flurry of students shared their conclusions, some of which were quite clever. Once the class had run out of dialogue, Amar knew that it was time to wrap up.

"The truth is that everybody lies. Nobody wants to hear the truth all the time because, frankly, the truth sucks. Let's be honest, telling the truth without fail is hard. Painful. Exhausting. And how many friends, lovers, spouses would you end up with at the end of all this truth-telling?"

Mallory stared directly at Amar. He paused, holding her gaze.

"We all lie. To say otherwise would be, you guessed it, lying. The question isn't about whether we *should* lie. The question is more about why we lie and knowing when we need to tell the truth. It's about understanding the moment when you simply must establish a baseline of honesty and trust in the relationships that matter the most to you. The ones you can't live without."

Amar's gaze lingered on Mallory for several beats of silence, hoping against hope that she would understand. That she might find it in her heart to forgive him.

"It also means understanding the culture you're dealing with. Next week we're going to talk about the ways in which business ethics differ across cultures. What holds true in North America might be very different in Germany, the UK, or dare I say it, China."

The buzz of animated chatter filled the lecture hall as the students filed out. Amar pulled out his cell phone and texted Mallory.

We need to talk. Will you meet me?

The five minutes it took for her to respond felt like an eternity. Hope flared as three wavy dots flashed across the screen before Mallory sent her response.

Where?

The one-word answer released the band of tension constricting his chest, and for the first time since Rani had showed up in his office this morning, he felt as if he could breathe again. Maybe he could fix things. Maybe there was a way to make Mallory understand why he had hidden the truth from her. From his family. From everyone.

Amar's phone rang. Assuming it was Mallory, he picked up the call without checking. It was Indira.

"You need to get here. All hell is breaking loose."

"I can't."

"That's not an option, Amar. You need to get your ass down here. Now."

16

THE HALF-EATEN DONUT HAD GROWN STALE. DETECTIVE MORELAND pitched it inside a paper bag and crumpled the remains. He dropped the bag onto the floor, where it rolled beneath his feet. Bradford frowned. Moreland ignored it. Over the years, they had become like an old married couple. Bradford's neurosis about keeping the car spotless was more than a little irritating. As much as Bradford hated clutter, Moreland couldn't stand the smell of the green tea Bradford drank.

If marriage had taught him anything, it was how to pick his battles, and neither of these hills, the smelly tea or the crumpled trash, were hills he wished to die on. Ignoring his partner's ire, he stretched his gaze across the busy street, to the job site where Tim Atwood worked.

"Every day, the same thing. He gets up, comes to work, finishes his day, goes home, drinks a protein shake, and watches *The Bachelor*. Same thing the next day. Lather. Rinse. Repeat," Moreland said.

"He knows we're watching."

"If so, he's smarter than he seems."

"You're not buying the regular guy act, are you?" Bradford asked, unimpressed.

"Three interviews, and his story hasn't changed. He says the night before Katie disappeared, they broke up. If that's true, what's his motive? You think he's lying about who broke up with whom?"

Bradford smirked. "Listen to you. *Whom.* You're so proper."

Pointedly ignoring the smart-assed remark, Moreland continued, "He's got an alibi."

"His parents," Bradford pointed out. "You don't think they'd lie to protect their kid? What if Katie broke up with him and he snapped?"

Moreland rasped his thumb across his stubbled chin and fell silent. Two weeks into the investigation and they still weren't any closer to figuring out what had happened to Katie. Her parents were frantic with worry, and who could blame them? It was as if, after her phone had been pitched into the ferns, she'd disappeared off the planet.

"Atwood's cell phone movements confirm his story. He did go to Abbotsford that night."

"What's to say Katie's body wasn't rolled up in a tarp stuffed in the back of his truck?" Bradford asked.

"Then what about her phone?"

"Atwood could have gone to her place that morning. Cleaned up whatever happened. Created a false trail."

"So, he fakes her going to the park for a run and pitches the phone where he knows we'll find it?"

Bradford's look skewered him to the seat. "You got a better idea?"

"What about the professor?"

"Dr. Hottie? That pretentious prick?" Bradford smirked.

"He was clearly lying about something. Did you see the way

that girl looked at him? Tell me you don't think there was more going on."

Bradford agreed. The tension inside the professor's office had been palpable. They had walked in on something, that was for damned sure.

"And then there were those texts on Katie's phone," Moreland pressed. "Katie bragging that she'd slept with the good doctor."

"She didn't actually say she slept with him. Innuendo. Bravado. Something to make her friends jealous, that's all. It doesn't *prove* anything. Aside from the calendar entry, we have nothing that links the two."

"He doesn't have tenure," Moreland pointed out.

"True," Bradford said. "But my money's still on Atwood and a lover's spat."

Bradford trailed off. Moreland gave a sigh. Dusk had fallen. The bright lights illuminating the job site began to shut off, plunging the high-rise building into darkness. Empty windows gaped like hollow eyes in the concrete and steel façade. They waited as one by one, the workers began leaving the job site. Spying Tim Atwood's truck, Moreland straightened in his seat.

This wasn't like all the other times. Atwood wasn't alone.

"Well, would you look at that," Bradford said, his interest piqued.

Bradford slid the gearshift into drive and tucked into the flow of traffic, carefully hanging a few cars back. Moreland kept his eyes pinned on the suspect.

"We need to get another look inside that truck."

17

THE BISTRO WAS LOCATED IN NORTH VANCOUVER, IN A SMALL PLAZA that overlooked the Lonsdale Quay. Mallory sat at a table for two by the window, staring out at the Burrard Inlet. Reflected lights from the downtown high-rises swam in the cobalt waves. It was beautiful here, in a perch poised above the ferry dock overlooking the city. The outline of the Lions Gate Bridge arched over the water to one of her favorite places, Stanley Park. Small, intimate, the bistro was the kind of setting you would choose for a romantic dinner, for new beginnings. Hope.

Mallory had already read the drink menu three times, an hour ago. Amar was late. Now she was beginning to wonder if he'd show. This was a bad idea. She still didn't know how to feel about the bizarre lecture he'd given on lying. Was he trying to excuse himself? Ask for her forgiveness?

It wasn't that simple. She'd asked him point-blank if he was in a committed relationship. She'd given him every opportunity to tell her the truth and he'd lied. And yet, here she sat, waiting. Like a fool. The waiter deposited a second glass of wine while deftly removing the empty glass from the table.

Her heart felt like lead in her chest.

She hadn't planned to fall for her professor. In fact, it had been the last thing on her mind the night she'd gone to campus to attend a lecture given by an activist—an inspiring woman whose relentless fight for women's rights in a part of the world where it was dangerous for a woman to speak her mind was heroic.

The auditorium was less than half full, which was a shame, but considering it was a Tuesday night with mid-terms around the corner, the lack of a crowd wasn't surprising. She recognized a few other students, but her gaze was fixed on her ethics professor sitting in the front row. Dr. Hottie. Though the nickname was juvenile, she couldn't argue its merits. With his strong cheekbones, straight nose, and dark eyes, he was impossible to ignore.

Mallory continued to watch him until the lights dimmed and the speaker took the stage. The talk was invigorating, and Mallory left inspired by the speaker's strength. She was still thinking about the talk as she sprinted through the heavy rain toward her car. She cranked the engine, praying to the automotive gods that this time the car would start. Her friends liked to joke that the engine sounded like a garbage disposal trying to shred a tin can. But the ticking sound she heard when she cranked the key was entirely new. Mallory's stomach dropped.

The car was a total money pit.

A hard rain fell, hammering the roof, and Mallory tugged a lever. The hood released with a pop. She climbed outside. Shivering in the cold rain, Mallory propped up the hood. She searched the alien topography of engine parts, hoping for a clue. Steam rising from a broken valve. Some other obvious sign of a problem. But it was hopeless. She wasn't a mechanic, hadn't even dated a mechanic. The sum of her automotive knowledge could be printed on the inside of a matchbook and there would still be left-over space.

She pulled out her cell phone and called her mother.

"Good lord, Mallory. Do you know what time it is?"

By now, calculating the three-hour time difference between Burnaby and her hometown of Kingston should have been second nature, but at times like these, it was easy to forget just how far away from home she was.

"Sorry, Mom."

Her mother heaved a massive sigh. "Okay, what's wrong this time?"

"My car won't start."

"That car of yours, I swear..." Mallory could hear the gears grinding inside her mother's brain, calculating the costs, resenting every red penny she shelled out to keep Mallory afloat. "Where are you?"

"School. I was at a talk."

"There must be someone you can catch a ride home with. Or a bus?"

The last bus had left campus hours ago. Getting home was the least of her problems.

"I can't leave the car here overnight. It will get towed, and even if it doesn't, how will I get to work?"

"It's the middle of the night, Mallory. What do you expect me to do?"

Mallory gripped the trunk lid and rested her forehead against her arm. She needed money to fix the car. Her mother knew it, but instead of helping, she seemed intent on making Mallory grovel for whatever good it would do.

"Never mind, Mom. I'll figure it out."

Mallory hung up. Drenched to the bone, she lowered the prop iron into place and closed the hood with a bang.

"Is everything okay?"

Mallory jumped at the unexpected sound of a man's voice. She swung around to face him. Rain dotted the lenses of his tortoise shell glasses and plastered his hair to his scalp. But even with all that, she recognized him. The sear of a blush surged through her all the way to her toes. *Dr. Hottie.*

"Dr....Saraf," she stumbled, almost using the nickname.

"Car problems?"

"The damned thing won't start."

"Want me to try?"

"Sure."

He slid behind the wheel and gave the engine a crank. The engine emitted a dry clicking noise but didn't fire. After the third try, he gave up.

"It's your starter."

"You know about cars?"

"I know a little about cars. The clicking noise is a dead giveaway."

Mallory closed her eyes. *Well, shit. How much is that going to cost me?* More than she could afford.

"Thanks, Dr. Saraf."

He handed her the keys with a regretful look. She shoved them into her pocket, cursing the car, cursing her bad luck. She would have to walk home in the rain.

"Need a ride?" he asked, as if reading her thoughts.

Could she seem anymore pathetic, dripping wet with a broken-down car?

"If it's not too much bother."

"Not at all," he said.

She followed him across the parking lot to a black BMW and climbed inside. The comforting smell of coconut and leather filled the cabin. She sank back into the seat, grateful to be out of the rain.

"Sorry, I'm drenched."

"That tends to happen when it rains."

He had a dry sense of humor and Mallory grinned. The powerful engine sprang to life on the first try, like it was showing off. Mallory relaxed into the warmth of the car and let her mind drift. What must it be like not to have to worry about money? A car like this. A boyfriend like him. She was so close to graduating, only a few more quarters to go, but damn it was hard. All uphill. And after that? What kind of job would she find? Although the kinds of hardships she faced were nothing like the struggles tonight's speaker had overcome, it was impossible not to worry about the future.

"Kind of late to be leaving campus," he said, making polite conversation as they pulled onto the street.

"I was attending Sheryl WuDunn's talk about oppression," she said.

"Me too. I found the way she summarized the economic benefits of educating women in third world countries particularly fascinating."

Mallory nodded and said, "Yes, and the story about the little girl in China whose parents removed her from school, and how she stood outside the schoolhouse so she could still learn, nearly broke my heart. It's hard to believe that today, places where this sort of thing happens still exist."

"Larry Summers, the former VP of the World Bank, once said that the biggest return on investment in the developing world would be to educate women. Gandhi viewed education as the key factor in emerging from poverty."

The heater enveloped her legs. It was too much to hope that her only shoes would be dry by morning.

"The path toward a better life," Mallory mused.

"Exactly so."

He was surprisingly easy to talk to. There were so many questions she wanted to ask—where he'd grown up, his family, what made him choose a life in academia, whether he liked teaching. She wasn't one of those lucky souls, born knowing what she wanted to do.

"So, what are you planning to do about your car?"

"I was thinking about burning it."

"Difficult to do in the rain, but not altogether impossible."

Mallory grinned. "Yeah, if I stabbed a hole in the gas tank, maybe…"

He laughed and the sudden thought that she could spend a lifetime listening to that laugh shocked her. The schoolgirl attraction she had initially felt turned into something deeper, a longing to connect that she had no business feeling.

"Perhaps I could offer a less extreme solution. I have a cousin who owns an auto repair shop."

She wasn't used to having someone offer help, especially someone she barely knew. She could have hugged him for his kindness, but there was no way she could take him up on it.

"It's so nice of you to offer, but I'm strapped for cash. I'll figure something out."

She could roll the car off a cliff into the harbor and then…

"Let's not worry about the money quite yet. More importantly, where do you live?"

"Near Brentwood Drive, where Parker meets Delta."

"Have you been to that new Thai place off Hastings?"

"No, but I hear it's good."

"I'm starving. Want to try it? My treat," he added, as if reading her mind.

Tomorrow, they'd go back to being student and teacher, but tonight, they were something else, and she wasn't ready for the magic of the moment to end.

"I'd love that."

Mallory could no more stop herself from falling for him than she could stop the rain from falling from the sky.

"Another?"

Rousing her from her memory, the waiter stopped by her table. He'd noticed her second glass was empty. She didn't remember drinking it. The soft rain struck the windows and rolled down the glass. She gazed out the window toward the ferry terminal where the SeaBus had just left the dock. Mallory checked the time.

The tables around her had filled with patrons, couples illuminated in soft pools of candlelight. She seemed to be the only single person in the place. She glanced at the empty chair, the phone, and ordered another glass of wine. Amar wasn't coming. She meant nothing to him. Someone to sleep with. A silly little girl.

Worse. A fool.

If she had a shred of pride left, she would leave now. Go home. But as the waiter dropped off a fresh glass, the pull of the past refused to relinquish its grip and she remembered how nervous she had been during their first dinner together.

She'd flipped through the pages of the menu trying to make up her mind, overanalyzing how each choice would make her look. She glanced across the table at Dr. Saraf, but he had already closed his menu and was pouring them both a cup of jasmine tea.

"You've already decided?" she asked.

He held her gaze, and she held his. She refused to look away, to let the hierarchy of teacher and student spoil this moment. She looked a mess, no longer soaked through but certainly out of place. She was used to that feeling, though. Her hair was mostly dry, but it still hung in damp strings that chilled her neck.

"I think I'll try their swimming angel."

"So, tell me, Dr. Saraf, do you make a habit of rescuing stranded students?"

"You're my first. Dr. Saraf sounds too formal for Thai. Call me Amar."

"Amar."

She liked the way it sounded. Amar Saraf. So exotic.

"You remember the last assignment?" he asked her.

"The paper on choosing a career," Mallory said. "Money versus passion, right?"

"Yeah. You were the only one in your class who didn't wax poetic on the moral imperative of following your dreams. May I ask why?"

Mallory felt a tiny sting of disappointment at his question. A few seconds ago, she had almost allowed herself to forget that they were student and teacher. They had become something else—a man and a woman enjoying each other's company. Seeing each other, as if for the first time. She felt the heat of a blush rush up her cheeks and dropped her gaze to her hands.

"Well, it's like I said. We're part of a generation that hasn't had to strive for much. Most of us come from nice homes. We've never gone hungry. Never had to struggle. The majority of my classmates have parents who are paying for their educations. They don't have student loans. They've never had to worry about money, so from that perspective, it's no wonder they think money isn't important. Money doesn't factor in as a primary motivation in their career choice."

Amar nodded, whether in agreement or acknowledgement, she couldn't tell.

"Exactly, so what makes your experience different from your classmates?"

His curious gaze pierced her, and Mallory looked away. She hadn't expected her essay to expose her vulnerabilities. She could say that she knew where her class would fall on the merits of pragmatism versus passion, and that she had taken the opposing view to distinguish herself, but she didn't.

"My parents fought over money when they were married, and even more so after the divorce. They're not paying for college. Thank god for student loans."

She gave a brittle laugh and glanced up at him, expecting to see pity in his eyes, but seeing admiration and understanding instead.

"University is expensive, and I'm going to need to come out of this with the kind of degree that will help me get a job."

"You don't love business?" he asked.

"I like business just fine, but love..." With a shake of her head, she trailed off. "Sometimes you've got to do what you have to do."

A thoughtful look crossed Amar's face and he nodded. "I understand. That's a mature perspective. So many of your classmates would rail at the injustice of not having their educations handed to them on a silver platter."

Mallory shrugged. "My grandmother always said I was born an old soul."

A companionable silence fell between them. Mallory studied his hands. His fingers were long. Well-shaped. There was no tan line or indentation, or any other indication of a wedding ring that she could see. She could imagine how his hands might feel skimming across her skin. A blush warmed her cheeks at the thought.

Mallory didn't realize how hungry she was until the food arrived. She dug into her phad thai like she hadn't eaten in days.

"Your parents must be proud of you for managing school on your own," he said between bites.

"My mother thinks university is a waste of money."

"And what should you be doing instead?"

Mallory shrugged and offered a wry smile. "In her world, she'd prefer I find a husband. Someone who'll take care of me. Of course that didn't exactly work out for her."

Amar set down his chopsticks and rested his chin on his fist. "She sounds a little like my mother."

"Really?"

"Don't get me wrong, education is very important in my family, but..."

"But?"

"My mother won't be happy until she marries my sister off to a doctor."

The ironic inflection in his voice made her laugh. "Maybe they *are* related. And what does your sister think?"

"Like you, she'd be more inclined to set the young doctor on fire than submit to my parents' will. Of the two of us, she's the engineer."

"What's her name?"

"Indira."

"Are the two of you close?"

"Yes."

She wanted to hear all about his sister, about his family, but as she looked around at the dining room, Mallory was surprised to see that they were the only table left. One of the workers had started tipping chairs up onto the tabletops in preparation for the nightly cleaning.

"I think they're ready to close."

"Oh," Amar exclaimed, glancing at the staff chatting amicably by the bar. "Shall we?"

He motioned the waiter over and paid the bill. Mallory zipped up her damp jacket and followed Amar into the rainy night. For the first time since arriving at the restaurant, the silence between them was awkward. She didn't want the night to end.

But he's your professor.

The low growl of the car engine rumbled through the cabin as he pulled out of the lot. She gave him directions to her place.

"Be it ever so humble..." she joked, feeling suddenly self-conscious of how sad the place must look to him.

"There is no place like home," Amar finished the line. "You know, that's a line to an old nineteenth-century song? The rest of it goes:

A charm from the skies seems to hallow us there

Which seek thro' the world, is ne'er met elsewhere
Home! Home!
Sweet, sweet home!
There's no place like home."

Amar parked in front of the house. His eyes glittered a soft shade of ebony in the dim lights from the dash.

"Thank you for the rescue. And for dinner."

"My pleasure, Mallory," he said.

A thrill coursed through her at the sound of her name on his lips. He was looking at her with a faintly bemused smile, as if he too was surprised to find himself here. The air between them was charged with the tension of the attraction she felt. With all her heart she wished this was a normal date and he would lean across the armrest and kiss her.

"I guess this is good night."

She tore her gaze away and reached for the door handle. He probably had an amazing girlfriend, or worse, a wife. Reluctantly, she opened the car door.

"Mallory?" A spark of hope lit in her chest as she turned toward him. "Your keys?"

"What?"

"Your car keys. My cousin will need them if he's going to work on your car."

"Oh, right."

Idiot, Mallory chided herself. She fumbled in her jacket pocket and was all thumbs as she struggled to separate the key from the keychain. He waited patiently for her to complete the simple task. Her fingers trembled slightly as she placed the key in his upturned palm.

"Thanks again," she said.

"What's your cell number? I'll ask my cousin to call you when it's ready."

She was about to recite the number when he handed her his

phone. Her heart thundered in her ears as she entered her number into his contacts list. It was still raining when she got out of the car and walked toward the house, the desire to look back almost too powerful to ignore.

How much time had she wasted? Their relationship was only a few months old, but she always seemed to be the one waiting. Here she was, sitting in the bistro, getting quietly smashed, while he was god knows where. Probably with his fiancée.

"Would you like to order some food while you wait?" the waiter asked.

She glanced away from the pity she saw in his face and shook her head. The waiter left. Like a fool, she picked up the phone and called Amar. Tears stung her eyes as the phone went to voicemail.

She typed in a text. Erased it. Placed her phone face-down on the table, willing it to ring. She remembered how nervous she'd been the day after he'd driven her home as she waited for him to call. Wondering what she'd say, how he'd act. When she'd seen the unfamiliar number flash on her cell phone's display, she picked it up on the first ring. It was Amar's cousin from the garage.

"We replaced your starter. Your car is ready."

"How much do I owe you?"

"Not to worry. It's been paid for."

The generosity of the gesture left her momentarily stunned. She cleared her throat. Forced herself to speak.

"Thank you."

"No problem. You can pick it up any time before seven."

He gave her the address. Mallory scribbled it down and hung up. She'd order an Uber and go pick it up after she finished school. Her phone buzzed. She saw a text from another unfamiliar number.

When does your last class end?

Amar. It had to be. Who else would ask?

MALLORY: Why? Are you a stalker?

AMAR: Maybe. ☺

MALLORY: If you really were a stalker, you would know that my last class of the day is yours.

AMAR: That makes it easy.

MALLORY: You think I'm easy?

AMAR: I think you might need a ride to your car.

MALLORY: In that case, you'd be right.

AMAR: I'll meet you at the car. Same place as last night.

A little buzz of excitement raced through Mallory. She veered into a restroom. Standing in front of the mirror, she smoothed down her hair and refreshed her lipstick.

"It's not a date," she told her reflection sternly, but her reflection looked unconvinced.

Mallory was all jitters as she walked to the parking lot. She kept her gait deliberately slow and forced herself to breathe. Amar waited exactly where he said he would. Their eyes locked. She felt a jolt of warmth rush through her. Then Amar smiled and Mallory knew that if she lived to be a thousand years old, she would always remember that smile.

"How was your day?"

Long. Boring.

"Good," she lied. "Yours?"

"Two lectures, a department meeting, three whiny students, and a crier. All in all, pretty average."

They pulled into the garage. Amar parked beside her car. A cool wind ruffled Mallory's hair as she followed him toward a man dressed in overalls.

"Mallory, this is my cousin, Rafi."

Mallory extended her hand, and he shook it.

"Good to meet you. That car of yours needs some work."

"Don't I know it?" she said, grinning. "Thanks for getting it running again."

"The keys are in it."

"Thanks."

While Amar spoke with his cousin, Mallory drifted toward her car. Now that the car was fixed, there would be no reason to see him outside of class again. And they would go back to what they were—a teacher and his student.

She smiled as Amar approached. "I can't thank you enough for your help."

Amar smiled back. He stood on the other side of the car door, gazing down into her eyes. A lock of hair blew across her cheek. Amar reached over and smoothed it back. He tucked it behind her ear. Mallory shivered at the sudden contact.

"Glad I was able to help."

"Your cousin seems nice."

"He is."

She was babbling, trying to extend the moment, and he knew it. She averted her gaze away from him to the traffic speeding by.

"Okay. I guess I should go."

"Mallory."

She glanced back. Amar placed a gentle hand under her chin and lowered his mouth to hers. Her breath caught at the unexpected kiss. His lips were soft, full. A flash of heat radiated through her, and in that moment, she felt as if nothing else existed. They were alone in the world.

The kiss ended all too soon. Pulling away, she met his gaze.

Falling in love with him was easy. Breaking up with him...well, that was going to shatter what was left of her heart.

18

EVEN FROM THE SIDEWALK, AMAR HEARD HIS FATHER YELLING. HIS stomach clenched as he took note of Falguni's car parked nearby. There were no secrets in their close-knit community. He'd known they would find out about the broken engagement eventually, though he'd hoped for more time.

Steeling himself for the parental onslaught, Amar opened the front door. His parents waited in the living room, along with Indira and Falguni. The dark expression on his father's face brimmed with anger.

"Is it true?" he bellowed.

"Amar, did you break off the engagement?" his mother asked.

The wadded-up tissues clenched in her fist told Amar that she'd been crying. He swallowed a lump of shame.

"Yes."

Before his father could speak, Falguni uncoiled from the sofa where she was seated beside his sister. Her red-rimmed eyes burned with hatred and bored a hole straight through Amar.

"You. Where is your honor? Where is your decency? Is this

how you were raised?" Falguni hissed. She approached Amar slowly, jabbing a finger toward his chest. "My daughter came to you innocent, and you used her, betrayed her. You've ruined her life."

"Me?" Amar said, incredulous. "You're blaming me? I did the honorable thing. I broke up with her."

"You dare speak to me of honor? You made a commitment to my family. A vow. And now you're throwing her away. Because of that whore?"

"Whore?"

"Rani told me that you've been...been sleeping with another girl."

"Amar, is that true?"

His mother looked stricken by the news, and a deep stab of guilt slashed through him. He'd tried, he'd really tried, to be the kind of man that everyone expected him to be, the kind of man resolved to live a life of obligation. But he refused to live a lie that wouldn't only ruin his life but would make Rani's life miserable too.

Indira was the only one who met his eyes. She rose from the sofa and strode to the middle of the room, positioning herself between Amar and her parents, and Falguni.

"Okay, that's enough," Indira interjected hotly. "Rani's not some innocent child Amar took advantage of. She's a grown woman old enough to make her own decisions."

"Enough," her father barked at Indira. "It is not your place to speak."

"Why, because I'm a woman?"

Her father's jaw clenched. He glowered at Indira, who refused to back down. In the face of his father's fury, his mother would have submitted, but not his sister. She stood strong. Defiant.

The silence that followed their heated exchange was deafening. Amar took a moment to assess the situation with fresh eyes.

Falguni couldn't have orchestrated the situation any more perfectly. By appealing to his parents, she had cast him in the role of the villain. She wanted to shame him. Humiliate him in front of his family in the hopes that they would force him into marrying her daughter, and his father was playing right into her hand.

"This isn't my fault. You've raised Rani to be submissive, to believe that her only inherent value is in becoming some man's wife. You have demeaned her, bullied her until she has no personality of her own. She's completely incapable of thinking for herself. What man would want a wife like that? I haven't ruined her, Falguni. You have."

"Amar!" his mother snapped and sprang from her chair. "I did not raise you to be disrespectful. Falguni has every right to be upset."

Indira raised her small hands, gesturing for silence. "Look, everyone needs to calm down."

"You're going to do the honorable thing, Amar. I demand it of you," his father shouted over Indira's head as if she hadn't spoken.

"I will not. She deserves someone who cares about her and I am not that man."

"Amar, you will apologize to Falguni at once. You will do your duty by Rani. I demand it."

Amar's jaw clenched. He stared silently at his father. He'd given in to so many demands. A lifetime of being told what was expected, how to behave. But this was one bridge too far.

"You can yell. You can rage. You can tell me how ashamed you are of me. How I'm not the man you raised, the man you expect me to be. And while that may be true, the answer is still no."

"Amar!" his mother cried.

For the first time in his life, he was directly defying his father's wishes. It was both liberating and terrifying. He loved them. He would support them. He would always be their son, but he would not sacrifice his happiness to satisfy his father's antiquated notion of honor.

"Amar's right. This is his life. He deserves to make his own decisions," Indira said.

His sister was the only one in his family who understood him, but her words had no effect on their father. He glared at Amar with disdain.

"Never have I been so ashamed to call you my son," his father said, turning his back on both his children.

"Mark my words, Amar Saraf, you will suffer for what you have done to my daughter," Falguni hissed.

"Mom!"

Indira's cry caught Amar's attention. He turned in time to see the color drain out of his mother's face. A fraction of a second later, she crumpled to the floor.

19

MALLORY LEFT THE BISTRO AND WAS DRIVING ACROSS THE SECOND Narrows Crossing when Shelby's text arrived. She was at the Library, a funky little off-campus bar. With a little coaxing from her roommate, Mallory joined her there.

Already buzzed from the wine, she quickly lost count of how many of these deadly little concoctions she had consumed. Served up in a martini glass, the sweet, potent cocktails were called a Crown of Thorns, and not only had they disappeared at an alarming rate, but they also left Mallory with a parched mouth and a spinning head. If all this drinking was supposed to take her mind off Amar, it wasn't working. She found herself thumbing through the trail of flirty text messages they'd exchanged when their romance had just been starting out.

Shelby had abandoned her the moment her ex, a guy named Hunter, arrived. The two of them were out on the dance floor, stuck together like human Lego blocks, while Mallory sat alone.

A passing waitress stopped by the table and gestured toward the empty glass.

"Another?"

Mallory sighed. While another drink was tempting, she declined. She needed water, Tylenol, bed. *Alone.* Unlike her roommate, who Mallory had no doubt would be spending the rest of the night with Hunter. And who could blame her? They looked perfect together. They were having fun, while she was wallowing.

How long would she spend torturing herself over her failed romance? Falling for her professor was so cliché. And she'd actually believed him when he said he wasn't married. Engaged. *Whatever.*

She'd let her hormones override her instincts and that made her dumb. *Dumb. Dumb.*

Mallory pushed away from the table and stood. Her head swam. She pulled out her phone to order an Uber. *Order. Uber.* For some reason, the fact that the words rhymed made her giggle.

She swayed. Grabbed hold of a nearby chair. Tried to steady herself. An arm looped around her waist and Mallory glanced up, half-expecting to see Amar. She recoiled from the face looming inches from hers.

"Brock? What the hell?"

"Relax, I've got you," he said.

Nothing about that statement made her relax in the least. The warm breath fanning her cheeks smelled like beer, and Mallory extricated herself from his grasp.

"I'm fine."

"Fine. Okay," Brock said, holding his hands aloft. "I was just trying to help."

"I'm fine," she repeated, as if saying it again might actually make it true.

"You said that already, but truthfully, Mal, you look a little...wobbly."

She felt more than a little wobbly. She was hammered, not that she'd admit that to him. It was Shelby's fault that she was forced to deal with Brock alone. God, he was such a letch. Which in her current state was a little more than she could handle.

"Where's this mysterious boyfriend of yours? Shouldn't he be helping you?"

"Boyfriend?" she spat, as if it was a curse word. Brock's eyebrows rose and she instantly regretted the slip. "We broke up."

She closed her eyes. Why had she said that? Now she'd never get rid of him.

"His loss."

Mallory struck the table and raised her palms, as if to say, *right*? They had finally found something they *both* agreed on. And really, it was time to go. She pushed away from the table and weaved unsteadily toward the bar. Brock trailed after her like a lost puppy.

He was *so irritating*. Why couldn't he leave her alone? Where was Shelby when she needed her?

Mallory sped up, trying to lose him in the crowd, but she stubbed her toe on a barstool instead. Thrown off balance, she careened toward the floor. Brock grabbed hold of her. Pinned her to his side. Her head spiraled in a dizzying blur of motion and she grasped for the edge of the bar.

"Easy, girl."

Mallory batted his hands away. "Look, I already told you—"

"You told me you're fine. I heard you both times. I just don't believe you."

Crap. Maybe he was right.

Mallory's top rode up. Brock's sweaty hand molded her bare midriff as she leaned against the bar. Signaling the bartender for her check, she fumbled inside her purse, hunting for her wallet. There was barely enough cash to cover bus fare, let alone the cocktails she'd consumed. She was going to have to use her credit card. She handed it to the bartender.

"I've got some Fireball back at my place," Brock said.

As if. Mallory wrinkled her nose at Brock's hot, smelly beer breath and inched a step away. The bartender returned. With a shake of his head, he handed Mallory back her card.

"Declined."

"What?" she called.

Come on. It wasn't *that* expensive. Shit. Now she'd have to use her debit card, which was something she didn't want to do. She was saving the money left in her bank account for groceries. But it couldn't be helped.

Brock handed two twenties to the bartender. Mallory gaped at him.

"No. Really. I've got it."

"It's no big deal, Mal. What are friends for?"

No big deal, he said, but she knew better. If she allowed him to pay for her drinks, she would owe him, and she didn't want to think about the kind of payment he'd expect.

"So, what about it? My place for a drink?"

She gave her head an emphatic shake. "Nope, I've got to go home."

"Aw, come on, you know what they say: All work and no play makes Mallory a dull girl."

Mallory shrugged into her coat and headed for the door, anxious to get away from him before his wandering hands found more than her bare waist. The sobering blast of cold air smelled like cedar and rain. She breathed in a deep lungful, trying to clear her head. Brock kept pace, refusing to take the hint. She whirled around to face him. Her hand on his chest stopped him cold.

"Why are you following me?"

"Christ, Mal, you can't walk ten feet on campus without seeing a missing persons flyer. Whoever took Katie Lord is still out there. It's not safe to walk campus alone."

As much as she hated to admit it, Brock had a point. The night she'd run into Amar on her way to the parking lot, someone had been following her. As if that wasn't bad enough, they'd texted that picture. And then there was the car break-in. The remote control. All the creepy things.

It was the whole reason why she'd gone to see Amar this morning. To tell him about what was happening. But then she'd seen him with...his fiancée. Oh. God. She still couldn't wrap her head around the idea that her boyfriend, ex-boyfriend, was engaged.

Suddenly, Brock following her seemed the lesser of two evils. Mallory stared through the swaying trees toward the parking lot lights. She wanted to go home. Crawl in bed. Forget this horrible day ever happened.

By the time she reached her car, Mallory's head was spinning so fast, she felt as if the car was moving. She rooted through her pockets. Finding her keys, she hauled them out, but Brock snatched them away.

"What? Are you kidding me? You're not driving."

"Who the hell are you to tell me what I can and can't do? I'm a grown-ass woman. Give me my damned keys."

"No way. Best case, you'll end up with a DUI. Worst case, you'll hurt yourself and someone else."

Dammit. He was right. She was in no shape to drive.

"Come on. I'll take you home."

Mallory huffed out a breath. Home was only a few miles away. Even drunk, she could walk it. But the idea that someone might be watching gave her pause.

"Okay, but give me my keys."

She held out her hand. Brock tucked the bundle of keys into her upturned palm and curled her fingers around them, as if she was incapable of hanging onto them herself. His fingers lingered around her fist and she snatched her hand away.

Brock's car was a brand-new Jeep Rubicon, the kind with the fog lights and a hard-shell convertible top. He opened the door for her, and Mallory clambered inside. She swayed a little at the head rush and fell gratefully into the passenger's seat. The interior smelled like coffee and pine. Five minutes after leaving the Library, they pulled up in front of Mallory's house.

"Thanks," she said.

She reached for the door, anxious to get out, when Brock's hand clamped onto her thigh.

"I had fun tonight, Mal," he said. "We should do it again."

His grip tightened, his palm sliding up her thigh. Mallory froze. Regretting the ride. Knowing this would happen.

Her fingers curled around the handle. "Thanks. See you in class."

"You can do better than that."

Brock swooped toward her. Her stomach curdled at the feel of his hot, wet lips on hers. She fought the urge to vomit. She pushed him away. Hard.

Anger lit his dark eyes.

"What the fuck, Mal?"

"Get off me."

"Bitch."

He muttered the word under his breath, but Mallory heard it as she scrambled from the Jeep, praying he wouldn't follow. Of all nights for Shelby to leave her stranded.

If Brock was the kind of guy who wouldn't take no for an answer, she was in deep shit, with only herself to blame.

Mallory slid down the hill toward the house. JoJo barked. The landlords' lights flickered on. For once, she was grateful for the ruckus.

Stones spat from beneath Brock's tires as he screeched away from the curb.

20

"OH, YOU NO LOOK SO GOOD, CHIQUITA," JOE SAID AS HE SKIMMED by Mallory, who was painstakingly removing dimes from the change drawer with shaky hands. This morning, with her head pounding and mouth dry, even simple tasks such as this one required a level of manual dexterity that she did not possess. "You know what they say—the only cure for a really bad hangover is death."

"Thanks, Joe. I'll keep that in mind," she mumbled and handed the customer back his change.

Given how she felt this morning, death didn't sound all that bad, really. When the lineup finally dissipated, she would beg Jenn for a couple of Tylenols. Hell, five minutes without the booming bass drum beating in her temples would be worth the lecture she would have to endure about how irresponsible and unreliable college kids were.

Despite the mountain of classwork piling up, Mallory had every intention of cutting class. Going home after work. Sleeping off the lingering effects of last night's Crown of Thorns. She understood now how the drink had gotten its name. Last night it had been all roses. This morning it was definitely thorns.

"What can I get you?" Mallory asked the next customer in line —a woman with Tammy Faye Bakker eyelashes and Texas fingernails.

"I'll have a decaf soy latte with an extra shot, and cream," the woman said.

Midway through jotting down the order, Mallory paused. "Wait, did you say soy?"

The woman rolled her eyes in an exaggerated you-must-be-the-stupidest-person-on-the-planet expression. "Yeah, soy. That a problem?"

"Uh...you want cream in a soy latte?"

"Yeah. Do I need to draw you a picture? Jesus. It's just coffee."

"Got it," Jenn cut in with a disingenuous smile.

Mallory rang up the drink and the line moved on.

"Next time you're too hungover to work, call in," Jenn said.

Mallory ignored her. It wasn't her fault that the moron with the drink order didn't realize that putting regular milk in soy was about as stupid as a vegan ordering steak tartare. The end of her shift couldn't come fast enough. Even if by some miracle the line eventually slowed down, there was no way she was asking Jenn for a Tylenol, or anything else for that matter. She'd rather deal with the skull-splitting pain than any more of Jenn's condescending remarks.

Traffic finally started to slow when Mallory glanced up to greet the next customer. Her stomach dropped. The fake smile died on her lips. Amar stood on the other side of the counter looking as if he hadn't slept. A heavy five o'clock shadow darkened his jaw, and he was wearing the same clothes he had worn the day before.

"Mallory, I'm—"

She raised her hands. "No."

"But—"

"No."

She gave her head a stubborn shake. He shouldn't be here.

"Mallory?" Jenn said.

"I need to take a quick break."

"But—"

Ignoring Jenn's objection, she moved out from behind the counter and headed for the door. Amar followed. The cold air raised goosebumps on Mallory's bare arms, but she barely noticed. Amar stood a safe distance away, hands thrust into his pockets, staring down at his shoes.

"I'm working, Amar."

"We have to talk."

Mallory crossed her arms and glared at him.

"Now? You want to talk now? We were supposed to talk last night. Or maybe you forgot. I spent an hour at the bistro waiting for you, like an idiot. I sent texts that you never answered. Not a word. And now, you show up here, expecting me to what? Believe that bullshit lecture you gave about how lying is noble, when all you're really trying to do is save your pathetic ass?"

Tears welled in Mallory's eyes. She hated herself for crying. She wanted to slap him. Hug him. She hated herself for wanting things to go back to the way they were, when she knew damned well there was no way they ever could.

"I'm so sorry, Mallory. I was on my way to the bistro when—"

Mallory held up her palm. "Tell it to your fiancée. I'm through listening. I'm through waiting for you. Believing you."

Loving you.

She'd humiliated herself enough for this man, and she wouldn't do it again. Despite her tough words, she was still standing on the sidewalk.

Amar's head dropped into his hands. He was the one who had hurt her and yet she felt sorry for him. It wasn't fair. She should hate him for what he'd done to her.

"Go. Just go."

Mallory shook her head in frustration and started for the door. Amar grabbed hold of her arm and roughly spun her around.

"For fuck's sake, Mallory, would you just listen?"

His strong fingers dug deeply into her flesh. She tried to pull away, but his grip remained firm.

"I broke up with her, okay? I—"

"And that's supposed to make me feel better? I asked if you were in a relationship and you lied to me, and now you think you're some kind of hero because you broke up?"

The door to the coffee shop opened and a voice called out. "Get your hands off her!"

All five-foot-six of Joe stood in the doorway. He looked like a pit bull ready to lunge. Amar released his grip and dropped his hands to his sides.

"It's okay, Joe," Mallory said, rubbing the red welts on her arm. "We're done. He was just leaving."

Amar looked every bit as shocked by his outburst as she felt. He backed away quickly, with his palms in the air. Tears brimmed in Mallory's eyes.

"You okay?" Joe asked.

Mallory nodded and moved past him. Trembling, she wiped her cheeks and went back inside.

"What was that about? Who was that guy?"

"It's nothing. I'm okay. Really."

"You're sure...?"

Joe trailed her to the counter, where the lineup of customers had doubled in size. She could feel Jenn's gaze, watching her every move, not because she was angry this time, but because she was concerned. Jenn and Joe were both worried about what they had witnessed, and she was barely holding it together.

They needed to get back to work. Forget about Amar. Once the last customer had been served, Jenn picked up a damp cloth and wiped down the espresso machine. Mallory tidied the counter-tops. Joe hovered nearby just in case Amar returned.

"Look, I get it," Jenn said, breaking the awkward silence. "You don't want to talk, and that's okay, but let me say this. If he doesn't make you happy, if he hurts you, promise me you'll ditch him."

Unable to meet Jenn's gaze, Mallory nodded.

"You promise?"

"I promise."

"Good. Because you don't want to end up like her." Jenn gestured toward the flyer with Katie Lord's face on it. "Another dead girl."

21

INDIRA'S FATHER WAS SEATED IN THE LARGE CHAIR BESIDE HER mother's hospital bed. After her mother's collapse, they had raced to the hospital, only to find that she had suffered a heart attack. In the two days that had passed, her father had barely left her mother's side. The ordeal had left him exhausted, and now, head resting on his fist, he snored loud enough to wake the dead. Indira set her laptop on the floor and strode across the room. Gently, she shook her father awake.

His dark eyes snapped open, and his gaze locked on Indira.

"Why don't you go home?"

Her father ran his hands through his ruffled hair as he glanced toward the bed where Indira's mother lay. A look of indecision surfaced in his weary gaze.

"She's strong. The doctor says she's getting better. Go home. Get some rest. Otherwise you'll be in the bed next to hers."

Her father's lips compressed, and he gave a brusque nod. Worry had aged him. While it was her father who everyone looked to for approval, her mother kept the family going.

"I'll call you if anything changes."

Of course he argued, but Indira had logic on her side, and eventually, he relented and went home.

She curled up in a chair beside her mother's bed. With her father out of the room and her mother sleeping, she was finally able to make a call she'd been wanting to make since this whole situation unfolded the day before. She called Amar.

His voice sounded gravelly. Emotional.

"How is she?"

"Come see for yourself. Dad's gone."

Amar sighed. She could imagine her brother, raking his hands through his hair the same way he had done when he was a kid, dealing with the frustrations of their upbringing.

"Okay, I'm on my way."

Indira set the phone down and gazed at her mother sleeping. There wasn't a day of Indira's life where her mother wasn't there, making breakfast, packing lunches, ordering her to clean up her room. Her father was a force of nature, the wind that blew through their family, but her mother...her mother was the earth itself, the foundation upon which their family was built.

While she had spent much of her youth fantasizing about moving away and the independence it would gain her, she had never once considered a life without her mother. The thought made her feel hollow, and she remembered the fear she felt when her mother had collapsed.

And her father. He relied on her mother to take care of him. She managed every aspect of their home life, which allowed him to focus on his business. Without her, he would be lost. Indira allowed her thoughts to drift. If this had happened after she'd moved to San Jose, how would she have felt, so far away from home when her mother needed her most?

It didn't matter. Her mother was going to recover. By the time Indira was ready to leave, her mother would be home, taking care of things the way she always did. The situation with Rani would blow over, and Amar would remain behind. He'd be here if they needed him.

Amar was as good as his word. Half an hour later, he arrived carrying a chai tea in a Starbucks cup, which he handed to Indira. The gesture was unexpectedly sweet, and she clutched the cup, grateful for the warmth radiating through her cold hands.

"I never said thank you."

"For what?"

Amar sat in the chair next to her and met her gaze. "For standing up for me."

Indira snorted. "For all the good it did."

"You know how focused Dad gets."

"Yeah, that's it. He's focused. Not pig-headed. Chauvinistic."

Indira glanced over her shoulder, at the bed where her mother slept. Amar understood. He knew how much she resented being overlooked.

"So, tell me about her."

"Who?" Amar asked, as if he didn't know.

"You're too pretty to play dumb," Indira said.

Amar smirked. "Her name is Mallory."

"Where did you meet her?"

"School."

"She's a fellow professor?"

Amar shrugged. "It hardly matters now. It's over."

22

LONG AFTER INDIRA LEFT, AMAR LISTENED TO THE SOUND OF HIS mother's breathing. Deep and even. He checked the monitors. As far as he could tell, everything looked normal. The doctors would adjust her blood pressure medications, and she would be fine. But she needed to relax. Avoid stress.

The thought that she might be seriously ill frightened him. He'd never stopped to consider what it would be like to look after his aging parents. This was the blessing of having a close-knit family. His aunties would help. They would cook. Look after his mother. But she would need his support. They both would.

His parents had been married over thirty-five years, their entire adult lives. His father, who had always seemed so remote, untouchable, would be lost without his mother. Until now, Amar had never really understood.

Devotion.

Their marriage had been arranged. His mother had barely met his father before the wedding. And now, over three decades later, they were still together. Their relationship was solid, and while they had never been the "crazy in love type," they both seemed content with their marriage. Their lives. Would it have ever been that way between him and Rani?

How would he have felt if it was Rani lying in a hospital bed, and not his mother? Would he have grown to love her someday, the way his parents had?

Love.

He missed Mallory with an ache that drove deep into his bones. But it was too late.

He'd blown his chance. She didn't want to talk to him or hear his explanations. He couldn't blame her. After his outburst at the coffee shop, he was lucky she hadn't called the cops. The stress, the sleepless night, everything had combined and clouded his judgement. There was no excuse for the way he'd acted. How he wished he could take it back and do things over. He would have been honest with her from the start, but none of that mattered.

Indira was right. Their relationship could never work. He had to forget her. Move on.

Amar gazed on his mother, who was lying in the hospital bed. He had never seen her look so small, so fragile. His parents had left their families, their homes, and moved to a new country. They had sacrificed so much to give him and Indira a better life, to grow up in a world where there was more opportunity. Advantages. Even Indira, especially Indira. Here, she could live independently. She could flourish in a career. She could be the person she wanted to be, as could any daughters he might someday have.

But what about him? Was he free?

The big questions, the ones that really mattered, had no easy answers. There were so many moving parts to a life. They included other people within your orbit who fit together into a whole, like a machine with inner workings and interdependencies. If he no longer had those people—his family—who would he be?

Would his life still work?

Amar was still contemplating that question when the nurses chased him from his mother's room. Visiting hours were over. The hospital's hallways were quiet, punctuated by the occasional laughter of the nurses as he made his way toward the elevator.

The closest ground floor exit was through the emergency room. He was heading for the exit when the glass doors slid open. A patient was being wheeled in on a gurney by two grim-faced EMTs followed by a dark-haired woman.

"Doctor. We need a doctor. My daughter, she—"

The desperate scream of the panicked mother cut through the tumult of the emergency room. The familiar tone gave him pause. The woman's dark eyes fastened on his face and Amar's stomach plunged. His gaze cut to the woman on the gurney. Beneath the oxygen mask, Rani's face was deathly pale.

"What's wrong?"

"You! She tried to take her own life."

Amar's mind wheeled. "What? How?"

Suicide?

The gravity of the situation pressed down on Amar, plunging him into a deep pool of regret and shame until he felt as if he couldn't breathe. This was his fault. He'd known she was upset, but he never imagined she would do anything so desperate.

"Get away from her," Falguni screamed. "You've already done enough."

Amar watched helplessly as the gurney wheeled through the doors into the trauma room and disappeared from sight.

———

ANOTHER SLEEPLESS NIGHT PASSED, filled with self-recrimination. All the things he should have done, shouldn't have done, played through his head on an endless, torturous loop. The only bright spot in the news of the day came from Indira, who texted him to let him know that his mother had recovered enough to be discharged from the hospital. The angry words he'd exchanged with his father had caused a rift that wouldn't be easily bridged. It kept him at home, when he normally would have been with his family.

He felt oddly disenfranchised getting the news secondhand. He tried to bury himself in his work, a new paper he was writing, but it was pointless. His thoughts were consumed with Rani and Mallory and the damage he'd done. It was the uncertainty of Rani's condition that sent him back to the hospital to check on her.

The volunteer at the information desk gave him Rani's room number. On his way to the elevator, he stopped by the gift store to pick up some flowers. He ran his gaze over the brightly colored bouquets wrapped in tissue paper and cellophane. Roses didn't send the right message. Carnations? No. Daisies?

Clutching the bouquet of yellow daisies in his hand, he rode the elevator to the fifth floor. Casting a wary gaze down the hallway, he searched for Falguni. The last thing any of them needed was another ugly scene. As he rounded the corner by the nurse's station, Falguni emerged from Rani's room and strode briskly toward the elevator.

Amar waited until the elevator doors closed before approaching Rani's room. The daisies, which had looked so cheerful in the gift shop, now seemed absurd. Trivial. What did you give a woman who tried to end her life?

He hesitated outside the door, wanting to turn around. But if he never went inside, never faced her, what kind of man would that make him? Every bit the coward his father believed him to be.

Rani sat in bed, gazing out the window at the gray morning sky.

"Rani," he called softly, not wanting to startle her.

The shock in her eyes at seeing him in the doorway quickly turned to anger.

"I hope it's okay that I'm here."

The words he'd practiced on the way to her room sounded feeble and he swallowed a lump of shame in his throat.

"My mother would be very upset if she found you here."

Amar nodded and wiped his damp palms on his jeans. "I wanted to make sure that you were okay."

His phone buzzed. He took it out. The text was from Indira. He quickly checked it, to make sure that everything was okay with his mother, and placed the phone face-down on the wide windowsill. Rani's eyes narrowed in suspicion and he felt another stab of guilt. She probably thought it was Mallory.

"Are you...okay?"

"I'm alive."

He gave her a feeble smile. "I'm glad."

She cleared her throat, shifting her gaze away from him toward a plastic water pitcher, placed on a rolling table three feet away from the bed. Amar skirted the foot of the bed and reached for it, relieved to break the awkward moment between them by doing something useful. He half-filled a plastic glass and handed it to her. She nodded her head in thanks and drank, her eyes downcast, refusing to meet his gaze.

"What did you come here for? Absolution? Forgiveness?"

Faced with the ugly consequences of his actions, Amar rocked back on his heels. He deserved her anger. He'd hurt her. Betrayed her. A better man would have broken up with her long before this point, but he was not that man.

"I understand what it's like to have a family who expects a lot from you," he said. "Sometimes it feels as if nothing you do is good enough. But you don't have to live your life based on what your mother wants."

Rani flinched, as if stung by his words. Looking lost, hopeless, she stretched her sightless gaze beyond him, to a place he couldn't follow. Tears surfaced in her eyes and he wished he could comfort her. Make amends for the pain he'd inflicted. But Amar didn't dare. Emotionally, she was raw. His actions could be too easily misconstrued.

"You can be more than a wife and a mother, Rani. You can find a job, go to school, have a career. Find meaning. There must be something you want to do, something you dreamed about."

A flurry of emotions played across her face as he waited for her to speak. Anger. Sorrow. Rani fixed her hollow eyes on him and gave her head a despairing shake.

"Why were the dreams of our parents not good enough? You keep looking for something more, Amar. Something better. But what if this is all there is? Why isn't it enough? Couldn't you be happy with a wife, a family?"

Amar raked his hands through his hair, wishing there was some way he could get through to her, but the uncomfortable truth was that despite the time they'd spent together, he didn't really know her. He'd never seen past the carefully curated image her mother had cultivated to what lay in her heart.

"Think, Rani. There must have been something else you wanted."

A single tear rolled down Rani's flawless cheek. "I wanted to marry you."

The words felt like splinters of glass in his heart. He shouldn't have come. There was nothing he could say. It was as if they spoke different languages.

"I'm being discharged today."

"That's good."

She refused to look him in the eye. She rested her hand on a stack of clothing folded neatly on her bed that he hadn't noticed.

"My mother will be back soon. I need to change."

"I'm sorry for the pain I caused you, Rani. I hope someday you can forgive me."

Amar stood at the foot of the bed, studying her. She looked so young, so vulnerable. Sorry couldn't begin to express the depth of regret he felt.

23

MALLORY DUMPED A PAIL OF DIRTY WATER DOWN THE KITCHEN SINK. Hell of a way to spend a rare Saturday morning off, but god knew the apartment could use a deep cleaning, and with Shelby spending the weekend with her parents, the timing was good.

Four days had passed since she'd last seen Amar. He hadn't called. He hadn't texted. It was over. It was really over. She should be glad. She bumped the volume of her Spotify playlist up a notch, hoping the music might fill the empty ache in her chest.

If ending our relationship was the right thing to do, why does it hurt so much?

With the walls of her apartment starting to close in, Mallory changed into her running gear. She jogged through the neighborhood at a punishing pace. When the rain changed from a mist to a downpour, she gave up and headed home.

Rounding the corner with her house in sight, Mallory slowed. A blue pickup truck approached from the opposite direction. The driver slowed and rolled down the window. The damp air stung her lungs as she struggled to regain her breath.

"I see you still haven't fixed your window," the driver called.

A jolt of recognition rippled through her. It was Tim. *Mr. Quad Grande Breve.* Her muscles tensed with apprehension. What was he doing outside her house? She thought about what Jenn had said, about Katie being dead.

Her gaze locked on his. Tim looked away.

"Sorry," he said, tugging at his ball cap and shooting her a self-conscious grin. "Didn't mean to scare you."

"I was just... What?"

She tried to remember what he'd said and couldn't recall a word. Tim waved a hand, gesturing behind her. "I was just driving by and noticed your car. The window. It's still broken."

"Yeah."

A dozen thoughts and images flashed through her mind in a rush. The car break-in. The Snapchat photo of her and Amar together. Was Tim responsible for all of it? Was he watching her?

The shiver that ran down Mallory's spine had nothing to do with the cold. Fear tasted like copper pennies in the back of her mouth.

"Sorry," Tim said again.

In a feeble attempt to hide her discomfort, Mallory forced a laugh.

"No, it's okay, I just didn't expect to see you here. Lost in my thoughts, you know." As if that had anything to do with it.

"Okay. Have a good one."

Tim waved and closed the window, easing the truck down the street. Mallory stood, rigid, her heart racing as she watched him go. It had to be a coincidence—seeing him here, right? But how could it be? There was nothing here. Just houses.

Her house.

Mallory slid inside the apartment and locked the patio door. The drapes squealed on the rod as she tugged them closed. The living room sank into shadows. The dead silence engulfed her, and she wished she wasn't alone. She'd feel safer with Shelby home.

Mallory cranked the music, hoping the noise would calm her nerves. The drapes were closed, and yet she felt as if she was being watched.

She really needed to get a grip. Tim wasn't stalking her. No one was. Chilled from her run, she peeled off her clothes inside the bathroom and stepped into the shower. The warm water felt good as it sluiced down her back and washed the dried sweat from her skin. She leaned into the spray, lingering until the last of the hot water was gone before toweling off.

Now that the apartment was clean, and she'd gone for a run, she needed something else to do, to keep her mind occupied. Homework? Netflix? Something.

Mallory coiled her damp hair in a bun and pulled on a clean pair of sweats. The music was playing so loudly, she almost didn't hear someone pounding on the patio door. JoJo barked. Mallory groaned.

Aw, shit. It was probably the landlord, coming to complain. She yanked open the drapes and stared out the patio doors.

She froze at the sight of the person standing on her doorstep. Catching her breath, she moved, cracking the door open an inch.

"Amar. What are you doing here?"

He looked exhausted, drained, as if he'd been run over by a truck. "Please, Mallory. I just want to talk. Can I come inside?"

"Talk? Talk about what? For fuck's sake, Amar, you were engaged. You are engaged. I don't know what you are besides a liar."

"Mallory."

Her name was a question, a plea, and she knew the smart thing to do would be to tell him to go the hell home, but the ache in her chest couldn't be ignored. She stepped back and allowed him to enter.

The apartment was small enough when she was alone and seemed to shrink now that he was inside. There was nowhere for her to go. No way to put enough space between them. She resisted the instinctive pull she felt toward him by falling back a step.

Amar paced to the threadbare couch in the middle of the living room and sat down. The failing springs groaned under his weight. He sat awkwardly with his hand covering his eyes as she waited for him to speak.

"You're right. I lied about Rani. I didn't think you'd understand."

"I don't understand. You lied to me. Used me. You betrayed my trust and now…" She trailed off, shaking her head. Grasping for words. "What do you want from me, Amar? Did I mean anything to you, or was I just another stupid girl? A distraction?"

Angry, heartsick, Mallory dropped her gaze away from his stricken face to the floor between her feet. All the moments they'd shared, all the hopes she'd dared to dream about how the two of them would build a life together, every single one had been predicated on a lie. She'd wanted so badly to believe him that she'd ignored the truth that was staring her in the face.

How could I have been so stupid? So naïve? So trusting?

"I didn't choose her."

The admission sounded as if it had been wrenched from the depths of his soul. The agony of each word hung in the air.

"Are you saying that it was an arranged marriage?"

Was that still even a thing?

Amar nodded. A muscle jumped in his jaw, but he said nothing, as if struggling to find the words to explain.

"It's the way my parents think things are done."

"And what about you, Amar? Do you think this is the way things are done? Is it okay for you to have a fiancée and a girlfriend on the side?"

Girlfriend. If that's what she even was. It's not like they went out on real dates. They'd kept their relationship under wraps because she was his student. Their relationship had always been complicated and now...

She tried to separate the facts from the emotions, but she couldn't. Anger, hurt, betrayal overwhelmed her sense of reason. And love. The intensity of the emotions she felt tore her apart. Her head pulling her one way; her heart, the other.

"You don't understand what my family is like."

"God, Amar, how could you do this to me? To her?"

A desperate pleading filled his eyes, but Mallory turned away. She needed to get out of here. Away from him. Somewhere she could breathe. Think.

"You're my student, I'm your teacher. This whole thing was wrong, and I'm sorry."

"That's all I was to you? A student?"

"No, but I shouldn't have—"

Mallory spun away from him, her hands covering her mouth as the pain of his words cut deep.

"I'm not some stupid kid you manipulated, Amar."

"That's not what I meant."

"Oh, no. Of course not. That's why you're giving me the I-should-have-known-better speech. You need to go. Now."

"Mallory."

He lurched toward her and Mallory spun away, knowing that if he touched her, she would break. Amar backed off. Showed his palms.

"I never expected...I wasn't supposed to fall in love with you. You were this lovely breeze that blew through my life and... meeting you changed everything. It changed me. For the first time in my life I thought about what I wanted. Not about what I should do, or what my family wanted me to do. God. Please, Mallory, you have to believe me."

Like a drowning man, he reached for her. She closed her eyes and allowed herself to be pulled against the hard wall of his chest.

Without him, it was as if all the color and life had drained from her world. In his arms, she felt whole.

"What about her?"

"It's over. I swear."

Mallory raised her head. Their gazes met. Truth glimmered in the depths of Amar's eyes and Mallory knew she was lost. She wanted so badly to believe him, and she could no more turn away from him than she could tear her heart out of her chest with her bare hands.

Her heart lurched as a surge of powerful emotions swept through her. He loved her. He'd said it. This wasn't just a fling. She wasn't just a girl. The force of his words washed away all remnants of Mallory's doubts.

"I'm so sorry," he murmured into the soft tangle of her hair.

Their lips met and she kissed him with all the passion she felt, as if every hour they'd spent apart had magnified the depth of her need. Amar shuddered at her touch. His fingers wound through her wet hair as he cupped the back of her head, deepening their kiss until they broke apart. Their breath ragged. Foreheads touching.

"I've missed you," she said.

MALLORY AWOKE to the sound of the alarm and Amar's breathing. Wrestling her arm free of the covers, she turned the alarm off and rolled onto her side, curling into the warmth of his body. Nuzzling her face against the hollow between his shoulder blades, she breathed in his scent.

"I have to go to work," she whispered.

"No. Stay," he murmured, his voice thick with sleep.

His hand reached for her, nudging her closer until she was pressed tight against his body. She sighed. The thought of skipping her shift and staying right here was tempting, but Jenn would throw a hissy fit and she'd probably lose her job. Just one shift at the café, and the rest of the weekend was theirs.

"You sleep. I'll be back in a few hours."

She slid free of his grasp. Pausing beside the bed, she bent to kiss his temple before heading to the shower. Thirty minutes later, she was on her way to work.

"Good morning," she chirped to Jenn, who eyed her with a skeptical look.

"You look like you just won the lottery."

"Something like that."

Mallory tied an apron around her waist and got ready for the morning shift. Even on a Sunday, there were people waiting to be let in. The minutes flew by as Mallory filled orders. She let her mind drift, to think about what her relationship with Amar could be like, when they were no longer hiding. Where they would go. Drinks with friends. Hiking in the woods. Museums. Concerts. She'd teach him how to cook and he... They would have long conversations about things that mattered to them both.

Over the course of the past twelve hours, it felt as if the whole world had changed.

"You're in a good mood," Jenn noted once the morning rush had subsided.

"It's Sunday," Mallory said simply.

She pulled her phone from her pocket and sent Amar a text. She expected a quick response, but nothing came. Maybe he was in the shower. Mallory pocketed her phone again and straightened up behind the counter.

Once her shift was over, Mallory shed her apron, pulling it over her head. She heard the sharp intake of Jenn's breath. Jenn's gaze was fixed on the inside of Mallory's bicep. The red welts she'd sustained during the argument with Amar had turned to ugly black smudges on her pale skin.

Jenn's mouth tightened in disgust. Mallory quickly dropped her arms, hiding the marks.

"See you tomorrow."

She left the Daily Grind and headed for the car. A mobile glass repair van was parked behind her rust bucket. A technician in a uniform was replacing her driver side window. Mallory stared at him with a startled look that made the technician grin.

"Mallory Riggins, right? Sorry for the delay. I'm almost finished here."

"Yeah... But who? How?"

"Apparently, it's a gift from a friend. That's all I was instructed to say. If you want more details, you can always call the shop."

"Thank you."

It was all she could think of to say, and his grin widened.

"Not a problem. With the Pineapple Express due to hit us next week, you'll be glad not to have to drive around with a busted window."

"Yeah. You can say that again."

Mallory arrived home to the smell of something delicious. Kicking her shoes off by the door, she found Amar in the kitchen stirring a pot. She wrapped her arms around his waist and peeked around his shoulder toward the pot on the stove.

"Hey, why didn't you text me back?"

"What?" Amar asked.

"I sent you a text."

Amar looked away. "I lost my phone a few days ago."

"Where?"

"If I knew that, it wouldn't be lost," he said.

Mallory laughed. "You've got a point there, Professor. Why haven't you replaced it?"

Amar shrugged and Mallory shook her head. She couldn't go six hours, let alone days without her phone.

"Maybe we should get you a replacement."

"Later. First, lunch."

"You made this?"

Amar's grin made her heart flutter. "Technically, I warmed it up."

He set the wooden spoon down on the countertop and pivoted toward her. The kiss they shared sent shimmering waves of heat wafting through her all the way to her toes.

"I could get used to this," she said.

Amar chuckled, a sexy sound she would never get tired of. "Lunch will be ready soon. Why don't you relax?"

Mallory released him. Her heart was as light as air as she turned from the kitchen and saw the vase filled with a dozen of the most gorgeous long-stemmed red roses she had ever seen.

"You got me flowers?"

The last guy who had bought her flowers had offered a sad little bunch of wilted carnations and acted as if he expected her to gush with gratitude, as if he'd done something heroic. She reached for the roses, sliding a lush petal between her thumb and forefinger. It felt like velvet to the touch.

"They better not be from your other boyfriend," he joked.

"Oh, he only brings pizza, never flowers."

Amar's smile faltered and Mallory laughed.

"Just kidding."

"I'll make you pay for that."

"You'd better."

He made a playful reach for her, but she dodged past him. Laughing, she retreated to the bedroom to change. Her shirt smelled like coffee grounds and sweat. Stripping it off, she launched it into the laundry basket. Rummaging through her drawers, she searched for something else to wear. If she was alone, she would have pulled on an oversized sweatshirt and some fuzzy socks. Instead she chose a close-fitted V-neck T-shirt that showed a bit of cleavage. After all, they still had the rest of the day ahead of them and one more glorious night before Shelby arrived home.

She emerged from the bedroom and found Amar plating lunch.

"And thanks for getting my window fixed."

Amar set the plates down on the table. "Yeah, of course. Really, Mallory, that car of yours. What happened?"

"It doesn't matter," she said as she pulled Amar toward her for a kiss.

24

INKY DARK FILLED MALLORY'S BEDROOM WHEN AMAR AWOKE TO THE sound of a scraping noise. It took him a moment to place it. *The patio doors. The roommate. She was home early.*

He glanced across the pillow to where Mallory lay sleeping. The soft inhale and exhale of her breaths were as soothing as the gentle waves lapping against the shore of a lake. He pulled the covers over her bare shoulder and eased from the side of the bed.

Eventually word of their relationship would get out, but it would be better for both of them if they kept it a secret a while longer. Mallory had agreed, saying that since she'd waited this long, a few more months hardly mattered. But if Shelby found him here, everyone would soon know.

Careful not to disturb Mallory, Amar dressed in the dark. On bare feet, he crossed the room and eased the door open. A slice of light shone beneath the bathroom door, and he could hear the sound of running water.

Amar crept silently out into the living room. His jacket was lying on the chair beside the couch. He scooped it up as he made his way to the patio doors. The wretched thing was heavy. He slid it along the rusty track. It groaned as if it was being tortured. Amar winced at the noise and stepped out onto the frigid patio stones. Cedar and pine needles stuck to his bare feet. He stooped to pull on his shoes.

The bathroom door opened, shedding a triangle of light into the hall.

"Mallory?"

Amar's pulse quickened. He closed the door with a thump and hurried up the pathway toward his car.

25

From somewhere up above, the dog barked, and she rolled over. In the dead of night, Mallory felt a chill settle over her. The bedroom was cold, and she burrowed deeper under the covers, reaching for Amar. The sheets were empty.

The clock read three a.m. She was alone. Mallory sighed and sank deeper into the pillows until she felt herself drift down into the layers of sleep once more.

She heard a noise. Footsteps approached the bed.

"Amar?"

No one spoke. She opened her eyes and searched the darkness. Saw the shadow hovering over the bed.

An electric current of fear jolted through her. It tasted like metal on her tongue. She tried to move, tried to scream, but she lay frozen in terror. Heart racing. Pulse pounding. A stab of silver descended. Lightning fast. A white-hot bolt of agony tore through Mallory's chest, stealing the breath from her lungs. A hand was pressed against her mouth and the scream died in her throat.

Somehow, she raised her hands. Tried to fight off her attacker.

But the knife descended again. Hard. Brutal. Relentless. Hot blood flowed down her chilled skin, soaking the sheets. Dripping onto the mattress. She tried to call out for Amar to save her, but no words came. Black dots flooded her vision. The shadowy figure moved.

And the knife came again.

Amar.

His name was a thought, a whisper, a cry for help, and then...

And then Mallory was gone.

26

Amar stood with his arms folded, leaning back against the table, while the students streamed into the lecture hall. With the engagement off and things finally back on track with Mallory, he felt lighter than he had in years. Maybe once the semester was over, he would tell Indira about Mallory, maybe even introduce the two. Mallory would like that. Introducing her to his parents was another matter. They were still reeling from the shock of his broken engagement. It would take time for them to understand, to accept that his life was his own.

Brock Sinclair entered the lecture hall from the door at the rear of the room and made for his usual seat. He slumped into the chair, looking uncharacteristically disheveled, as if he was on the tail end of a three-day bender.

Amar kept a watchful gaze out for Mallory, but as the last few students trickled in and the doors to the lecture hall closed, she had not yet arrived. *Late again.*

Tonight's topic was the effects of globalization on business ethics. Amar focused the conversation on intellectual property rights in China. Sweeping his gaze across the class, he spied Brock, who looked half asleep with an elbow on the desktop and his fist propped against his stubbled cheek.

"Mr. Sinclair, please share with the class your thoughts on how Chinese companies differ from other international companies with respect to how they deal with their IP."

Roused from his stupor, Brock jerked upright in his seat. His gaze dropped to the cell phone he had cradled in his hand and Amar grinned.

"Let me assure you, Mr. Sinclair, the answers won't be found within the first few links of your Google search."

The class laughed and Brock reddened, not used to being caught unprepared. Amar paused long enough for the laughter to subside before opening the question to the class.

"Anyone care to share their observations?"

"Chinese companies are so used to having their IP stolen that they often don't post detailed or accurate product information to their websites."

"That's true, Ms. Anderson. Are there other examples?"

"Piracy," another student piped up from the back. "Back in the day when you had to buy software, within a four-year period, the cost of Photoshop rose from four hundred dollars a copy to nearly a thousand. As it reached its peak, you could pick up a pirated copy of Photoshop from China for free."

"Right, so even your prized English bulldog could look like a super model. Has the tendency toward piracy changed over time?"

Amar motioned toward another student and gestured for him to speak.

"Growing competition from other developing countries has forced China to change their approach to copyright protection and infringement."

At least someone had done the reading, and the class gained energy around the discussion.

"Now we're hitting on the fundamental truth of the matter. There are two things in business and life that spur change—pain and happiness. In business, pain means the fear of lost sales and negative growth while happiness is the opposite."

Amar paused, letting the students fill the silence with their own thoughts. A door at the back of the auditorium opened. He looked up, half expecting to see Mallory scurry inside, scrambling to find the closest open seat. Amar frowned as he recognized the two detectives who had shown up in his office last week asking questions about Katie Lord.

A rush of anger filled him at the intrusion. The last time they'd barged in on him, he'd been very clear that if they wanted his time, they had to book an appointment, and now they had the audacity to interrupt class. Ignoring their arrival, Amar continued with the lecture, elaborating on his point.

"In business, happiness comes in the form of new opportunities and growth—whether it be new products or a rise in the company's profits."

But as the detectives started down the aisle toward him, Amar could no longer ignore their presence. He brought the lecture to an abrupt end and dismissed the class.

"Detectives Bradford and..." Amar snapped his fingers, as if trying to recall the second detective's name.

"Moreland."

"I assume you gentlemen aren't here to learn more about copyright infringement in China, and unfortunately, I have no more wisdom to impart about the matter upon which we last spoke."

The two detectives exchanged a glance that made Amar's blood run cold.

"This isn't about Katie Lord," Detective Moreland said.

"Then what?"

"You need to come with us."

"Where?"

"To the station."

Amar took in their expressions, their stances, both of which signaled a clear shift from their previous visit. Whatever this was, it was serious. They had no intention of being deterred.

"Please tell me, detectives, what could possibly be so compelling that it couldn't wait until after class? Or perhaps showing up unannounced during one of my lectures is your version of a power play, designed to intimidate me in front of my students?"

"It's about Mallory Riggins."

27

GROWING UP, AMAR'S FATHER HAD OWNED A CROWN VICTORIA. Riding in the back seat of that car had felt as smooth as floating on a cloud. Safe. Privileged. The back seat of this squad car couldn't have been more different. Dirt and tiny bits of refuse were ground into the crevices of the molded plastic back bench, which smelled faintly of vomit. He wrinkled his nose and crossed his arms, trying to avoid touching anything, which was almost impossible. Every time the car turned a corner, he was thrown off balance.

The half hour ride to the police station was spent in silence. With each passing mile, Amar's irritation grew. They were trying to scare him. Bully him. It wasn't going to work.

The detectives led Amar to an interrogation room, no bigger than a closet, and left him there. He sat with his legs casually crossed, as if this were no more stressful than drinks with a colleague, aware they were watching.

They returned half an hour later.

"Mr. Saraf..."

Amar cocked an eyebrow. "Dr. Saraf."

"Can we get you anything? Coffee? Water?"

"How about a Moscow mule—Kettle One and Top Hat, if you please." The detectives regarded him with a puzzled look and Amar shook his head. "Never mind."

Aside from currying favor, the other reason for offering him a beverage was to collect his DNA, something he was in no hurry to provide. He folded his hands on the table and waited for them to continue.

"We know you've been seeing Mallory Riggins."

They were studying his expression closely, but Amar's expression didn't change. "Seeing a student isn't a crime, nor is it expressly forbidden by the university."

"But it is frowned upon and seeing as how you don't have tenure—" Bradford trailed off, baiting him. "She's got to be what? Fifteen years younger than you?"

"Is that a question, detective?" When Bradford didn't answer, Amar offered a chilly smile. "She's twenty-two years old, which is well beyond the legal age of consent, and makes the age difference between us nine years. I do understand that mathematics can be challenging."

The slight downward tug of Bradford's mouth told Amar that his barb had hit the mark.

"Still, nine years."

Amar both understood and ignored the insinuation. He wasn't a pedophile, and he hadn't coerced Mallory into a relationship, no matter what Bradford might think. Perhaps the cop had teenaged daughters of his own. Whatever the reason for his attitude, Amar saw little point in explaining to him that Mallory wasn't like most of his students. The one gift bestowed upon her by her estranged and dysfunctional parents was a maturity well beyond her years.

"Ms. Riggins is old enough to make her own decisions about who she wants to see, even in the eyes of the law. And before you pursue the next obvious line of questioning, if our relationship was discovered by the university, I might receive some form of censure for not exposing the relationship to the administration. Even if I had, the next step would be to submit Mallory's papers for independent grading to ensure that her academic performance was being assessed objectively, which I assure you it has. In addition to being an intelligent woman, she is also an exemplary student. So, gentlemen, I do hope there is a legitimate reason for bringing me here. Tell me that you haven't wasted my time based on a series of harmless text messages. Otherwise I'll assume that I am free to go."

Amar rose from his seat but was stopped by a hard, verbal slap. "Sit the fuck down."

"I see you're playing bad cop today, Detective Moreland," Amar said breezily as he resumed his chair.

Though his annoyance at being detained flared, he returned their stone-faced glares with a pleasant smile.

"When was the last time you saw Mallory Riggins?"

"What does it matter?"

"Answer the question."

"I expected to see her in class today, but she wasn't there."

He didn't answer what they'd asked, and the incongruity pushed them off stride. The detectives exchanged another look, an unspoken signal, a clear indication that they had spent years working together, establishing their roles. Like most police, they assumed their suspects were stupid, easily intimidated, and he had done nothing wrong.

"Where were you last night?" Moreland demanded.

"At home."

"Alone?"

"Last time I checked."

"All night?"

Amar offered a chilly smile. "Do I need a signed note from my mother?"

A hard glint of anger flashed in Detective Moreland's eyes. "You think this is a game, you pompous son of a bitch?"

"Ah, profanity. You know a lot of people think that excessive use of profanity is a symptom of a limited vocabulary or a low intellect, but that's never fully been proven."

"Shut the fuck up."

"Shown here." Amar gestured toward Moreland, as if making a point.

"Do you have anyone who can account for your whereabouts last night, *Dr. Saraf*?" Bradford asked.

"Why?"

"Just answer the damned question."

Amar folded his arms and returned their stares. They were legitimately angry, and not just because he was making them look foolish. There was something else behind their questions, although he didn't know what. Whatever it was, they were guarding it, treating it like a secret—a grenade they were planning to launch at him.

"Well, gentlemen, I do have to confess to having watched enough *Law and Order* episodes to know that either I am free to go or..."

"Or?" Bradford leaned across the table far enough that Amar could smell the sour stench of his coffee breath.

"Or you need to charge me."

"Is this fun for you? Do you think this is a game?"

It was a game. It was called chicken and Amar had no intention of being the first to blink.

"We have a witness who says he saw your car parked outside Mallory's house last night. We have traffic camera footage that shows your car leaving her neighborhood."

Witnesses? Traffic cameras? Whatever he was driving at, Amar wasn't about to give an inch.

"So?"

"So maybe you're right after all, *Dr. Saraf.* We can't hold you here indefinitely without just cause. But we can hold you while we collect more evidence."

"Evidence?"

He cocked his head, waiting for a response. The two detectives exchanged a glance that caused the hairs on the back of his neck to rise.

"She's dead," Bradford said flatly.

"Murdered," Moreland added. "Stabbed fifteen times."

A shock wave crashed over Amar. He tried to focus, to process what they had said, but he couldn't make sense of the words.

"Mallory? Dead? No. It can't... She can't be. It's..."

Impossible.

Barely able to speak, Amar covered his face with his hands.

"Dr. Saraf."

"Amar. Call me Amar..."

The two detectives slid a manilla file across the table, then they left the room. Amar stared at the folder, promising himself he wouldn't look. Knowing that what was inside, once seen could never be unseen. Would change him forever. Amar turned his head away, knowing he shouldn't look.

28

AMAR SAT ALONE IN THE INTERROGATION ROOM, THE HIDEOUS ARRAY of photographs spread out on the table. His stomach churned. A wave of heat washed over him. He doubled over as if he might be sick. Amar squeezed his eyes closed, trying to purge the images from his mind, but he couldn't. They were indelibly etched into his brain. Part of him now.

None of this felt real. It was as if this was happening to someone else. Not him. His world had been ripped free of its moorings and he had been cast into a nightmare too horrible to contemplate. Nothing made sense. He couldn't wrap his mind around it.

There had to be some mistake. Mallory couldn't be dead. They'd been together only yesterday. They had finally put Rani behind them and had a shot at building a future together, one that wasn't predicated on a bed of lies. The memory of their final happy hours together cut deep. He pressed his palms to his eyes. Tried to breathe.

Oh, Mallory.

Time ceased to exist for Amar as he floated in an ocean of grief and loss. The sound of the door opening roused him, and Detective Bradford walked in. Amar straightened in his chair, his spine as rigid as steel.

"I know how hard this must be on you. You loved her, right?"

Amar bristled at the false note of pity in Bradford's voice.

"Look, nobody blames you for what happened. Sometimes things get out of control. We see it every day, the way a woman can do things that drive you beyond reasonable limits."

He knew what they were trying to do. Build a rapport. As if they were two regular guys talking about how an argument with his girlfriend had gone off the rails. No big deal. Except in this case, they weren't just talking about an argument. Mallory was dead. Murdered. And they honestly believed that he was to blame.

How stupid or desperate did they think he was? He hadn't hurt Mallory. But...but he could feel the trap they'd set for him. He was without a witness, an alibi. A solid way to prove to them without a doubt that he was not their guy. Amar's throat tightened. He struggled to draw a breath.

"It's time I exercise my right to have a lawyer present."

Bradford shrugged at his request. "I want to help you, Amar, but the only way I can do that is if you tell us what happened. We can work with the DA and do what's best for you. Once the lawyers get involved..."

He trailed off. It didn't take a genius to pick up on the implication of what Bradford had in mind. *A deal. They were talking about a deal.* As if they expected him to confess.

"I'm afraid I've got nothing more to say, Detective Bradford."

Bradford's face hardened. The good cop routine vanished in a heartbeat.

"Fine. You won't mind if we take some pictures while we wait."

"Pictures?"

"Cuts. Scratch marks. In cases like this it's routine."

Amar's eyes narrowed. "I assume it's also routine to obtain a warrant before requiring me to submit to any type of examination."

Bradford's smile was thin. "Rest assured, Dr. Saraf, the warrant is on its way."

As promised, the warrant arrived, served by a smug-looking Detective Moreland. Amar's fingers curled into fists when they asked him to strip. He removed his sweater. The police officer photographed every inch of his torso. Inwardly, Amar seethed with the indignity of the moment.

"Extend your arms to the side, palms up."

Amar did so. More photographs were taken. Palms up, palms down. Both hands. Then he was told to remove his pants and the humiliating process was repeated as the detectives stood by and watched. They were enjoying this. Seeing him stripped down. Laid bare. Exerting their power over him. Then he was ordered to remove his boxer shorts.

Amar's stare extended beyond the detectives and fixed on a point on the wall directly across from him as every part of his body was exposed, studied, cataloged with clinical precision. As if he was no longer a man, a person, but a frog laid out on a slide, ready to be dissected.

Though his expression remained blank, inside, he was filled with shame. His chin trembled and he clenched his jaw tight, not wanting them to see his humiliation. His fear.

After their work was complete, he dressed quickly. Moreland held up two large cotton swabs, and Amar opened his mouth. The insides of his cheeks were swabbed. Twice. The two detectives left with the sealed evidence bag, and once more, Amar was alone.

He had no idea how much time had passed until the door opened once again and a different officer entered the room.

"Dr. Amar Saraf, you are under arrest for the murder of Mallory Riggins."

Panic rang in his ears. In a matter of hours, everything he'd known had been ripped from him. Mallory. His life. His family. His freedom. What would happen to him now? He'd never felt more scared. More alone.

The officer cuffed Amar and shepherded him out of the station and into the back of a police car. The drive to the jail, a squat concrete facility on East Cordova, seemed all at once too long and too short. He stared at the streets filled with high-rises, pedestrians, and traffic that streaked by. His thoughts had turned inward into the desolation of the moment.

The gates opened and the car drove around the facility. A set of retractable doors gaped open like the jaws of a whale and the officer entered. The car rolled to a stop inside the bay. The doors behind them rumbled and shuddered to a close. Despite the bright overhead lights, Amar felt a darkness envelop him, as if he might never feel the sun on his face again. Through a haze of panic, he heard the cop speak into his radio. The car door opened, and he was guided onto a platform and into the custody of a correctional officer.

Amar trembled as he was led inside. The endless maze of empty hallways reeked of bleach and sweat. The very sound of their echoing footsteps filled him with dread. This was the kind of place that could swallow a man whole. It was all happening fast— too fast. Last night, he'd held Mallory in his arms. This morning, he'd awoken in his own bed, completely unaware that, within hours, his whole life would come to a crashing halt.

He couldn't stop it. He couldn't stop any of it. A stone-faced guard guided him through the process like he was a cow being prodded down a chute.

Photos. Left. Right. Straight on. Next, fingerprints. His hands were sprayed with alcohol and rolled against a glass pad. The guard grunted. His fingers were wiped. Sprayed again. Readjusted until the system was satisfied with the quality of the prints.

Once they were finished with the formalities, Amar was steered into a doorless room. No windows. No light. Just a box made of concrete blocks stacked like LEGO bricks with no hope of escape.

For the second time that day, Amar was forced to suffer the indignity of shedding his clothes in front of a stranger.

"I have the right to make a phone call."

"After you've been processed."

"I need to call my lawyer—"

"Later."

"Now. I know my rights."

For the first time since being led inside the building, the guard's expression cracked and slid into a smirk. "Are you a lawyer or did you get that from TV? Now strip."

The cool air settled on his damp skin and Amar shivered. He stood naked in front of the guard. Holding his arms close to his body, he watched as his clothes were bagged. Sour bile crept up the back of his throat as the guard ordered him to squat, and he was subjected to a full body search.

What kind of a man did work like this, dealing with the dregs of society day after day in a grim building devoid of light? Amar was handed a bulky, oddly shaped garment. Made of a sturdy nylon fabric, it weighed about four pounds. There were no buttons or strings. Designed to slip over the shoulders, it looked like a long vest with Velcro strips.

Amar eyed it with disdain. "What's this?"

"A smock."

"Why do I have it?"

The guard offered a thin smile. "Because it can't be made into a rope or a noose."

Amar blinked as the full weight of the guard's implications sank in. "You think I'm going to commit suicide?"

The guard shrugged. "Not my call. Standard procedure in

cases like yours. Unless you want to march into the cell block buck naked, I suggest you hurry up."

They honestly thought that he might kill himself. The concept was so foreign, so bizarre, that Amar had a difficult time wrapping his head around it.

The guard gestured for him to get a move on, and Amar struggled his way into the smock. He barely had time to settle his glasses in place when he was shuttled out of the room.

"It's time to make your call, Professor."

29

"DON'T BURN THE ONIONS LIKE YOU DID LAST TIME. YOU'VE GOT TO watch them."

"I know, Mom," Indira called from the kitchen, swearing softly under her breath.

Every day since her mother had been discharged from the hospital, Indira had made the same thing for lunch. On the first day, she had glanced away from the pan to scan her work email and the onions had singed, but since then, she hadn't made the same mistake. But that didn't stop her mother from micro-managing her through the process.

Indira, and her female cousins, had been taught to prepare a vast array of traditional dishes with the expectation that someday they would assume responsibility for cooking the food served at their family celebrations. Many of those same cousins were now married and worked alongside her mother and the aunties, but not Indira.

She plated the food and left the kitchen, handing it to her mother.

"You had the pan too hot. See?"

Her mother picked at the onions that admittedly were a few shades darker than the perfect golden brown, but who cared?

Her mother was driving her nuts. She missed her apartment. Her dog. Her life. It took every ounce of restraint she possessed not to snap back with some smart-assed remark, but that would be disrespectful. Indira unclenched her jaw and forced her shoulders to relax as she returned to the kitchen to brew her mother's favorite tea.

"Get the one Rani and her mother gave me for my birthday."

Without responding, Indira complied. She dug through the cupboard until she found the brightly colored tin of tea. Falguni had gone on at length about how expensive it was, but Indira thought it smelled like cat urine.

Indira warmed up the milk. Once the tea was ready, she loaded it onto a tray alongside her mother's favorite teacup. Holding her breath, she hauled it into the living room.

"What was your brother thinking, giving up a girl like Rani? She comes from a good family. Her father was a doctor, you know, back in India. Shame he died so young. Amar could do far worse. Sometimes he is as stubborn as you. I wish I could knock your heads together. Maybe then you'd both show some sense."

"Thanks, Mom, that's very helpful," Indira quipped.

Her mother's mouth pursed, a frown forming between her eyes. She wagged a finger Indira's way.

"Amar is acting like a fool. It is high time he took his place as the head of the family. I'm not the only one who thinks so. Your father is losing patience with him too."

"Amar should marry who he wants, when he wants."

"And when will that be? You tell me. What have I done to deserve such rebellious children? Home from the hospital a week now and your brother has not come. Why? What excuse can he have for not coming to see his own mother?"

"It's only been a few days and he probably thinks that you and Dad are still upset about Rani."

"Well, he's right about that."

Her mother huffed out a dissatisfied breath. Indira made a mental note to text Amar and nag him into visiting Mom. She'd had about all the complaining she could take. For a few precious minutes there was peace as her mother ate. Once lunch was finished, Indira ferried the empty plate into the kitchen, where stacks of dirty dishes waited. Warm water hissed as the sink filled. She was reaching for the bottle of dish soap when her phone rang.

Indira checked the number. Unknown caller flashed across the screen. She dismissed the call with a swipe of her thumb. From the living room, the television blared. Indira had barely made a dent in the mound of dishes when the phone rang again. Wiping her soapy hands on her jeans, she picked up the call, fully prepared to give the telemarketer a blast of hell when she heard Amar's voice.

"Indira..."

The bright edge of fear in his tone set her pulse racing. "Amar? What's wrong?"

"Listen. Just listen. I've been arrested. I need a lawyer."

Indira shut off the faucet and moved away from the sound of the television, struggling to hear over the roar of panic filling her head.

"A lawyer? What's wrong? Are you okay? Are you hurt?"

A burst of static filled the line and Indira's pulse spiked.

"Amar!"

"They think I've...they think I've killed my girlfriend."

Indira shook her head. *What*? She couldn't have heard him correctly. He wasn't making sense.

"Rani's dead?"

"Not Rani. There's no time to explain. Indira, please..."

"A lawyer. Yes. Where are you?"

"Jail."

"What?"

Indira's mind reeled as Amar relayed his location and ended the call. She stood in the kitchen, staring at the phone clutched tightly in her hand. Trembling. Trying to process everything her brother had said.

Moments later, Indira's brain kicked into gear, setting her into motion.

"Mom, I have to go," she called on her way down the hallway toward the door.

"Go? Where are you going? Who will cook your father's dinner?"

"I'll order take-out and have it sent."

"Indira!"

"I'll call an auntie."

Surely someone would keep an eye on her mother until her father arrived home from work. Indira sent a blaze of text messages on her way to the bus stop, cursing the commute. The only family lawyer she knew was a friend of her fathers. And Sabina. Her friend from work was a corporate lawyer, but she would have other contacts.

By the time the SkyTrain rumbled across the city limits, Sabina still wasn't answering her phone.

"Dammit."

She left Sabina another brusque voicemail as the neighborhoods sped by. Indira was already on her feet when the SkyTrain rumbled into her stop. The sidewalks were choked with people. Indira elbowed her way through the crowd and hurried toward Yaletown. She had never been so happy to see work.

Without her access badge, she was forced to stop at the reception desk.

"Buzz me through," she said, gesturing impatiently toward the glass doors leading to the office.

"Where's your pass?" the security guard asked, barely tearing his eyes from the screen long enough to shoot an indifferent gaze her way.

"I don't have it."

"Then you'll need an escort."

Indira flung her hands wide in frustration and marched toward the desk. She leaned across the poured concrete surface, giving him no choice but to look at her.

"Seriously? You know me. I work here."

He looked unimpressed. She wanted to rip into him, tell him that for fifteen bucks an hour, they'd hired a fence post instead of a guard, but insulting him was pointless.

"Fine. Call Sabina Dewan."

"Who are you?"

"Good god." Indira pressed a palm to her forehead and summoned the few scraps of patience she had left. "I'm Indira Saraf."

Moving at a pace that could best be described as glacial, the guard picked up the phone. Indira paced the lobby, willing Sabina to respond.

"She's not answering."

"Try again."

Preparing to rage text Sabina, Indira pulled the phone from her pocket when a fellow developer, a friendly guy named Jon, emerged through the glass door. Indira cut a sideways glance at the guard. He stared blankly at the wall with the phone pressed to his ear when Indira lunged for the opening.

"Hey!"

By the time his sizable bulk had risen from the chair, she was already inside. She sprinted up the open staircase, taking the steps two at a time, betting the guard in the lobby couldn't be bothered to chase her down. At the top of the landing she paused, out of breath and huffing. A few heads swiveled in her direction as she threaded her way through the desks, beelining it toward Sabina's office.

Indira skimmed past the glass-walled conference rooms and rounded the corner. She turned into a short, L-shaped corridor where the management offices were located. Sabina's office was on the left, second to the end. A frustrated growl escaped her as she peered through the glass door. The lights were on, but the office was empty. A red trench coat hanging from a hook on the wall told her that Sabina hadn't ventured far.

Spinning on her heel, Indira almost ran headlong into Dylan. He was striding down the corridor with his laptop in hand. His surprised expression was quickly replaced by a smile.

"I thought you were off today. Is your mother feeling better?"

Ignoring his question, Indira said, "Sabina. Where is she?"

"What's wrong?"

"I need her. Now."

"Okay."

Dylan launched the calendar application on his phone. "She's in the Grouse Nest," he said, hooking his thumb toward the meeting room at the end of the hall. "But—"

Before Dylan could finish, Indira reached the door. The blinds were turned, making it impossible to see inside. Not caring who she interrupted, Indira entered. The conversation stopped mid-sentence. Sabina looked up in surprise.

"Indira, I thought Dylan said you were out." Preet smiled.

Indira was rendered momentarily speechless when she heard Dylan say from behind, "So sorry for the interruption, but Indira needs to give Sabina a heads-up on a situation."

"Now?" Preet asked.

"I'm afraid it can't wait. But since you have a few minutes on your hands, why don't I show you the latest build? The team's been making great progress."

He flashed that charming smile of his, the one that was guaranteed to distract Preet and prevent her from asking more questions. Sabina rose quickly from her seat and left the meeting room.

"What's wrong?" Sabina asked and gestured down the hallway toward her office.

"Sorry. I tried to call." The door to Sabina's office had barely closed when Indira blurted out, "It's my brother, Amar. He needs a lawyer."

"Why?"

Raising her palms, Indira struggled to explain. "The police have him. They think he...might have hurt his girlfriend."

"Assault? Has he been arrested?"

Indira hesitated, as if saying the words out loud might make the horrible situation Amar faced real. She swallowed. Forced out the word.

"Murder."

A heartbeat passed as Sabina studied her, then she grabbed her phone.

"Simon Chen, please. Tell him it's Sabina Dewan."

Indira waited, silently wringing her hands. This was bad. Really bad. She had never heard Amar sound so panicked.

"Simon."

Sabina's greeting roused Indira from her thoughts.

"Yeah, it's been a while. I'm calling for a friend." She gave a soft chuckle at the lighthearted banter on the other end of the phone before continuing. "No, seriously. My friend's brother has been arrested. Not sure of the details, but he needs someone to represent him, and I thought of you. His name's Amar Saraf. Can you go?"

Shifting the phone away, Sabina asked where Amar was being held. Indira's voice shook as she rattled off the address of the institution. Sabina relayed the information.

"You're a doll, Simon. This weekend. The martinis are on me.

Thanks."

Indira pulled in a breath as Sabina hung up.

"He's going?"

Sabina nodded. "He probably won't get in tonight, but try not to worry. Your brother's in good hands. Now what do you know about the girlfriend?"

"Not much."

The truth was even less than that. A few weeks ago when they'd had dinner at the brewery, Indira had guessed Amar was seeing someone else, but he'd refused to say anything.

"If they've already arrested him, they must have some solid evidence. I don't want to scare you, Indira, but you may need to brace yourself for some unpleasant realities."

"What do you mean?" Indira snapped. "Whatever they think Amar has done, they're wrong."

A shuttered expression crossed Sabina's face and Indira's worry spiked.

"He didn't tell you about the girlfriend or why the police are holding him."

"So?"

"So why not? Why the secrecy?"

Indira felt sick, unsettled by Sabina's probing questions. She shook them off.

"I'm sure it's going to be okay. Just a misunderstanding. Thanks for calling your friend. I should go."

"I'm sorry. I'm not trying to upset you. I don't know the details of what's happened, or what part the police think your brother played, but I do know this. There are reasons we keep secrets from those we love the most."

Sabina's words froze Indira to the core. She tried to force a smile and failed.

"Just wait. We'll be laughing about this tomorrow. You'll see," she said, hoping with her whole heart it was true.

30

AMAR SPENT THE NIGHT TOSSING AND TURNING ON A THIN MATTRESS inside a cell that reminded him of the poverty he'd seen in his father's home country of India. They had made several trips to the small village north of Noida where his father had been born. His upper-middleclass upbringing made them look like kings compared to the lives of their cousins. It was an eye-opening and humbling experience and provided a rare insight into the forces that shaped his father's life.

Hard work and an education, his father had preached, were the path to success. Though his father's own education was limited, he had moved to Canada and worked hard, building a successful business and a life for his family. Amar understood the value of education and had made it the center point of his life.

Never forget where you came from, his father had said more times than Amar could recall. But his life, the life his father had given him, was far away from the village streets, and inside his cell, every noise, every shift in the environment, was cause for alarm.

Time seemed endless in this foreign land, and the hours that crawled past seemed like days as his restless mind dragged him down roads he had no wish to travel. Every time he closed his eyes, he saw the shocking crime scene photographs the police had taken inside Mallory's apartment. His mind refused to reconcile the fact that the woman torn apart on the bed was Mallory—the girl he loved.

He tried to forget. Forget the fear. The grief. Everything. But forgetting was impossible. Sleep continued to elude him as the beam of a flashlight shone through the window, piercing the dark, catching him fully in the eyes. All night long, the pattern repeated in fifteen-minute intervals.

Suicide watch.

Standard procedure in cases like his. Amar flipped on his side, away from the beam of light, and faced the wall. From the bunk below he heard his cellmate softly snoring and prayed this interminable night would end.

At five a.m., the alarm went off, rousing the inmates from their bunks. Breakfast was a grim affair served on trays within the cellblock. Amar fought back a wave of nausea as he stared at a lumpy mound of powdered scrambled eggs.

"You should eat," his cellmate said.

Michael Schiff, a heavyset man in his forties, inclined his head toward Amar's tray. Amar sipped the bitter coffee and shook his head. His stomach roiled at the thought of eating. He nudged the tray back with his elbow.

"You don't want to pass out in court."

There was a pragmatic reality to the statement that Amar couldn't deny. Swallowing the bitter taste in his mouth, he managed a few bites of powdered eggs.

They came for him at last, making an elaborate show of cuffing his hands and his ankles, and he was reduced to shuffling awkwardly down the hall pillared between two bulky and silent guards. He wasn't violent or dangerous, and yet here he was, being treated as if he was the worst kind of criminal. The clatter of heavy chains mocked him with each step. Amar was led to a windowless room where he was supposed to meet his lawyer.

Simon Chen didn't look much older than one of Amar's students. He was tall, slight, and sharply dressed in a custom-fit Armani suit. He looked well-rested as he sized Amar up with an appraising glance.

"Uncuff him," Simon said to the officer, who complied with a grunt.

Once they were alone, Simon gestured to the chair on the opposite side of the table and Amar sat, feeling shell-shocked. He took a moment to compose himself before meeting Simon's gaze.

"How are you holding up?"

"I'm okay."

Amar was a million things, but okay wasn't among them. Given the enormity of the situation, it was all he could think of to say.

"Tell me what happened."

"I didn't kill Mallory Riggins."

Simon's neutral expression never changed. He absorbed Amar's statement with a nod.

"Why don't you start by telling me about your relationship with Mallory?"

It was harder than it should have been, admitting to a stranger how he found himself in a relationship with one of his students. He could imagine what a predatory light the situation cast him in —a professor using his power to manipulate a student into a sexual relationship with him. But it hadn't been like that. He hadn't planned it. He couldn't help how he felt, and if he couldn't convince his own lawyer that he had genuinely loved Mallory, how was he going to convince a jury? Amar shuddered at the thought.

He started speaking, haltingly at first, but the memories took hold, pouring out of him. By the time he finished, his voice was hoarse, his throat bone-dry. Like the most assiduous of students, Simon's pen scratched across the pages of a legal pad, recording copious notes. A rapid-fire volley of questions followed. What time had he left Mallory's house? Where did he go?

"Home. Alone."

Simon dutifully recorded his answer. At last the pen stilled.

"You're going to get me out of here, right?" Amar asked.

Simon set the pen down and folded his hands on top of the legal pad. "We're going to push for bail, but given the violent nature of the crime, the prosecutor will fight us."

Amar exhaled sharply, as if he'd been sucker punched. How many nights would he have to spend in a cell until the real killer was found? Weeks? Months?

Black wings of panic thrashed inside Amar's chest. He pressed his palms into his weary eyes.

"It's going to be okay, Amar. You're not alone. I'm going to be with you the whole way. I won't lie. This is going to be a marathon, not a race, but you can do this."

Amar nodded and dropped his hands to the table.

"Good. I need you to promise me that you won't say a word to anyone about the case. Not your cellmate. Not the guards. Every word you say in here can be twisted and used against you. Got it?"

"I understand."

"Okay, the arraignment is going to go fast. The judge is a hard-ass, but your record is clean. You've got a good job. Family ties to the community. Speaking of which, your family, they will be here, right?"

Amar shook his head. Needlessly exposing his mother to this kind of shock in her condition was unthinkable. Her blood pressure was already dangerously high. The last thing she needed was to stand by while her son was publicly accused of a horrific crime.

Simon frowned. "I understand this is hard, but a supportive family humanizes a defendant, especially during a trial."

"Trial?"

The thought of it terrified him.

Simon's smile radiated confidence as he gripped Amar's arm. "Don't worry. In all likelihood, it will never get that far."

Amar wanted to believe Simon, but hope was a luxury he couldn't afford as he waited for the arraignment to begin.

An hour later, for the first time in his life, Amar was led into a court of law. Gray light spilled through the large, arched windows. Rain struck the glass, and Amar was overcome with a feeling of detachment, as if this was happening to someone else. Not him. Then his case was called.

Hearing his name spoken in open court was surreal. Again he had the sense that the Universe had tipped on its axis and he'd landed into an alien world. Simon nudged him, indicating he should stand. Amar rose slowly to his feet and faced the judge, a dour-looking bald man with a bloodhound's sagging jowls. The judge scanned the page he held in his grasp before his cool gaze settled on Amar.

"Does the defense waive the formal reading of the charges?"

"We do, Your Honor."

"Due to the heinous nature of the crime, the Crown believes that the defendant poses a clear danger to the public. As such, it is our request that the defendant remain in custody."

A deep silence settled over the courtroom. Amar struggled for breath, knowing that the next ruling would dictate the kind of hell he would face over the weeks and months to come.

"Your Honor, because of my client's clean record and close ties to the community, we believe bail should be granted."

Hope cut deep, like a painful shard of glass thrust into his heart, as he waited for the judge's ruling.

The judge's gaze rested on Amar for a single beat.

"Bail is denied."

Amar rocked back on his heels. Simon placed a steadying hand on his shoulder.

He was glad that his family was not here to witness his shame. As a man accused of murder, how could he look them in the eyes? How could he face his family, his colleagues, his friends? From this day forward, even if he was proven innocent, they would never look at him the same way. Might they not always wonder if he'd escaped justice, if somehow he'd been responsible for Mallory's death?

The date of the next hearing was announced. Two weeks from today. The panic ringing in Amar's ears intensified, mercifully drowning out the monotonous legal speak that damned him to a purgatory spent behind bars while he awaited his fate.

"It's okay. We expected this," Simon said, as if trying to bolster Amar's sagging spirits, but there was little comfort in his words.

He was innocent of the crime he had been charged with, and yet, the road that stretched out before him was a perilous one. There would be a jury. A trial. Every piece of his life would be scrutinized, and his family would be forced to deal with the humiliation as every bad decision, every secret he'd ever kept, was revealed in open court, laid bare for the jury to judge.

On his way out of the courtroom, Amar raised his head and locked eyes with his sister. The shock of seeing Indira, here to witness his shame, struck Amar with the force of a gavel blow. The dark circles beneath Indira's eyes spoke to the restless night she'd endured. In them, he sensed the same fear he felt—that he had been trapped in a nightmare from which there was no escape. Tears of sorrow streaked down her cheeks as he was led from the courtroom.

31

INDIRA SAT IN THE GALLERY, BARELY ABLE TO BREATHE AS AMAR WAS led away. She felt as if her soul was being ripped in two. Her whole life, Amar had been there—her friend, her protector. Never had she imagined that his life, their family's lives, would be destroyed by the murder of a woman she had never met.

As the shock wore off, Indira slid from her seat and left the courtroom with her head bent low. She felt adrift in a sea of dread, overwhelmed by the enormity of what her brother now faced. The courtroom doors closed behind her and she emerged out into a corridor filled with a sea of people, each navigating the treacherous waters of the legal process, just another soul among the many caught up in the wheels of justice.

She thought about her parents and a fresh wave of despair crashed over her. How would she tell them? What would she say? She could barely believe this was happening herself. The news would crush them.

Up ahead, she caught sight of Amar's lawyer, striding through the crowd, heading for the entrance. Indira hurried toward him, not slowing until she reached his side.

"Hey, what happened in there? How could they refuse bail?"

Simon stopped and turned his gaze on her. "You're Amar's sister?"

She nodded. "Indira."

"I'm Simon Chen. I was going to call you when I got back to the office."

"We can talk now. I'll walk with you." She matched his long stride and together they emerged from the courthouse and into the gloomy day. "Sabina said you were good. How could you let this happen?"

Simon's expression remained steady as he turned west onto Cordova. The cobblestone streets and brick warehouses of Gastown lay a few short blocks away.

"Ms. Saraf—"

"Indira," she corrected him.

"Indira, as I told your brother, it's not time to worry yet. This is only the first step. I'll be in touch with you and your family as I prepare Amar's defense."

"What's going to happen to my brother?"

Simon's eyes looked a thousand years old as he glanced down at Indira, and she realized that she had been pushed into a world she knew nothing about. Courtrooms and legal strategies were a world inhabited by other people, not by Indira or her family.

She pulled in a deep breath and released it slowly.

"I need to see him."

"I know and you will."

"When?"

"Weekly visits are permitted. I'll get you on the list."

The answer, though accurate, was wholly unsatisfying. She hated thinking of her brother in there alone, with all he must be thinking and feeling.

They moved silently through the crowded sidewalks until they reached the parking lot where Simon had left his car. He clicked a button on the remote. The lights of a Tesla flashed.

"I'll schedule some time for us to talk soon. Come the trial, Amar is going to need the support of you and your family. Can I count on you?"

Indira nodded. "Of course. I'll do anything to help my brother."

"Good."

They shook hands. Simon's grip was strong, reassuring. He left Indira standing in the rain. Her gaze skimmed across the crowded streets toward the nearest SkyTrain station. With Amar remanded in custody, she had no choice but to tell her parents. What would she say? How was she going to break the news that their only son had been arrested for murder?

They'd be confused. Scared. Like she was.

Turning her back on the SkyTrain station, Indira drifted through the streets of Gastown, toward the familiar landscape of Yaletown. She couldn't face her parents. Not yet.

She caught sight of a pub on the corner near her building. She'd gone there a few times after work with her team. Indira crossed the street, deciding that a drink might steady her nerves and give her time to think.

One drink might not be enough. She might need two.

INDIRA AWOKE WITH A START. In the early morning light that filtered through the blinds, she realized three things. First, she wasn't in her own bed. Second, she'd consumed enough tequila to make her feel as if she'd been run over by a tank. And third, she couldn't remember the name of the guy who was tangled in the sheets beside her. A tattoo of an eagle in flight was etched into the pale skin stretched across his muscular left pec, one wing unfurled across his shoulder. Between his dark crew cut and the insignia tattooed on his right bicep, she knew he was military. Or former military.

It wasn't much to go on, but it was enough to propel her out of bed and onto her tiptoes. Hunting around for her clothes, she hastily dressed on her way to the door, determined to disappear before her companion awoke.

On bare feet she padded a silent trail toward the door. With her boots in one hand, and the doorknob in the other, she almost jumped out of her skin when she heard his deep voice.

"I want to see you again," he said.

Looking rumpled from sleep, the guy from the bed didn't appear to be disturbed in the least by the fact that he was standing buck naked in the middle of his living room. Indira's gaze strayed to all the obvious places, traveling from his broad shoulders, well-toned chest down the ripple of his six-pack abs, then lower still. She averted her eyes away and jammed her bare feet into her boots.

"Yeah, sure," she mumbled. "I'll call you."

"I'm Jason. You have my number?"

She gave a hasty nod before heading out the door.

She had no intention of calling him. Last night, she'd gone out for a few drinks to forget about court, and Amar, along with every-thing else, and had left, drunk off her ass, with a stranger. *Stupid.* Indira was no prude, but facts were facts. This guy was a head taller and outweighed her by a hundred pounds or more, and if he'd decided to play rough, there wasn't much she would have been able to do to stop him. At the very least, she should have texted Sabina to let her know where she was going. He was just another in the growing list of things she wanted to forget.

The morning air was cold. A thick blanket of fog hung over the street. She didn't recognize the neighborhood. Small houses rimmed with chain-link fences crammed the block. Pale green paint was peeling off the monkey bars in the empty schoolyard across the street. She checked the placard outside the school, taking note of the name. Port Coquitlam?

Indira groaned. She knew where she was. Checking her phone, she searched for the nearest SkyTrain station, which was a dozen blocks away. Indira shivered in the chilly morning as she made her way toward it.

Walking a mile or so in bare feet and boots was another thing to add to the growing list of stupid things she'd done this week. By the time she climbed aboard a westbound train heading downtown, blisters were already starting to form on her heels.

Indira propped her elbow on the window and rested her temple against her fist. Her eyes closed as the train rumbled down the tracks toward home. Bone-weary and wincing from the pain of the broken blisters on her heels, Indira exited the SkyTrain station and walked the short distance to her building in bare feet.

Entering the apartment, a shot of relief pierced Indira. She was grateful to be home at last. Hazel circled her legs three times, tail thumping, toenails clicking on the floor as she did a happy dance. Indira reached down and scratched the dog's head.

"I know. You need to go out."

She slapped some Band-Aids onto her feet and took the dog out for a quick jaunt. Hazel's protest at returning to the apartment so soon was short-lived. Not for the first time, Indira was struck by how lucky she'd been to have adopted such a good-natured dog.

Inside the apartment once more, she unclipped the leash and tossed Hazel a few dog treats. Hazel devoured them, tail wagging the whole time. Stripping off her clothes, she stepped into the shower, hoping the hot water might wash away last night's hangover.

Drying herself off, she got dressed. A few Tylenols, a glass of water, and then maybe, maybe she could face her parents. She couldn't stall any longer. She had to tell them before they found out through someone else.

Hazel watched from the hallway. Her tail swung in a hopeful wag.

"Sorry to do this to you, girl," Indira said. "I have to go see my parents. I know. I don't want to do it either but..."

Indira left the condo and ran the gauntlet of public transit across the lower mainland. She arrived in White Rock soaked from the rain.

One look at Indira and her mother gave her head a disapproving shake. "Look at you, you're dripping on the carpet."

At a time like this, who gave a damn about carpets? It took all the patience Indira could muster not to snap back. She drew in a breath and let it out slowly as she advanced into the room.

The look on her face gave her away. Instantly, her mother tensed.

"Indira, what is it?"

"Where's Dad?"

"At work, of course."

"We need to call him."

Forty minutes later, her father arrived home.

"What is so important that I have to leave work in the middle of the day?"

Ignoring his irritation, Indira shepherded him into the living room. She placed a pot of tea on the table, which no one touched. Her parents stared at her—her father with irritation, her mother with worry. Indira twisted her hands together and forced herself to speak.

"I have something I need to tell you both and it's not going to be easy to hear."

Her parents exchanged an anxious glance. Her father's face darkened. Disapproval showed in the hard line of his mouth.

"You're pregnant?"

Had the situation been any less dire, Indira might have laughed at the absurdity of the accusation. Instead, she shook her head gravely.

"It's about Amar."

Indira moved beside her mother's chair and lowered a comforting hand onto her shoulder. Her mother's condition was fragile. The shock of the situation was bound to take its toll. She wished there was a way to soften the blow, but as the silence stretched on, worry got the best of her mother.

"What is it, Indira? You're scaring me."

"Amar's been arrested."

Her mother's face paled. Her thin hand fluttered to her chest, palm pressed against her heart.

"Mom, are you okay?"

Her mother managed a nod before her father burst in.

"Amar? Arrested? For what?"

Indira swallowed. "He's been charged with murder."

Her father rocked back on the couch as if he'd been struck. Her mother curled forward, narrow shoulders hunched over her knees, as if the pain was an arrow pierced straight through her heart.

"It can't... I don't..." Her mother's words were muffled by a sob. She buried her face in her hands, shoulders shaking with her grief.

"It's okay, Mom."

Indira crouched by the chair. She ran her palm helplessly across her mother's back, consoling her, wishing there was something she could do to ease her mother's pain.

"When? When did this happen? Why did you not tell us sooner?"

Indira's spine straightened at the attack. She rounded on her father.

"This isn't about me. It's about Amar."

"He needs a lawyer."

"He has a lawyer. A good one. I've already taken care of it."

"You? Why would he call you instead of—?"

He bit off the words, but Indira knew full well what he was going to say. *Instead of me.* As the head of the household, he was the decision maker, and yet Amar had chosen to confide in her.

Her father looked away, his jaw working as he struggled to contain his anger. "Who is he accused of killing?"

"They think he killed a woman he was involved with."

Her father's nostrils flared. "This woman, is she the same woman he was cheating on Rani with?"

Indira closed her eyes. "It doesn't matter, Dad. All that matters is that Amar didn't do this. Proving his innocence is the only thing we should be worried about."

Her mother raised her tear-stained face. "Where is he?"

"He's being held in custody."

"Bail?" her father, always the pragmatist, asked.

"Denied."

He flinched at the word and lapsed into silence. Indira left her mother's side and poured them all a cup of tea. Her mother's hands shook so badly, she couldn't hold it. She placed it back on the table with a clatter. Her father stared fixedly at the floor.

"What do we do next?" he asked.

It was the first time she could remember him asking her opinion about anything that truly mattered. They were both looking at her now as if she might have the answers. Indira pulled in a steadying breath.

"His lawyer wants to meet with us. I'll call him."

32

Days had passed since the arraignment in an unbroken stream of monotony that made each day seem like ten.

The prisoners streamed into the day room, flowing around Amar like water around a rock. He lowered himself into a chair near the back of the room, wishing he could disappear.

"Amar," Michael, his cellmate, called. "We're playing cards. Come on."

Amar shook his head. With a sigh, Michael broke off from the knot of inmates gathered around a table and approached.

"It's not good to isolate yourself. The other guys will see it as an insult—like you think you're too good for them."

"No."

He didn't care what the other prisoners thought. He had no intention of integrating himself into this place. This world was not his. He *was* better than them. He was a highly educated man, innocent of the crime for which he stood accused, while these other men had done unspeakable crimes. They weren't his friends. His peers.

Michael lifted his thick shoulders in a shrug. "Suit yourself."

Turning away from Amar, he joined the card game. Near the front of the room, another group of inmates flocked around a television mounted high on the wall, squawking like seagulls. Tuning out the noise around him, Amar let his mind drift. He imagined being miles away, in his small office at the university. It had only been a few days since he'd last set foot on campus, and yet, it felt as if it had been another life.

"Saraf."

Surprised by the summons, he looked up sharply at a husky guard with a thick beard.

"Move it, Professor. Your lawyer's here."

Amar was shuttled to the room where Simon waited. The guard left. Grabbing a fresh legal pad, Simon gestured for Amar to sit, anxious to get started.

"Walk me through every detail of that night."

"Again? Haven't we already covered this?"

Simon nodded. "Every detail is important. I don't want to miss anything."

Amar drew in a breath and closed his eyes. He walked through every painstaking detail of that night, from the moment he pulled up in front of Mallory's apartment, to the time he arrived home. Simon interjected, asking questions and jotting notes. The process left Amar feeling hollowed out, as if he had lived a lifetime within the span of an hour.

"They're going to expedite the DNA testing and use the results to cement their case."

"To what end? I've never denied that I was at Mallory's."

"Or that you had sex with her."

Amar lifted a hand, conceding the point. "Consensual sex."

"With your student." Simon paused, letting the emotional weight of the nuance sink in. "They also have an eyewitness who saw your car outside Mallory's place the night of the murder. They have text messages and other evidence of your relationship. From their perspective, they believe their case is solid."

"You're saying I'm fucked."

"No, but they have offered a deal. If you plead guilty to second degree murder, they'll recommend twenty years with the chance of parole."

"Twenty years? Are you serious? They call that a deal?"

Simon laced his fingers together and rested his chin on his thumbs. His measured gaze settled on Amar, who steeled himself for what was coming next. The barely controlled panic welling within him made it hard to think. His pulse throbbed like a hammer inside his skull.

"If you're convicted of murder one, the aggravating factors, including the violence of the crime, you could be looking at life without parole."

"I won't plead guilty for something I haven't done."

Simon gave a measured nod, as if he expected Amar's response.

"Okay then," he said. "I suggest we do everything we can to expedite a fast trial."

"Won't we need as much time as possible to prepare our defense?"

"The more time we give them, the stronger their case gets. Instead, we'll force them to present their case and poke as many holes in it as we can. We'll hire experts to scrutinize every piece of evidence, look for sloppy procedures, whatever we can find to discredit their case. Challenge them where they're weak. They don't have a murder weapon, and as for motive, they're going to claim that after your fiancée's suicide attempt, you were trying to salvage your relationship in order to hide the indiscretion from your community."

Amar lowered his head and pressed the pads of his thumbs to his eyes. "I killed Mallory to appease Rani? That makes no sense."

"Nevertheless, the more pressure we can put on the prosecution, the more I like our chances."

"I would never hurt Mallory, or any other woman, and yet they're trying to cast me as this monster..." Amar broke off and swept his hands in a broad arc, grasping for words to express what he felt. "Who could do this? Who is capable of such violence, such hate?"

"We don't need to prove your innocence, Amar. We only need to cast doubt."

"Doubt?" It seemed like a weak substitute for the truth.

An overwhelming wave of panic crashed over him, dragging him under, until he could sense his life being ripped away. He'd already lost Mallory, and now he was going to lose his job, his family. Everything he'd ever wanted, hoped for, gone in an instant.

Amar grasped for something to hold onto—a nugget of bravery. Resolve. Hope that, between the two of them, he and Simon would find a way out.

"It's going to be expensive," Simon said.

"How much are we talking?"

Simon quoted a number that sent Amar's mind reeling. If he sold everything he owned and mortgaged his condo, he still couldn't come up with that kind of money.

How had his life come to this?

33

In the hours since his lawyer left, Amar's thoughts were consumed by the wreck his life had become. Mallory was dead, and he was their best and only suspect. And what could he prove? That she'd been sleeping peacefully in her bed when he left?

Who else would have done this? Why weren't the police looking for other suspects? Was he going to spend the rest of his life in this hellhole paying for a crime he didn't commit? Unanswerable questions looped inside his head, consuming his thoughts until there was nothing else.

A few inmates in the pod squabbled like toddlers over what television show they were going to watch. Amar ignored them. Visiting hours had arrived and the guard read the list of prisoners who had people waiting for them. Amar looked up in surprise as the guard called his name.

He pushed away from the wall and fell in behind the rest of the inmates, who lined up like cattle in a chute. The group was herded off to the visitation area, where a row of narrow stalls waited. Each stall was bordered by shallow walls rising up from a shelf, like a slimmed down cubicle you might find in a public school or library. A thick barrier of plexiglass separated the prisoners from their visitors. An old-school telephone was affixed to the left-hand side of each stall.

He peered through the glass. A quick rush of love filled him as he caught sight of Indira. Seeing her felt like arriving home after a long and harrowing journey to the one person who could bring you comfort. But those emotions were quickly overshadowed by the shame he felt at bringing her here. What indignities had she suffered to be admitted to such a place? And what must he look like, here behind the glass, dressed in clothes that weren't his own, sharing his fate with men such as this?

Amar took a seat and lifted the receiver.

"You shouldn't have come," he told his sister.

"How could I not?"

The horror and pity he saw in her eyes pained him, and Amar looked away.

"How's Mom?"

In the second or two it took for Indira to frame her thoughts, he understood the truth. They were ashamed. Horrified. Who wouldn't be?

"They're worried about you. We all are."

Amar nodded. He tried to imagine how difficult it must have been for Indira to tell their parents the news. In the span of a heartbeat, so many emotions passed through his mind, each more difficult to articulate than the last. He felt hopeless. Heartsick. Afraid.

He couldn't tell Indira any of this. Looking into her eyes, he could already see she was worried.

"How are you?" she asked, interrupting the painful flow of his thoughts.

Turning away from the tears in her eyes, Amar gave his head a gentle shake.

"You have to know that I didn't do this. I never would have hurt her."

Mallory. He couldn't bear to say her name.

"You lied. You said she was your colleague."

There it was. The faintest hint of accusation in her voice. Amar's gaze dropped to his hand, which was curled into a fist.

"You asked if she was from school. I said yes."

"You know I thought she was a colleague, not a..."

Student. Indira stopped as if she couldn't bring herself to say the word, as another of his lies was revealed. Shame welled within him and he wished he was back in his cell, where he wouldn't have to face her disappointment.

"You shouldn't be here," he said again in a voice that was barely audible.

"I won't abandon you."

In those words, he heard his sister's fiery spirit and knew, beyond a doubt, that she meant what she said.

"There's something I need you to do."

Like a keen student, Indira straightened in her chair. "Of course. Anything."

Amar dropped his gaze and swallowed; his throat had gone suddenly dry.

"I need to talk to Dad."

"I'll tell him. Mom hasn't been well. I don't know if he'll come."

"I could call," Amar offered.

Indira nodded. "That might be best."

As much as he hated the idea of asking his father for money, it couldn't be helped. But more than that, he wanted to look his father in the eye and tell him that he was innocent. He needed his father, his family, to believe him.

"Tell me about her. Mallory."

The mention of her name cut a deep fissure through Amar's soul. He pulled in a ragged breath.

"We met one night after a lecture when her car wouldn't start."

He could still remember how beautiful she'd looked standing in the rain, holding her cell phone and staring desperately at the car. It had been impossible not to overhear the conversation with her mother, or the distress in Mallory's voice. She'd seemed so alone.

"She was your student?"

Amar nodded. "One of hundreds, but she didn't become real until that night. She called her mother for help but—" He shrugged, his mind drifting back to Mallory standing in the parking lot, drenched with rain. "There was something about her —a maturity beyond her years. She was smart, curious. Funny. In a world filled with cynicism, she was sweet."

Refreshing. At a time when he felt like he was suffocating— engaged to a woman he didn't love with the specter of a whole planned life looming over him—Mallory was like a spring breeze. The promise of a new start. A life he had never imagined.

"Did she know about Rani?"

Amar shook his head. "Not until after I broke off the engagement."

It was a small lie. He pictured the stricken look on Mallory's face the day she'd walked into his office and found him with Rani. The betrayal that surfaced in her eyes at Rani's deliberate kiss. That had happened days before Rani's failed suicide attempt. Amar saw no benefit in sharing the humiliating details with his sister.

"How did she react?"

"What does any of this matter?"

Amar tipped his palms skyward and shifted his gaze from Indira, down the deserted hall. He couldn't talk about this. Thinking about Mallory, how young she was, how vulnerable, ripped something loose inside him. Indira seemed to understand. She let the thread of conversation drop, pursuing another tack.

"What do you think happened to her?"

"I don't know."

"Come on, Amar. There must be someone. An ex-boyfriend?"

Indira waited for his response. Much to his horror, Amar realized he didn't know much about Mallory's life. They'd never spoken about previous relationships. She seemed to get along well with her roommate. Unlike many of her peers, Mallory's life, outside her tempestuous relationship with her mother, wasn't steeped in drama. It was one of the things he'd liked about her.

"She was a pretty girl. There were probably dozens of guys who were interested in her. She never mentioned... But there was this one guy in my class who did seem to hover around her. Brock Sinclair."

He remembered seeing Brock in class the day Mallory was killed. He'd looked rumpled, disheveled. Not at all like his usual self. Why hadn't he told the police about Brock? He would mention him to Simon.

Perhaps Brock was the seed of doubt his lawyer was looking for.

34

AFTER LEAVING JAIL, INDIRA TOOK THE TRAIN HEADING TOWARD Burnaby, her mind churning through the conversation with Amar, more certain than ever that he had not committed this crime. But somebody had, and now that her brother sat awaiting trial, the police would be focused on building their case against him rather than hunting down the real murderer.

It didn't take long to find Brock Sinclair on social media. His parents owned a small ski hill in the Okanagan Valley called Summit Peak, and his feed was split between pictures of snowy days spent on the slopes and pub nights with his friends. Medium height. Athletic build. Bronze skin. Dark hair. Indira scrolled through the avalanche of selfies, wondering if she was looking into the face of a killer.

If she had any hope of figuring out what had happened on that awful night, she needed to learn more about Mallory. The news articles mentioned a part-time job. It was that thought that led Indira from the train station to the place where Mallory worked.

A makeshift memorial grew on the sidewalk outside the Daily

Grind. Cellophane-wrapped bouquets of flowers, dewy with rain, lay propped against the building beside a soggy teddy bear. Seeing the outpouring of grief from the community, Indira's heart ached with the tragedy of the situation.

She would find the truth. She would dig until the secrets buried with Mallory were revealed. For Amar, who deserved his freedom. And for Mallory, who deserved justice. Rain streamed like tears down her face. Indira rose and headed toward the door.

The mood inside the coffee shop was subdued. Half a dozen patrons littered the tables, and there was a small lineup near the cash register. Indira took in the surroundings. Natural light poured through the windows, reflecting off the dull metal chairs. Pendulum lights swung from the high ceilings, casting circles of light onto the dark wooden tables. The earthy smell of the coffee filled Indira with a sense of warmth.

Behind the cash register, a young man with dark hair stood taking orders. Beside him was a woman in her thirties with short hair and red-rimmed eyes. She looked as if she'd been crying. Indira stood in line behind a tall guy in a plaid shirt and a North Face jacket.

"Sorry to hear about Mallory," he said to the cashier as he paid for his drink.

The dark-haired man nodded. Indira had come thinking she might be able to learn more about Mallory from the people who had worked with her, but now that she was here, she was at a loss for where to begin. It didn't seem right, asking questions of people who were still so clearly grieving.

She averted her gaze away from Mallory's coworkers to the community announcement board. A missing persons poster was pinned to the surface. For a moment, Indira just stared, stunned by how closely the missing girl resembled Mallory. Unaware the line had shifted, she was still staring at the poster when the cashier called.

"Ma'am?"

Was she old enough to be called ma'am?

"Who is that?" Indira asked, gesturing toward the flyer.

"Katie Lord. She's been missing for three weeks," the clerk said.

"Did you know her?"

"She and her boyfriend were regulars here, but since she went missing, we hardly see him." The cashier lifted a shoulder in a half-hearted shrug.

"Afraid to show his face," the woman by the espresso machine said.

The muttered statement spiked Indira's interest. "What makes you say that?"

"Guilt. Why else would he stop coming in?"

"Wow," Indira said, raising her eyebrows. "That's kind of spooky."

Ordering a chai tea, she dug in her pocket and paid for her drink.

"So sorry, all this must be hard on you guys."

The cashier nodded and handed Indira her change. She deposited the coins into the tip jar.

"Did you know Mallory?" he asked.

Indira hesitated, not wanting to lie, but also not wanting to tell them that her brother was accused of the murder. She grasped for something that was true.

"We both went to Simon Fraser."

"It still doesn't seem real, you know? I keep expecting her to walk through the door."

The corners of his mouth tugged into a wistful smile and he gave his head a shake. Indira pulled her cell phone from her pocket and clicked on a photo of Brock Sinclair.

"Did you ever see this guy in here?"

The cashier's face hardened. "Are you a cop?"

Indira snorted and ran her palm across the shaved stubble on the side of her skull. "With this hair? Are you kidding me? I was just wondering because this guy was in our class too. He always kind of gave me the creeps, and I just thought...well, I don't know. I suppose it's crazy."

She shrugged and was about to pocket the phone when the guy gestured for it. He studied the photo more closely. Her hopes plummeted as he shook his head.

"He's not one of the regulars."

He handed the phone to his coworker. She barely glanced at it before she shook her head too. The woman gave the phone back.

"If you ask me, it was the guy she was arguing with," she said.

Indira's interest spiked. "Who?"

"A few days ago, she was arguing with some guy outside the shop. Dark hair. Older than Mallory. He looked Middle Eastern, or something. He grabbed her arm. No telling what might have happened if Joe hadn't gone outside to break it up."

Indira froze. Middle Eastern? Or did she mean Indian? Amar?

"What was his name?"

The woman shook her head. "Don't know. Mallory didn't say, but she was sure shaken up over it. Later, I saw bruises on her arm. She tried to brush it off, but I've been in enough bad relationships to know trouble when I see it."

Indira felt a sinking sensation at the pit of her gut. It had to be some kind of misunderstanding. The brother she knew would never hurt a woman, especially not a woman he claimed to love, but he fit the vague description.

Joe shot his coworker a sideways glance and said, "I thought you were convinced it was Mr. Quad Grande Breve."

"That creep?" she snorted.

"What creep?"

"The name's Tim something-or-other and his girlfriend was Katie Lord." She pointed to the missing persons poster that Indira had been studying minutes ago. "Any idiot could see that he was hot for Mallory. Always flirting with her. I told her to watch out for him but..."

She trailed off with a shrug and Indira made a mental note to read everything she could about Katie Lord. If the woman was right and the guy whose girlfriend had just gone missing did have a thing for Mallory, Brock Sinclair might not be the only suspect on Indira's list.

35

DEAD ON HIS FEET, AMAR SHUFFLED OUT OF HIS CELL. LAST NIGHT had been another hard night among many to come. Another breakfast, and he pushed the food around the tray with his fork, telling himself to eat, but unable to do so. He grimaced as he sipped the bitter coffee and tried not to think about the day ahead —classes he would never teach, the girl he would never see again.

No matter what happened from this point on, his life would never be the same. Losing his job at the university was inevitable. If he got out of here, he could try fighting it, but the fact was, no parent would want their child taught by a man who was accused of killing a student. No one would ever look at him the same way. And Mallory... She was gone.

The well of grief he felt every time he allowed himself to think about her threatened to pull him under. The ritual of the morning meal was followed by cleaning the cell, followed by time in the day room.

Midmorning he was led to a room where Simon waited. The

expression on Simon's face looked equally grim as Amar resumed his seat.

"The DNA tests came back from the sheets, and the other bodily fluids they recovered from the body. They're a match."

Amar nodded dully. "We knew that already."

Simon grimaced. He stood with his hands on his hips, angled away from Amar, looking like a man who had something to say and was trying to find the best way to say it.

"There's something else."

"What?" Amar asked, with a growing sense of dread.

Simon plucked a file folder off the top of a stack and flung it across the table at Amar. He opened it. His stomach dropped as he scanned the contents of the police report.

"How did you even find out about this? I was never charged."

"Never charged?" Simon scoffed.

His jaw tightened and he rubbed his forehead, his frustration palpable.

"Why didn't you tell me?"

"It was years ago. It didn't matter."

"Didn't matter? You're charged with first degree murder, Amar. Everything matters. As your lawyer, I can only defend you if I know everything. This..." He jabbed a finger toward the police report. "This is the kind of thing they can use against you."

"But—"

Simon silenced him with a raised palm. A bright spark of anger lit inside Amar's chest. It had been so long ago, a part of his past he'd left behind, wanting to forget everything about that period of his life, and now, here it was, emerging at the worst possible moment.

"So?"

"What?"

"Are you going to tell me what happened?"

Amar released a breath through his clenched teeth and shook his head.

"I met her at a party. Graduate school. We had all been pushing really hard and...and needed to blow off some steam. I'd never seen her before. She was friends with Jasmine, a girl in my doctoral program."

She'd been perched on the arm of a chair, like a rare and beautiful bird. Fine features. Blue eyes. Bright red streaks threaded through her dark, wavy hair. Cigarette in hand. She was talking to a guy, or rather, listening to him, or pretending to. Her eyes wandered, as if bored with the conversation. The guy she was with was too full of himself to notice.

The program was full of those types—people in love with the sound of their own voices, as if they had some rare and precious wisdom they couldn't wait to bestow on the masses. Amar watched her, all the while thinking that she was the most beautiful woman he'd ever seen.

Somehow, after inhaling another glass of liquid courage, he worked up the nerve to talk to her, but she had left her perch on the chair, and taken flight, bypassing the restroom, her excuse for abandoning her date, and headed outside. Amar followed.

Music bled through the windows, shattering the serenity of the small backyard. It was early summer. The humidity of the day lingered in the dewy night air. The smell of cigarette smoke carried on the slight breeze and she stood staring into the dark.

The sound of his footsteps startled her, and she whirled around to face him.

"Christ, you're a quiet one."

"Needed a breath of air, that's all," Amar said.

She was so lovely that it was hard not to stare. He tore his gaze away from her and surveyed the tall line of maple trees outside the fence. She had enough men staring at her. He needed a different angle.

"God, how do you stand those people?" She waved her hand toward the windows, the tip of her cigarette glowing in the dark. "They're so full of themselves. I don't know why I let Jasmine drag me to these things."

She shook her head and ground her cigarette out on the railing of the deck. Once extinguished, she flicked it out onto the darkened lawn and blew out a long trail of smoke.

"Did you come here with one of those twats?" she asked.

Amar flashed a lopsided grin. "I am one of those twats."

"You?" She emitted a gravelly laugh. "Sorry."

"Don't be. You're right about most of them. That guy you were talking to—"

She held up a hand. "Don't even. Michel. Luc. I don't remember. Seriously, who gives a fuck about game theory?"

"Yeah, it's his current obsession."

"And you, what are you obsessed with?"

Her eyes rested on his face. Amar gave a dismissive laugh.

"I won't bore you with the details of my dissertation. I'm afraid it's frightfully dull. Besides, isn't that why we're here? To forget about the tedium of academia for a while?"

This won him a thin smile.

"How novel. A man who isn't obsessed with his work."

"And what are you obsessed with?" Amar asked, surprised by the depth of his desire to know.

Her smile widened. "Why don't we get out of here and I'll show you."

Though Amar was sorely tempted, his instincts urged him to play it cool.

With a shake of his head, he said, "No."

"No?"

Her eyes widened slightly, betraying her surprise.

"Afraid you're going to miss something?"

Amar grinned. He was right. She was the kind of woman who

was used to getting what she wanted. The only hope he had of capturing her interest was to be unexpected.

"I can't just leave here with you."

"I suppose you've got a girlfriend in there," she said, her gaze drawn to the golden light spilling through the window, illuminating the side of her face.

"No."

"Then why not?"

Amar ran his gaze lightly over her, not saying a word. The hush of the night was filled with chirping crickets as she waited for him to speak. Allowing a playful smile to tug at his lips, he stared down at her eyes.

"It has nothing to do with them. It's you."

"Me? What have I done?"

"You're trouble."

She pulled in a mocking gasp and swept her hand to her chest, pretending to look affronted. Amar's smile disappeared.

"And besides, I don't even know your name. You're just this strange woman at a party, who smokes cigarettes and labels everyone with an education a 'twat'." Feigning indifference, Amar tipped his palm up in a shrug. "Why would I be any different?"

"Well, not everyone," she said in a tone that was decidedly flirtatious.

Amar glanced back at her, as if daring her to go on.

"Jasmine, for example, she's not a twat."

A chuckle erupted from the back of his throat. He crossed his arms. "And..."

"And you're not bad. So far."

She gave him a once-over that set his pulse racing. He kept his expression cool.

"You don't even know my name," he said.

"So? You don't know mine either and still..."

He waited for her to say more, but she didn't. She heaved a sigh and shrugged her shoulders as if readying herself to go.

"Amar," he said. "My name's Amar."

Her face broke into a smile and he thought that he had never seen anyone more lovely.

"I'm Callie." She stuck her hand out toward him and he shook it. Her long fingers clasped his in a grip that was surprisingly firm. "Well, Amar, now that we have formalities out of the way, what do you say we get out of here?"

She tipped her head to the side and he gave his one-word answer.

"Absolutely."

Turned out that Callie had two obsessions. The first was art. She was a painter. Her work was modern. Abstract. Erratic. But he couldn't deny that there was something compelling about her paintings. An unexpected use of color. That first night he'd studied her canvasses in silence, while she fixed them a couple of drinks.

"I'm talking to a gallery about a showing," she said as she handed him a glass.

He lowered his nose toward the rim and gave it a sniff. Vodka and something sparkling. Not much else. He took a sip. Swallowed. Hid a grimace. It was strong.

"I can see why. They're remarkable."

"You think so?" She gave a throaty laugh. "My last boyfriend said they were shit."

"Then your last boyfriend was a shit."

That made her laugh even harder. Amar followed her to a threadbare couch pressed up against the wall of the cramped living room, which doubled as her studio. He could feel the heat of her thigh brush against his, and he took another sip.

"Oh my god. He was a shit, but a talented one. He's sold a few of his paintings to a gallery on Rue St. Paul, near the Port."

"So? That makes him what? Successful?"

Without meeting his eyes, Callie smiled. "He's a conceited asshole."

"See? My point exactly. Who cares what he thinks? It's what you think that matters."

She turned toward him then and Amar was caught by the intensity of her gaze.

"You are different," she said, leaning toward him.

Her lips met his in a kiss that made his pulse leap. She was confident. Aggressive. Unlike any other woman he'd met. Callie drew back.

"I like different."

For the next few weeks they were inseparable. They stayed at her place, drinking late into the night and sleeping away the morning. Several weeks later, Amar discovered her other obsession. Drugs. At first, she'd brushed off his concerns, chiding him about his puritanical values. He'd tried to convince himself that she wasn't a junkie, but there were times when she'd disappear for hours on end, and stumble back home altered.

He never knew where she went, and she refused to tell him. A few months into the relationship, the arguments began. Amar pressured her to clean up and focus on her art. Callie railed against him, declaring that she didn't need him telling her what to do. She was just fine thank-you-very-much.

Then the impossible happened. Callie got a show booked. And for the next while, their relationship reverted to the way it was at the beginning. Bright. Exciting. And she was the woman he'd met outside the party. The woman he couldn't get enough of.

The gallery was small, near the university. The gallery owner was effusive in his praise, and Callie preened. Opening night, she looked stunning, and as the patrons flocked in to revel over her work, Callie glowed. Everything was going perfectly.

Until her ex strode in.

The moment Callie saw him, everything changed. Amar watched helplessly as she tried to ignore him. He walked in like he owned the place. He raked his gaze across the canvases with an inscrutable look.

Amar eased toward Callie, settling his hand in the small of her back as her ex drew near. No sooner had he touched Callie when she pulled away from Amar, drawn, as if by a magnet, to the man she had once called a shit. Amar stiffened as the sting of jealousy took hold. He hung back as she held out her arms and the two embraced.

Body language had a rhythm of its own and he studied each intonation, each inflection. She leaned in and grazed his raspy cheek with her lips, desperate for attention, for approval, which her ex gave sparingly. It seemed he too understood the value of holding back. The more he withheld, the more she wanted, and a half hour later, his glass of wine empty, Amar left the gallery. Alone.

Callie didn't come home that night. Or the next. On the third night, she let herself into the apartment.

"Oh!" she said, catching sight of him, as if surprised he was still there.

For the past three days, Amar had run the gamut of emotions, starting with anger, moving on to jealousy, betrayal, and ending in despair. Without saying a word, she stood by the door, as if waiting for him to do something.

He didn't ask where she'd been. He already knew. From the look of her bloodshot, hollowed-out gaze, he knew she was on the back side of a three-day binge with her ex, and he was supposed to do what? Forgive her? Pick up the pieces?

Amar's fingers curled into fists as he stared at her.

"I'm glad you're here," she said.

And just like that, a blade of hope sliced through him, and he was filled with a sense of self-loathing so deep, he had to look away. She stepped toward him, and he could smell the stink of the drugs oozing from her pores. The cigarettes. The sex.

She stopped a foot away and waited in silence until his gaze swept back toward her before she spoke.

"He understands me," Callie said.

Those three words broke something inside Amar. She reached toward him, but he batted her arm away.

"Whore."

He had never used that word in his life, but the depth of her betrayal tore through him and the word slipped out. Callie jerked away and gave a hard laugh.

"Poor Amar," she sneered, brushing past him.

She dug her pack of cigarettes out of her purse and flung it on the couch with such force, the contents spilled out.

"I thought you were better than this," he said, his voice filled with disdain.

"You know, you're just like them! Another grad school douchebag with an overinflated ego." She slashed her hand through the air, the burning coal of her cigarette pointed toward the door. "You think you're better than me. Smarter. But you're not. You've been playing a part. Hiding who you are."

"Me? You're so desperate for attention, for *his* approval, that you threw yourself at that piece of shit, hoping somehow that the meager-talented-fuckwit will shore up your crumbling self-esteem. The only shred of talent you have is in that pretty face, and even that—"

Amar bit off the hateful words, but it was too late. They had both gone too far.

"Get the fuck out!" she screamed.

"He doesn't care about you. He doesn't want you."

She whirled on him with wild eyes. Her hand collided with his cheek. The crack of her slap was deafening. His head snapped back. The hate in her eyes burned as hot as coals and a black rage overcame him. Trembling with a surge of adrenaline, he slapped her back.

She reeled away with a gasp, a hand planted against her cheek. "You sonofabitch."

She grabbed a jar of brushes off a shelf and hurled it across the room. He ducked. The jar exploded against the wall. She grasped a paint-smeared putty knife and whipped it at his head. The sharp edge caught his cheek and opened a fissure in the flesh. He felt the sting. Raised his fingers to the wound and pulled them away. Blood covered his fingertips.

The last bit of Amar's control ripped loose, and he lunged at her, forearm raised, connecting with her chest, pushing her back, back, back. She stumbled over the leg of an easel and it crashed to the floor. The canvas flew. Amar's vision narrowed, focused on nothing but the satisfying flash of terror he saw in her eyes.

He drove her into the wall. Her teeth snapped together with a crack. His forearm rammed against the base of her throat and he pressed. The chords of her neck stood out. She struggled, tried to push him away, but he was too strong. Veins pulsed in her forehead as her face turned red.

Amar never heard the crack of the door opening. Voices yelling. It wasn't until the cops ripped him away from her that he came back to himself to see Callie crumpled to the floor. Holding her throat. Sobbing.

The memory faded and Amar fell silent. He opened his eyes to find himself seated once again in a concrete room across from his lawyer.

"Did she drop the charges?" Simon asked at last.

Amar pulled in a shaky breath and shook his head. "No. The charges were dropped after..."

"After what?"

A bitter taste filled Amar's mouth and he swallowed. He raked a hand through his hair. He'd been so deeply ashamed of what had happened that he had never told another living soul what he'd done.

"Two days later Callie was found in her apartment. Dead. An overdose."

A somber silence fell across the room.

"Why does any of this matter?"

"The prosecution will argue that the episode with Callie shows a pattern of violence against women. Callie was going to leave you, so you beat her. They have a witness who will testify that she saw you grab Mallory outside the coffee shop. Mallory had just found out that you'd been lying to her. She was about to break up with you, and you snapped."

"But I didn't."

"No, but that's what they're going to say. They're going to paint you as a violent guy and this..." Simon lowered his palm to rest on the closed file folder. "This police report strengthens their case."

Amar had never told his family about Callie or what had happened to her, and now they were going to find out about every stupid, awful thing he'd done in a court of law. He dropped his face into his hands and imagined how all of this would play out. The jury would hate him. They would believe the prosecution. He was charged with first degree murder, and for the first time since entering this concrete crypt, the idea that he would spend the rest of his life here felt like a distinct possibility.

"Do you think I should take the deal?"

Simon sighed and shifted in his chair. He met Amar's desperate gaze with a grim one of his own. "I'm afraid that's no longer an option."

36

"WHY ARE YOU READING THAT FILTH?" INDIRA'S MOTHER SNAPPED.

Her red-rimmed eyes lifted from her needlework and settled on Indira's father. He sat in a chair by the window. A copy of *The Vancouver Sun* lay sprawled on his lap. From a few feet away, Indira glimpsed the photographs inserted into the layout beside the article. Mallory smiling for the camera. A stone-faced Amar in court.

In his haste to close *The Sun*, the newspaper crumpled, and he tossed it aside.

"What else am I supposed to do? Just sit here while the newspapers convict my son?"

He lurched from his chair and strode to the front of the living room, staring out the windows at the neighborhood. Where once they had exchanged friendly greetings with their neighbors, they were now met with chilly stares. Her father turned away from the windows in disgust.

"You. You have spent a lifetime ignoring instead. Maybe if you had paid more attention to our children instead of turning a blind eye, we would not be in this situation. Indira would be properly married and Amar—"

Her mother's stricken expression turned to anger at the accusation hurled her way.

"Maybe if you had given them more room to grow, they would not have felt the need to rebel."

"How dare you speak to me that way! In my own home."

"Stop. Just stop," Indira burst into the room, silencing them both.

Since Amar's arrest, she had taken on the burden of the daily chores. Cooking. Cleaning. Making sure that everything was taken care of while her parents wallowed in their grief. Her father shot a sideways glance in her direction.

"And you, with your shaved head and tattoo."

"Oh, so now you want to drive her away too—"

"Mom." Indira held up her palms, all too aware of the tattoo, visible on the inside of her wrist.

She suppressed the urge to hide it, knowing there was little point in doing so. Her father had already seen it. Despite what he thought, she was not ashamed. Besides, this had nothing to do with her tattoo. Being cooped up in the house wasn't doing either of her parents any good. All this pointless bickering was driving her insane.

"You should go to work tomorrow, Dad," Indira said, but her father didn't respond. He stared moodily out the window as if she hadn't spoken. "Why don't you go see Ranjit?"

Her uncle Ranjit and her father were as close as two brothers could be. If there was anyone who could snap her father out of his funk, it was him.

Her father dismissed the suggestion with a snort. "How can I face him? How can I face anyone with—?"

"You have nothing to be ashamed of. Amar is innocent," Indira insisted, but her father's dead-eyed look said something different.

"My son is locked up, accused of the most heinous act, and you think that I, his father, should not feel ashamed?"

The indignation that burned in her father's eyes lit a spark of anger in hers.

"How do you think Amar feels? He needs us, his family, to stand up for him, to show him that we believe him no matter what. Hiding here, inside the house, only makes him look more guilty. Don't you understand? You need to go to work with your head held high because you know that he has done nothing wrong. And, Mom, you need to let the aunties come and visit with you. Wouldn't it be nice to have a cheerful voice in here for once?"

The days had grown shorter, and with the dinner dishes dried and put away, the sky had faded from gray to black. Indira felt a deep restlessness growing within her. Unlike her father, she would have preferred to immerse herself in her work. Anything to distract herself from the nightmare her family was going through.

She heaved a sigh as she felt the futility of the situation descend upon her shoulders. She had to do something. Hazel had been cooped up in the apartment all day. It was time for her to go home.

"Is there anything you need?"

"All this commuting, Indira. Such a waste. When are you going to move home?" her mother asked.

Never. She wasn't going to move home. In fact, she was planning to take a job in San Jose, not that she had any intention of sharing this information with her mother until things with Amar were settled.

"I'll be back in the morning," she said, dodging the question.

From the hallway, she could hear her parents murmuring in disapproving tones about how stubborn and impractical she was being, but she wasn't the one being unreasonable. She was here, taking care of them. What more did they expect of her?

Indira barely noticed the rain as she hurried to the bus stop, still fuming, refusing to admit that there was a certain practicality to their argument. She had some vacation time banked, but once that ran out, what would she do? Quit? Without a job, the expense of her Vancouver condo would eat through her savings at an alarming rate, and it wasn't fair to leave Hazel alone so long. She thought about how, for the rest of her life, time would be measured in before and after. Before Amar was charged and after...

She couldn't bear to finish the thought. With every fiber of her being she wished that none of this had happened to Amar, to her family. To Mallory.

On the long commute back into the city, she scoured the internet for anything she could find on the murder investigation and her brother. She stumbled onto a video clip of Mallory's parents. She knew she shouldn't watch—it was painful enough dealing with her own parents—but clicked on the video anyway.

Mallory had her father's dark hair and her mother's bright eyes. Mallory's father stood facing the camera, his face ravaged with grief. Mallory's mother stood behind him. She refused to look at him, at anyone. She stared at the ground, her anger palpable, as he began to speak.

"Mallory was the best daughter any father could have wanted, and losing her has left a hole in our lives that can never be filled." His voice cracked with emotion. He wiped his eyes. "We want to thank the Vancouver police for their work in making such a quick arrest. As a parent—"

Whatever he was going to say was cut off as Mallory's mother stepped up beside him, taking center stage.

"As a mother, I just want to say that not only did this man, Amar Saraf, use his power and influence to manipulate his way into her life, he murdered her in cold blood."

Mallory's mother's eyes were dry as she glared into the camera. Her rage robbed Indira of her breath. Mallory's father looped a consoling arm around his ex-wife's shoulder, but she quickly shrugged it off.

"I wish Canada had a death penalty. Life in prison could never begin to pay for what this man stole from us. How many more of our daughters have to die before we put a stop to monsters like him?"

The brutality of the comments posted beneath the video stunned her. So many people posted about his guilt, not just of Mallory's murder, but also unhinged conspiracy theories linking him to Katie Lord's disappearance. The public wasted no time in connecting the two cases and convicting her brother in the court of public opinion.

So much hate. So much certainty despite a lack of evidence.

Given the overwhelming swell of public outcry, what chance did Amar have of finding an unbiased jury pool, or a fair trial? The fact that he was having an affair with a student made things worse. Women's groups posted daily, stories claiming how this case was the very exemplification of an abuse of power. Sexual harassment. Quid pro quo.

The rush to arrest her brother left little doubt in Indira's mind that the police weren't looking for other suspects. They were already biased against her brother and were looking for any evidence they could find to back up their case, which left Simon Amar's best and only hope at building a defense and gaining his freedom.

But she had two names—Brock Sinclair and Tim Atwood. Had the police even considered them potential suspects? In their rush to judgement had they even considered that there may have been other people in Mallory's life who posed a threat?

Indira swayed with the movement of the train as they sped down the tracks through New Westminster and Burnaby, rocketing toward the downtown. Nighttime had fallen across the city. A thousand lights from the high-rise condos penetrated the gloom and lit up the charcoal sky. Over a half million people lived in the downtown core, but Indira had never felt more alone.

Then a thought began to take shape in the back of her mind. If the software they were creating could be used to track a customer's purchasing patterns, perhaps it could be leveraged for something more. What if she could adapt it to lock in on the cellular signals of the two other suspects on her list? What were their connections with Mallory? Where were they the night Mallory died?

If she found evidence supporting an alternative theory of the crime, one that gave the police another suspect to focus on, they would have to listen.

She knew she should be rushing home to let Hazel outside— Hazel who had spent the day alone while Indira looked after her mother—but Hazel would have to wait just a little while longer. Brakes squealed as the train pulled to a stop and Indira joined the throng of people flooding through the open doors and out onto the platform. She squeezed through the edge of the crowd and raced up the escalator.

Emerging out into the cold, rainy night, she jogged the ten blocks toward work, grateful that it was after hours. The office would be empty. She would have time to fire up her laptop and pull down the latest version of the application's code.

Indira's heartbeat raced with anticipation as she swiped her card key across the door sensor, waiting impatiently for the access system to beep and for the door locks to disengage. The red light flashed green, and Indira sprinted up the stairs.

The faint light of flickering monitors cast a ghostly glow across the sea of workstations. Indira sank into the chair behind her desk and felt the tension of the past few days melt away. This felt normal. Like home. She opened the lid of her laptop and hit the power button. With a few quick clicks of her mouse, she was synching the source code files for the marketing application onto a USB drive she'd inserted into her laptop. Her heart sped up as she watched the familiar filenames flash by on the screen, a combination of exhilaration at the idea of actually *doing* something that might help Amar at odds with the unmistakable pang of guilt she felt in her gut.

In the quiet of the office, there was no denying the ethical ramifications. What she was doing was wrong. She was stealing code, or at least using it for purposes for which it wasn't designed. Hadn't she argued with Preet and Dylan that using someone's cell phone data to track their movements, their patterns, was unethical? And yet here she was downloading code that she planned to use to do the same thing for different reasons.

But if she left Amar's fate in the police's hands, he might spend the rest of his days locked up behind bars for a murder he didn't commit. And that was something she couldn't live with.

The sound of footsteps at the top of the stairs brought Indira to her feet. She whirled on her heels, using her body to hide the monitor from view. Dylan looked every bit as startled to see her as she was to see him. Reaching behind her back, Indira turned off the monitor.

"Indira. What are you doing here?"

She flashed a nervous smile. "I was about to ask you the same thing. Kind of late to be working."

He returned her smile and slowly approached, swinging his hands wide. "I left my wallet here. How's your mom?"

The night her mother had been admitted to the hospital, she'd emailed Dylan asking if she could take a couple of days off. Dylan had responded quickly, assuring her it was fine. And when she'd asked to extend her absence, he hadn't balked. His kindness only made her feel worse.

"She's at home now, still recovering. I've got a few weeks of vacation I haven't used..."

Dylan stood a few feet away, looking down at her. Shadows

hooded his blue eyes, and she saw the concern he felt deep in their depths.

"Sounds serious. Take all the time you need. We'll figure it out later."

The stab of guilt she felt twisted inside her gut. Not only was she stealing, but now she was lying to her boss and he was being so kind.

"Preet told me about the offer."

"The offer?" Indira questioned, without the faintest recollection of what he was talking about.

"Yeah, at the team celebration. Preet brushed it off as girl talk, but I could tell there was more to it." He breathed out a sigh and looked away. "Look, I know that we haven't always seen eye to eye, and that you were upset when I was promoted to team lead but—"

Indira shook her head, cutting him off. "I don't—"

"No, let me finish," he said, turning his gaze back to her and meeting her eyes. The pull of him was like a magnet and she couldn't look away. "You're the best engineer on the team, Indira, and...and I really like working with you. The architect role is a great opportunity, and while I would understand if you took it, I just wanted to say..."

Indira was startled when Dylan broke off, partly because the Dylan she knew was never at a loss for words, and partly because she intuitively sensed that there was more behind his objection than just work. They had been coworkers. Rivals. Never friends. And the way he was looking at her now made her wonder if there wasn't something else about their relationship she had overlooked. As she stood here with him in the darkened office, the sparks of attraction between them were undeniable.

"I don't want you to go. The team wouldn't be the same without you."

"Thanks," she said, barely able to breathe.

She took a step back and bumped against her desk. Her laptop chirped, notifying her that the code download was complete. Dylan stood, waiting for her to say something more, but what else was there to say?

"With Mom sick, it would be the wrong time to move and..."

"And?"

"My brother—"

Indira broke off. The temptation to tell another soul about the hell Amar was going through was palpable, but something stopped her.

"What about your brother?"

"Never mind," she said, flashing a fake smile.

The way Dylan's eyes narrowed, she knew he didn't believe her. She had to get out of here before she blurted out the whole sordid mess.

Turning away from Dylan, Indira reached for her messenger bag. Using the bag as a shield, she pulled the thumb drive from its slot and shoved it into her pocket.

"I've got to go."

She sidestepped past Dylan and rushed toward the stairs.

37

INDIRA ARRIVED HOME TO A VERY ANTSY HAZEL, WHO DANCED around her legs, clearly anxious to go outside. Though she wanted nothing more than to fire up her laptop and get to work, Hazel's needs took precedence, and she walked the dog to the park. The rain didn't seem to bother Hazel as she sniffed at every patch of grass, every tree, every sidewalk between Indira's apartment and the park. By the time they made it home, Indira was thoroughly drenched.

She toweled off and changed into her warmest sweats while her laptop powered up. The development environment they used at work was already installed and configured on her home laptop. All she had to do was download the source code and compile. Hazel groaned and placed her chin on Indira's leg. The dog's soulful blue eyes looked up at her. Indira scratched behind Hazel's ears.

"I know you want to play, but I need to get some work done first. How about a treat instead?"

At the mention of a treat, Hazel's tail swung in delight. Indira smiled. She was lucky to have such a good-natured dog. Indira rolled her chair away from the desk and was about to head into the kitchen when her computer chirped. An error message flashed on the screen.

Missing files?

She rolled her chair back toward the monitor to take a deeper look. *Crap.* There were at least half a dozen files missing. Maybe more. The download must have stopped when she closed the laptop's lid, and now it would take days, maybe longer, to reconstruct all the missing files. *If* she could. It wasn't all her code. There were other developers working on the project. She would need to reverse-engineer what was missing and figure out how those pieces worked. And that would take something she didn't have. Time.

Shit. Shit. Shit.

Instead of trying to download the files, she should have taken her laptop, but somehow the thought of using company property on top of stealing code seemed worse. And if she accessed the source code depot at work, she would leave a trail. If Dylan found out what she was doing and why, she could be fired. Maybe even sued.

A knock at the door set Hazel off, and she began to bark. The deep, throaty woofs would surely piss off the neighbors, who had already complained about the dog. Swearing under her breath, Indira jerked away from the desk and stalked to the door. Yanking it open, she found one of her aunties on the doorstep holding a casserole dish.

One look at Hazel was enough to make her auntie yelp in fright. Indira snapped her fingers and pointed to the dog.

"Go."

Hazel looked deflated. She hung her head and skulked into the living room, doing what she was told.

"Don't worry about the dog. She's harmless."

Her auntie cast a skeptical look in Hazel's direction and followed Indira inside.

"Oh, Indira. How are you? With the news about Amar, we've all been so worried."

Indira took the proffered casserole dish that her auntie had brought. The scent of lemongrass waved off the spiced yellow lentils and made her stomach rumble. She set the dish on the kitchen counter, safely out of Hazel's reach.

"How are your parents? I've tried to call, but they're not answering the phone. We've all been so worried. What can we do?"

Indira shrugged, wishing that her parents would open up and let the family help, but the only help they seemed to accept was hers.

"They're taking it hard," Indira admitted. "I've been trying to get them out of the house, but you know how stubborn Dad can be."

Her auntie splayed her hands in a helpless gesture. "And what about Amar?"

Before Indira could answer, there was another knock at the door. Hazel gave a muted woof. *Seriously?* She didn't have this many visitors in a week, let alone a single night. For a brief second, Indira closed her eyes.

Her auntie's gaze followed her to the door, with Hazel close behind. She glanced out the peephole and her heart dropped.

Dylan.

A flurry of thoughts sped through her mind at the sight of him. She opened the door. Hazel craned her thick neck around Indira's legs and pointed her snout in Dylan's direction. She inhaled with a deep sniff.

Dylan held his curled fingers toward the dog. Hazel's tail thumped the wall.

"At least one of you looks happy to see me," Dylan said.

She ran a hand self-consciously across her hair, which had dried into a frizzy mess. And she was wearing sweats that, despite Sabina's comments about her pathetic wardrobe, even she wouldn't wear out. And her auntie was here watching everything.

"Hey," Indira said, trying to sound casual. She nudged Hazel out of the way and blocked the door. "What's up?"

"May I come in?"

How did he even know where she lived?

Indira tried to dream up an excuse to deny him entry but came up blank. She swallowed hard and tossed a glance toward her auntie. "Now's not a good time."

"Nonsense, Indira. Who is this?"

Her auntie's look contained more than simple curiosity. Resigned to her fate, Indira backed away from the door and beckoned him inside.

"I'm Dylan," he said, offering his hand.

Her auntie shook Dylan's hand and eyed him with a guarded look. "How do you two know each other?"

Indira suppressed a groan, but the question didn't seem to bother Dylan. He slid his hands casually into his pockets and gave her auntie a smile.

"We work together."

"He's my boss," Indira said, in a desperate attempt to stem the flow of questions she knew would come next.

"Your boss? Are you working so late?"

"It's not—" Indira shook her head. She had meant to signal that Dylan wasn't her boyfriend and had exposed another line of questioning instead. "Never mind."

Picking up on the awkward vibe, Dylan said, "Maybe I should go."

"Dylan's just here to talk to me about a work matter. How about I give you a call tomorrow?" Indira said to her auntie.

Indira's auntie reached for her purse and shot a sideways glance at Dylan. "I could stay..."

"No need. I'm fine," Indira assured her, knowing that having her auntie overhear the next part of the conversation would only make things worse.

She had no doubt that as soon as her auntie left, she'd call other members of the family and they'd generate their own crazy theories on exactly why Indira's boss stopped by her apartment at night, not to mention the inappropriateness of a single woman entertaining a man alone in her apartment.

Screw it. This was her apartment. Her life. If they didn't like it, they were going to have to learn to deal with it. Indira nearly had to push her auntie out the door.

"I'll call you tomorrow," her auntie said.

"Fine."

Indira closed the door and caught her breath.

"Sorry about that. My family can be...protective," she admitted, having barely avoided calling them nuts.

"They care. That's a good thing." Dylan paused. "I suppose you know why I'm here."

"I've never liked guessing games. Why don't you tell me?"

Dylan's gaze remained locked on Indira's face. If he'd come here to accuse her of stealing, she wished he'd just get on with it. She already felt guilty enough, and the waiting was making everything so much worse.

"I—"

"You—"

They both started talking at once. Dylan gave a small shake of his head.

"You first," he said, sweeping his hand in a courtly gesture.

Indira hung her head. "I'm sorry."

"About?"

A burst of anger radiated through her. "Stop playing dumb."

"Dumb?" Dylan's lips quirked up in a half-grin that she wished she didn't find charming. "I've been accused of worse."

She huffed out a frustrated breath. Turning her back on Dylan, she stared out the large windows at the city lights burning like beacons in the dark, as if the answer to her dilemma lay somewhere out there.

"I assume you've figured out what I was doing at the office."

If he checked the source code logs, he would have seen that she'd logged in. He also would have seen the list of files she'd downloaded onto the thumb drive. It didn't take a genius to piece the rest together, and Dylan was brighter than most.

"I suppose you've come to fire me, for taking the code. If it makes things easier, I'll resign."

Pivoting away from the windows, she stalked across the room and snatched the thumb drive from her desk. She'd been stupid to believe she could get away with it. She was a lousy person and an even worse thief.

"Here. Take it. I'm sorry. I shouldn't have done it, but I was just so—"

So desperate. So scared her brother would spend the rest of his life in jail that she was willing to risk her own freedom to save him. Now that she'd been caught, there was no choice but to face the consequences.

She tossed the drive to Dylan, who caught it with a bemused look.

"You think I'm going to let you quit?"

"What else can I do? I stole the code, all right? I took it because I wanted to—"

The reason she'd taken it didn't matter. Why would Dylan or anyone else in the company care about her intentions? Dylan stood without saying a word. When she finally looked at him, she saw that his eyes were not filled with accusation, but with empathy. Somehow that made her feel worse.

"Please, would you just tell me what's going on?"

Indira exhaled, knowing the only choice she had left was to tell Dylan the truth.

"My brother has been accused of murder and I was hoping…"

Dylan waited for her to say more, but when the protracted silence that followed dragged on, he picked up the trail of her thoughts.

"You were thinking that maybe you could use the geodata tracking module and extend the predictive analysis piece to work on his case?"

Indira gave a brittle laugh. "Stupid. Right?"

Closing the distance between them, Dylan placed a comforting hand on her shoulder. Tears welled in Indira's eyes and she looked away from him, out the windows into the rainy night.

"It's not stupid at all."

Dylan dropped his hand away and strode to the couch, retrieving the backpack he'd placed on the floor. He zipped it open and pulled out a laptop.

"I checked the logs. You didn't get everything."

"You're okay with the fact that I was stealing code?"

"Not exactly. I prefer to think of it as your request to work from home."

He handed her the laptop. With trembling hands, she took it and clutched it to her chest.

"Why are you doing this?"

"After you left, I Googled your brother and I saw a bunch of news articles about the…situation he's in."

"He's innocent."

Dylan paused and met her eyes. She wanted so badly for him to believe her, but she couldn't tell whether he did. Maybe he was like everyone else. Maybe he thought her brother was every bit the monster they described in the media. But if that was true, then he wouldn't be here trying to help.

"Look, Indira, I can't imagine how hard this must be for you and your family. I won't pretend to know what I would do if I were in your shoes, but if this can help you figure out what happened, even for your own closure, I understand why you need to do this."

Raising her eyebrows, Indira said, "You're not mad?"

Dylan's smile was back. He shook his head. "What can I say? I miss having my best engineer on the project. And if you happen to write some code that helps the team, that's a win for everyone, right?"

38

AMAR ENTERED THE VISITOR'S ROOM BOTH EXPECTING AND DREADING the sight of Indira waiting on the other side of the glass, but he stopped in surprise as he saw the person sitting there. The guard unlocked the cuffs that bound his wrists. He rubbed the chaffed skin and slowly approached the glass.

Rani sat bolt upright in the visitor's chair, looking like a frightened deer. She wasn't alone. There were a half dozen other people —friends, family members—waiting to speak to their loved ones, and she was the only one who looked this scared. Her wide eyes darted warily around the room, as if worried she might be attacked, as she waited for Amar to pick up the phone.

Finally he did. She had never looked so lovely. The delicate bones in her were more pronounced, as if in the time since their breakup, she had lost weight. Emotion brimmed in her dark eyes as they locked on him.

"You shouldn't be here," he said, seeing the way one of the men who was visiting another inmate looked at Rani. His gaze slid over her body, full of want. Behind this glass there wasn't a damned thing Amar could do to protect her.

"Neither should you."

Amar didn't know what he expected her to say, but it wasn't this. He had betrayed her, broken her heart. He was incarcerated for murdering his lover, and yet, for some reason he couldn't begin to understand why she'd come.

"Does your mother know you're here?"

Rani shook her head. He was both surprised and not surprised. He hadn't thought that she had kept much from her mother, but they both knew how upset Falguni would be at the thought of her precious child in a place like this. For once, Amar couldn't blame her. This was no place for a young woman to come, especially by herself.

Fatigue showed in the dark shadows beneath Rani's eyes. She looked like a woman suffering, but from what, he couldn't say.

"How are you?" he asked.

She shrugged. "They have me seeing a therapist."

"Really?"

The idea that her perfect daughter might expose the less flattering pieces of their family life must infuriate Falguni, including the habitual breakdown of her self-esteem by an overbearing mother. Amar kept his opinions to himself, knowing that they would do no good. The psychological damage this mother had caused her daughter would take a lifetime to unravel.

"It was one of the conditions under which I was released from the hospital."

"That's a good thing. Is it helping?"

"Who knows?" A ghost of a smile crossed Rani's face then quickly faded. "I hate to think of you in here."

"Why did you come?" he asked again, meeting her gaze.

"I had to see...I had to see that you were okay."

The words sounded as if they had been torn from someplace

deep inside her. There was pain in the admission, and something else, an emotion he couldn't name.

"How is it?" she asked, eyeing the concrete box in which he sat with a look of trepidation.

"Terrible."

He should have lied. Said he was fine. But his lies had already cost him dearly. Still, the honest admission caused her pain. He could see it in her face.

"Is there anything I can…do?"

The simplicity and generosity of the offer touched his heart. After everything he'd done to this girl, his callous treatment, he didn't deserve her compassion. Her pity.

"You want to do something for me? Don't come back."

"You're upset I'm here?"

Amar shook his head. "This is no place for you."

A pulse of silence passed between them, then Rani took a breath and swallowed, as if gathering her courage. She leaned toward the plexiglass barrier and shot a fleeting glance over her shoulder, as if worried someone might overhear.

"It's time we told your lawyer the truth," she said.

Amar's forehead furrowed. The truth about what? Their engagement? His betrayal? The breakup? The suicide attempt? How would telling Simon any of this be relevant to the case?

"I don't understand."

Rani paused, licked her lips, and drew in a breath.

"We need to tell your lawyer the truth about the night that girl was killed. You were with me. All night. I know you lied to protect my honor, and that our families…if they knew we were…intimate before the marriage ceremony, they would not approve. But that doesn't matter anymore."

His hard stare pierced Rani. What was she doing? Why was she saying those things? A ripple of shock coursed through Amar as a sudden understanding dawned.

An alibi?

She was offering him an alibi.

Why? After everything he'd done to her.

"I can't let you do this."

"Please, Amar. Do not let pride stand in the way of your freedom. We could tell the truth, and once you're free, we can be married. Like we planned. Everything could go back to the way it was—the way it was supposed to be before all this happened."

She pressed her hand to the glass, wanting to touch him, to connect with him, but Amar couldn't move. He sat stone-still, processing the terms of the deal.

A marriage in exchange for his freedom.

39

WITH A DISSATISFIED GRUNT, INDIRA PITCHED THE EMPTY COFFEE TIN into the recycling bin and went rooting through her cupboards, searching for the backup supply, only to discover that the tin she had just finished was the backup. She heaved a heavy sigh and rubbed her bloodshot eyes. Just her luck that today of all days, she'd run out.

Maybe it was for the best. All the caffeine was making her jittery. She had spent the night making tweaks to the code and had completed a pull of geodata for every cell phone that had pinged within a one-mile radius of Mallory's apartment on the night of the murder. The data points from each individual cell phone formed golden strands that were projected onto a map of the city. The complex overlapping data strands formed a series of patterns so dense, they were impossible to interpret. It was like trying to isolate the path of each individual pen stroke contained within a spirograph drawing.

The problem was simple. The application was originally designed to identify the patterns of an individual user—where they went, what they shopped for. The data for each user formed a profile that could then be tracked and refined over time. Indira was attacking the problem from the opposite angle. Instead of focusing on an individual user, she was focusing on a place. Instead of showing all the places their target user named Sunny liked to shop and learning that she most often bought shoes from a little boutique on Robson Street, it was showing all the people, including Sunny, who shopped at that boutique. Identifying a single user's cell phone signal from the thousands of people who shopped in the store was like trying to locate a specific silver Prius from the miles and miles of lined up traffic clogging the Trans-Canada Highway at rush hour. There was way too much data.

Indira pushed away from the desk and raked her hands through her hair. There had to be a better way. She would either have to redesign the algorithm or find a more efficient way to parse through it. Rising from her chair, she paced the room.

Morning light streamed through the patio doors leading out to a micro-balcony. She cracked the patio door opened and breathed in the cool air—a combination of rain and car exhaust. Through the gaps between the high-rises, she had a peek-a-boo view of False Creek. Runners and cyclists carved a path beside the water that started at Science World—a structure that looked like a space-aged golf ball for giants—and curved along the edge of the downtown core, winding around the jagged edge of English Bay to Stanley Park. It was an area that she and Hazel had walked more times than she could count. But this morning, the serenity of the scene failed to bring comfort as her mind churned through the possible solutions to her current dilemma.

She had to find a way to solve the problem.

Her visit to the Daily Grind had left her with two viable suspects—Mallory's classmate, Brock Sinclair, and Katie's boyfriend, Tim Atwood. Once she locked into their signals, she could isolate their cell phones from the rest of the noise. Finding their cell phone numbers was one problem she could definitely solve.

Revived by the fresh air and refocusing her plan, Indira returned to her desk. No sooner had she launched a web browser, poised to begin her search, when her cell phone rang. *Now what?*

It was her father calling. Tempted to ignore the interruption, Indira silenced her phone, but the kernel of guilt in her chest sprouted roots. With a grimace, she picked up the phone.

"Hi, Dad."

"Indira, you must come and stay with your mother."

"Why? Aren't you already there?"

"I must go to the store to pick up groceries and her prescriptions."

"I'm right in the middle of something, Dad. Can't she stay by herself for a few hours? I could call one of the aunties—"

"What is more important than your mother? She is not feeling well."

Indira rubbed her burning eyes and suppressed a groan. If doling out familial guilt was a sport, her father would be an Olympic gold medalist.

"Indira?"

Jaw clenched, she slammed her laptop shut. "I'm on my way."

Indira ran the gauntlet of public transit, arriving at her parents' house an hour later. Anxious to be on his way, her father waited by the door. They exchanged a terse greeting as he left. Indira found her mother napping in her favorite chair by the window. Not wanting to disturb her, Indira cleaned up the morning dishes. By the time her mother awoke, the tea was ready. Like the dutiful daughter they expected her to be, she set it on a tray and carried it into the living room.

A trickle of fear raced down Indira's spine as she caught sight of her mother's flushed cheeks and fever-bright eyes. The morning tea was forgotten. Indira dropped the tray on the table and hunkered down beside her mother's chair.

"Mom, are you okay?"

Her mother's icy fingers curled around hers. "A headache. That's all."

But it was more than just a headache. Instinctively, Indira knew that something was very wrong.

"Would you like something for it? Tylenol?"

"I've already taken some pills. They're not helping."

Brushing Indira's worry aside, her mother stood, only to sit back down with a thump.

"Oh!" She winced and pressed her fingers to her temples.

Indira's heart thudded with worry. "Just sit."

Stress. With all the stress the family had been under, it was no wonder her mother wasn't well. She'd been on blood pressure medication for years, but ever since the hospitalization a few weeks ago, she'd been weak.

Indira searched the house for her mother's portable blood pressure machine and found it in the master bedroom, on the floor beside the bed. Grabbing it, she hurried back into the living room, where she found her mother sitting with a bloody tissue pressed against her nose.

Indira's worry turned to dread.

"Let's check to see where you're at, okay?" she said in a breezy tone that belied the depths of her concern.

She knew the risks—another heart attack, a stroke. Fastening the cuff firmly around her mother's arm. She pushed the button. The machine cranked to life and the blood pressure cuff filled. Indira waited impatiently, wishing that Amar was here with them. He would know what to do. Somehow, he was the one who could sweet talk his mother into doing what was best.

"I'm calling Dad."

"No, Indira, I'm—"

"Don't tell me you're fine. It's either Dad or I'm calling 911."

Her mother lapsed into a brooding silence while Indira made the call. Twenty minutes later, her father's car streaked past the driveway and parked in front of the house. Easing her mother from the chair, Indira guided her toward the door. The drive to the hospital was mercifully short. The car had barely come to a halt when Indira jumped out.

"Wait here. I'll get a wheelchair."

"I can walk," her mother snapped.

"No. You will wait for Indira."

Under normal circumstances, Indira would have resented her father's commanding tone, but not today. Her mother scowled. Knotting her arms across her chest, she waited inside the car until Indira returned, and they wheeled her inside.

Her mother's blood pressure caused a subtle stir among the admissions staff. She was whisked back to an examination room and hooked up to an array of machines for observation.

They waited hours for a doctor to come.

———

IT WAS WELL past dark when Indira left the hospital's emergency room with her mother, who had been issued a prescription for a different type of blood pressure medication, along with strict instructions to get some rest and avoid stress at all costs. Like that was possible, given the circumstances. On the way home, Indira's father dropped her off at the nearest SkyTrain station and she rode the train downtown.

She should be beat, but still wired from the stress of the day, she took Hazel out for a quick walk and then picked up the investigation where she'd left off. Rummaging through the trash bins of the internet, Indira found what she was looking for—the cell phone numbers of her two suspects, along with Katie Lord's. The fact that at least one of the suspects, Katie's boyfriend, knew both girls had to mean something. She wasted no time plugging the phone numbers into the algorithm and let the application work its magic.

Thousands of data points dropped off the map. Indira's breath caught in anticipation as she waited for the updated results to display, certain that somehow, miraculously, it would pinpoint the presence of one of her two suspects.

The process indicator chugged along the screen as the results were compiled.

"Come on. Come on," Indira muttered as the map redrew.

With a fraction of the original data to process, it shouldn't take this long. Every lag felt like an eternity when finally the results displayed.

Nothing. Not a single ping from either of the phones she had identified showed anywhere near Mallory's house that night. In fact, she couldn't see Brock's information at all. Frustration pulsed between her temples and she slammed her palm on the desk.

Hazel jumped, gave a startled bark, and Indira shushed her.

Something was wrong. It had to be.

A glitch in the application? A bug? Indira didn't know.

Refocusing on the problem, Indira began to troubleshoot. She broadened the window of time for her search, starting with the day Katie disappeared and ending the day after Mallory's death. Seemingly endless seconds chugged by as her laptop parsed the data and the new rendering of the map was displayed.

She checked Tim Atwood's cell signal first. The night before Katie disappeared, his cell phone signal showed him eighty kilometers away in Abbotsford, where he apparently had spent the weekend. At least his cell phone continued to ping at various spots within the Abbotsford city limits. Was this why the police hadn't arrested him? Because he had an alibi?

Indira turned her attention instead on Brock Sinclair, the guy her brother believed had a thing for Mallory. Like most of her test subjects, Brock was a creature of habit. Deep golden lines were carved into the digital map, documenting the patterns of his daily life. *Home. Starbucks. School.* Though his movements during the daylight hours were mind-numbingly consistent, his evening routines varied. But it wasn't the patterns of Brock's daily life that sparked her interest. It was the fact that the river of geodata flowing from his phone dried up shortly after Katie disappeared.

Why? What happened? Had he changed his number or gotten a new phone?

The timing seemed too coincidental to be anything but deliberate. It was the kind of thing a clever man might do to cover his tracks if he had committed a crime. Like a kidnapping. Or something even more deadly.

She had to get eyes on him. Get hold of his phone. There were a handful of reasons why the stream of geodata may have come to an end, and Indira needed to isolate the cause. He might have turned off his geodata, or worse, he could have ditched the phone altogether. Without his phone, she wouldn't be able to track his movements on the day Mallory died.

Geodata was the river of information that fed into the predictive algorithm—the powerful turbine that transformed the data into an actionable predictor of future behavior. And according to the application, chances were good that he would be hanging out with his buddies at an off-campus bar called the Library.

Indira looked down at Hazel, sprawled artlessly across the floor beside the desk.

"I'm going to get a closer look at this guy. Hold down the fort for me, would you?"

THE LIBRARY WAS EXACTLY the kind of place Indira hated and

Sabina loved. Indira slipped through a crowd of Abercrombie & Fitch models in their skinny jeans and scanty shirts. She seated herself in a booth by the back with a bird's-eye view of the bar. The drink menu was stuffed inside a hollowed-out cover of a Nancy Drew book. For a college kid hangout, the haughty list of cocktails carried an equally exalted price. Her mouth curved in a wry smile as she scanned the cocktail names—Tequila Mocking-bird, Gone with the Gin, a Pitcher of Dorian Gray Goose, Rum-eo and Juliette. The Animal Farm was essentially a thinly-veiled White Russian. The person who'd come up with this list was not only a well-read drunk but was a hair shy of being a comedic genius.

"What's your poison?" the waitress asked, yelling over Abba singing about the dancing queen. Dressed in a period costume, she looked like a sexy version of Jo March from *Little Women*. "The Carl Sagan Cosmos are on special. Six bucks a shot."

Indira skipped past the Grapes of Wrath and ordered a Call of the Wild. It was a witty play on a Jack Daniels and Coke, which, she also knew from social media, was Brock's drink of choice.

"I'll need to see your ID."

Indira wasn't surprised. Though she was in her mid-twenties, she looked younger. She handed over her ID without argument. The waitress eyed her with the skeptical look of a woman who'd been passed a hundred fake IDs.

"It's the hair," Indira said, running her palm along the shaved strip on the right side of her scalp.

Satisfied by the explanation, the waitress handed back the ID and scribbled down Indira's order.

Groups of people gathered around the scarred wooden tables. Pendulum lights dangled from the ceiling, casting soft orbs of golden light.

Indira's gaze floated across the sea of patrons until she found him. From the back, he could have been mistaken for Amar. He was just under six feet tall, with broad shoulders and dark, wavy hair. Though not heavily muscled, Brock Sinclair had an athletic build and looked fully capable of overpowering someone of Katie Lord's size, or Mallory's for that matter.

Brock was with a couple of guys she recognized from the snapshots posted to his social media sites. Empty glasses littered the center of the table, and if the drinks they hoisted in their unsteady hands were any indication, they would need another round soon. Indira was too far away to hear what Brock was saying, but whatever it was, it had the other two swaying with laughter.

Indira could only guess what they were talking about. *Classes? Frat parties? Katie Lord and what he had done with her remains?*

They were still reeling with laughter as the waitress dropped off Indira's Call of the Wild. She took a sip and winced. *Gross.* The damned thing tasted like a combination of cherry-flavored NyQuil and lighter fluid. She choked down a swallow. Her phone buzzed with a text notification and she picked it up.

SABINA: What are you up to?
INDIRA: Are you checking up on me?
SABINA: No... Maybe...?
INDIRA: I'm out for a drink.
SABINA: With whom?

Indira smirked at her friend's perfect grammar. She raised her phone. Zooming in on Brock and his buddies, she snapped a photo and sent it to her friend.

SABINA: Hello, handsome. Who's that?
INDIRA: The last guy to see Katie Lord before she disappeared.

A full fifteen seconds went by before Indira received a response.

SABINA: What? You're stalking the guy?
INDIRA: Stalking? Harsh. We're having a drink at the same place. 😊
SABINA: Get out of there. Seriously. He could be dangerous.
INDIRA: Don't worry. He doesn't know he's being watched, let alone who I am.

The waitress stopped by Brock's table and unloaded a fresh round of cocktails from her heavily laden tray. Their lame attempt to hit on her was nothing short of pathetic. Indira watched the spectacle from the safety of her booth. The waitress's condescending smile didn't deter them from almost spraining their necks as they watched her walk away, as if her only function in life was to fetch their drinks and inflate their teeny tiny boy parts.

Indira's phone buzzed again. Sabina continued to question the wisdom of Indira's stakeout, but Indira brushed off her friend's worries by solemnly swearing to text Sabina the moment she got home. In the meantime, Indira ordered another cocktail as she continued to watch and wait.

The boys were doubled over in raucous laughter when Indira discovered something that made her hair stand on end. *Lover boy has a type.* The girl who passed by Brock's table could have been Mallory's doppelganger. Though she'd never met Mallory in person, she'd seen enough pictures online to peg the resemblance. Medium height. Slender build. Dark hair and light blue eyes. The eerie similarity to the dead girl gave Indira chills. The girl took no notice. She glided past the table and joined a group of friends at the bar.

Brock said something to his compatriots. With a swagger in his step, he pushed away from the table and started toward the crowded bar. Indira chugged her drink, grimaced, and went after him.

Brock elbowed his way through the thick ring of college students who swarmed around the bar like flies. At times like this, being small had its advantages. Indira slid between the press of bodies until she reached the bar. The heavy-handed scent of Brock's cologne, a manly, woodsy brand reminiscent of campfires and pine trees, made her eyes water. She thumped an empty tumbler on the bar, drawing his attention.

"Who have you got to screw to get a drink around here?" she asked.

The crass line caused Brock's wide mouth to break into a grin. Waving the empty glass in the air, she caught the bartender's attention. He pointed at her.

"Call of the Wild," she yelled over the crowd noise.

Brock flashed the victory sign. "Make it two."

Turning his back on the Mallory lookalike, he focused his attention on her.

"That's a hefty drink for a little girl like you."

"I can handle it," Indira assured him with a cocky smile.

The bartender served up the drinks and the two clinked glasses.

"Here's to Buck."

"Who?" Brock asked, wrinkling his brow.

"Buck," Indira said. "You know, the dog from *Call of the...* Never mind."

Indira took a hit of her drink and Brock laughed. "I'm totally messing with you. Jack London, right? It's a classic. First book I ever read."

Ice cubes jammed at the lip of the glass, causing a flood of sticky alcohol to spill down Indira's chin. Brock's eyes glittered with amusement, and she wiped her mouth with the back of her hand.

"I like a girl who gets into her work."

Staring hard at Brock, Indira snapped her fingers. "Hey, don't I know you? Business ethics with Dr. Saraf."

"Dr. Hottie, you mean? Or is that Dr. Death?"

A wave of anger surged inside Indira. She masked it with a smile.

"You don't really think he killed her, do you?"

"Mallory? Oh, hell yeah. I caught the two of them smashing outside the school one night."

Smashing? As in having sex?

"Shut up. You're not serious!"

Brock snagged the phone from his pocket and swiped his thumb across the screen. *His phone.* Indira's eyes were drawn to it like a beacon. He scrolled through an endless array of photos, searching for something. Seconds later, he held it up for Indira's inspection. The phone was the whole reason she had come here in the first place. All she had to do was find a way to take it. She tried to pry it from his grasp, but he refused to relinquish his hold. Instead, he held it inches from her face so she could see the screen.

A trickle of cold dread filled Indira as she took in the scene. It was her brother all right. He and Mallory were locked in an embrace.

"Where did you get that?"

With a haughty smirk, Brock pocketed the phone. "One night after class, I was heading to my car and there they were, pressed up against the side of a building."

"No shit?"

"No shit," Brock confirmed, taking a hit from his glass. "According to Mallory, they broke up and he went berserk."

Indira shivered as she remembered what Mallory's coworkers

had said about the argument they'd witnessed outside the coffee shop.

"Did you show that to the cops?"

Brock shrugged. "No need. The cops zeroed in on Dr. Hottie pretty quick. If you ask me, he's not going to see the light of day again."

The anger rushing through Indira turned darker and it took every ounce of her self-control not to fling her drink in Brock's face. Mallory was dead, brutally murdered, and this smug sonofabitch was gloating over the fact that her brother had been charged with a crime that, if convicted of, could cost him his life. Of course he wasn't going to go to the police. Why risk implicating himself?

"I thought for sure that what happened to Mallory had something to do with Katie's disappearance," Indira said.

From the way Brock flinched at the mention of Katie's name, Indira knew she had struck a nerve.

"Katie and Mallory are both gone. How creepy is that?" Indira made a face.

Brock's eyes narrowed. "What did you say your name was?"

"Sabina," Indira lied.

"You were in our business ethics class? Why don't I recognize you?"

"Probably because you were too busy lusting after Mallory."

She gave him a sly smile, but his gaze hardened, his thoughts turned inward, and Indira sensed his interest slipping away. Desperate to get her hands on his phone, she tried another tack.

"Here." She held out her palm and eyed him with a look of expectation.

"What?"

"Your phone. Give it to me."

"Why?"

"Do you want my number or not?"

He stared at her for half a second, then handed over his phone. A Pixel.

"Would you mind getting me another?"

Indira held up her glass, which still contained two fingers of alcohol. She downed it in a single gulp.

"Pretty please?"

She rattled the ice cubes in the glass and gave him her best flirty look. Brock nodded and turned away, trying to catch the bartender's attention. Knowing she only had a few seconds; Indira went to work. She clicked on the settings icon and selected security. She tapped the Pixel imprint option. A screen popped up asking to re-enter the device's PIN.

"Here. Enter your code," she said, holding the phone out to Brock.

His brow wrinkled in confusion. "What? Why?"

Indira held her breath. In order to program her print into the phone, she needed him to re-enter his PIN. She could only hope that he was drunk enough, or horny enough, to play along.

"I must have clicked on the wrong button. Fucking technology, right?" Indira's lips tugged up into a lopsided grin. She lifted her shoulders in a helpless shrug. "So do you want my number or not?"

Brock exhaled sharply and entered his PIN. Handing the phone back to her, he signaled the bartender. Indira tapped the pad of her index finger rapidly against the sensor until the fingerprint setup was complete.

Brock had finally gotten the bartender's attention when Indira grabbed his arm.

"You know what? Screw it. I have a bottle of Jack at my place. Want to get out of here?"

She swayed against him. A moment of hesitation passed, and then Brock shrugged. He slammed his drink back and thumped the glass onto the bar.

"Why not?"

A light, misting rain deepened the sense of gloom outside the bar. He swayed slightly as they cut through a narrow alley leading to the street. Brock spun Indira around and pressed her against the wall. There was no time to think as he pressed his lips against hers in a hard kiss.

Repulsed by his touch, Indira fought the urge to shove him away. He pulled back, breath ragged, planting his hands against the wall, and kissed her again. This time his cold hands slithered beneath her leather jacket. She did her best to ignore his wandering hands and reached inside his coat pockets until she found his phone. Sufficiently distracted, he seemed not to notice as she tucked it into her pants.

Brock pulled away and stared down into her eyes.

"My place is only a few blocks away," he said.

"I just remembered. I have to work in the morning," she said, ducking beneath his arm.

Indira tried to skitter away, but he was too quick. He grabbed a fist full of her collar and hauled her back, pinning her against the wall. Indira's head cracked against the brick. Sparks of pain shot through her skull.

"Where do you think you're going?" he rasped into her ear. "We were just warming up."

"I said no."

The chunky metal zipper of her leather jacket scraped across the side of her throat. Indira tried to shove him back, but he was too heavy. Too strong. She sensed a violence in him that turned her blood to ice.

"Not so fast, little girl. I'm not done with you yet."

"No means no, asshole."

Brock's face convulsed in anger. He released his grip on her collar and barred his forearm across her neck. A pulse of panic raced through her. She couldn't swallow, could barely breathe, and she hadn't thought this through. She was afraid. The situation had escalated faster than she'd imagined and now she was trapped. Manhandled by a guy she believed could be a murderer.

"Wait," she tried to speak, but it came out as a croak.

With her neck pinned, she couldn't move, but she angled her gaze down the alley, hoping, praying that someone would come along. Ten feet down the alley, the hiss of tires sped down the wet streets, but there were no pedestrians in sight.

"A little prick tease, happy to play games, and just like that, I'm supposed to let you go."

Brock's elbow shifted, completely cutting off the flow of air to Indira's trachea. Indira struggled against him, but he outweighed her by seventy pounds. She couldn't breathe. Black spots bloomed in front of her eyes and she felt herself slipping away.

"Hey!"

The sound of a stranger's voice echoed from down the alley. A man. Brock's weight shifted. He stepped back, dropping his arm to his side, and suddenly Indira could breathe again. She coughed, pulled in a shuddering breath, and blinked the tears from her eyes.

"You okay?" the guy called to her.

Ignoring his question, Indira jerked her knee up, full force, and drove it into Brock's crotch. His breath left him in a boozy whoosh. His knees buckled and he crumpled like a paper doll to the asphalt, emitting a strangled cry.

"You okay?" the guy called again.

Indira held up her hand and shuffled off in the other direction, leaving Brock in a pathetic heap.

40

THIRTY MINUTES LATER, INDIRA ARRIVED HOME, ADRENALINE STILL buzzing through her veins like an electrical current. Bypassing Hazel, she headed straight to the cupboard above the fridge where she kept her liquor and poured herself a shot of Crown Royal.

Stupid. That was stupid. What had she thought was going to happen?

Tonight's escapade proved that Brock was the type of guy capable of hurting Katie, or worse, killing Mallory. He had a quick and violent temper.

The third shot burned all the way down her raspy throat, but at least it steadied her nerves. If that Good Samaritan hadn't shown up when he had, there was no telling what might have happened. It was a sobering thought.

Hazel sat by Indira's feet, watching her with a judgmental look.

"I know. I know. You don't need to tell me how stupid I am for baiting a sociopath," Indira said.

Hazel's ears pricked up. With a woof, she rose and spun toward the door. Indira froze. It was late. The dog must have heard some-thing. Had Brock followed her home?

Someone rapped on the door. Indira jarred into motion. Peering through the peephole, she released a breath and unlocked the door.

Sabina threw her arms around Indira, enveloping her in a fierce hug.

"You were supposed to call," Sabina said.

"Sorry. I'm okay."

"When you didn't text, I got worried."

Still gripping Indira's shoulders, Sabina stepped back.

"I'm fine. I'm—"

Realizing that Sabina hadn't come alone, her gaze collided with Dylan's. His blue eyes were filled with concern. Oblivious to the human drama playing out, Hazel's head stretched toward Dylan, and Indira heard her sniff. He scratched the dog between her ears and Hazel's tail thumped.

"For the love of god, Indira, how could you put yourself in danger like that? Promise me you won't do anything that dumb again."

Indira muttered something akin to a promise as she took in the sight of them. A pang of envy filled her. Were Sabina and Dylan a thing now? Sabina hadn't mentioned anything to her, but then, she'd been so obsessed by what was going on with Amar that her friend could have mentioned a Las Vegas wedding and a secret baby and it might not have registered. They looked good together —he was a head taller than Sabina and had those blue eyes...

As if reading her thoughts, Sabina said, "We were at a work thing when I got your text. I was worried. We thought we should check on you."

"The team released a beta today," Dylan explained. "After how hard they've been working, I owed them a beer. One beer turned into more. You know how it goes."

Indira did know. She missed being part of a team. She missed going to work every day when the biggest worry she had was meeting a deadline. That life seemed so simple. So far away.

"Indira," Sabina exclaimed, catching sight of the marks around Indira's throat.

"What?"

"Are those choke marks?"

Indira's hand rose to her throat. The abrasion caused by the jacket's zipper was bumpy to the touch.

"It's nothing. I'm fine." But even as she said it, her voice cracked.

A quiet anger infused Dylan's voice. "He did that?"

Indira looked away, ashamed. She tried to cover the marks on her throat, but Dylan gently brushed away her hand. Picking up on the shift in mood, Hazel growled and inched closer to Indira's side. She wedged her sturdy body between the two. Dylan eased away, giving Indira and her dog some space. Hazel sat, still keeping her eyes on him.

"I'm okay. Really," Indira said, wishing they'd leave it alone.

She, of all people, didn't need to be reminded of how badly her half-baked plan could have ended.

"You could charge the bastard with assault, you know."

"Spoken like a lawyer," Indira said in a lighthearted quip that fell flat.

"Look, Indira, I know you're worried about your brother, but it's not your job to prove his innocence. Leave the investigation to the professionals," Sabina urged.

"The police? They're convinced he's guilty. If I leave it to them, he'll be convicted."

"Then trust Simon to do his job. He'll find a way to clear Amar's name."

"Innocent people are convicted every day, Sabina. You know I'm right."

Raising her hands in surrender, Sabina shot a pleading look at Dylan, as if he could say something that might change Indira's mind. But Dylan had drifted away from the conversation. He stared at the map displayed on Indira's monitor.

"You got it working," he said, studying the data with a practiced eye.

"Of course," Indira scoffed, as if he doubted her abilities. "It wasn't hard. With a few tweaks to the code, I locked into Brock's signal. But here. Look at this." She pointed to the screen. "The day after Katie Lord's disappearance, the data just stops. Oh!"

She'd totally forgotten about the phone—the whole reason she'd gone to the Library in the first place, not to mention how she'd let that degenerate paw her. Indira's coat was slung across the back of the couch where she'd pitched it. Grabbing it, she rifled through the pockets until she found what she was looking for.

Dylan's head cocked at the sight of the phone.

"What's that?"

"Nothing,"

Ignoring the fact that she sounded like every guilty teenager on the planet, Indira thumbed the power button and the phone sprang to life.

"Is it *your* cell phone?" Dylan asked.

She could have lied, but what was the point? She could tell by the way he asked that he already knew the answer.

Sabina gasped. "Oh my god, Indira. You stole *his* phone?"

"I *borrowed* it."

"So *that's* why you were stalking him."

"I wasn't stalking him. I just needed to find out why his cell phone trail ended."

"Look, Gretel, these aren't breadcrumbs on the forest floor you're following, they're crackers," Sabina mocked. "This is someone else's property. It's called stealing, Indira, and in case the facts escaped you, it's a crime. So, tell me, exactly how did you liberate the phone?"

Dylan and Sabina just stood there, staring at her. A scalding blush crept up Indira's cheeks.

"I...uh...distracted him."

"You *distracted* him?" Sabina asked, sounding far too much like a lawyer for Indira's liking.

"Look... Whatever."

She gave her head a dismissive shake. It didn't matter how she'd gotten the phone. Now that she had it, she thumbed the settings button and checked the number. With a small stab of disappointment, she confirmed that it was the same phone she'd been tracking. So why wasn't she getting any geodata? Dylan held out his palm. Reluctantly, she handed him the phone.

"He turned location services off."

Dylan held up the phone, displaying the settings screen. The location services for all Brock's apps were turned off, including Google. Indira groaned. That's why she was unable to pinpoint his phone the night of Mallory's murder.

"But why?"

The timing of it was too coincidental. She headed back to the monitor and focused on the date and time Katie Lord had disappeared from the park. Narrowing the number of data inputs into the map that represented several weeks of geodata markers, Indira zeroed in on the one golden data-strand that showed his whereabouts that morning. Using Google Earth, she created a video that played back his movements. Together they watched as the dot representing his coordinates moved across the map.

Online conspiracy theorists and amateur detectives alike had expounded on the theory that the same guy who'd snatched Katie had gone on to kill Mallory. Small hairs prickled on the back of Indira's neck as she watched the video replay. If this was right, she may have just uncovered the link she was looking for.

The data showed a complete departure from his morning routine. Not only had Brock skipped his morning coffee at Starbucks, but he also hadn't gone to school. His phone pinged within a two-block radius of the park around the time police suspected that Katie had gone missing.

Dylan hovered behind her, peering over her shoulder. He was standing so close, the scent of his cologne, sandalwood and cedar, filled her senses. If she turned her head even slightly, they would be nose to nose. Trying to ignore his proximity, she kept her gaze fixed on the screen.

"Brock may well have been the last person to see Katie alive. I'll need Katie's data to be sure, but if I prove it..."

"It still doesn't link him to Mallory's death," Sabina said in her cold-voice-of-reason, lawyerly way.

"No, but why haven't the police locked in on him?" Indira asked.

"We don't know that they haven't. For all we know, he's already been cleared, but the fact that they questioned him at all might explain why he turned off his geodata. Besides, there were probably dozens of people in the park that morning."

Dylan pulled away and shook his head.

"Police need to write their warrants in a way that tightly constrains the amount of data they pull. They can request the data from a cell phone tower for a small window of time, and even then, it can take weeks or months before they receive the data," Dylan said. "This isn't a cop show that needs to be solved in forty-two minutes."

"How do you know that?" Indira asked. "About the warrants, I mean?"

Dylan shrugged. "A friend of mine's a cop. Over beers one night we were shooting the shit and he was saying that we have access to data they could only dream of. Everything in law enforcement is tightly regulated for obvious reasons. No one wants Big Brother watching everything they do."

"So maybe they haven't picked up on Brock yet because they don't have access to his cell phone data."

"It's possible," Dylan said.

"Then I have to tell them. I have to..."

"Tell them what?" Sabina asked, cutting into the argument. "That you're using an application you can't show them because of the non-disclosure agreement you signed and admit that you're using the application for purposes other than those for which it's designed, which, by the way, is also a violation of your employment agreement. And how are you planning to explain that you're able to identify the signal from his phone? Not to mention how you know he turned location services off?"

At times like this, having a lawyer as a friend really sucked. Sabina took advantage of Indira's silence to drive her point home.

"I suppose that while you're at it, you're also going to mention that you stole the suspect's cell phone, which means that even if for some reason they believed you, which they won't, they can't check his cell phone because it's missing. Or that it's been tampered with."

"They could still subpoena his phone records," Indira grumbled defensively, but was quickly silenced by Sabina's scathing look.

A brief silence enveloped them. Though Sabina's points were valid, worrying about her own legal jeopardy wouldn't do Amar any good. She had to find a way to use this information. She just needed to be careful. Smart.

"It doesn't matter if I get in trouble. If this could help Amar, I've got to try."

Sabina shook her head in exasperation. "Fine, but if you get arrested, don't call me."

Indira bit back a retort as Sabina strode to the door. Dylan followed in her wake. Hand on the knob, he turned back toward Indira.

"If you get arrested, I'll totally bail you out."

His stage whisper was followed by a wink before he closed the door.

41

AMAR WAITED AS LONG AS HE COULD BEFORE MAKING THE CALL. HE dialed the number, as familiar as the back of his hand, and waited for the line to connect. His mother picked up. She sounded frail and a little scared as the automated system asked if she was willing to accept the charges. Another little stab of humiliation pierced Amar as she hesitated, then said yes.

Amar's throat ached with emotion. He swallowed before he spoke.

"Hi, Mom."

"Amar?"

Her voice trembled on the other end of the line. He closed his eyes. It was late afternoon, and he could picture her in the kitchen preparing dinner, as she had thousands of times when he was growing up. For so many years, he'd taken her for granted, how she'd stayed on top of what was going on in the lives of her children. On hard days she would make his favorite dish or prepare a special dessert for Indira just to cheer them up.

"How are you feeling?"

"Oh," she drew in a shaky breath, and he could hear the tears she was holding back. "I'm okay."

"Indira says you haven't been well."

"They worry too much about me. I'm made of stronger stuff than they know."

As a child, he'd believed that his parents were indestructible, but now he knew better. He worried about his mother's high blood pressure. The stress of his incarceration and the heart attack she had suffered following Rani's suicide attempt put her at greater risk. He hated everything he was putting her through. When he got out, if he got out, he would make it up to her. But for now, all he could do was send her a gentle nudge in the right direction.

"They worry because they care. Please listen to them. They want what's best for you, and I need you to stay strong. Can you promise me that?"

"Okay," she said in a trembling voice, her emotions so close to the surface he could sense them. "How are you?"

"I'm hanging in."

"Are they treating you okay? Are you eating?"

He answered the obligatory questions, careful to gloss over the details, until finally the questions ran out. Silence stretched across the phone line, as there was nothing more to say. From the way her breath shuddered, he knew she was crying. He hated this. Hated himself for causing her such distress. Kilometers away, in this concrete box, he had no way to comfort her.

Amar swallowed the sadness he felt and asked, "Is Dad home?"

After a brief hesitation, his mother said. "He's right here."

"Thanks, Mom. I love you."

She didn't answer. Couldn't.

Her voice broke. "Here."

The phone was handed off. "Dad?"

"Amar."

There was none of his mother's softness in his father's tone. It was all sharp edges and hard planes. He could sense his father's frown.

"How are you?" Amar said, carefully probing his father's mood as he had done a million times over the span of his life.

"How am I? How do you think I am?"

Over the past few days, he'd thought of little else but how he was going to broach this conversation with his father. He knew it was going to be hard, but now he realized that it was so much worse than he had imagined. Amar bowed his head and pressed his thumb and forefinger to his tired eyes. He burned with shame at the thought of what his father must think of him right now. All the lessons on being a good man, all the expectations of what it meant to be a good son, had been shattered with his lies.

Amar cleared his voice and forced himself to continue. "Look, I'm calling because...I...I need your help."

"You need my money," his father interrupted, cutting straight to the bone, as usual.

"Yes."

"How much?"

Amar told him the number that Simon had quoted. The chilly silence that followed seemed to last a lifetime.

"The business, it is not so good since—" His father broke off.

"What's wrong with the business?"

"I have lost customers. Stores that have bought from me since the early days are finding other suppliers. Restaurants who I have given deals to no longer seem in need of produce. Food is rotting in the warehouse."

Pride was one thing his father always had in abundance. For his father to admit this kind of weakness, Amar knew the situation was far worse than he was letting on. Word travelled fast in their tight-knit community, and he knew that his father was being punished for what their friends, their neighbors, and everyone else believed that Amar had done. It was his fault that his father, who had worked hard all his life to provide for his family, was at risk of losing everything because of him.

"I'm sorry, Dad."

His father grunted. Amar died another small death as he waited for his father's response.

"It will take time, but I will get the money."

"Thank you. And Dad?"

"What?"

"I'm sorry," Amar said again, needing his father to hear it.

Sorry didn't begin to scratch the surface of what he felt, but his father had heard enough. The call disconnected and dial tone filled the line. Amar hung up.

An hour later, the smell of bleach cut through the greasy stench of the brown lumpy food filling his dinner tray. He didn't know what it was—some kind of beef, he supposed. Avoiding it, he shoveled his fork into the grayish-green peas over to one side and popped it into his mouth.

He thought about his mother's kitchen, how every year for his birthday, she'd made a virtual feast. So many family celebrations. He missed them with an ache that bored deep into his being. He tried not to think that he might never talk to his cousins again or sit at his mother's table.

A lump formed in Amar's throat. He dropped his fork into the brown mass and shoved the tray away. It scraped against the table, drawing the attention of the men sitting nearby.

A white guy, bald, over six feet tall, with a heavily muscled physique, turned to stare at Amar. He had the build of a stonemason, or a logger, or a guy who jackhammered cement. His fists were as big as the head of a sledgehammer and probably twice as strong.

"Aw, you don't like dog?" he goaded in a gravelly voice.

Amar ignored him. He straightened his spine and was about to rise from the table when the man grabbed his arm. A half dozen other muscle-bound lackwits gathered around the table, waiting for him to react. Amar struggled to contain the black anger that expanded inside his chest.

"Finish it," he demanded.

"I'm not hungry."

"I'm not hungry," the man mimicked in a high, lilting falsetto. "So proper, Professor. I said eat."

Amar jerked his arm free of the Neanderthal's grasp. The onlookers fixed their hungry stares on him, like a salivating pack of dogs. Spoiling for a fight. Amar sat down with a thump, elbows resting on the table, his fists clenched.

"Too good for you?"

"It's fine."

"They don't eat cows where you're from?"

Amar knew that it didn't matter what he said. This moron was looking for a fight—a reason to degrade him. He knew he should shut up and just let it go, but after the humiliation of the call he'd made to his father, he couldn't.

"I suppose you're more fond of pigs," Amar said.

The skinny man sitting across from Amar sucked in a breath. The stonemason's piggy eyes burned with anger.

"What did you say?"

"Pigs," Amar repeated, setting his fork aside. "Or are they too close to your kin? Too much like cannibalism for your taste? Oh, sorry. That's a polysyllabic word. Do you need me to break it down for you, or perhaps we could find someone to translate it into basic redneck idioms?"

He managed to block the first punch but the next one plowed into his face. A bone-crushing pain exploded behind his eyes. His glasses flew, and a paralyzing flash of white temporarily blinded him. Amar dodged the second blow. He rolled aside, and the man's knuckles crushed into the hard floor. The sound of crunching bones was followed by a curse. Amar moved quickly until, suddenly, he was the one on top, throwing punches. All the shame, the humiliation, the rage he felt roiled to the surface and packed every blow.

Dimly, he heard the far-off yelling of the guards, the rush of footsteps as they converged, pulling him off the man who lay bleeding on the floor.

"Enough," one guard yelled. "Calm the fuck down."

A guard gripped each of his arms as they hauled him back, away from Piggy. Blood dripped from a gash on his cheekbone where the first punch had landed. His throbbing hands started to swell.

"My glasses," he said.

A guard bent to retrieve them. The frames were twisted, broken beyond repair. He was led down the maze of halls toward the infirmary. Now that the rush of adrenaline was starting to wear off, the pain in his head pulsed. The bones of his hands throbbed.

He hadn't been in a fight since the third grade. He'd forgotten how much it hurt.

A thin man with wire-rimmed glasses and a large hook nose awaited them. "Amar Saraf, I'm Dr. Lencioni."

Amar flinched away from the laser beam of a penlight boring painfully into his eyes, but the doctor held him in place with a strength far greater than suggested by his wiry frame.

"How many fingers am I holding up?"

"Three," Amar mumbled.

The small act of speaking sent a bright shimmer of pain rippling through his skull. Fingertips probed his orbital sockets and prodded gently across his cheekbones. Amar winced.

"Good. Nothing broken." The doctor dropped his hands away and picked up his chart. "You've got a mild concussion, but all things considered, it could have been worse."

"My glasses were broken."

"Yes. We'll contact your optometrist and get your prescription. They won't be Armani's, I'm afraid."

The man's lips spread into a thin smile. Amar couldn't tell whether he was joking or not. He remained silent as the doctor jotted notes into his file and moved onto Amar's hands.

"Can you straighten them?"

Amar splayed his fingers, pain arcing along his swollen joints. Then he curled both of his hands into fists. The doctor nodded, as if satisfied by the movements.

"On a scale of one to ten—"

"Four," Amar said, interrupting before the question could be fully asked, although the throbbing in his head felt more like a six.

"Good. All in all, you've fared well. Better than expected. The last guy who tussled with Cecil Evoy spent two days in a coma."

Aw, shit. That probably meant that the stonemason, or his friends, would be gunning for him.

"Two Tylenols should do the trick. If you feel nauseated, tell the guard."

Amar nodded. Once the pills were dispensed and consumed, he was led back to his cell.

42

INDIRA KICKED OFF THE COMPILE FUNCTION BY PRESSING A combination of keys on her keyboard. Filenames scrolled past at warp speed. Hours had gone into redesigning the code, and she could hardly wait to test out the results on the geodata for the next best suspect on her list, Tim Atwood—Katie's boyfriend.

The whole point of the application was to look for patterns, to identify the things that people did every day. Track their habits and their buying patterns in the hopes of being able to appeal to their wants in a way that made the company money. But when it came to the men on her suspect list, it was the times that they broke with their patterns that she cared most about. Like Brock.

The two breaks in his normal routine made him an excellent suspect. The first was the day he skipped school and went to the park, where she believed he was stalking Katie Lord. The second was a day, not long after Katie was gone, when he'd turned location services off on his cell phone—a deliberate action convincing Indira that he had something to hide.

Now that she had the information she needed from Brock's

phone, she should get rid of it. She could either return to the Library and pitch it under a table or kick it under a dumpster in the alley where he'd attacked her. Both were viable choices. First, though, she could install a stealthy application allowing her to collect information from his phone on the sly. She picked up his phone, fully intending to navigate to a website that would allow her to download the spyware she needed. Her thumb hovered above the install button when she stopped herself.

What was she doing? Harvesting the data that was already available was one thing, but tampering with his phone was something else altogether. Just a few short weeks ago she'd argued that the product was invasive and unethical. Now here she was, seriously considering hacking some guy's phone. This wasn't just an ethical line she was crossing; it was a criminal act.

It would be so damned easy to justify her actions under the guise of clearing her brother's name but that would be a lie. Still, Indira couldn't deny that there was a tiny little part of her that enjoyed hacking his phone and stealing his data.

Just then her phone buzzed, intruding on her thoughts. A text message from Dylan asking her to meet him at the brewery.

What for? Had he found something out? Curiosity consuming her, Indira grabbed her coat on her way out the door.

———

FRIDAY NIGHT and the Yaletown Brewery was bumping. Hundreds of patrons filled the place, their voices pitched to a deafening roar trying to make themselves heard over a blistering version of Jet asking are you gonna be my girl. Indira navigated through the press of bodies, searching for Dylan. She spied him sitting at a table with Sabina and a guy in a green canvas jacket.

He hadn't mentioned bringing someone else, and the idea of

inviting a stranger into a private conversation didn't sit well. Catching sight of her, Dylan waved.

"Indira, this is the cop friend I told you about. Jason Black."

Her jaw dropped as she met his gaze. *It was him.* The stranger with the eagle tattoo whose apartment she had tiptoed out of the morning after Amar's arraignment. She remembered how he looked, buck naked and asking for her number while she crept out the door. A flush surged up her cheeks. Indira blinked to wipe the image from her mind.

"It's you," he said.

"Wait, you two know each other?" Dylan asked.

Barely recovering from the shock of seeing him again, Indira cleared her throat and said, "Uh, yeah. We met playing pool."

"And you never called," Jason replied pointedly.

Sabina covered her mouth and stifled a laugh. Dylan, on the other hand, didn't look amused.

"I'm surprised you remembered," Indira said offhandedly, as if the whole thing was no big deal.

"Oh, you'd be surprised the things I remember."

Is it hot in here?

In desperate need of a drink, Indira signaled the waiter. Seconds later, he appeared. Dylan drained his IPA and asked for another. Indira ordered a porter. The waiter gestured toward the other two, but Jason and Sabina shook their heads.

"So, you work with Dylan?" Jason asked.

"We both do," Sabina answered, smiling brightly.

"Small world."

Just when she thought she couldn't stand another second of this torture, Dylan ended the awkward moment by refocusing the conversation.

"I thought you might want to tell Jason about your suspect."

"Suspect?" Jason asked.

"How much do you know about the Katie Lord disappearance?"

"Enough," Jason said. "We're still looking for her body."

Sabina shuddered at the blunt remark. "Wait. I thought she was just missing. You think she's dead?"

"A girl with that kind of digital footprint doesn't go silent without some reason," Jason said, meeting Sabina's worried gaze.

Indira nodded. "That's what I thought too. I don't know how much Dylan has told you about the technology we've been developing but...but I have good reason to think that one of Katie's classmates, a guy named Brock Sinclair, may have been the last person to see Katie on the morning she disappeared."

Indira paused, waiting for a reaction from Jason that didn't come. He sat there so silently, she wondered if he'd heard. Dylan nodded, encouraging her to go on.

"I also think there's a high likelihood that he was stalking Mallory Riggins too."

The waiter arrived with their drinks, delaying Jason's response. Indira took a swallow of beer, steeling herself for the onslaught of questions she felt sure would come. Jason stared at her for a second before a cynical smile broke across his face.

"You know, I love a good conspiracy theory as much as anyone else, but theories are a dime a dozen. We cop-types tend to prefer evidence."

The sarcastic remark set Indira back a step, but Dylan didn't look thrown in the least by Jason's reaction.

"Look, I know how this sounds, but the data tells a story. Indira's information is good. We can walk you through it. Show you what we're talking about."

Jason took a swallow of beer before he answered. "Even if I thought you had the faintest fucking clue what you were talking about, it's not my case."

"You're telling me that if we had evidence that proved what we were saying was true, you wouldn't at least bring it up?"

"Evidence? Maybe. But this—"

Jason raised his hands dismissively. A surge of irritation pulsed through Indira. He thought they were crackpots making shit up, but this was real. Drawing in a calming breath, she regrouped, determined to do more than just make him listen. Somehow, she had to make him believe.

"The data doesn't lie. The guy's name is Brock Sinclair. He took a business ethics class with both Katie Lord and Mallory Riggins," Indira said, pressing her case, forcing him to acknowledge her.

"Along with dozens of other students, I'm sure," Jason countered.

"The same class taught by Amar Saraf."

Recognition flashed in Jason's eyes at the mention of her brother's name.

"Exactly. Saraf knew both victims, and for all I know, he was sleeping with them both," Jason said.

"Having an affair with Mallory Riggins doesn't prove his guilt."

Indira broke off, simmering with anger. How could anyone think that her brother was capable of committing such a heinous act? Dylan placed a hand on her shoulder. The gesture was meant to comfort, but Indira shook him off.

"Amar is Indira's brother," Dylan explained.

Why had he said that? With that one sentence, he'd destroyed any credibility she might have had. Jason would assume that her claim was solely based on the need to save her brother. But this was more than just a theory. She had data.

She felt Jason's gaze bore into her, but she refused to look up, afraid how much of her inner thoughts her gaze might reveal.

"Forget it," she snapped. "If he doesn't want to listen, we're wasting our time."

She jumped off the stool and landed on the floor with a thud.

"Wait. This guy—Brock Sinclair—he attacked Indira," Sabina said, stalling Indira's exit.

That got Jason's attention.

"What?" he asked. An undercurrent of steel rippled beneath the single word.

"Do you see the marks on her neck?"

Sabina gestured across the table toward Indira. Another wave of embarrassment struck her, and she raised her hands, wanting to hide the marks, but Dylan gently restrained her.

"Let him look," he said softly.

Reluctantly, Indira dropped her hands to her side.

"I wanted to get a closer look at him," she said, leaving out the part where she'd cyberstalked him to the bar and stolen his cell phone.

"You tracked this guy down by yourself?" Jason demanded harshly.

Indira rolled her eyes. "Spare me the lecture. I've already heard it from the two of them. The thing is that I have geodata that puts him in the vicinity of Katie Lord before she disappeared, and if my confrontation with him last night is any indication, he's not afraid to hurt a woman."

Jason leaned back in his chair, looking thoughtful, and took a long pull from his beer.

"If he did that, you should file a police report. Charge him with assault."

"That's it?" Indira asked, staring at him in disbelief. "You're not the least bit curious about this guy and what role he could have played in Mallory's murder? I thought you were the good guys. I thought you were supposed to help, but I guess now that you've already arrested an innocent man for the crime, it doesn't matter all that much whether he actually did it. All that matters is closing the case."

It was a low blow. With a small burst of satisfaction, she saw

Jason flinch. Their eyes met. He stared at Indira for a long moment. He was angry, and while that was good, it hadn't changed his mind.

"I'll see you later," Indira said to her friends.

Tossing some money on the table, she started to leave.

"Indira, wait—"

Dylan caught her arm, but Indira extricated herself from his grasp. Talking was pointless. Jason needed evidence, and come hell or high water, she was going to find a way to get through to him.

She was going to make him believe.

43

IT TOOK NO TIME AT ALL FOR INDIRA TO LOCK IN ON JASON'S CELL phone signal. She already had his number. He'd insisted on reciting it while she'd had one foot on her way out the door.

Aside from the shock of seeing him again, what bothered her most about their surprise meeting was that he hadn't had the decency to hear her out—to listen, let alone try and understand why she was convinced that Sinclair was wrapped up in Katie's disappearance. Her family members notwithstanding, Indira wasn't used to being summarily dismissed. She was a professional. An engineer. A damned good one. If it weren't for Amar, she would have written him off as an arrogant cop and never thought of him again. Good riddance. But the need to prove Amar's innocence compelled her to spend half the night crawling through Jason's cell phone data until she'd found what she was looking for. A way to prove the tech worked and that she wasn't full of shit.

The next morning, Indira waited a full two hours into Jason's shift before dialing his number. He was slow to pick up.

"Black," he answered tersely.

"That's some greeting. What ever happened to hello?"

"Who is this?"

"Indira, Dylan's friend," she said, savoring the momentary hesitation on the other end.

"Oh, hey. How did you get my number?"

"Uh, you gave it to me, remember?"

The unbidden image of Jason standing stark naked in his living room flashed through her mind. On the other end of the line, Jason chuckled, as if he remembered it too.

"I'm glad you called. I'm at work, so I don't have much time. About yesterday—"

"It's fine," she said, cutting him off. "This won't take long. You think that what we do is hocus pocus, so I did a little checking of my own. You have a buddy named William Garner."

"Hey, wait. You're cyberstalking me?"

"Yeah. No. Not stalking, really."

"What would you call it?"

"Research. It doesn't matter. From your cell phone data, I was able to see that you and Will have lunch together every couple of weeks."

"Yeah, so?"

"What if I told you that today at 1:35, your friend will stop by Glowbal for lunch?"

Glowbal was a trendy little steak and seafood place on West Georgia. Super popular with the business crowd.

"Don't tell me you hacked their online reservations system," Jason said.

"Hardly. I didn't need to. I figured it out using Will's cell phone data."

"If he didn't make a reservation, how could you possibly know unless he texted a friend of his—?"

"You know, for a cop, you're a lousy listener. I didn't need to hack anything. Will doesn't even know he's going there yet. If you don't believe me, why don't you stop by Glowbal for lunch? See if you can make a liar out of me."

"I don't have time for games, Indira. I'm on duty. I can't just swing by Glowbal because you have a half-baked theory about where one of my friends might be."

"It's not a theory. It's a fact. Besides, even cops eat lunch. Just stop by Glowbal, that's all I'm asking. If I'm wrong, you can dismiss me as a nutcase, but if I'm right..."

"If you're right, what?"

Indira sighed. "Just do it, okay?"

Not waiting for a response, she hung up, resisting the urge to count the hours before he called back. The phone rang a full ten minutes earlier than she expected.

"So, was I right?" she asked, skipping the greeting altogether and getting straight to the point.

Jason sounded less amused. "Will says he's never heard of you. In fact, according to him, he had no plans to stop at Glowbal. It was a total spur-of-the-moment thing. So how did you know?"

The question made her smile. At last, he was curious.

"Will's a salesman. The first Friday of every month, he visits his clients in Gastown. But downtown is busy and it's nearly impossible to get into Glowbal at noon, so he schedules a few of his Robson Street accounts over the lunch hour so he can land at Glowbal after the worst of the rush has passed. He's done the same thing four times in the last six months. He skipped last month because his kid had a doctor's appointment."

"You know about his kid's doctor's appointment?"

"It's all there in the data. People follow patterns, Jason. Once you learn their patterns, you can predict what they will do. So, now do you believe me? Are you willing to check out Brock Sinclair?"

"Okay, even if what you say about patterns is true, you can't use that kind of data to predict crime."

"Can't I?"

Jason sighed heavily on the other end of the phone, like she should know better. "I've got to get back to work."

"I'll see you later."

AN HOUR and a half before the end of Jason's shift, Indira wound her way up the hillside through a residential neighborhood at the base of Burnaby Mountain. It wasn't much of a mountain really, not compared to the real mountains that lay northwest of the city. The faint shadow of Grouse Mountain was still visible against the fading charcoal sky. Beyond Grouse lay the twin peaks of the Lions. Although it was too dark to see them, she pictured them in her mind, their shapes as familiar to her as the houses on the block where she grew up.

It was a Tuesday night, and according to the analysis she'd done on the pattern of police reports for this area, she knew that Tuesday nights were the quietest night of the week. That made the timing perfect.

Two blocks short of her destination, she sent a text—an address—and waited for a ping back. Jason's response was quick, which was a good sign that he wasn't engaged in another call.

JASON: What's this?
INDIRA: Brock Sinclair's address.

Indira watched the wavy dots flash across the screen as Jason furiously typed in a response.

JASON: Are you serious? Don't do it.
INDIRA: I'll be at his door in five minutes. Better hurry.

JASON: He's in Burnaby. My jurisdiction ends at Boundary Road.

INDIRA: Then I guess I'm going in alone.

Indira placed the phone in her coat pocket. She felt it buzz. Seconds later, it rang. She ignored Jason's call and continued up the street toward Brock's place. The issue of jurisdiction had crossed her mind. Jason worked for the Vancouver Police Department and Burnaby fell under the purview of the RCMP. In her mind it was a technicality that was easily overcome.

The streetlights were on, casting yellow globes of light on the houses lining the street. The small house where Brock lived had seen better days. The cheap tile and turquoise paint gave the place a run-down look, especially compared to the modern-looking stucco palaces that flanked either side. Little by little, many of the houses built in the 70s during one of Vancouver's booms were being bought, torn down, and replaced with McMansions. Progress, she supposed. But the continued gentrification of the city drove families farther and farther out into the sprawl of the suburbs beyond Surrey and White Rock where her family lived.

The porch light was on. The tall cedar trees surrounding the house cast long shadows across the yard. Indira thumped up the stairs, her heart pounding as she tried to anticipate how Brock would respond. She rapped on the door and waited.

Brock Sinclair answered. Standing in bare feet, he wore a ragged black T-shirt and jeans. Not the kind of thing you would wear to a club. In any other circumstance, Indira would have found the look of shock on his face amusing, but the fury in his eyes gave her pause.

"What the fuck are you doing here?"

"I thought you might want this."

Indira slid his phone from her back pocket. Having already removed her fingerprint from the device's storage, she held it up, just beyond his grasp. Brock lunged for it and she stepped back, safely out of reach.

"You stole it."

"I *found* it," she countered.

She backed quickly down the staircase. He came after her.

"Give me the damned phone."

"Are you sure it's yours? Maybe we should call it. Find out."

"Listen, you little bitch, you'd better hand it over, or else..."

"Or else what?"

She was goading him like a third grader, and it was working. Anger turned his face scarlet. A vein pulsed in the middle of his forehead.

"I never should have let you walk out of that alley."

"Like you had a choice. You couldn't have stopped me if you tried."

A door opened. An elderly woman, dressed in a pink bathrobe, stepped out of the neighboring house. She stared across the unkempt lawn at them.

"What's going on? Are you okay?" she called to Indira.

"He's threatening me," Indira called back.

"Threatening you?" Brock said, slapping his palm against his chest, as if he was the picture of innocence. Not a stalker or a killer. "You're the one who showed up at *my* house with *my* phone."

He leapt forward, striking her hand, and knocked the phone from her grasp. It sailed a few feet in the air and landed face-down on the sidewalk. Indira heard the glass break. Brock's face convulsed in anger as he bent to retrieve the phone.

"Look at what you did."

He pitched the broken phone at Indira. She ducked out of the way. Hands clenched into fists, he advanced.

"You get away from her."

The neighbor's cries were drowned out by the roar of a car

speeding down the street. Indira kept her gaze locked on the asshole. Behind her, a car door slammed.

"Stand back!"

A feeling of relief washed over her at the sound of Jason's voice.

"I saw everything, officer," the neighbor called. "He was threatening that young woman."

"Thank you, ma'am. I've got this. Please take a step back, Mr. Sinclair," Jason said, coming to a stop beside Indira.

"That bitch stole my phone. She showed up here and wouldn't give it back."

The look Jason shot her was a mixture of grim resolve and resentment, knowing full well she'd forced his hand.

"I found his phone and was returning it to him when he lost his mind," she said.

"Liar!" Brock shouted.

Jason held his hands up in a calming gesture.

"No need to shout, sir. Let's go inside where we can talk privately."

"I'm not letting you or her anywhere near me or my house. That bitch kneed me in the balls," he yelled, his eyes spitting fire at Indira.

"After you tried to choke me."

She stomped toward him, continuing to goad. Jason held out an arm, barring her approach.

"I saw the marks on her throat. She must have really pissed you off," Jason said to Brock.

"Me?" Indira swung toward Jason. "If he did that to me, imagine what he did to Katie Lord."

Shock rippled across Brock's face. His expression darkened. "I didn't do anything to that girl."

"Her name's Katie. Try saying it without flinching, asshole."

Brock took a menacing step toward Indira. Jason's hand inched toward his holster.

"I should charge her with libel."

"Libel is written. Slander is spoken. If you're going to accuse me of something, moron, at least get the nomenclature right. But in this case, neither apply since you're obviously guilty."

"Calm down, both of you. I've just got a few questions, Mr. Sinclair. Did you know Ms. Lord?"

Brock hesitated. "We may have had a few classes together, but I wouldn't say I *knew* her."

"You didn't run into her at the park the morning she went missing?"

From clear across the yard, Indira heard the neighbor's gasp. Brock heard it too, and his lips curled back in a snarl.

"I run at the park sometimes. Is that a crime?"

"Were you going for a run on the morning of November eighth?"

"Maybe. I don't remember."

"Lie all you want, but I can prove you were with her the day she disappeared," Indira shouted. "It's all on your phone."

Jason shot a fierce look at Indira and she lapsed into a mutinous silence. She caught the flicker of panic that surfaced in Brock's gaze as he moved quickly toward the house. Jason pointed at the cruiser, in a silent command, but Indira refused the order. He couldn't make her *do* anything. The only reason the police knew anything about Brock was because of her, and she wasn't about to let Brock talk his way out of this.

Brock stomped up the stairs and into the house. He tried slamming the door shut, but Jason stopped it with his boot.

"Look, I get it. Women can be infuriating. If Katie is anything like her..." He jerked his thumb at Indira. "I totally understand how things could go south. She's right about one thing though. We have proof that you were the last person to see Katie before she disappeared."

"I don't have to talk to you," Brock said, his voice cracking with fear.

"You're right. I don't know if you've met my colleagues, Detectives Moreland and Bradford, but let me tell you that once they get a whiff of what we've found, there will be no deals. I'm the best shot you've got."

As Indira looked on from the sidewalk, Brock's shoulders slumped. The speed with which he turned from smug asshole to broken kid was impressive. Perhaps Jason wasn't entirely without skills.

"Okay, I saw Katie in the park that day," he blurted. "But I didn't do anything to hurt her, I swear."

"Okay," Jason said in a voice that was so relaxed, he might have been talking to one of his friends, and not a suspected kidnapper. "How about I come inside, and you can tell me your side of the story?"

Brock jutted his stubbly chin Indira's way. "No way. Not with her."

Jason glanced over his shoulder and their eyes met.

"Wait for me in the car."

"But—"

One look at Jason's face and Indira knew it was pointless to argue. Pissed off and out of options, she stomped toward the squad car and slammed the door shut. Ignoring her, Jason followed Brock inside the house. Left alone with nothing to do but obsess, the minutes dragged past. After what seemed like an eternity, another car pulled up. Two men dressed in suits got out and entered the house.

Half an hour later, Jason finally emerged. He strode back to the car where she waited, leaving the two men behind.

"Well?" Indira asked.

"Do you have any idea how much danger you put us both in?" Jason snapped.

She flinched at the anger in his voice. "If it wasn't for me, he never would have admitted that he was with Katie."

"And you think that justifies your actions? Is this a game to you?"

"No."

"What if I'd gotten another call? What if he'd attacked you?"

"I did my research. Tuesday nights are slow."

"You think that justifies anything?"

Struggling to rein in his temper, Jason shook his head and fell silent. Indira bit back a retort and waited for his anger to cool.

"So, what did he say?"

"He claims he met Katie at the park. Total coincidence. They flirted, considered going for coffee, but ended up at his place instead."

"And then?"

"He says that they had consensual sex, before she freaked out."

"Freaked out?"

Removing a hand from the steering wheel, Jason tipped his palm in the air. "Katie's engaged. He said that she started freaking out about what her fiancé would do if he found out she'd cheated on him."

"And then?"

"And then she grabbed her clothes and left."

"Bullshit," Indira said, not buying a word of it and hoping to god that Jason wasn't buying it either. "You know he's lying, right? Katie Lord hasn't been seen since the day she left his apartment. She's probably dead, buried in a shallow grave somewhere."

"Maybe," Jason said, sounding unconvinced.

"What do you mean, maybe? He's obviously lying. Not only was he the last guy to see her, but the only reason he admitted to having sex with her is because he knew you'd find out. You know I'm right."

"Having sex with someone and knowing them isn't exactly the same thing."

The irony of Jason's statement was not lost on her. Indira stared out the window, stubbornly avoiding his gaze.

"He may be lying, but we need to check out his story. Moreland and Bradford will get a warrant to search the house and the Jeep. If they find any incriminating evidence, they'll bring him in."

Indira snorted, knowing all too well that the evidence, or lack of it, didn't tell the whole story.

"The data doesn't lie. No one has seen Katie since the day she left the park with him. I'm right about this."

"Did you steal his phone?"

Indira shot him a defiant look. "Can you prove it?"

Jason shook his head and kept his gaze focused on the road.

"Look, it was a good lead, I'll give you that, but it doesn't stand on its own. It's not a replacement for a thorough investigation of all the angles."

Evidence? All the evidence Jason needed was staring him in the face and yet he refused to believe it. Indira crossed her arms and gazed stubbornly out into the night at the gentle, misting rain. They crossed Boundary Road and entered Vancouver proper.

"Thank you."

She said it so quietly, she wondered if he'd heard her. Jason met her gaze across the darkened cabin of the car.

"For what?"

"For coming when I texted. I know you didn't have to."

A beat of silence passed between them before he spoke.

"You can thank me by doing two things, Indira. First, promise me you won't do anything that crazy again. When you back a desperate person into a corner, there's no telling how they will respond."

Indira drew in a steadying breath and nodded. "Okay. And second?"

"And second, I'm off in an hour. It's in the public's best interest for me to drive you home. Who knows what kind of trouble you could get into without me around."

Indira couldn't stop herself from smiling. "No need, Officer Black. I'm quite capable of making it home by myself."

Jason cocked an eyebrow. "If you say so."

"Do you think all women are helpless?"

She'd meant the remark as a slight, but Jason grinned.

"Hardly. I grew up with three older sisters who routinely kicked my ass."

She tried to imagine him with sisters. The thought of family struck a nerve. Until now, she'd managed to block out the details of her brief and awkward history with Jason, but now, vivid flashes of the night they'd spent together raced through her mind.

"So how long have you known Dylan?" Indira asked.

Normally, she avoided small talk at all costs, but now, alone in the car with him, she needed a distraction—a way to focus on something other than their one-night stand.

"Since high school. We played hockey together."

With his build, she could easily imagine Jason playing hockey, but Dylan?

"You were obviously the goon on the team, but Dylan doesn't strike me as the hockey type. Too smart."

"Fastest right wing I've ever seen. Great at spotting patterns."

"Still is," Indira said under her breath.

"Are you and Dylan a thing?"

Indira sucked in a breath. He was just full of awkward questions. "No. Why?"

"Just trying to figure out where all of the pieces fit. You work together?"

"Yeah, I work with a lot of guys, but you know, it's better not to

get involved with anyone you work with." She could have short-
ened the sentence to say, *it's better not to get involved,* but she
thought it best not to elaborate. "I prefer to keep my relationships
simple."

"Huh," he said.

"What?"

"Nothing."

"It's not nothing. You were thinking something."

Jason slowed the car for a stoplight, keeping a sharp eye on
traffic as she waited for his response.

"You give off a vibe."

"A vibe?"

"Yeah. Most girls are easy to read. You're not."

"Is this because I didn't call you? The hot cop routine doesn't
work on everyone, you know."

"Yeah," he chuckled, and shot her a searing sidelong look that
would have melted Sabina on the spot.

A fierce blush surged up her cheeks and she turned her gaze
toward the passenger's window, deciding that small talk was a very
bad idea.

"So, asshole ex-boyfriend or daddy issues?" he asked, as if it
had to be one or the other.

The dime-store psychological analysis made her bristle.

"We're not all walking clichés, you know."

"Okay," he said, as if he didn't quite believe her.

"How about you? Hero cop complex or do you just like
carrying a gun?"

Not put off by her cheeky remarks in the least, Jason smiled. "I
like helping people, but truth be told, I do like my gun."

The police station's lights beckoned through the gloom.
Outside the entrance, Jason pulled to a stop. Grasping the door
handle, Indira glanced his way.

"Hey, thanks again for checking on Brock."

"I'd like to say it was my pleasure but—" He let the sentence hang and Indira returned his grin. "Sure you don't want to wait for me? We could grab something to eat."

"Are you asking me out on a date?"

"Maybe."

"Not tonight."

"Got plans?"

Indira shook her head. "I've got work to do."

"I'm not sure I like the sound of that."

With a laugh, Indira climbed out of the squad car and closed the door.

44

GRABBING AN UBER FROM THE STATION, INDIRA WENT STRAIGHT home. An hour later, she'd all but put Jason from her mind when the intercom buzzed. Knee-deep in code, she was working her way line by line through a file, trying to isolate the source of a crashing bug, when the intercom buzzed again. By the third interruption, it became painfully clear that the person vying for her attention was not going away.

It was probably Sabina. She loved her friend, but really, the incessant pinging to ensure that she was okay was getting on her nerves. A minute later, the person she had buzzed through on her phone knocked. Indira blew out a breath and pushed away from the screen. She yanked the door open and stopped mid-greeting when she saw who it was.

Dylan. And he hadn't come empty-handed.

"I didn't know what kind of pizza you liked, so I got a meat option and a vegetarian."

Before she could say a word, he handed her the boxes and held his hand out toward Hazel, who was only too happy to welcome visitors who brought food.

"I like meat," Indira said, setting the square boxes down on a nearby cupboard.

"A girl after my own heart."

Her stomach growled at the mouthwatering smell of Canadian bacon, pepperoni, and melted cheese. She got them both plates, paper towels, and a beer as they dug in. They were seated on the couch across from each other, while Hazel placed her head on the coffee table, staring up at them with a puppy-dog look designed to melt even the hardest of hearts, but Indira wasn't moved.

"Dogs don't eat pizza," she told Hazel, whose tail wagged.

"A dog can dream," Dylan said, tossing Hazel a thin slice of pepperoni, which she caught mid-air before it hit the floor.

"No more. Next thing I know, she'll be hunting squirrels in the park because you gave her a taste for meat."

"I gave her a taste for charcuterie, not children," Dylan said, rolling his eyes dramatically at Hazel.

The dog licked her chops while Dylan grabbed another slice.

"How'd it go with Jason?"

How did he know she'd been with Jason? She supposed that Jason must have mentioned it. The look in Dylan's eyes told her that his interest wasn't entirely casual.

"Well, Brock, the scumbag, didn't admit to killing Katie Lord, but he did admit to sleeping with her, which is pretty mind-blowing if you ask me."

"Interesting. What about Mallory?"

"They had a common class, but because he turned the location services off on his phone, I've hit a bit of a wall." Indira set her plate on the coffee table and pointed her finger at Hazel. "Don't touch."

Dylan devoured his second slice in silence and was well into his third when he asked another seemingly casual question that made her hair stand on end.

"So, how well do you and Jason know each other?"

Not him too. After Jason's barrage of awkward questions, she was disinclined to answer more.

"Not well. Hardly at all. Why do you ask?"

Dylan took a gulp of beer and shrugged. "No reason... It's just that Jason isn't exactly what I'd consider discriminating in the girl department."

"And I suppose you're a paragon of virtue?"

Apparently, all Dylan's witty retorts had dried up as he wiped his fingers on a paper towel and stacked his plate on top of hers.

"I don't want to see you get hurt, that's all."

"Thanks for the warning," she said, and was tempted to leave it at that. After all, who she dated was none of his business. But since he was here on his time off and he'd brought pizza, she said, "We're not dating."

Despite his neutral expression, Indira noticed the corners of his lips tug up a fraction.

"So, what have you been working on?"

Relieved to have once again reached familiar footing, Indira rose from the couch and retrieved her laptop.

"So, I started tracking the other guy's cell phone, Tim Atwood, Katie's fiancé."

Indira launched the map application, which showed the golden strands outlining Tim's movements in the weeks leading up to Katie's disappearance through Mallory's death. Tim was a predictable guy. Most of the lines covering the map were thick strands, showing the repeated patterns over and over again.

Indira launched a new module in the application. The cursor spun while the new function loaded. Once it was ready, she pushed play.

"Watch this."

A red dot showing Tim's GPS location traced a new line across the map.

"You animated it?"

"Yeah, I'm using Google Earth to create a video that plays back his timeline over a period of days and weeks."

A broad smile unfurled across Dylan's face. "Cool."

With a small burst of satisfaction, Indira turned her attention back to the map. "He wakes up, heads to the coffee shop where Mallory worked, drops Katie off at campus, and then he goes to work. For weeks and weeks the same pattern plays out until the night before Katie disappears. After that, he stops going home every night. Instead, he sometimes goes here."

She touched a new coordinate on the screen.

"It's near Mallory's neighborhood. He's not here every night, but often enough to establish a new pattern."

Dylan leaned in, studying the data with a fresh eye.

"Have you pulled it up on Google Maps?"

Indira nodded. "It's a house, like Mallory's, cut up into apartments and rented out by some guy from Hong Kong. I've been trying to trace the deed through a public records website, but when I try to link to it, the damned thing crashes. Almost immediately. I've been through the integration code line by line and I still can't figure out why."

She thrust her palms in the air, frustrated that after hours of debugging, she was no closer to figuring out the problem.

"Mind if I take a look?"

"Please."

Dylan reached for the laptop. His hand collided with hers. The brush of their fingers sent a rush of warmth through Indira. She folded her hands in her lap, grateful he couldn't hear the sudden racing of her heart.

Indira studied Dylan as he scanned each line of code, hoping to god that she hadn't made a stupid mistake. She would die of embarrassment if he happened upon something obvious—something she should have caught herself—but then she'd been staring at the code for so long that she might have looked right past it. Sometimes a fresh set of eyes was gold.

"Here's an issue," he said, typing a few small adjustments in her code. "It's not a big deal, it's not causing your crash, but it will make the search a little faster. Maybe it's this..."

He implemented a few more changes as he processed the lines. Indira remained silent, watching Dylan work, his fingers flying across the keys, admiring the quick machinations of his mind. Giving a small grunt of satisfaction, he kicked off a recompile.

"There. Let's try that."

"Thank you," Indira said awkwardly. "For being here. I mean."

Never, in a million years, would she have asked for his help. In her family, relationships were overloaded with expectation. You didn't just date someone for fun. Every date was assessed through the lens of whether this person was a potential match. It was one of the main reasons why Indira preferred to keep her relationships simple. Transactional. Free of expectations. But Dylan...Dylan was a colleague and, up until a few weeks ago, her favorite sparring partner.

But lately, something had shifted. She didn't quite know what to make of it. He must be worried about her. Why else would he spend his evening debugging code instead of doing whatever it was that Dylan did when he wasn't at work?

"How are you holding up?"

Indira shrugged. She dropped her gaze to the floor, trying to articulate the jumble of emotions she felt—worried that she wouldn't be able to track down another suspect, and even if she did, that the police might not take her seriously. She'd given Jason no choice but to confront Brock. And when she thought about Amar and the enormity of what he faced, the real panic started to set in.

Tears surfaced in her eyes. Dylan rested a hand on Indira's back. The warmth of his touch was a comfort.

"He's my only brother. We're close. Without him, my family... my family just doesn't make sense. That's why I've got to do this."

She gestured toward the laptop.

"What if—?" Dylan trailed off, letting his hand fall away.

"What?" Indira prodded him, half dreading what he might say.

"What if in the process of doing this, you find out that your brother isn't who you thought he was?"

Dylan's question cut uncomfortably close to something Sabina had said, about how the people you're closest to lie. Indira remained silent a long time. She'd spent countless hours unable to sleep, wrestling with the possibility that Amar might be holding something back. She knew there were parts of his life he kept hidden from her parents, but the brother she'd grown up with was incapable of murder.

"I have to believe in Amar. I have to find the truth."

Slowly, Dylan turned toward her, and in that instant, she became aware of everything—how close they were sitting, the subtle flecks of green in his amazing blue eyes, the rapid beating of her pulse.

Dylan's gaze remained locked on her as he leaned closer. Startled by the intensity of the moment, Indira didn't pull away. His mouth descended so achingly slow that Indira's breath caught. His lips touched hers, softly. Tentatively. His hand curved around her neck, his mouth shifting, and the kiss deepened.

The harsh buzz of the intercom shattered the moment and the two broke apart. Dylan swore softly at the intrusion. Indira moved from the couch, heading toward the door. What was that? She ran her fingers across her lips, still trying to process what had just happened.

She pressed the button, hoping against hope that it wasn't her auntie. If her auntie arrived to find Dylan in her apartment again, there would be no end to the rumors.

"Hey."

She was startled by the sound of Jason's deep voice. "How did you get my address?"

"You're kidding, right?"

Right. He was a cop. Indira swallowed. She could sense Dylan watching her as she pressed her thumb on the buzzer. An instant later, Jason was there. His gaze slid past her and rested on Dylan.

"I'm not interrupting, am I?"

The awkwardness of the moment struck her full force. He'd asked her out, and she'd turned him down. And now Dylan was here. How had everything gotten so complicated?

"We were just working," Indira said. "What are you doing here?"

"Just wanted to make sure you made it home safely."

Indira's eyes narrowed at the excuse. If he was that concerned, he could have texted.

Toenails clicked on the floor and Hazel thrust her head past Indira toward Jason. She eyed him with a suspicious look.

"Oh, hey. Who's this?"

Without waiting for an answer, Jason hunkered down, allowing Hazel to sniff him before scratching her chin.

"Hazel. As you can see, she's not much of a guard dog."

"Don't listen to her," Jason crooned. "I think you're doing a fine job."

Hazel's tail thumped the wall as she reveled in the attention. Indira sighed. She backed away from the doorway as Jason entered.

"Hey, man," Jason said, locking eyes with Dylan. "Is that the application you were telling me about?"

Indira nodded and followed him into the living room, where Dylan sat on the couch with the open laptop resting on his knees.

"I'm still trying to wrap my head around what that thing can do. It's fucking spooky if you ask me. A total invasion of privacy."

"He sounds like you, minus the expletive," Dylan said wryly.

The objections that Jason raised bore a striking resemblance to the ones she had voiced the day Preet had presented the new product direction. Now that she needed the software to track down suspects, she hadn't just blurred the ethical boundaries that had once been so clear to her, she'd destroyed them.

Stripping off his coat, Jason sniffed the air and spied the pizza boxes on the kitchen counter. He lifted one of the corners and peeked inside.

"Do you mind? I'm starving."

"Help yourself," Indira said.

"Vegetarian?" Jason asked with a slight wrinkle of his nose, as if the whole thought of pizza without meat was absurd.

Grabbing two beers from the fridge, she handed one to Jason and the other to Dylan.

"Any updates on Sinclair?" Indira asked.

"We searched his Jeep and his house. Nothing obvious, and based on what we've got so far, my theory that the Lord case has nothing to do with Mallory's murder stands."

Indira crossed her arms and fixed him with a hard stare. "What makes you say that? They're essentially the same age, they go to the same school. Hell, they even look alike."

Jason loaded a few slices onto his plate and took a seat. Hazel licked her chops and gave a soft whine that Indira ignored.

"There are similarities on the surface, I'll give you that, but when it comes to the actual crimes, they're very different."

"How so?" Dylan asked.

Jason chewed a piece of pizza and swallowed. "Remember what I said about police work? We now know that Katie Lord left the park with Sinclair willingly."

"According to that asshole, who has every reason to lie," Indira said.

Jason acknowledged Indira's skepticism with a nod of his head. "Okay, sure, but so far we haven't uncovered a shred of evidence to contradict his story. No signs of a struggle. No blood. Nothing to indicate that he actually hurt her."

Indira looked away in frustration. Sinclair was the best lead they had and yet Jason continued to brush it aside without giving it a second thought.

"Look," Jason said, softening his tone. "I know this isn't what you want to hear. The guy's definitely a douchebag, but that doesn't make him a murderer."

"What about the fact that he knew Mallory too? He had a photo of Mallory and Amar on his phone, which is proof that he was stalking her."

"Let's say you're right about Katie, and she was abducted and murdered. If that's the case, it sure as hell didn't happen at Sinclair's house, or there would be evidence all over that place, and there's not."

"It's not impossible that he took her somewhere else."

"Impossible, no. Improbable, yes. Someone would have seen something or heard something. He's got roommates, and the one thing I know about college students is that they're not known for their discretion."

Indira clenched her jaw and kept silent. It was obvious that nothing she was going to say would change Jason's mind, not without some hard data to back up her supposition. The fact that Brock had turned off his geodata location was significant. There was a reason he didn't want to leave a trail.

"Whoever killed Mallory didn't lure her away. They didn't bring her to a secondary location. They killed her in her apartment while she slept. That's a very different crime. The way she died, the stab wounds. It's total overkill. It speaks to a personal motive."

"What if Sinclair was obsessed with Mallory and she rejected him? The photo on his phone proves he was stalking her."

"Or he happened across them by accident and snapped a photo?"

Indira sighed in frustration. "Why aren't you tearing his life apart?"

Jason fell silent. Indira glanced at Dylan, imploring him to take her side, but instead, he sat quietly staring at his feet.

"You're just like everyone else. You think my brother killed her."

Dylan's head came up. She saw the one thing she didn't want to see surface in his eyes. Pity. Indira swallowed the bitterness she felt and looked away. As if sensing her distress, Hazel left her perch beside Jason and crossed the room to set her chin on Indira's knee. Absently, she stroked the dog's head.

In the awkward silence that followed, Jason stood.

"Look, as I was leaving the station today, I overheard something. It hasn't hit the news yet, but when it does, I didn't want you to be surprised."

A sudden chill swept through Indira and she steeled herself for whatever was coming next.

"It's about Mallory," he continued. "According to the autopsy report—"

"You don't have to say it. Amar told me that he was with her that night. There's bound to be DNA."

Jason shook his head gravely. "That's not it. The DNA results aren't back yet. Mallory was pregnant."

45

AMAR SAT AT THE TABLE, HIS EARS RINGING WITH SHOCK, STRUGGLING to wrap his head around the question his lawyer had just asked. It couldn't be real. None of this felt real. But as Amar dropped his hands away from his face, he knew that this was no nightmare. This was about as real as things could get.

"Amar, did you know she was pregnant?" Simon asked again.

It couldn't be true, could it? They'd only been together a few months. If she'd been pregnant, surely she would have said something. If she'd known... If she'd...

Amar covered his face with his hands, trying to think through the panic and pain filling his mind at all that had been lost. Not just one life, but two. The terror Mallory must have felt in the final few seconds of her life was more than he could bear. *Dear god.*

A baby.

"You didn't know."

Overwhelmed by the horror of the situation, Amar couldn't speak. He shook his head, his mind incapable of formulating words.

"It was early. I suppose it's possible she didn't know. There's no record of Mallory buying a pregnancy test. Nothing was found at the crime scene."

Amar curled his fingers into fists. Propping his elbows on the table, he pressed his knuckles to his cut lips and forced himself to think beyond Mallory and whether she knew she was pregnant, and all that it had meant. A child. *Their child.*

It took several minutes to organize his thoughts.

"The prosecution is going to play this as if Mallory told me, and I freaked out—" Amar closed his eyes, crushed beneath the brutal weight of the situation. "The jury will think that I...that I killed her."

Simon's grim expression confirmed what Amar already knew.

He was fucked.

"There is zero chance a jury believes that I didn't know about the baby. And if I had—"

"If you had?" Simon prompted him.

Amar shook his head. Given his current situation, it was impossible to imagine what he might have said or how he might have felt.

"It wouldn't have been terrific news, but we would have come to an agreement."

"An agreement? As in an abortion?"

Amar shrugged. It was against his family's religion, against his upbringing, against everything he thought he stood for, but he'd be lying to himself if he pretended that it wasn't a viable choice. Mallory was young, too young to be a mother, and he...he knew how his family would have responded to the news.

"I suggest we work on that line," Simon said. "Okay, so when you're asked, you answer truthfully. You didn't know Mallory was pregnant, and if you had known, you would have supported her. End of story. No talk of marriage. No talk of abortion."

Amar nodded.

"The prosecution is going to say that you killed her because you were desperate to hide the fact that you were having an affair with one of your students from your colleagues, your parents, and your fiancée. And then, given the situation with Callie in Toronto, they're going to argue that finding out Mallory was pregnant was a trigger and you snapped."

"That's not what happened. I never hurt Mallory. How many times do I have to say it?"

"There are witnesses at the coffee shop who saw you arguing a few days before she died. One of the staff members said that Mallory had bruises on her arms. Although Mallory didn't tell her that you caused them, the witness believes that Mallory was in an abusive relationship and was afraid for her safety."

The argument outside the coffee shop came back to Amar in a rush. He'd been upset. Frustrated. He'd grabbed Mallory, but he'd never meant to hurt her.

Everything was so fucked up and it was all his fault. If only he could go back to the night in the parking lot when he'd happened upon Mallory and her broken-down car. If he'd just driven home that night without offering help, everything would be different. He'd be a free man. Mallory might still be alive.

"Did you grab her? Outside the coffee shop?"

Amar closed his eyes and nodded.

For a long time, he sat without saying anything. Until this moment, he'd believed that the truth mattered, that a new suspect would emerge, and he'd be cleared of the charges. Now he realized that he was caught in a trap he might never escape. And when the jury learned of Mallory's pregnancy and when DNA confirmed that he was the father of her unborn child…he would be convicted of murder.

"What if I told you that I lied about where I went after I left Mallory's? What if I told you that I had spent the remainder of the night with Rani, my ex-fiancée?"

Simon sat perfectly still, studying Amar with a thoughtful look. Absorbing the enormity of what Amar had just said. Simon planted his elbows on the table and leaned toward Amar.

"Let me be clear about this. Are you saying that you have an alibi?"

Amar nodded. "I was with my fiancée, Rani."

"And she'll testify to this?"

Amar swallowed hard before answering.

"Yes."

Simon stood and paced the length of the room in silence. Amar waited for him to speak.

"I don't know, Amar. The prosecution will claim the fact that you didn't divulge your alibi immediately proves you're lying."

"In my culture, pre-marital sex is frowned upon."

"Still, you'd have to admit that you were sleeping with two women."

"Just because I'm guilty of infidelity doesn't make me a murderer. I'm innocent of the crime, and as such, I was protecting my fiancée from the shame and ridicule she would face if the truth were known."

Simon stopped pacing and stared at Amar.

"Your sister claims that she has evidence that someone else was stalking Mallory."

An electric pulse of hope shot through Amar. "Who?"

"Brock Sinclair. Indira says he had a photo of you and Mallory on his phone. Between your fiancée's testimony and another suspect, maybe..."

Simon broke off, letting the sentence hang.

"I don't have to prove you're innocent, I only need to raise enough reasonable doubt that a jury won't convict. Was there anyone else who could verify your presence at your fiancée's house? A neighbor? Your future mother-in-law?"

As much as Falguni now hated him, she wanted a good

marriage for her daughter. Maybe...maybe if he went along with the wedding, she would lie for him.

He hated himself for thinking this way, but what other choice did he have?

"Yes. Yes, she will testify," he said.

46

Soaked to the bone from the punishing rain, she clawed through the mud beneath the ragged ring of stones encircling the weed-infested garden bed, searching for the key she'd buried months ago. The cold stones turned over in her hands. *Nothing.* Nothing but rocks and dirt and mud.

How could that be?

The key was nowhere to be found. He must have moved it.

A growl of frustration rumbled low in her throat as she rose and brushed the mud from her knees. The effort depleted her already drained reserves. She cast a weary glance over her shoulder and down the street to where cheerful lights spilled from the windows of the other small bungalows crowding the streets of the working-class neighborhood.

Shuddering from the cold, she climbed the concrete stairs and pounded on the front door.

Where the hell was he? He was always home by now.

Unless...unless the thought of going home to an empty house was just too much for him to bear. With his fiancée still missing,

Tim would be worried sick. She imagined the weeks he'd spent, staring at the ceiling, unable to sleep. Wondering what had happened to her. All of the horrible things she must have endured.

Maybe Tim was driving around right now searching, hoping against hope that he might find her.

Endless seconds ticked by as she stood on the porch, shivering in the bitter wind. Unable to endure the bone-chilling cold for a second longer, she descended the stairs. Her dirty neon green Nikes squealed on the wet concrete as she neared the garden bed to retrieve a stone.

It took no effort at all to smash the rock through the small window next to the door. She stuck her hand through the hole in the glass, careful not to cut herself on the jagged edges, and unlocked the front door.

The welcoming warmth of the house enveloped her. Tears of relief stung her eyes. *Home.* After everything she'd been through, it felt so damned good to be home at last.

Tears slid down Katie Lord's face. She drew in a shuddering breath.

Still shivering, she crossed her arms and padded down the hallway toward the bathroom. She needed to wash the filth from her body. For the first time in weeks, she wanted to feel clean.

She turned on the water. Steam billowed from behind the shower curtain and filled the room as Katie stripped off her soiled clothes and stepped beneath the spray.

God. Yes. The hot shower felt amazing. She lathered herself from head to toe twice, scrubbing her skin until it was pink, and then did it again. Washed her hair. Then finally, using Tim's razor, which was delightfully sharp, she shaved her legs and under her arms before rinsing off. Tim hated it when she used his razor, but he'd be so happy to see her that he'd forgive her for anything.

Wrapped in a thick towel, Katie emerged from the bathroom, just in time to hear the key rattle in the front door.

Confusion and anger darkened Tim's face as he took in the broken glass. Setting down the bag of groceries he was carrying, he reached for the bat he kept near the door and gripped it tight in both hands. Straightening up, his expression turned to shock as he caught sight of Katie.

Every day since she'd disappeared, Katie had imagined what it would be like when she finally saw Tim again. How he'd look when he first walked through the door to find her standing inside their house waiting for him. He'd be shocked, yes, but he'd be happy too. Deliriously happy to have her home safe. She'd run into his arms, he'd kiss her, and everything would be like it was before.

A stab of shock and anguish pierced Katie. Of all the times she had imagined this scene, it had never played out quite like this. Tim wasn't alone. The girl from work—*that girl* was with him.

Tim lowered the bat. The girl dropped a bottle of wine.

The bottle shattered on the slate tile entryway. Red wine flew in all directions. Katie jumped back with a cry.

"Katie," Tim said, his face ashen, as if he'd seen a ghost.

Hot anger seared through Katie's veins. "Well, isn't this cozy?"

"Oh my god, Katie."

He stared at her, unmoving, as if he couldn't quite believe she was real.

"Don't just stand there," Katie snapped at the stupid twit beside Tim. "Clean this shit up."

Jolted into motion by the sound of Katie's command, the girl scurried from the room. Moments later she returned with a towel and knelt on the floor, swabbing up the wine, while Tim finally recovered his power of speech.

"Katie, where have you been?"

Tears welled in Katie's eyes as she glared into his hateful, cheating face.

"Where have I been? Where have I been?" Her voice rose to a shrill pitch bordering on hysterics. "I was kidnapped. Tied up. Tortured. While you were supposed to be grief-stricken and wracked with guilt, wondering what had happened to your fiancée... All that time, you were fucking her?"

Katie flung her hand in a wild gesture toward the girl kneeling at Tim's feet. Her chest heaved with her ragged breath. She wasn't even that pretty. She was too skinny. She looked like a pointy-faced scarecrow.

"You sure didn't waste any time, did you?"

Tim snapped out of his daze and stepped toward her. Katie raised her hands, warding him off. He didn't deserve to touch her. Not with that skank so close by. How could he do it? Bring her into this house? Their house?

"What is wrong with you?" she screamed, directing her venom at the girl. "You knew he was engaged, and you didn't care. You went after him anyway."

"We broke up," Tim said weakly.

Katie shot him a withering stare. "We argued. Couples argue all the time, but you... The first chance you get, you go out and... and sleep with her? I loved you. I trusted you. I thought we were meant to be, but you..."

Tears streamed unchecked down Katie's face. She stared at the ruins around her—at the drops of wine dripping down the walls like blood, the white carpet drenched with red that would never come out, the stupid look on Tim's lying, cheating face.

"I thought you'd be happy to see me. I risked my life fighting like hell to get back to you, and this...this is what I get?" Katie's voice broke on the words. "I'll never forgive you for this, Tim. You don't deserve me. You don't deserve to be happy. I hope you both rot in hell."

Trembling with rage, Katie marched past the two of them, skirting the spilled wine and shattered glass toward the door. The cool night air soothed her burning cheeks. Her bare feet struck the front porch steps, and Katie stopped.

Only then did her anger subside long enough to realize that she was still wearing a towel.

47

THE PING OF A TEXT MESSAGE ROUSTED INDIRA FROM SLEEP AND SHE picked up her phone. It was from her auntie—the one she'd asked to stay with her mother today so she could continue to work on the case.

I can't go today. Rashi has a cold and I need to take her to the doctor.

Irritation spiked as she read the text. Her cousin Rashi always had something. A cold. The flu. Either the girl's immune system was eggshell fragile, or she was looking for a reason to skip school again. Either way, it didn't matter. Her auntie couldn't make it, so Indira's plans would have to wait. She could bring her laptop with her, but what were the chances she'd have a moment of peace to work?

Indira regretted the thought. Someone had to be there in case her mother's condition took another turn for the worse. How would she feel if something happened to her mother and she wasn't there to help? With Amar in jail, they needed her more than ever.

After taking Hazel for a walk, she jumped in the shower and

took the SkyTrain south. Forced to lay off some of his staff, her father had started working again. In the few days that had passed since Indira had last been in her parents' home, her mother was looking better. The dark circles beneath her mother's eyes were beginning to fade. It was a good sign.

"I thought you were too busy to come," her mother said in lieu of a greeting, and Indira's teeth clenched.

She willed herself to find the patience not to snap back a retort. "You're looking well today. How did you sleep?"

"I haven't slept well since your brother was arrested but at least it's not so bad since I stopped taking those pills."

Her mother's answer gave her pause.

"You mean the pills the doctor prescribed?"

Her mother's hand waved, dismissing her concerns. "They make me feel awful. Doctors don't always know what's best. I went back to the old medication I was using. It's better."

An argument surfaced in Indira's mind, but she held back. She knew her mother well enough to know that if she tried to bully her into taking the pills again, her mother would only resist, and the ensuing argument would cause her blood pressure to spike. Typically, this was the kind of discussion she would offload onto Amar, but since he was no longer here, she'd talk to her father instead. Her mother would listen to him. In the meantime, she would keep a close eye on things today. Maybe it was a good thing her auntie had canceled. Clearly, her mother needed watching.

"You've been cooped up inside for days. Let's take a short walk," Indira suggested.

Her mother made a face. "It's raining."

"I'll bring an umbrella. Come on. The air will do you good."

Despite her mother's grumbling, they bundled up and went outside. A light, misting rain fell from the slate gray sky. They set off at a fraction of Indira's normal pace, but even that seemed too much for her mother, who lagged a few steps behind. Indira slowed and threaded her arm through her mother's, providing extra support.

"Have you and Dad talked about going to visit Amar?"

Indira's mother shook her head. "I don't think I could bear to see him in that place."

"It's hard, I know, but we have to stay strong for Amar."

Her mother turned away, but Indira had already seen her tears.

"Amar's innocent. You know that?"

Her mother didn't respond. Unsettled by her mother's silence, Indira wondered how much her parents understood about Amar's legal situation and the perils they faced. The trial would be hard. Her parents would be forced to face truths about Amar that would mortify them. The affair. The baby. And there would be no shielding them from the brutality of the crime.

As they turned the corner, Indira recognized one of their neighbors, a young woman pushing a baby carriage. The boy was a toddler now. Sitting up, his legs jutted from the front of the stroller, feet almost brushing the ground.

"Oh, your son, he's getting so big," Indira called with a friendly smile.

The woman ignored Indira's greeting, staring through them as if they didn't exist. The wheels of the stroller rattled and thumped as she steered it off the sidewalk and crossed the street, carving a wide berth onto the road as if they carried a disease.

Indira felt her mother shudder, but she shook off the slight.

"When the trial begins, we have to be there to support Amar."

"We have spoken with your brother's lawyer. He has said this also."

Indira's mother heaved a weary sigh as they rounded the final turn and headed back toward the house.

"I do not know if I can do this—see Amar in that place."

"You can. You must. You're stronger than you know."

"You're so much like your father. Stubborn. Strong. Your brother is more like me—ruled by his heart. At times like this, I think being stubborn is better."

Indira felt a tug in her chest at her mother's admission. Her whole life she had been chastised for her willfulness, called head-strong, worse than stubborn. Hearing it referenced as a strength rather than a burden buoyed her spirits. Emotion swelled within her and she gave her mother's arm an affectionate squeeze.

"Even if I sometimes burn the onions?"

Her mother managed a tremulous smile. "There are more important things in life than onions."

They returned home. The walk had tired her mother out. Indira cleaned up the dishes from lunch, happy to be of use, while her mother napped. She opened the fridge and scoured the shelves, thinking about dinner plans when the doorbell rang.

Indira rushed to answer, but the sound of the bell had already awoken her mother. She expected to find one of the aunties wait-ing. Instead Falguni stood on the doorstep with a vase filled with yellow tulips in her hand. It was an unwelcome surprise. Rani was with her.

"Hi," Indira said with little enthusiasm.

"We brought these for your mother."

Falguni thrust the vase of tulips into Indira's hands. Without waiting for an invitation, Falguni slipped past Indira into the hall-way. Rani followed close on her mother's heels. Neither one of them made eye contact with Indira as they passed through the doorway into the living room.

Now that they were inside the house, it was too late to tell them her mother was sleeping. Indira followed them into the living room and placed the vase of tulips on a table by the window. Indira's mother smoothed a self-conscious hand over her hair.

"Oh, I am afraid you caught me napping."

"It is good to see you," Falguni said. "You're looking well."

"Thank you. You must forgive me. I had not planned on guests."

"We were worried about you and wanted to come by."

Her mother motioned Indira toward the kitchen, obligating her to make tea and fix a plate of treats for their guests. Under normal circumstances, Indira would have resented being sent to the kitchen, but today she was grateful for any excuse to avoid sitting with Rani and her pernicious mother. The murmur of voices drifted down the hallway. Once the tea was brewed and the refreshments arranged, Indira joined the conversation, unwilling to abandon her mother to deal with these two alone.

"Indira, did you know of this?" her mother asked, startling Indira from her silence.

"What?"

"The engagement is back on?"

An instant of shock seized Indira as she absorbed what her mother had said. "What engagement?"

"Rani's and Amar's, of course," Falguni said with a cat-like smile.

Engaged? Why now?

Amar should be working with Simon on his defense, not worrying about a wedding. And why would Rani want to renew her engagement with a man who had cheated on her, who stood accused of murder? It didn't make any sense.

"Amar's in jail," she said. "I doubt he'll be marrying anyone."

"But he won't be there long," Falguni said, smugly.

"What? How do you know that?"

"You'll find out soon enough. Suffice it to say that we should start working on the preparations. Soon, your mother and I will have something to celebrate."

Indira turned her gaze on her mother, who, for the first time in weeks, looked hopeful. Silently, she cursed them both for planting such ridiculous notions in her mother's head.

"You don't have the faintest clue what you're talking about."

"Indira," her mother snapped. "I will not have you speak so to our guests."

"But, Mom—"

Indira's cell phone rang, cutting her off. She checked the display and broke away from the group, grateful for the interruption. Eager to leave the ridiculous argument behind, she answered Jason's call.

"Hey," she said, pulling in a calming breath. "What's up?"

"Where are you?" he asked in a clipped tone.

Indira recognized it as his cop voice and her stomach dropped.

"At my mother's house. Why? What's wrong?"

"You need to turn on the news."

48

WORD OF KATIE LORD'S SUDDEN REAPPEARANCE CAUSED A RIPPLE that spread across the local media outlets and made the national news. Katie soon found herself at the center of a media firestorm. Her interview on the news was pure napalm. The handsome anchorman who sat across from her was so nice. His sympathetic look made Katie feel as if he really cared.

"When the news about your disappearance was reported, Katie, I must tell you, I feared the worst. I'm both relieved and amazed to have you here today."

Katie blinked away the mist of tears that had formed in her eyes.

"It's a miracle, Brian, and I thank the Lord for His grace. There were days...many days...when I feared I wouldn't make it back at all."

Her voice broke on the words and she averted her gaze. He placed a reassuring hand on top of hers.

"Could you walk us through what happened?"

Katie dabbed a tissue to her eyes and cleared her throat.

"I was in the park, jogging, when these two men came up behind me. They jumped me and placed something—a mask, a blanket—over my head. Everything was dark. I couldn't see. I was dragged back to a van they had waiting and thrown inside."

"Did you scream?"

Katie nodded and dabbed at her eyes again.

"I tried. But they put tape over my mouth."

"While they were dragging you to the van?"

"After."

She swallowed hard. The anchorman's perfect eyebrows compressed, as if he was trying to reconstruct the timeline.

"Before, like when they were dragging me. One of the men had his hands over my mouth so I couldn't scream."

"That must have been terrifying."

"It was. And you know what it's like when you panic, not everything is clear. Sometimes the details get a little messed up."

He nodded; he had such soulful eyes, and Katie sniffed.

"So after that, what happened?"

"They drove for a really long time while I was in the back. And then they brought me into the house. I couldn't see anything, of course, because my face was covered. I was tied up in the basement and they would take turns..." Katie choked down a sob. "Hitting me. And doing...other things..."

Katie gulped and dabbed away her tears.

"How did you escape?"

Head bowed, Katie drew in a shaky breath and then answered. "They let me go. One night when I was still tied up, they blindfolded me and took me to the van. They drove me out to a service road near Buntzen Lake and told me I had to stay there, blindfolded, for an hour before I could walk back. You know, to give them time to get away."

"They let you go? I'm surprised they weren't worried about being identified."

"Well, I never did see their faces, Brian. They wore masks. And gloves."

"Do you think these men could be the same men who killed Mallory Riggins?"

Katie shook her head. "No. No, I don't think so."

"Why not?"

"Well, when would they have had time? They were with me."

"The whole time? Both your captors?"

"Yeah."

"You were never left alone?"

"Well, sometimes, but..."

Katie raised her palms and trailed off. The anchorman swept his gaze away from her and back to the camera.

"Well, Katie. I want to thank you for sharing your harrowing story and tell you again how glad I am that you made it home safely. Welcome home."

Katie blinked her eyes and turned her tremulous smile up to full wattage.

"Thank you, Brian."

IT WAS weird watching yourself on the news, Katie thought as she turned off the television. She didn't look bad. The stylist and the makeup artist had done a good job. Nothing was overdone. But they were right about one thing—the camera really did add ten pounds. Her face looked positively bloated.

Katie's phone was blowing up with messages from her friends. She was frantically typing back when she heard a knock on her door.

Tim.

Her first thought was that *finally* Tim had dumped that bitch and come crawling back to her. Of course he'd be riddled with guilt. But you know, after everything *he'd* put *her* through, she might not take him back. After all, he had cheated on her.

The knock on the door was louder this time and Katie rose from the couch.

Maybe she shouldn't be *too* hard on him. After all, she had met that guy in the park and...well... Maybe she should be more Christian and forgive him for his mistakes.

Katie arranged her face into an appropriately somber mask before opening the door. Her expression turned to shock as she saw who was standing there.

It was the police.

49

INDIRA TURNED HER PHONE OFF. SHE DIDN'T WANT TO TALK TO Sabina, or Dylan, or her family. The news about Katie's sudden and dramatic reappearance hit her hard. The whole theory that there was a connection between Katie's disappearance and Mallory's murder had completely fallen apart, and now she was back to square one with no good suspects.

Hazel, as if sensing Indira's mood, stuck close to her side. Indira scratched the dog behind her ears and Hazel's thick tail thumped the ground.

"Good girl. You've been so patient."

In her mind, Brock was still a viable suspect, but without cell phone data or any other evidence that showed he was at Mallory's place on the night she died, there was no way she could prove anything, and she'd figured out where Katie's ex-fiancé was spending his nights. His new girlfriend lived less than a mile from Mallory's house.

A feeling of hopelessness descended, threatening to crush her under its weight, but Indira wasn't ready to give up. There had to be someone else. There had to be some way she could find out who killed Mallory.

Turning back to her computer, she decided to take another tack. She would run a community algorithm for all the people associated with Mallory and Amar—everyone in their digital social circles. Then, once she had that data, she would run it through the application to see if there was anyone from either social circle whose phone pinged near Mallory's place on the night of the murder.

It was like trying to find a needle in a hundred-acre field of hay. A broad-based speculative search like this one required the kind of deep-linking, machine-learning computing power that far exceeded the processing capabilities her laptop possessed. Instead, she would configure the search to run in the cloud, harnessing the power of networked super computers housed in data centers across the country. Across the world. Even then, it would take time.

It took hours to configure the resources to run the search, but finally, once all the pieces were in place, Indira kicked off the search and let it run. She was tired. Beyond exhausted, but her mind refused to power down. Too much was riding on the outcome of her search. Her subconscious churned through the endless possibilities, wondering what she was going to do if...

She cut the thought off before it had time to fully form. This was going to work. She was going to find something. She had to. For Amar. For Mallory. For Mallory's baby. For herself and her family.

Her shoulders cramped from spending endless hours hunched over the keyboard, and she stood, stretching her arms wide over-head. A tension headache boomed behind her eyes and she rolled her head from side to side, stretching the knotted muscles.

Closing her eyes, she tried to empty her mind. So many jumbled thoughts and emotions spun through the circuitry of her brain. She drew in a deep breath and let it out the way they'd taught her in the one meditation class she'd attended, trying to clear the brain buffers. She'd never figured herself for the meditation type, but she was desperate enough to try just about anything. Minutes crawled by and her restless mind refused to yield.

Half an hour later, a knock at the door triggered a bone-jarring explosion of barking that jolted Indira from her seat.

"Hazel! Quiet."

Looking up with chastened eyes, the dog gave a muffled woof as Indira trudged toward the door. She checked the peephole and there he stood.

Jason.

He was dressed much the same way he had been the first night they'd met, in faded jeans and a green canvas jacket. A light stubble clung to his jaw. Indira felt an odd sensation, a flutter at the pit of her gut at the sight of him. He looked good. Way too good for this time of night.

"You were right about Katie Lord," she said as she opened the door.

"Technically, I was only half right. While I didn't think her case was linked with Mallory's, I thought she was dead. I come bearing gifts."

He handed her a six-pack of Kootenay Ale. Indira's mouth twitched. She could use a drink. Hazel woofed softly, wagging her tail with such force her whole backside swung. Jason hunkered down and scratched her ears. Indira didn't think it was possible for Hazel's tail to wag any harder, but she was wrong. The dog's pink tongue shot out and planted a wet kiss on the side of Jason's face. Jason laughed. Straightening, he wiped his face on the sleeve of his jacket.

"Sit," Indira ordered.

The dog instantly complied, and Jason looked impressed.

"She's well trained."

"As a pit bull in the city, she has to be."

He gave her a knowing nod and pulled a bottle from the carton. The bottle hissed as he twisted the cap free and handed it to Indira.

"I noticed you're not a lager fan. Hope this will do."

Forgoing a glass, Indira took a sip. It was good, still cold, the flavor more malty than hops. Given the choice between meditation and alcohol, she'd take a beer any day.

Crossing the living room, she sank into the corner of the couch. Jason sat on the other end with a beer bottle resting on his leg. An awkward silence fell between them. It was the first time they'd been alone together since she'd been inside his cruiser. Other memories flashed through her mind. Playing pool at the bar. The feel of his hand on her hip. Waking up beside him.

Indira shook her head. Why did he have to be so damned attractive? They had nothing in common. He was a cop. When it came to her brother's case, they were on opposite sides of the fence.

Still, here he was.

"Arrest any bad guys today?" she asked, taking a sip of beer and shaking off the thoughts that had no business forming in her mind.

"A few. How was your day?"

Indira shrugged. "I spent half of it at my parents' house keeping an eye on my mother. She's been sick. The other half, well..." She waved a hand toward her computer.

"What's wrong with your mother?"

"She's recovering from a mild heart attack. She has high blood pressure, and the stress of Amar's situation isn't good for her. But you've already heard enough about my problems."

Jason's answering smile was as unexpected as it was gentle. "She's lucky to have a daughter who cares. Not all families work that way."

"You're close to your family?"

What he'd said during their ride along about having three sisters stuck with her. She imagined him in the center of a big, bustling family.

"My mother died when I was young. I was adopted."

"I'm sorry," she said, feeling like they'd somehow crossed a boundary into deeply personal and painful territory.

"Don't be. My dad's a retired cop. My mom's a teacher. And my sisters, well...they're a force to be reckoned with."

The mention of his sisters beckoned thoughts of Amar and pierced her heart like a sliver of glass. Growing up, they'd been so close. He'd been her only confidant, and now, she might lose him.

Indira looked away, but not before Jason saw the glimmer of sadness in her eyes. She directed her gaze out the window to where thousands of city lights gleamed in the night sky. In the heavy silence that followed, Indira marshalled her emotions, struggling to keep everything she felt inside.

"Are you okay?"

It was hopeless. She'd thought she was doing better, but just like that, with those few words, her resolve shattered. Tears flooded over her lashes and tumbled down her cheeks. She lowered her face to her knees.

"It's going to be okay, you know."

Jason reached across the couch and laid his hand on her knee.

"Sorry. I'm not usually this much of a mess but—"

"But you're scared and worried. I get it."

Jason's strong arms wrapped around her, and Indira let go. She felt it all—the panic that she wouldn't be able to solve the puzzle that held the key to her brother's freedom, the fear that if she didn't, her family might never be made whole. She couldn't stop her family from falling apart. Her body shook with the force of her heartrending sobs.

Jason held her. He stroked her back in slow, comforting movements until the storm of tears subsided. She pulled away and curled her knees into her chest, as if forming a barricade between them. Too ashamed to meet his gaze, she wiped her face on the sleeves of her sweater and forced a shaky laugh.

"Sorry. I probably look like I've been run over by a train."

"I won't lie. You do look pretty awful," he said.

His blunt statement drew a sharp breath. She couldn't tell whether he was joking or not. Then she caught the slight curve of a faint smile. She smiled too.

"You're kind of an asshole, you know?"

"My sisters wouldn't argue with you."

The tears dried on Indira's cheeks and for the first time all night, she dared to look at him. Really look at him. Past the handsome exterior to the good, solid core of him, and she wondered if this was the real Jason. A person whose shoulders you could cry on. A guy who didn't care if you looked a mess. The kind of person you could count on when your world was shattered, when your whole life was falling apart.

"Seriously, why did you come here tonight?"

Jason hesitated. He took a sip of beer and stared at the bottle, as if choosing his words carefully.

"I knew the news of Katie's reappearance would be hard for you to hear. I didn't want you to be alone. And..."

Jason trailed off, letting a silence hang between them until Indira couldn't stand it a second more.

"And?"

"And I wanted to see you."

The intensity of his gaze unnerved her. The way he looked at her, it was as if he could see into her heart. She didn't know which one of them moved first, but Jason leaned toward her and their lips met in a searing kiss. With a thump, his beer bottle hit the table, and he pulled her into his lap.

Indira straddled him, her body responding to the demands of

his mouth, his hands that molded her back, pressing her against his hard chest. It was all happening so fast. There was no time to think. Her pulse raced, breathing ragged as she pulled away, looking deep into Jason's molten eyes, swept away by the depth of her need. She wanted him.

His mouth pulled away from hers, branding a blazing trail from her jaw down the slender column of her throat and she emitted a soft groan, her head tipping back as she lost herself in the swirl of dizzying sensations sweeping through her. His strong hands drifted beneath her sweater, sliding up the curve of her back. Indira's breath caught as he tugged the sweater from her shoulders, over her head, and tossed it to the floor.

Indira slid off his lap, onto her feet, and stood in front of him. She met Jason's gaze. She extended her hand, and he took it. With a tug, she pulled him from the couch and led him to the bedroom. Hazel followed along, but Indira shooed her outside and closed the door.

IT WAS STILL DARK when Indira woke. Jason was asleep. The deep, even sounds of his breathing soothed her. Silently, she slid from the sheets and crept from the room, easing the bedroom door shut behind her. Hazel was asleep on the couch. Her ears pricked up at Indira's approach.

Out of habit, Indira fired up her laptop. She grabbed her coat and Hazel's leash from the hook. The morning walk was mercifully short. The deep, earthy smell of coffee greeted her as she opened the condo's door.

Jason was up. The bedroom door was ajar, and she heard the shower running. In an effort to distract herself from the thought of the naked man in her bathroom, Indira poured herself a cup of coffee and strolled to her desk.

The search she'd initiated the night before was still running. She clicked on the application instead and brought up Amar's cell phone data. She narrowed the search parameters to the night of Mallory's death, wanting to see when Amar had left Mallory's apartment so she could use it as the basis of comparison when the search was finally done.

Whoever had entered Mallory's apartment would have done so after Amar had left. If she could zero in on the timeframe, she could narrow the search parameters. The screen updated. The new results displayed. Indira took a hasty step back.

No. Amar said that he'd left Mallory's after midnight. But then why did his phone ping outside her house three hours after he had gone?

Was he lying? What else didn't she know?

Sabina's words came back to her about family and lies. A chill passed through her as a thought began to form.

She'd never once questioned her brother. She'd believed him, no questions asked. But as Dylan was fond of saying, the data didn't lie, and the data displayed on her screen directly refuted Amar's account. Indira covered her face and tried to think over the roar of panic that blew through her mind.

Jason emerged from the bedroom with a towel wrapped around his hips. "Is everything okay?"

Concern filled his eyes. Indira's gaze flicked to the monitor and Jason looked at the screen. A pulse of fear shot through her. Hands shaking, she reached toward the monitor, desperate to turn it off before he had a chance to absorb the implications of what it showed. He restrained her hand with a gentle grip and leaned closer to the screen.

"Whose phone is this?"

It was too late. He'd already seen. He'd already grasped the significance of the data displayed. The location. The time. It wouldn't take him long to connect the cell signal to Amar and then—

Jason let his hand drop and Indira thumbed the power switch. The monitor went dark.

"What the hell was that?"

Indira's throat went suddenly dry, and she averted her gaze.

"Nothing. A mistake."

"The hell it is."

"Amar already admitted that he was at Mallory's house."

"The timeline's wrong. You know it is. The medical examiner pinned the time of death between two and four a.m. That proves—"

"It proves nothing—"

A knock on the door cut Indira off midsentence. Hazel barked. Indira shushed her with a look. She crossed to the door and gazed out the peephole. Emitted a groan. She didn't think it was possible for this morning to get any worse.

Pressing a finger to her lips, she gestured toward the bedroom. Jason understood. He flashed a you've-got-to-be-kidding-me look but quietly retreated to the bedroom as Indira caught her breath. Pressing her palms to her burning cheeks, she answered the door.

"Good morning, Auntie. You're here early."

"It's about your mother," her auntie said, sliding through the doorway past Indira until she was inside.

A shard of fear lodged in Indira's chest. She'd turned off her phone last night. If something had happened, there was no way the family could have contacted her.

"Is she okay?"

"Yes, but I was doing some reading online and I realized—"

Her auntie trailed off. She crossed the living room to the sofa, where she picked up Jason's coat. Indira's stomach lurched. The two beer bottles from last night were still on the coffee table. If her parents found out that she had a man inside her apartment, she would be forced to move home for sure.

Her auntie held up the jacket with an accusing look. She couldn't lie and say it was hers. It would wrap around her twice and hang down to her knees.

"It's...it's Amar's. He left it here and I...I was missing him last night, so I wore it out to walk the dog this morning."

From the inscrutable look on her auntie's face, Indira couldn't tell if her auntie had bought the lie. Reaching for the jacket, she folded it across the back of the sofa. Her auntie's expression softened and the tightness in her chest eased.

And then Hazel gave a whine. She was sitting by the bedroom door, her nose pressed against the crack. The dog gave an audible sniff.

Indira snapped her fingers, summoning the dog to her side. Hazel gave a huff of dissatisfaction and didn't budge an inch. Indira snapped again.

"Hazel!"

This time, the dog obeyed. The tick-tack of toenails filled the silence as the dog strolled to her side. Hazel sat by her feet. Her auntie flinched, crossed her arms, and eyed the dog as if she thought Hazel might attack.

"You were saying?"

"I was saying that the tea your mother's been drinking has an ingredient in it that's bad for people with high blood pressure."

"But she's been drinking that tea as long as I can remember. Surely—"

"Not that tea. The tea that she got for her birthday. From Rani and Falguni. The godawful stuff that smells like goat pee."

"Oh," Indira said.

"You should throw it out today, before she drinks any more of it."

"Of course."

Indira had no idea what her auntie was talking about, and whether there was any validity to the claim, but she was anxious to say whatever she could to placate her auntie and get her out of the apartment.

As if picking up on her desperation, her auntie placed a balled fist on her hip and fixed Indira with a skeptical look.

"There's something off about you today. What's going on?"

"Nothing," Indira said. "It's just with all the stress. Mom. Amar. You know."

Indira raised her palms and her auntie nodded. She pulled Indira into a hug.

"I know. It's been hard on everyone."

"Thanks for dropping by. I'll head over to Mom's and get rid of that tea."

"Good. Tell her I will come by later, after I run my errands."

Her auntie headed toward the door and the tension in Indira's shoulders eased. She was almost in the clear. Then she heard a thump from the bedroom. Her auntie shot a sharp look at the bedroom door. Indira gave a nervous laugh.

"Hazel," she said, hooking a thumb over her shoulder toward the dog, who was returning to her post by the bedroom door. "She's such a klutz."

Only after her auntie left did Indira feel like she could breathe. A second later, the bedroom door opened, and Jason strode out.

"Who was that?"

"My auntie, and before she comes back, you need to go."

Grabbing his jacket off the couch, she shoved it into his hands and prodded him toward the door.

"Indira, we need to talk about this."

He was right. They couldn't ignore what he had seen, but it would have to wait. She needed to talk to her brother first.

50

It was a day of firsts. Katie had never been on the news before, nor had she ever been inside a police station. The detectives were nice enough. They were off right now getting her a pop and a sandwich. She had barely eaten anything since she'd gotten home.

These rooms sure were small. She looked around to see if she could find the cameras they used for recording. A light reflected off a tiny lens in one corner.

She wasn't worried about being recorded. Heck, it was a whole lot scarier being in a news station with those big cameras pointed at you, with the whole world watching. Her sudden reappearance was the news story of the day. She wouldn't be surprised at all if she got a call from that good-looking hunk of a man, Michael Strahan, from *Good Morning America*. They liked to tell true crime stories like hers in their broadcast. Just the thought of it excited and terrified her all at the same time.

Just then the door opened, and the two detectives came back in. Detective Bradford placed a turkey sandwich and a Diet Coke on the table in front of her. She'd have preferred a roast beef sandwich and a real Coke, instead of the diet drink, but after seeing herself through the lens of the camera, maybe the sugar-free version was for the best.

"So, Katie, can you tell us, in your own words, what happened?"

In her own words. Well, of course she was going to use her own words. What else was she supposed to do? Speak in tongues?

Katie pulled the tab on the pop can and took a sip. Then she began.

She told the story the same way she had on the news. Well, almost the same way. She tried to remember how she had phrased things. But it was hard. The details shifted a little. The two detectives listened without interrupting. They weren't exactly mean, but the way they were staring wasn't at all as sympathetic as that nice anchorman, Brian, had been.

She waited until she was finished before opening the sandwich and taking a bite.

"Thank you, Katie. I know this must be hard for you," Detective Bradford said.

She nodded, chewing on another bite. Detective Bradford was kind of cute. A little too old for her. But he had nice hair and the kind of dark eyes she liked. Katie snuck a secret glance at Detective Bradford's left hand. The sight of the gold wedding band brought her up short.

Married?

Well, she wasn't the type of woman who went after a married man.

"If you don't mind, we have some questions."

Katie sighed and nodded, waiting for them to begin. They looked at each other the way gentlemen do to see which one of them is going to start. Detective Moreland took the lead.

"So you say that these two men took you from the park?"

"Yes. I couldn't believe it. Getting attacked during the daytime. It was so shocking."

"See, we have a witness who says he left the park with you."

"Witness? What witness?"

Katie put the sandwich down and wiped her sweaty palms.

"Brock Sinclair. He said he met you at the gazebo that morning. The two of you talked."

"Oh yes, that's right," Katie said, flashing a nervous smile. "I totally forgot about seeing him. Brock and I chatted for a little bit and then once the rain stopped, I finished my run. I like to go all the way to the reservoir. After I talked with Brock, that's when I was attacked."

Moreland and Bradford exchanged a glance that made Katie's stomach churn.

"Mr. Sinclair says that the two of you went to his house."

A bubble of gas rose in Katie's throat and she masked a burp with her hand.

"Oh, I'm so sorry. Excuse me." She wiped her mouth. "He is most certainly mistaken. Why would I go to his house? I'm engaged."

Bradford leaned back in his chair. There was a look in his dark eyes that Katie didn't like as he took over the questioning.

"So, he's lying?"

Katie leaned forward, meeting his level gaze.

"That's exactly what I'm saying, detective. Honestly, if I had a dime for every time a boy lied about me, I'd be a rich woman."

"He lied? You didn't leave the park with him?"

Why was he asking her the same thing over again? She wasn't dumb. This was her story.

"Either he's lying, or he's mistaking me for someone else."

"So, if I told you that we found security camera footage of the two of you leaving the park together the morning you disappeared, what would you say?"

"I'd say that it was someone who looked like me, detective. Young. Pretty. There must be hundreds of girls who look alike on campus. Besides, that security camera footage, I mean, it's so bad. How can you really tell who you're looking at anyway?"

Detective Bradford shrugged and met his partner's gaze.

"Why don't you wait here and finish your sandwich while my partner and I take a moment?"

Katie nodded. Suddenly, her appetite had fled. She gave the second half of the sandwich a regretful look. For the second time since she'd arrived at the station, the detectives left her alone in that horrid little room.

They returned fifteen minutes later carrying a laptop. Setting it down on the table, Detective Moreland raised the lid.

"I'd like you to look at something," he said.

"Mug shots? I thought you kept mug shots in binders. But then, I suppose that's pretty old school."

Moreland gave her a brittle smile. "Mug shots?"

"Of the men who abducted me."

"I thought the men wore masks. You couldn't see their faces."

Katie froze.

They were trying to trick her, to trip her up, make her doubt the validity of her own story. It was so unfair. After everything she had been through. The cops were as bad as Tim.

"Well, of course I wouldn't be able to identify them, but I figured that wouldn't stop you from showing me pictures."

Moreland didn't respond. He punched a button on his laptop and waited. Then he spun the laptop around to face her. With the touch of another button on the keyboard, the video began to play.

Katie sucked in a startled breath. This wasn't one of those blurry, black and white, low-resolution cameras. The footage was crystal clear.

There she was in her running gear, right down to her lime green Nikes. And there he was. Brock, with that dark curly hair and those eyes. The video taken by a neighbor's camera showed them entering his house. The detective sped through the footage until an hour later, there she was, leaving the house, clearly distraught.

She covered her mouth and looked away, mortified. The lid of the laptop clicked shut. The detective's gaze rested on her and Katie swallowed.

"What's really going on, Katie?"

Tears, real tears, filled her eyes.

"I didn't mean to lie," she said. "It's just that…"

Detective Moreland handed her a tissue, and she blew her nose.

"It's' okay. We know that situations can get out of hand, sometimes. We just need to know what really happened."

The truth sounded so stupid. It came rushing out of her all at once.

"You see, my fiancée was cheating on me with this girl from work. And I…I thought that if I…disappeared for a while, he might really miss me. He'd be sorry that we fought. And all that talk about breaking up would just blow over."

"How does Brock fit into this picture?"

"Oh, him? He doesn't."

"He says the two of you…"

"Okay. We went to his place, but I was just planning to get some water. I'd been running and I was thirsty and…"

"And?" Moreland prodded.

"And okay, one thing led to another and we…you know…"

"You had sex with him?"

Her cheeks flushed a deep flamingo pink. Having to talk about private things with these two men who were old enough to be her father was beyond humiliating. If it was possible to die of shame, right now she'd be dead.

"He didn't force you?" Moreland asked.

"No. No, he didn't force me," she hissed. "It was a mistake. We're all allowed to make mistakes, aren't we? Jesus forgives the sinner, and dammit, I've sinned."

"It's okay, Katie," Detective Bradford said.

He was being nice to her again now that she'd confessed.

"So this story you told, about the abduction, it was untrue?"

Katie nodded.

"There were no men. No van. No house."

Again, Katie nodded. They were silent a good long time. Katie cleared her throat and took a sip of her drink.

"So, if you weren't tied up in a house somewhere, where have you been?"

"I stayed in one of the foreclosed houses a few blocks away. You know, one of the nice ones. Not one of those—what are they called? Zombie houses where the crackheads and the gang-bangers hang out."

Detective Bradford's lips twitched in amusement. Katie watched him try to smother his grin. He was laughing at her. The smug sonofabitch.

"Is that all? Can I go?"

"Not yet, Katie," Moreland said.

"Do you need me to sign something?"

She just wanted this over with, so she could leave the police station and forget that any of this had ever happened.

"You're not going to tell Tim, are you?"

It would be the worst, if he found out. She'd look stupid. And pathetic. No doubt he and that girlfriend of his would get a real kick out of the whole sordid mess.

"Breaking into a house is trespassing, Katie," Detective More-land said.

Katie stared at him in shock. Surely to god, he couldn't be serious.

"The house was foreclosed. No one owns it. No one lives there."

"The bank owns it."

"Well, they should be thanking me. I was keeping an eye on the place."

"Perpetrating a hoax is also a crime."

"I wasn't perpetrating anything. I'm a grown-ass woman who has the right to disappear. I don't have to tell you, or that lying snake, Tim, where I'm going."

"But then you went on the news and told a story about being abducted."

Katie fell silent. The two detectives were staring at her in a way that made her squirm. After everything she'd been through, they were going to charge her with some trumped-up crime. No matter how bogus.

Katie straightened in her seat and stared the detectives directly in the eyes. She didn't have to put up with this horseshit. She had rights.

"I want a lawyer," she said.

51

AMAR SAT ON HIS BUNK AND STARED BLANKLY AT THE WALL. EVER since Simon had dropped the bombshell of Mallory's pregnancy, he'd thought of little else. She hadn't known, couldn't have known. If she had, she would have told him. And yet, the day Rani had dropped by his office, Mallory had come by unexpectedly too, obviously upset about something.

Was it this? Was it about the baby?

Everything had blown up in such a spectacular way that he'd never known for certain why she had chosen that morning to stop by. Afterwards, their equally spectacular and brief reconciliation had been so wrought with emotions that there had been room for little else.

And if she had told him...

He replayed the flimsy statement he'd given to Simon, his assertion that they would have come to an agreement. *An agreement.* What a load of shit. Amar closed his eyes and tried to imagine Mallory, how she would have felt when she realized that she was pregnant. Happy? Afraid? Terrified?

Yes. All these things and more. And he... If she had come to the office that day to tell him the news, how would he have reacted? He would have liked to think that he was the kind of man who would have supported her, held her, told her that it was going to be all right and meant it.

But that was a lie. He would have been shocked by the news. Angry. Upset. Worried about how his parents would have taken the news, so worried in fact, that he would have failed Mallory. Again.

He would have pushed her to get an abortion, and if that hadn't worked, he would have found a way to distance himself from the whole situation. Paid her off. Abandoned her to face the situation on her own.

The truth was ugly. He didn't like admitting it, but trying to pretend otherwise was futile. It was time he faced the man he really was. A man who'd entered into a sham engagement to please his family, and now, he had agreed to marry Rani so she would lie for him.

He was a liar. A coward.

Amar opened his eyes and released the breath from his lungs. He was going to spend the rest of his life paying for his failures, either trapped within these four walls for a crime he didn't commit or trapped in a marriage with a woman he didn't love. By committing perjury, he would gain his freedom and lose whatever was left of his soul.

"Saraf, you have a visitor."

Amar stared out the cell door at the waiting guard. Feeling as if he had aged decades overnight, he slowly eased off the bunk and shuffled out of his cell. In the weeks that had passed since his incarceration, the maze of hallways had grown familiar. They approached the visitor's area, and he waited as the guard unlocked his handcuffs. Gazing out through the plexiglass, he saw Indira waiting on the other side. The metal cuffs slid from his wrists and he rubbed at the chaffed skin.

He seated himself on the plastic stool behind the glass and picked up the phone. Only then did he register the stony look on Indira's face. She'd never looked at him that way before, like he was a stranger. He felt something shift inside him. A rising panic filled his chest.

"What's wrong?" he asked at once. "Is Mom all right?"

"She's fine. She's—"

Indira bit off the words with a shake of her head, which only made Amar worry more.

"You lied." She hurled the accusation at him. It landed like a blow. "The phone, Amar. Your phone. You said you left Mallory's place at midnight."

Amar shook his head. "What are you talking about?"

"Midnight, Amar. But I looked at the data and..."

Amar watched a barrage of conflicting emotions play across his sister's face. She wanted to believe him, needed to believe him, and yet something stopped her. Losing faith in himself was one thing, but the thought that he might lose Indira too was a thousand times worse.

"Your phone, Amar, it pinged off a cell tower near Mallory's house at nearly three in the morning, three hours after you said you'd left."

"No, that's not true. I didn't have my phone. I'd lost it."

Indira stared through the plexiglass at him, the look in her eyes as cold as snow.

"The data doesn't lie."

"I've lied about a lot of things, Indira, but not this. Never this. I didn't kill Mallory. You have to believe me."

She grimaced and shook her head. "I want to but how can I?"

An agonized beat of silence passed between them. A deep sadness filled Amar. If Indira didn't believe him, no one would.

"Falguni stopped by Mom's house the other day. She says the engagement is back on. Is it true?"

"Yes."

Tears filled Indira's eyes. She jerked her chin in a sharp nod.

"Why? You don't love her. I don't understand."

In silence, Amar regarded his sister through the glass. She would figure out soon enough why he was doing it, and then she too would come to understand what kind of man he was.

"Okay then," Indira said and hung up.

Amar watched her go, devastated by the realization that he had lost something precious. No matter what happened from here on out, his relationship with Indira would never be the same.

52

Jason entered the station and continued through the break room toward the cubicles where the detectives sat. Both Moreland and Bradford were nowhere to be seen.

"You lost, Officer Black?" Through the thick fringe of her dark eyelashes, Carla Jones looked up from her computer screen.

Her blunt words were softened by a semi-flirtatious smile. He and Carla had gone out once or twice, but it had never progressed beyond beers after work. She seemed to be willing, but he...he just wasn't feeling it. There was something missing for him. Indira wasn't wrong when she said that office romances were a bad idea. Still, he hadn't quite believed her when she said that nothing was going on with Dylan. He had definitely sensed something between them.

Jason shook off the thought. He tipped his head in the direction of the detective's bullpen.

"Any idea where they are?"

"They're in with the chief, answering a bunch of questions about the Katie Lord debacle. Can you believe that shit?"

Carla shook her head and Jason hitched his shoulders in a shrug.

"Pretty crazy. Imagine going to those lengths to keep your hooks in a guy. The whole time I was thinking that the boyfriend killed her."

"That's what we were all thinking," Jason said. "Just goes to show you that even the best of us can get it wrong."

Carla gave a low whistle and reclined back in her chair. "So, handsome, isn't this your day off?"

"Yeah, there was something I needed to check on."

Carla shook her head. "Pathetic. You need a girlfriend, eh?"

"So my sisters tell me," he said, brushing off Carla's insinuation.

And god knew it was true. They were always trying to set him up with one of their friends. Or friends of friends. It wasn't like he had any problems meeting girls, but relationships were another matter. Since he'd broken up with his last serious girlfriend, he'd been careful to keep things light.

When he'd met Indira playing pool, he'd thought she'd be fun. But Indira wasn't like most girls he knew. She was all chain mail and spikes. That girl's defenses had defenses, and yet, for some reason, he couldn't stay away.

Last night, he hadn't gone there intending to hook up. She needed a friend, and he knew damned well that if the situation were reversed and it was one of his family members behind bars, he would do just about anything to protect them.

He understood the instinctive need that drove Indira's actions and he worried about how she'd deal with it when she was forced to face the facts. Her brother was lying. The look on her face this morning confirmed that reality was starting to intrude, eroding her confidence. When she'd tried to hide the cell phone data, he knew she fully understood how bad it looked for her brother.

If Amar's phone had pinged at three a.m. outside Mallory's

house, that definitely fell within the window the medical examiner outlined for Mallory's time of death. But instead of turning to him for support, Indira had pushed him away.

"Earth to Jason." Carla snapped her fingers in front of Jason's face.

"Hey, can you run a number for me?"

"Sure," Carla said. Straightening in her chair, she rested her fingers on her keyboard. "Shoot."

Jason rattled off the number he'd seen on Indira's screen from memory. Carla typed it in. In no time at all, the LexisNexis database returned a match. Carla read the result, which confirmed what Jason already knew in his gut. It was Amar's number.

"Thanks," he said.

"Any time. If you're up for a beer later..."

She let the offer hang, and Jason gave a nod. "I know where to find you."

He swung away from her cubicle, still thinking about Indira's search results. Something still bothered him. Something about the timing didn't line up.

Jason crossed to the detective's bullpen and studied the whiteboard. Photographs of Mallory Riggins and Amar Saraf were taped near the top, along with other relevant facts about the victim. Date of birth, age, height, weight. Beneath that was a timeline of the critical events leading up to the murder.

Jason mentally walked through the evidence. Mallory at work. Mallory at home. And Amar. Amar's car being tagged by the traffic camera on his way to the victim's house. The time the neighbor saw his car parked outside. The time the license plate reader application registered Amar's plate number leaving Mallory's neighborhood.

All the puzzle pieces were on the board, but at least one of them didn't fit.

"Look what we have here, a baby cop," Bradford said.

He and Moreland stopped outside the cube, regarding Jason with curious looks.

"Solve the case yet?" Moreland asked.

"No, but..." Jason trailed off.

He was a beat cop, not a detective, but the answer was here, somewhere on the board. He just needed to find it.

"Give you a hint. It's this guy," Moreland said, pointing to the photo of Amar.

"Yeah, but the witness and the data from the license plate reader show Saraf leaving Mallory's house just past midnight, three hours before the time of death."

Bradford's jaw tightened. "So he left and then came back."

"But why? Why would he come back three hours later to kill her? Why not do it at midnight before he left? Your theory is a crime of passion, right? Three hours later, his rage would have cooled."

The two detectives exchanged a glance.

"Look, I get it. You're interested in becoming a detective. You've got good instincts, Black, but second-guessing our case isn't going to get you there."

Jason raised his hands in a reassuring gesture. "Trust me, I'm not trying to poke holes in your case; it just doesn't make sense. If he did return to Mallory's house that night to do what you said he did, why didn't the license plate reader register his car?"

Moreland squinted at the board. "He must have taken a different route. There are at least several dozen possible routes, a maze of neighborhood roads and unmonitored intersections between her place and his."

"Or a different car," Bradford said dismissively. "It doesn't matter. He's our guy."

"Okay. It was just a thought."

Jason left the two detectives standing inside the cubicle, knowing that arguments weren't enough to sway their opinions.

They had enough evidence to charge Amar, and the district attorney felt good enough about the case to bring it to trial. He'd need more than conjecture to challenge their thinking.

He needed evidence.

On his way out of the station, Jason pulled his phone from his pocket and dialed Indira's number. Indira's phone went straight to voicemail. Jason swore under his breath. After the way they'd ended things this morning, he wasn't the least bit surprised.

The beep sounded in his ear and Jason left a message.

"Look, I know you're angry with me, but you need to call me back. We've got to talk."

53

JUGGLING THE AWKWARD LOAD IN HER HANDS—A BOTTLE OF WINE, A bag filled with Thai take-out, and a DVD—Indira knocked on Sabina's door. Sabina lived in one of the expensive new condos on Pacific Avenue overlooking English Bay. The way Sabina's snooty neighbors looked down their noses at her, as if she were a transient, caused Indira's hackles to rise.

Okay, she'd be the first to admit that she wasn't looking her best. The black jeans she wore were ripped at the knee, making the ratty graphic T-shirt look even more ghetto. Her leather jacket was soaked through with rain and her hair looked like a train wreck. New growth sprouted from the shaved portion of her head, making her look as unruly and disheveled as a hedgehog.

More like a junkie than a transient, she decided, though neither option was great. Ignoring their sidelong looks, Indira kept her chin up and knocked on Sabina's door.

"Holy crap, Indira," Sabina said, taking her in. "Are you okay?"

Fresh from her hot yoga class, Sabina wore yoga pants, a tank top, and her hair in a stylish messy bun. It always amazed Indira how Sabina could sweat through her class in ninety-degree heat and still come out looking gorgeous.

"I hope you don't mind. I brought Thai, and this." She handed the DVD to Sabina, who read the title with a smile.

"Oh, dear. You're pulling out the big guns tonight. Come on in."

Sabina's condo was as lovely as she was. Painted in a soothing palette of grays and pinks, the urban design was clean and sleek. Everything was feng shui perfect. Even the potted orchid on the bookshelf by the balcony thrived.

A look of concern flickered in Sabina's eyes as she took stock of Indira.

"I don't need to ask how you're doing. I can see that for myself."

Indira ducked her head and unpacked the takeout boxes. Sabina set two plates onto the quartz countertop. Indira filled them.

"I don't want to talk about Amar," she said, her voice gravelly from emotion.

Sabina knew better than to press. They took their plates into the living room. Indira gazed out the balcony doors toward the cobalt blue expanse of English Bay, stretched out across the horizon. Lights from the bobbing cargo ships flashed like beacons in the night.

The tranquility of Sabina's apartment soothed her, and it felt good to be somewhere other than her apartment or her parents' house. Here, she didn't have to worry about dealing with her father's moods, or looking after her mother, or the Pandora's box of data waiting on her laptop.

"How's work?" Indira asked, picking a safe avenue of discussion, far away from her current worries.

"Okay. The team is making good progress. The executives seem pleased and Preet is letting Dylan run things."

"That's good."

"Speaking of Dylan, he's worried about you."

"Worried? Why?"

Sabina tossed her head and gave a humorless laugh. "Well, let me think about that. You're basically tracking down a killer solo and one of the guys you're stalking attacked you. So, yeah, I can see his point."

"Okay, for starters, I'm not stalking anyone. And second..."

"And second, you're working with the hot cop?"

Sabina's powers of perception were scary good. Indira struggled to keep her expression flat, but apparently the look on her face gave her away.

"Ah, now I'm worried that I'm going to have to break Dylan's heart," Sabina said, giving her head a regretful shake.

"What? Why?"

"You're falling for the hot cop. Speaking of which, why didn't you tell me that you and Jason hooked up?"

Indira shrugged. "It was no big deal."

"You should have seen the look on Dylan's face when he picked up on the subtext of that conversation. You were playing it cool, but Jason... Let's just say it wasn't hard to figure out. I can't fault your taste. I mean who doesn't like tall, dark, and delicious?"

There was more to Jason than the way he looked. He was the kind of guy you could count on. Who showed up when you needed him, willing to listen. But then he was also a cop, and what he'd seen on her computer this morning put them both on precarious footing. What if he used what he'd seen in the cell phone data to cement the case against Amar? How could she forgive him? Or herself?

All of this remained unsaid as Sabina studied her with a shrewd look.

"Anyway, about Dylan," Sabina said.

"Why are you so worried about Dylan unless...? Oh."

Sabina was so busy playing the field that Indira had never

stopped to consider that maybe she had feelings for Dylan. That would certainly explain her interest.

"Oh, what?"

"You like him."

"Me?" Sabina said, planting a hand over her heart, as if shocked by the implication.

"You're the one who keeps talking about him."

"And you're the one he keeps talking about. He's not into me. He likes you. God knows why. You're always so busy pushing everyone away that you can't see what a good guy he is."

"Have you told him?" Indira asked, peeking over at her friend through lowered lashes.

"Told who what?"

"Now who's playing dumb?"

Sabina averted her gaze to the window and fiddled absently with a stray lock of hair. Every guy Sabina had wanted had thrown himself at her feet. But apparently, not Dylan.

"Just tell him how you feel."

Sabina's smile was wistful. She gave her head a small shake. "No. Maybe."

Indira didn't push. Whatever her friend was feeling, she was going to have to work it out for herself. All Indira could do was listen.

"So, you're upset about something. Is there anything I can do?" Sabina asked.

"I didn't come here to talk about Amar but..."

"But?"

"I saw something today that I wish I hadn't seen."

"And you're worried about it?"

Indira nodded. She supposed that was why she had come. Although she didn't want to tell Sabina what she had found out, or about the fight she'd had with Amar, she needed to talk to someone about how she was feeling. If she'd never started her own investigation, she'd have never questioned Amar's guilt.

"You love your brother, right?" Sabina asked softly.

A misty film of tears filled Indira's eyes. She blinked them away. How was it possible she had more tears? She'd already cried rivers today.

"Then just love him."

"But what if he—?" Indira broke off, unable to speak the words.

"What if he didn't? The only one who knows what happened for sure is Amar. It is absolutely okay for you to just be there for him. No matter what."

"I don't know if I can do that," Indira said. The conflicting emotions she felt were tearing her in two.

"You can't choose how you feel, but you can choose how you respond. In the end, that's all you can control. Your choices. Your actions."

54

FOR THE FIRST TIME IN WHAT SEEMED LIKE FOREVER, INDIRA LEFT home without turning her computer on. She spent the long commute ignoring the news, the incessant pinging of her cell phone, and focused instead on her mother's well-being.

Her mother spent the day resting, which was good. While she and her mother might never see eye-to-eye on most things, they had settled into a more comfortable rhythm of late. Indira no longer burned the onions, and her mother no longer complained.

With her mother napping in the chair, Indira scoured her mother's cupboard, searching for the box of tea from Falguni. She found it and popped it into her messenger's bag. Her auntie was always reading blogs about miracle diets and wonders of herbal supplements. Quite likely, her auntie's claims were bogus, but it wouldn't hurt to get rid of the tea. Her auntie was right. It did smell like goat urine. She'd take it home and stuff it into the trash, where her mother wouldn't see.

It was after six. Her mother was doing needlework when her

father arrived home. He looked tired. Defeated. Hanging his coat up in the closet, he shuffled into the living room.

"How was your day?" Indira asked.

Her father shook his head. "Orders are down. It hasn't been a good month."

"Things will get better," she said, hoping to cheer him. "I've made ramja for dinner."

Indira served the kidney bean curry dish over rice.

"Didn't Indira do a good job on dinner?" her mother asked, casting a hopeful look her father's way.

He gave a grunt and nodded dully. It was the first nice thing her mother had ever said about her cooking and Indira appreciated the effort she was making, even if she was only picking at her food.

"Mom, you have to eat."

Her mother nodded and took a half-hearted bite. Indira sighed. Amar's incarceration weighed heavily on all three of them. Her attempts to carry conversation fell flat. After cleaning up the dishes, Indira left. She arrived at her apartment building ready to call it a night, when she spied a familiar figure waiting by the door.

"Dylan?"

"Hi," he said. He dragged his hand through his wet hair and offered a smile. "I hadn't heard from you in a few days. I thought I'd check in."

"Not much going on."

"Mind if I come up?"

Sabina was right. He was worried about her. Indira shrugged.

"I should warn you, I'm lousy company."

"Yeah, but I've gotten used to your surly ways."

She laughed at his teasing tone as he followed her inside the building. They rode up the elevator in silence. Hazel was waiting by the door. She broke out in a big dog happy dance when Indira stepped inside.

"Ugh, I have to take the dog out."

"You look beat. Why don't you let me do it?"

Aside from her brother, she'd never let anyone else walk Hazel, but tonight she welcomed the break.

"I usually take her down to the park. It's a few blocks away..."

"Off Homer Street. Yeah, I know the one."

Dylan removed Hazel's leash from the hook by the door and clipped it to her collar.

"Careful, she has a thing about Yorkies."

"I'll keep that in mind." Dylan grinned.

Indira picked her keys up off the counter and tossed them his way. "Let yourself back in."

"Cool."

Hazel hesitated, looking back at Indira as if confused. Dylan tugged on the leash and Hazel followed him out the door. Indira was grateful for the brief respite. She kicked off her shoes and headed to the couch. After a busy day of cooking and cleaning, sitting down felt amazing. Sinking back into the cushions, she had just drifted off when the intercom buzzed.

With a sigh, she lurched off the couch.

"You've got my keys," she called into the speaker.

"What?"

Startled by the sound of Jason's voice, she grasped for something to say. "Nothing. Sorry."

"Buzz me up. We need to talk."

His timing was abysmal. She was exhausted. Dylan would be back any minute and she didn't have the energy for another awkward conversation.

"If it's about the other night—"

"It's about Amar."

Indira pressed the button. A burst of adrenaline revived her, and she yanked open the door, staring down the hall, waiting for the elevator to arrive. Jason trudged toward the apartment, looking as tired as she felt.

"I've been trying to call you. I left messages."

"I turned my phone off."

For a fraction of a second, he closed his eyes, reminding her of Amar fresh out of patience and at the end of his tether.

"Can you pull up the data from Amar's phone?"

"Why?"

"There's an anomaly in the timeline."

"If you're planning to use what you saw on my screen to send my brother to prison—"

Anger sparked in Jason's eyes. "Christ, Indira, if you constantly assume I'm the enemy, then this isn't going to work."

"I'm not even sure what *this* is."

She threw her hands up in the air. What were they anyway? Friends? Lovers? She didn't know, and she sure as hell didn't have the emotional capacity to deal with another person's expectations on top of everything that was happening to her family, to Amar.

Jason's expression hardened. "Dammit, you're the most infuriating woman I've ever met. You're convinced we're working at cross-purposes when I'm only trying to—"

The key rattled in the door and Jason stopped short. Inwardly, Indira groaned.

Dylan entered the condo. For a long moment, the two men stared at each other, then they both turned toward Indira as if expecting her to explain.

This was messed up. She'd kissed Dylan, slept with Jason, and this was why she avoided relationships. She wished she could sink through the floor and make the whole complicated situation disappear.

The only one oblivious to the rising tensions in the room was Hazel. She skittered across the floor, delighted to have more company, and did the happy dog dance while Dylan struggled to unclip the leash. Hazel raced over to Jason and thrust her snout into his palm. Patting the dog's head, he studied the two of them, as if trying to read the situation.

Dylan placed the keys on the countertop. Indira cleared her throat, which had gone bone-dry.

"How about a beer?" she asked.

Thank god she'd put the four beers left over from the six pack into the fridge. Ignoring Dylan's questioning look, she retreated into the kitchen. She handed one bottle to Dylan and another to Jason before opening her own. Gesturing them into the living room, she sat on the chair. Jason and Dylan occupied opposite ends of the couch.

Indira wracked her brain, trying to figure out a way to break the tension, when Dylan spoke.

"I stopped by to see how things were going," he said benignly.

Indira picked up the thread. "I was tired, and Dylan offered to take Hazel for a walk. I lent him my keys so he could let himself back into the building."

A blush crept up Indira's cheeks. She wasn't fooling anyone. Like a guilty suspect, she'd offered too many unnecessary details. Dylan turned to look at Jason, the only one of the three who hadn't yet explained his presence.

"There's something about Amar's cell phone data that doesn't fit the timeline," Jason repeated for Dylan's benefit.

"What?" Dylan asked, sounding hopeful.

"Maybe we should just leave it alone," Indira said.

"I know you're worried, but you've got to trust me. Otherwise, I can't help you. Please, Indira. Let's just take a look."

He was annoying. Persistent. There would be no peace until she did as she was asked. Indira sighed as she rose from the couch to retrieve the laptop. Launching the application, she saw that Amar's cell phone data was already loaded. Dylan and Jason had left their perches. They gathered behind her chair until all three of them were peering at the screen.

"Yeah," Jason said under his breath. "That's what I thought."

"What do you mean?" Dylan asked.

"See here?" Jason pointed to the map. "Amar's cell phone pings near Mallory's house close to three, but the LPR on Lougheed clocked his car heading out of the neighborhood just after midnight. There's no evidence on the traffic cams showing his return a few hours later."

"LPR?"

"License plate reader," Jason explained. "If he returned, both his car and his cell phone should have registered in the area."

A stab of hope pierced Indira. For the first time all day, the weight of dread lifted from her chest.

"He wasn't there."

"Let's back it up," Jason suggested. "Let's start with the day before the murder."

She felt it again, the sense that she was reopening Pandora's box—the sick feeling at the pit of her gut that the secrets Amar was keeping could destroy their family forever. But hiding from the truth was no longer possible. She had passed the point of no return. Jason would keep probing until he found the answers he was looking for and she could no longer protect Amar.

Indira's forehead furrowed, and with a growing sense of dread, she watched the geodata render to the screen.

"What the hell?"

Amar's story and the geodata diverged. Indira covered her eyes, wishing she had never seen, wishing she could deny the truth. But the data didn't lie. People did.

Amar had lied to the police. To her. It was the only plausible explanation.

Unless...

"I went to the jail to see Amar yesterday. He said he'd

misplaced his cell phone and hadn't taken it to Mallory's. I thought he was lying but..."

"Where was the last place Amar's cell phone location matched his known patterns?" Dylan asked.

Buoyed by the logic of Dylan's statement, it took less than thirty seconds for Indira to change the parameters of the search. She loaded a week's worth of data into the video application and let it play back.

The days before Mallory died followed a familiar pattern. Amar slept at home. He left for work at seven-thirty. After classes were through, he stopped by the gym. An hour later, he went home, where he spent the night. Several days before the murder, the data showed a slight deviation. Amar got up and went to school, but after school, he didn't go to the gym. He went somewhere else.

To the hospital.

"Was he visiting your mom?" Jason asked.

Indira shook her head. By the date in question, her mother had already been discharged. She wracked her brain, trying to figure out what Amar was doing at the hospital. Then she remembered what Jason had told her, about Mallory being pregnant. Had something happened with the pregnancy?

Amar said he didn't know anything about the baby, but what other explanation could there be?

"After leaving the hospital, the phone doesn't go to Amar's place, or Mallory's. It goes somewhere else."

Dylan reached for the laptop. His fingers flew over the keyboard as he located the address and typed it into Google Maps. Zooming in on the neighborhood, Indira studied the house.

"Do you know who lives here?" Dylan asked her.

She didn't recognize it. It didn't belong to anyone in her family.

"I can find out," Jason said.

55

DETECTIVE BRADFORD ENTERED THE SMALL INTERROGATION ROOM. He flashed the young woman sitting stiffly behind the table a reassuring smile. Skirting past her, he took a seat in a hard chair on the opposite side and placed an unopened file folder on the bare surface. She eyed it with a look of trepidation.

"Thank you for coming down today, Ms. Khatri," Detective Bradford said.

Rani Khatri was an attractive Indian woman in her mid-twenties with light skin and dark eyes as wide as a doe's. She released her death grip on her purse only long enough to fiddle with her head scarf before clutching it to her chest once again.

"Is this your first time in a police station?" he asked lightly.

Acknowledging the question with a faint nod of her head, she remained silent. Bradford crossed his legs and leaned back in his chair, adopting a casual stance, designed to put the woman at ease.

"Do you know why we've asked you to come in?"

After a slight hesitation, Rani swallowed. "You wanted to talk to me about Amar."

Bradford's smile widened. "That's right. How long have you known Amar?"

"Nine months."

"How did the two of you meet?"

"Through our families."

"Your families know each other?" Bradford asked.

Rani shook her head. "Not exactly. We met through a match-making site, and our mothers—our mothers encouraged the match."

"A dating site? Like Match.com?"

"Not really," Rani answered, licking her lips. "That's about dating. This one is more serious."

"Like a marriage site?"

"Yes," Rani said.

"You and Amar are engaged, is that right?" Bradford asked.

None of this was new information, but he asked it anyway, in the hopes that treading over familiar ground would encourage her to relax and open up, but her body language remained tense. Scared. She looked like a jackrabbit ready to bolt.

"Tell me about Amar."

"He's a professor at Simon Fraser University. He teaches business."

It was an oddly impersonal description that he could have found on a professional networking site. He waited for her to say more, hoping she would fill the awkward silence, revealing something that would help provide insight into who she was, or her relationship with Amar. He'd hoped for a flicker of emotion that would indicate how she felt about her fiancé, or the ghastly situation he found himself in, but there was nothing. She remained silent. Stoic. A few more awkward beats passed between them before he forged ahead.

"What about his family?"

"He comes from a good family. Well off. His father runs a distribution company, supplying food to restaurants and markets. It's a very good business. Everyone knows him. Amar's parents moved to Canada shortly after they were married. He and his sister were born here."

"And you?"

A flicker of apprehension lit her eyes. "Me? My mother and I moved here ten years ago, after my father died."

"I'm sorry for your loss. I lost my father too when I was young. Heart attack."

Rani didn't respond. She showed no signs of softening as Bradford continued.

"So tell me about your relationship with Amar. Was it love at first sight?"

The corners of her mouth lifted into a soft smile. Her shoulders dropped and the lines in her face relaxed as she answered.

"It was awkward at first, you know, meeting someone for the first time. Would he like me? Would we have anything to talk about? But Amar's intelligent. He has such interesting things to say, and soon..."

"Soon what?"

"Soon we were engaged."

If Bradford was expecting a declaration of love, he didn't get it. Maybe that was to be expected. On the surface, it seemed to be an arranged marriage between two consenting adults, not what some of his Indian friends would have called a love match. The key was to keep her talking. See what else she might reveal.

"So you were engaged. Your families must have been pleased."

Another smile. "Yes."

"Every mother wants to see her daughter married. My own wife was so excited when our daughter got engaged, you would have thought she was planning her own wedding." Bradford chuckled at the memory.

At the mention of her mother, Rani flinched, and Bradford knew that he'd hit on something important. Had Rani's mother pressured her into the engagement? Was Rani the type of woman who was hardwired to please her family? The answers to each of these questions represented a piece of the puzzle, a truth that, once uncovered, he hoped would reveal more about the motive behind the murder.

"You must have been heartbroken when you found out that Amar was involved with one of his students."

The sudden inflammatory statement landed with the force of a bomb. Rani's chin snapped up. A hard flash of anger surfaced in her eyes and she quickly looked away.

"You knew about the girlfriend, right?"

Rani refused to answer. The simmering look of contempt in her eyes required no translation.

"Is that why you tried to commit suicide?" Bradford asked gently.

Rani bowed her head and covered her face, but not before he saw her tears. *Shame.* She cried without a sound. He'd seen other kids do that, kids who had been abused by their parents in the most awful way, and he wondered what this woman had suffered.

He let her cry without interruption, hoping for a glimpse of the emotions that lay beneath the surface. But when Rani's hands dropped away, he saw the cold expression in her eyes and knew that whatever secrets she held locked deep inside her, she would guard them with her life.

"Can I leave now?" Rani's voice shook, but Bradford heard the metal behind her words. He was losing her.

"Just a few more questions, Ms. Khatri. When you found out that Amar was seeing Mallory Riggins, did you break up with him?"

"He didn't care about her. It was just that...there was so much pressure about the wedding. His family. My...my mother can be overbearing sometimes and Amar...he was just tired of the pressure, you know?"

"So he didn't break up with you?"

"Never. In fact, he broke up with her."

"Then why did you try to commit suicide?"

Again, Rani refused to answer. Bradford watched her, thinking back to Amar, who had sat in the very spot his fiancée now occupied and claimed that he had loved Mallory. Had he lied to the police or to his fiancée? Or was he lying to them both to save himself from the awful things he had done?

"The night of Mallory's murder, Amar says he spent the night with you."

Rani failed to meet his eyes. "He did."

It was the answer he expected, and Bradford nodded. Leaning forward in his chair, he finally opened the file folder that he'd placed on the table between them. It was filled with the crime scene photos taken at Mallory's apartment. Like a moth to the flame, Rani's gaze was drawn to the photos. They rested on the gory images for a brief instant, before fluttering away. Her fingertips pressed against her pursed lips, as if the sight of them made her sick.

Bradford wanted her to see them. To shock her and make her rethink her commitment to the guy.

"Ms. Khatri, Rani, we have physical evidence that on the night she died, Amar had sex with Mallory. Are you telling me that after he's made love to another woman, he came to your house and spent the night in your bed? Am I supposed to believe that a strong woman like you would allow yourself to be treated so callously by the man she's supposed to marry?"

He saw the revulsion, the shame on her face as he forced the issue, forced her to face exactly what kind of man she was involved with.

Rani straightened in her chair, gripping her purse so tightly, her knuckles turned white. The chair squeaked on the tile floor as Rani abruptly stood.

"Go ahead and think I'm weak. Go ahead and play your mind games. I'm telling you, detective, that Amar was with me. You need me to swear to it? I'm doing just that. If you don't believe me, you can ask my mother. She was at home that night too. She awoke when Amar arrived. He didn't leave the house until the next morning."

"Where did he sleep?"

"In my bed."

"With your mother in the house? She was okay with that?"

"I'm not a little girl."

Bradford paused and met her gaze. This time she stared back. Unflinching. Rani crossed the room with purposeful strides and flung the door open. It cracked against the wall.

"Ask her, detective," she spat over her shoulder. "Ask my mother."

"Oh, don't worry, Ms. Khatri. We will."

56

A QUICK PHONE CALL PROVIDED JASON WITH THE INFORMATION HE needed.

"The house belongs to a Lin Xia but Xia is out of the country."

"Which makes him a dead end," Dylan said.

"So that's where the cell phone tracking data diverges from Amar's story. We need to figure out why he went there and why he would lie about it."

Indira rounded on Jason, her hand flaring out in a frustrated arc. "Why are you always so quick to assume my brother's lying?"

"You're no use to anyone, your brother included, if you can't be objective," he snapped back.

Indira recoiled from the rebuke. She hated the way she felt. Angry with Jason. Angry with herself. Furious with Amar for getting involved with a student, lying about it, and putting her in a no-win position of defending him against everyone else. She wasn't a cop. She didn't know the first thing about solving crimes.

Dylan placed a calming hand on her shoulder, but Indira shook it off.

"Stop," she said in a shaky voice. "I thought I could do this but—"

Her chest tightened. She couldn't breathe. The walls were closing in. Turning her back on the two of them, she crossed to the patio door and stepped outside.

The wet wind struck her face. Goosebumps rose on her arms, but she didn't care. At least, out here, away from the laptop and the gnawing truth, she could breathe again. Hazel lumbered out onto the tiny balcony, toenails clacking on the hard surface, and leaned her bulk against Indira's side. Indira dropped her hand to rest on the dog's back, grateful for the comfort her reassuring presence brought.

"Are you okay?" Dylan asked softly.

He stood just a few feet away, on the edge of the patio door. Indira swallowed hard. Her throat ached from the force of the emotions she held back. It would be so easy to fall apart and let him pick up the pieces, but what about tomorrow, and the day after that, and the day after that?

She couldn't rely on Dylan or Jason to fix things for her, and their relationships were already too complicated.

"You need to leave. Both of you."

"But—"

"I'm sorry. I can't do this anymore."

A beat of silence passed. The Dylan from work would have argued, tried to sway her with reason. But now he hesitated. As if sensing her fragility, he decided not to push. It made her feel weak. Deflated. As if somehow, she had failed herself and her brother. She thought she was so strong, but she wasn't strong enough to face this.

"Okay."

Resignation filled Dylan's voice. Hushed tones murmured in the room behind her. She sensed Jason's gaze, but ignored it, unable to face the expression in his eyes. Seconds later, the door closed, and Indira's shoulders slumped. Finally alone, the enormity of what she felt overwhelmed her. The hopelessness. The fear. The reality that there was nothing she could do to protect Amar from the perils he faced.

Indira bowed. Burying her face in Hazel's fur, she allowed herself to break.

———

A PATTERING SOUND struck the windows as the gathering mist gave way to rain. Indira burrowed under a blanket. Curled up on the couch, sleep eluded her. Outside the condo, traffic hummed along the Vancouver streets as people went on with their daily lives while her life was falling apart.

Her cell phone pinged a few feet away with text messages she had no wish to read. Dylan checking in on her. Sabina worried about her lack of response. She could lie and say she was fine, but after everything she'd been through over the past few weeks, she couldn't stomach any more lies.

Or maybe it was Jason. Probably not. He struck her as the kind of guy with a low threshold for drama. Their fledgling relationship would wither on the vine, and she supposed it was just as well. She liked him. She was attracted to him, but no matter how strong the chemistry between them was, it couldn't withstand the painful reality of Amar's situation. If Amar was convicted of killing Mallory, could she ever look at Jason without blaming him for not taking her brother's side?

From the other end of the couch, Hazel groaned. Indira closed her eyes, thoughts racing inside her mind along an infinite loop of dread. Was Amar innocent? What about the data on his phone? Could she still love him if he'd done the crime?

Every theory had blown up in her face. Nothing but conjecture and dead ends. Jason was right. She was just as guilty of confirmation bias as the cops, manipulating the data to fit her theory of the crime. Like Brock Sinclair. She'd believed in her bones that he had killed both Katie and Mallory. She would have staked her life on it, and worse, his.

And then Katie Lord had returned alive and well with some bullshit story about how she'd faked her own kidnapping. For attention. Because her boyfriend had broken up with her. Of all the stupid, pathetic, narcissistic things that Indira had ever heard...

Wait. What if...?

A sudden thought struck her. Indira sat bolt upright and threw off the blanket. Hazel snorted, bolting awake as Indira lurched off the couch and headed toward her desk.

She flicked her computer back on. Ignoring Amar's data, she cleared the query and focused instead on finding Rani's phone.

The phone pinged from the same location as Amar's had. Lin Xia's house. That couldn't be a coincidence.

Her heart raced in anticipation as she retrieved Rani's geodata from the weeks preceding Mallory's death and fed it into Google Earth. Nerves rubbed raw from lack of sleep, she paced the room as she waited. It seemed to take forever. Once it completed, she played back the animation.

A pang of disappointment tore through Indira as she realized that on the night of the murder, Rani hadn't left home. Her hunch turned out to be nothing more than another half-cocked theory.

But then, as she reversed through the timeline, she felt the hairs on the back of her neck rise. The data scrolling across her screen told a very chilling tale. Rani's phone pinged a half dozen times at places associated with Mallory—the Daily Grind, the SFU campus, and at Mallory's house.

Inside Mallory's house.

Heart pounding from the adrenaline spike caused by the sudden revelation, Indira stared at the map, letting the ramifications fully sink in. Seconds later, once the shock wore off, her mind kicked into gear. She checked the date and time of Rani's unexpected visit. A week and a half before the killing. In the middle of the night. And it wasn't just a drive-by either. She'd taken her time.

Indira's stomach dropped as she reviewed the data. Hands trembling slightly, Indira reached for the mouse. Opening a fresh search window, she navigated to a public records database and typed in the address where Mallory lived. The results popped up on her screen. Ten years ago, the owners of the house filed a permit to build a large extension off the back. As part of the filing, they were required to submit updated architectural blueprints of the entire structure, which included the plans for Mallory's apartment. Indira downloaded the file.

Overlaying the plans onto the Google Earth map was a trickier piece of coding than she'd anticipated. Stitching together the disparate and granular data was about as graceful as attempting to replicate her mother's intricate needlework with cable wire. It took most of the morning and a couple failed attempts to get things working, but when she finally did, the results were absolutely heart-stopping.

Indira's gaze was riveted to the screen as the geodata played back.

Rani entered the house through the garage. She spent several minutes presumably searching the kitchen and attached living room before heading toward the larger of two bedrooms, located across from the bathroom. Rani spent almost no time there. Long enough to open the door and close it again.

Quickly reversing course, Rani crossed the small, shared living space and entered the second bedroom. The time stamp read 2:41 a.m.

The image that formed inside Indira's mind turned her stomach to ice. She pictured Mallory in bed, sleeping, completely vulnerable. Unaware that there was someone else in the room. Watching her. And Rani...

The hate Rani must have felt standing over her rival sent chills racing through Indira.

Had she gone there with the intention of murdering Mallory and lost her nerve? Had something spooked her?

Why? Why leave, only to come back weeks later?

When Amar broke up with her, something inside Rani must have snapped, and like Katie Lord, killing Mallory was her one last desperate hope of regaining the life she thought she had lost. She must have believed that if Mallory was gone, Amar would come back to her.

As far-fetched as the theory was, it made a bizarre kind of sense. Rani was obsessed. The fact that she was still willing to marry her brother after everything that happened proved the depth of her commitment. He'd cheated on her. He was accused of murder. What woman in her right mind would stand by him unless...unless she knew he wasn't guilty? The only way she could know that for certain was if she'd done the crime herself.

Indira's hands jerked back from the keyboard and she rolled away from the desk. How had she missed it? She'd been so convinced of Brock Sinclair's guilt that she had turned a blind eye to the truth that was staring her in the face.

She couldn't prove that Rani had killed Mallory but this...this was motive.

She had to tell Jason.

Indira dialed Jason's number, but the call went straight to voicemail. He was at work. Too busy to pick up. A frustrated growl escaped her. She had to talk with him. Explain the logic behind how she had arrived at her findings. His voicemail beeped and she hung up. A message wouldn't suffice.

Indira was on pins and needles, hoping that Jason would see the missed call and call her back. The minutes dragged by like hours, each more excruciating than the last. She was going insane sitting here. She had to do something.

Indira grabbed her cell phone and called Sabina.

"What are you doing?"

Her friend laughed. "Drinking coffee. Reading the news. Why?"

"There's somewhere I need to go and..."

"And?"

"And I need a wingman."

57

Most of the houses crowding the block were typical box-style structures made of brick and stucco. Their low-pitched roofs and iron balconies dated them as part of the construction boom that hit Vancouver in the 1970s, which was what made this house stand out. It was a two-story modern Craftsman with a dark stone and cedar façade and a "For Sale" sign planted out front.

Sabina pulled her car to the curb. "What do you think a place like this goes for? Two, three million?"

Indira shrugged. "Mom says that Rani's father was a doctor. They have money."

"This kind of money?"

"Jason says the owner is overseas. They're probably leasing it from him."

"Good luck finding another place this nice."

The lights were on inside the house. Falguni's late model Mercedes was parked in the driveway. Indira climbed the stairs to the front door and rang the bell.

"You're sure you want to do this?" Sabina asked, eyeing her with a skeptical look.

"Relax. It will be easy."

"If you say so." Sabina shrugged.

At the sound of approaching footsteps, Indira tensed. A different version of Rani opened the door. Indira had never known Rani to look anything short of perfect, but with her face scrubbed clean of makeup and her hair scraped back into a careless pony-tail, she looked years younger. Run-down, as if she hadn't been sleeping. Dark circles shadowed her large eyes as she glanced away from the phone in her hand, surprise registering on her face.

"Indira, we weren't expecting guests."

"I hope you don't mind my dropping by unannounced. I brought you something." She thrust the plain pink bakery box into Rani's hands. "May I come in?"

Rani shot an apprehensive glance over her shoulder, reminding Indira of the way Hazel looked when she was about to disobey. Backing away from the door, she allowed them to enter.

"Coconut barfi. It's Amar's favorite. I thought it would be a nice treat on such a gloomy day. This is Sabina Dewan. She's a wedding planner."

"A wedding planner?"

"Oh, yes. She comes highly recommended."

Rani eyed Sabina with an incredulous look, as if she couldn't quite figure out what Indira was doing here and why she would have brought someone like Sabina along. Indira smiled.

"You look shocked."

"Well, I...I am. Last time I saw you, you seemed upset to learn that the wedding was still on."

Indira wrapped an arm around Rani's shoulders and gave her a sisterly hug. She steered them down the hall to the large living room.

"I'm sorry. It was unkind. I was just so shocked, you know, with everything going on. I came to apologize for my behavior and to bring someone who could help."

"Help what?"

"Plan the wedding, of course."

As if suddenly remembering her manners, Rani gestured toward the pristine white sofa and loveseat, which looked straight out of a showroom.

"Please sit. I'll get my mother and make some tea."

"Thank you. Tea would be lovely."

Rani left the room while Sabina and Indira took a seat on the off-white sofa opposite the windows. Sabina set her purse down.

"Wedding planner? Are you kidding me?" she murmured. "I'd be better suited for the role of divorce attorney."

"How hard can it be? Number of guests. Food. Where to hold the reception. Here, I downloaded some questions. Keep them busy while I..."

Indira slid a folded sheet of paper from her pocket and handed it to Sabina.

"While you...?"

Sabina raised her eyebrows and let the question hang. Indira answered with an enigmatic smile. Rising from the sofa, she approached a grouping of framed photographs that hung on the wall. Family photos. Most were old. Some went back decades. From the style of dress and the landscape, she could tell they were taken in India. Her parents had similar photos of aunts, uncles, grandparents, and cousins that she and Amar had never met.

One photo caught her eye—an image of a younger Falguni in her mid-twenties beside a much prettier girl. A relative of some sort. The two young women bore a passing resemblance to each other, but the resemblance the prettier woman bore to Rani was striking.

Sometimes family characteristics skipped a generation. Her

own mother was always going on about how much Indira resembled her grandmother.

Indira's musings were cut short by Falguni's entrance. Like Rani, she looked exhausted. Puffy bags sagged beneath her eyes. Her hair looked slightly mussed, as if she had just woken from a nap.

"What a surprise. We weren't expecting guests." The cool note in Falguni's tone was far from welcoming.

"Please excuse the intrusion. What a lovely group of family shots. I was particularly struck by this one." Indira pointed to the photograph of Falguni with the younger woman. "Is this your cousin?"

"Sister," Falguni said.

"I didn't know you had a sister."

"She died shortly after that was taken."

"Oh, I'm sorry," Indira said, drifting away from the wall, back to the sofa where Sabina waited. "I brought a friend with me."

Indira introduced the two women, and Falguni took a seat. Rani entered the room bearing a tray. The coconut barfi was arranged on a chipped china plate and tea was served.

"What makes you think we need a wedding planner?" Falguni asked, glaring over the rim of her teacup at Indira.

Indira brushed the question away with a dismissive wave of her hand.

"Who couldn't use a wedding planner? I mean, there are so many details, and since Mom's been sick, she hasn't been able to help out as much as she would have liked. You shouldn't have to do all the work yourself."

Sabina hid an amused smile behind her teacup and Falguni frowned.

"I really don't think—"

"Oh, please," Sabina interrupted, setting her teacup down.

"We don't have to make it anything formal. We could just talk, jot down some ideas. How would that be?"

When Falguni didn't object, Sabina forged ahead.

"How big a wedding are we talking? Last week I finished one with three hundred guests."

Rani shot an apprehensive glance at her mother before answering. "Nothing that large. Maybe a hundred and fifty guests or so."

"That's a good size. Have you already decided on a venue?"

"Not yet," Falguni answered. "The date is..."

"Flexible," Rani finished.

"Good." Sabina smiled. "That's good. It gives us plenty of options."

Pleased to see how easily Sabina fell into character, Indira rose from the couch. "Excuse me. Would you mind if I used your restroom?"

Rani gestured toward the hallway. "It's down there. Second door on the left."

With a nod, Indira left the room. The deeper into the house she went, the shabbier things looked. Bypassing the powder room, Indira headed for the stairs. Taking them two at a time, she climbed on tiptoes, careful not to make a sound.

She paused at the top of the staircase and studied the layout of the rooms. Straight ahead, a set of double doors opened onto the master suite. Another bedroom and bathroom lay to the left. Creeping silently down the hallway, she peeked through the open door to the master suite.

Heavy drapes blocked the light, casting the room in shadows. Indira ducked inside. This room lacked the carefully cultivated showy quality of the rooms downstairs. The bed wasn't made. The duvet cover was thrown back, revealing rumpled sheets, as if Falguni had risen in a hurry. Steep mounds of dirty laundry were piled against the wall, emitting the faint odor of jasmine and sweat.

Indira thought about her mother's room, which was always meticulously neat. Her mother couldn't stand clutter and had spent most of Indira's teenage years haranguing her about leaving a mess. Even with her health failing, her mother would never let her house fall into such disarray.

Using the flashlight app on her phone, Indira swept the light across the room, looking for a reflection of glass, plastic, something shiny in the shape of her brother's Google Pixel device. Dresser drawers hung open. Costume jewelry littered the top of the chest. Nothing. No phone.

She moved to the nightstand, which was piled high with magazines and pocket novels. A pair of reading glasses perched precariously on top. She opened the drawers and rummaged through the contents. Bills. Lots of bills. Some marked in yellow. "Past Due" written in bold letters.

A pill bottle rumbled off the table and rolled across the floor. Silently cursing her clumsiness, Indira dropped onto all fours and shone the light under the bed skirt. Amid the thick dust, she caught sight of the bottle. Grasping it, she shone the light on the prescription label. Restoril. Indira snapped a photo and set the bottle back on the nightstand. A quick Google search told her what it was for. Insomnia.

Scrambling to her feet, Indira exited the bedroom and hurried down the hall. Voices floated up the stairs. Below, she could hear Sabina's valiant attempts at making cheerful conversation and knew she had to hurry.

Much longer and they would notice her absence.

The second door opened to a large, impersonal bathroom. Bypassing it, Indira moved to the closed door at the end of the hall. It was Rani's room. She recognized the subtle scent of Rani's perfume—orange blossoms and spice.

Like Falguni's room, Rani's was messy. Filled with cheap furnishings. Clothes were strewn everywhere—on the bed, on the carpet, and heaped on the closet floor. There was makeup, perfume, shoes.

Above the dresser hung a mirror with photographs pressed into the frame. Snapshots of friends and family. There was one of Rani with Amar. Rani beamed at the camera with her arm wrapped around Amar's. Her brother's smile was stilted and failed to reach his eyes. There was a photograph of Rani as a toddler being held by a man. The man looked to be Rani's father. She recognized the woman standing with them as Falguni's sister. Adoration softened the woman's face. Joy lit her eyes. A pang of sympathy passed through Indira as she studied the photo. How much better would Rani's life have been if she had been raised by this woman instead of Falguni?

She was taking too long. Tearing herself away from the photographs, she moved to the bedside table. Falguni's nightstand had been stacked with books but Rani's had a shiny new tablet device. Half-empty bottles of nail polish were carelessly strewn on top of the tablet's screen. Indira shook her head. Careless.

Brushing the bottles aside, she flicked on the power button. The lock screen flashed, demanding a PIN. She made a few random guesses. Not surprisingly, they were rejected, and with time quickly running out, Indira gave up.

She opened the drawer. Digging beneath the box of tampons, she found what looked to be a journal. Rani's handwriting swirled across the pages in an airy, slanted script. Pen and ink drawings cluttered the margins.

Indira had no idea that Rani was an artist. The drawings, though hastily penned, were unmistakable. Falguni angry. Amar smiling. And... Her pulse rocketed as she caught sight of another familiar face. Mallory sleeping. Or dead. *Holy shit.*

She slid the journal beneath her sweater and tucked it into the waistband of her pants, anxious to see what other secrets it contained. Near the back of the drawer, a flash of black plastic caught her eye.

A phone.

Indira snatched it from its hiding place. It was a Google Pixel with a simple black case, just like her brother's.

Indira thumbed the power button, but nothing happened.

It was dead.

"What are you doing?" Rani demanded.

Caught red-handed, Indira froze, grasping for something to say. Fury filled Rani's eyes as she strode from the doorway into the room, ripping the phone from Indira's hand.

"What are you doing in here?"

"I was looking for the bathroom and I..." Indira stammered, knowing full well that whatever excuse she could come up with would sound feeble. "What are you doing with my brother's phone?"

The anger that drained from Rani's face was replaced by a frigid stare.

"It's mine."

"But yours was downstairs. It has a purple case. You were on it when we came."

"It's an old one."

"Then why does it have the same case as Amar's?"

"Get out of my room."

Indira's gaze dropped to the pocket where Rani had stuffed the phone, but as if sensing her intent, Rani stepped away, putting some distance between the two.

"I said get out."

"Rani! Indira!" Falguni called from downstairs, jolting Indira into motion.

Rani cast her suspicious gaze around the room, as if convinced Indira had stolen something. Indira emerged into the hall. By the time she reached the top of the stairs, Falguni stood at the bottom, arms folded, frown lines carved deep into her furrowed brow. She looked furious.

"What were you doing up there? Stealing?"

"Stealing? No, of course not." Indira reached the bottom of the stairs and gestured for Sabina to fall in. "I hope my friend was able to help. We should probably be going."

Sabina's lips parted in surprise at the sudden turn of events. Grasping her purse, she rose from the sofa and followed Indira toward the door.

"Well, it was lovely meeting you both. If you need any help with the wedding—"

"We won't be needing your services."

Falguni slammed the door. As they rushed to the car, Indira resisted the urge to look back.

"What the hell was that about?" Sabina asked, turning the key in the ignition and pulling away from the curb.

"She caught me snooping in her room."

"Oh, crap. No wonder she was angry. I hope it was worth it."

"I think she's got Amar's phone."

"What?"

"I found one just like his in her nightstand. It's got the same case."

Sabina shifted her gaze away from the road and fixed Indira with a thoughtful look. "Is there any way to know for sure?"

Indira shook her head. "It was dead. Without power, I can't ping it."

"According to Amar's alibi, he spent the night at Rani's. If that's true, he could have accidentally left his phone at her place, which is why it's there," Sabina reasoned, putting as much distance between them and Rani's house as quickly as she could. "That place gives me the heebie-jeebies."

Indira had often teased Sabina about driving like her

grandma, but today, she grabbed the armrest as Sabina took the corner fast enough to make the sedan's tires squeal. Within seconds they left the cul-de-sac behind and navigated down the maze of secondary streets leading to the highway.

"I did find something else." She wrestled the journal from beneath her sweater and held it up.

Sabina gaped. "How long do you think it will take them to figure out it's missing?"

"I saw something in here."

"What?"

The rain pounded the car's roof as she quickly searched through the pages, her mind leaping ahead.

"Rani was obsessed with Mallory. I wonder what else is hiding inside that house. I need to call Jason. Tell him what I saw. Maybe he could get a search warrant."

"On what grounds?" Sabina asked. "Breaking into her house and snooping around Rani's room would hardly qualify. You're going to need more than that."

"We didn't break in. We were invited."

"Whatever," Sabina snorted. "I'd hardly call that a lawful search. I—"

The sight of a car hurtling toward them cut Sabina off. A bright flash of silver blinded Indira. Squealing brakes, crunching metal, and breaking glass exploded in a deafening crash. The force of the impact drove Sabina's car sideways through the intersection. Indira's head cracked into the side window.

The journal flew from her hands.

58

Indira's eyes opened. A lightning bolt of pain spiked through her skull and she cringed. The bright lights were blinding, and she squeezed her eyes shut again as she waited for the pain to subside. Dizzy, disoriented, she eased her lids open once more and took in her surroundings. Where was she?

A gauzy halo of light blurred her vision.

"It's okay. You're safe."

She turned her head toward the familiar voice. Even that small movement sent another blistering web of pain shooting through her skull. The intensity of it left her breathless. She blinked again, until at last her vision cleared.

Jason. Dressed in uniform. Looking uncharacteristically grim.

"What happened?" Indira asked.

"You don't remember? You were in an accident. Your car was broadsided. You're in the hospital."

The hospital? She didn't remember anything about the car, or the accident, or... It explained why her head hurt and her body ached as if she'd been hit by a concrete slab. An image surfaced through the fog of her mind.

Sabina. Driving.

"Sabina. Is she okay?"

Moving closer to the bedside, Jason took her hand. "She's getting the best care."

A rush of panic filled her. "That's not an answer."

"Do you remember anything about what happened? Where were you going?"

"Going?"

Indira searched her memory, but it was all a blur. Snatches of images. Nothing more. Tears leaked from her eyes and she carefully shook her head.

"We're still trying to locate the other driver," he said. "It was a hit and run. There were no witnesses. We're canvasing the neighborhood to see if there are any cameras that we can pull footage from."

"Who would do that? Just leave us there?"

"Don't worry. We'll find them."

"Why can't I remember? I need to get out of here."

Indira shifted on the bed, sending embers of pain sparking through her skull. She gasped in another breath. Jason restrained her with a gentle hand.

"You're not going anywhere. After a blow to the head like the one you took, short-term memory loss is common. Get some rest. It will come back to you."

"But Hazel—"

She couldn't leave the dog alone. Jason squeezed her hand.

"I'll pick her up and take her to my place."

"But—"

"Indira!"

The shrill note of panic in her mother's voice cut Indira's objections short. Jason released her hand and stepped away from the bed. Her parents and two of her aunties flocked to the bedside, brushing Jason aside.

"Indira, what happened?" her mother cried.

Stress had drained the color from her mother's face, leaving her pale and drawn. Her hand flew to the bandaged cut on Indira's forehead and stroked it, as if her touch could take away the pain.

"It's okay, Mom. I'm fine," she said reassuringly.

"When we heard you were in an accident..."

Her mother's mouth quivered as she struggled to hold back tears. She shook her head, as if unable to utter the words. Indira patted her mother's hand and glanced past her family to where Jason stood. Their eyes locked. He held her gaze for a long moment before he turned toward the door.

———————————

Hours later, when Indira's father finally convinced them that she was going to be okay and that she needed her rest, they left. Indira closed her eyes, soaking in the relative quiet, grateful to be alone. Her head throbbed from the concussion she'd sustained. She needed time to think, to remember.

The only good news of the day was that Sabina had made it out of surgery and was in stable condition. The feeling that she was somehow to blame for the accident plagued Indira, though she didn't know why.

What had they been doing?

The lapse in memory unnerved her and guilt weighed heavily as she sank lower in the bed. A soft tap at the door roused her from her thoughts. Indira looked up, expecting to see Jason, but found Dylan instead.

Looking pale and anxious, he approached the bed. "I heard about the accident. Are you all right?"

"Reports of my death have been greatly exaggerated," she answered wryly.

The crooked smile she expected never came. Concern filled his eyes. His expression remained somber.

"What happened?" he asked.

"Apparently we were at a four-way stop when a driver plowed straight through the intersection and into us. We never saw it coming."

Dylan shook his head. He carefully perched on the side of the mattress and reached for Indira's hand. His fingers curled around hers and everything about the unexpected contact felt wrong. Indira let her hand rest in his for a few seconds before pulling away. Dylan's expression shifted. A question surfaced in his blue eyes.

"It wouldn't work," she said, skipping ahead a couple steps to the inevitable question that lay between them.

"What?" he asked, though she suspected he already knew.

"You. Me. Us."

A deep hush fell between them. She felt a heavy weight descend upon her chest. She'd be lying to say that she wasn't attracted to him, but something held her back.

"Is this about Jason?" Dylan asked.

Leave it to Dylan not to shy away from the unvarnished truth.

A heated flush warmed Indira's cheeks. She tore her gaze away from his and smoothed the wrinkles from the hospital sheet covering her torso with her clammy palms.

"It's not what you think."

"If you say so."

She cringed at the bitterness in his voice. "If you and I...if we were to become...a thing...how would that work? You're my boss."

Dylan cocked his head and peered down at her with that crooked half smile of his that she liked so well.

"You haven't been to work for weeks, and when you do come back, there's always that architect's role."

He was right. Her objections were lame. As usual, Dylan's quick mind had already identified the crux of the problem, which couldn't be so easily dismissed.

Jason.

Though neither of them had acknowledged it, what had started out as a casual fling had run deeper.

Several seconds passed as Dylan waited for a response. A flicker of pain crossed his face and he rose from the bed.

"Anyway, while we're on the topic of work, HR's been asking questions. I've been covering for you, but it's probably time to make some decisions about when and if you're planning to come back. Once you're out of here, give me a call. We'll talk."

They'd started out as rivals and ended up as friends. At least she hoped they were still friends. A twinge of loss twisted in her gut as she watched Dylan walk away.

59

Indira signed the patient release forms in a rush, anxious to be on her way. She shuffled slowly down the hall toward the elevator and rode it to the seventh floor. Sabina's room was located across from the nurse's station.

The lights were dim when she entered. The woman lying on the bed barely resembled her best friend. Sabina's face was bruised and swollen. Part of her hair had been shaved away. A neat row of staples caught the light, closing the gash on Sabina's head. Indira's knees weakened. She sank into the chair beside the bed. A cast covered Sabina's arm from her hand well past her elbow.

Indira studied her friend, taking stock of her injuries, wishing she would move. A twitch. A shake of her head. Something. The Sabina she knew was always in motion, and even when she sat still long enough to enjoy a social drink, that mind of hers was still going a mile a minute. Indira found Sabina's unnatural stillness deeply unsettling.

The sound of rubber soles on the tiles alerted Indira to the nurse's presence.

"She needs her rest," the nurse explained in a tone that was kind but firm.

"But she's going to be okay?"

"She's getting stronger."

Though it wasn't the ringing endorsement she was hoping to hear, Indira took it as a good sign. Leaving the hospital, she clutched the cell phone in her pocket, barely waiting until she exited through the heavy sliding doors to call Jason. He picked up her call on the first ring.

"How are you?"

"I'm out."

"What do you mean, out?"

Indira stopped at the corner along with a dozen other pedestrians, waiting for the light to change.

"I'm out of the hospital. How's Hazel?"

"Wait. I thought they were going to keep you another day for observation."

"Turns out I'm okay."

She sensed Jason's disapproval in the silence that followed. "Are you with your parents?"

Her parents didn't know about her discharge. He was the first person she had called.

"No."

"Jesus, Indira." She heard him expel an exasperated sigh. "Where are you?"

"I'm heading to the SkyTrain station. Are you home? I'd like to check on Hazel."

"You should be resting."

"I didn't call for a lecture."

Gentle vibrations shook the sidewalk as the SkyTrain rumbled overhead.

"Don't worry about Hazel. She's fine. She misses you. I took her out for a run before work. I'll drop her by when my shift is over. That is, if you feel up to it."

She missed Hazel and longed for the familiarity of home. A blanket. Her couch. Her head was pounding. The short walk from the hospital had taken a toll.

"Yes. That would be great. I could order Chinese."

It felt natural. Almost as if they were a real couple and she sensed Jason's smile. "Sounds like a date."

"Hey, since you're at work, I was hoping you could check something for me."

"What?"

"There should have been a green journal in Sabina's car. Can you see if they found it?"

"Your journal?"

"No."

Jason paused. "If it's not yours, then who does it belong to?"

While she was in the hospital, snippets of Indira's memory had returned. She remembered going to Rani's house. The journal she'd found in Rani's room. The drawing of Mallory she'd found inside. She was anxious to find out what other secrets it contained. Whether there was something in there that might help bolster Amar's defense.

"Rani's. Amar's ex-fiancée."

Current fiancée. Whatever.

"Is this going to be another story like the one about how you ended up with Brock Sinclair's phone?"

A ghost of a smile tugged at the corners of Indira's lips. "Are you asking as a cop or as my...?"

She almost choked on the word boyfriend. The half-finished thought hung between them. On the other end of the line, she heard Jason chuckle, as if he'd read her mind.

"As what, Indira?" he prodded her.

Grateful he wasn't here to see her blush, Indira shook her head. "Nothing."

One by one, she trudged up the two flights of stairs toward the SkyTrain's platform. Before the accident, she could have run up six flights of stairs and barely broken a sweat. But now, fatigued from the effort, she shuffled aside to let her fellow commuters pass. Her pulse thundered inside her head, where a blistering headache raged. Her bruised ribs ached with every breath. Sparks of pain lit up her knee. She angled the speaker away from her mouth so Jason couldn't hear her labored breath.

"I found something in the data implicating Rani's involvement. I'll tell you about it later. In the meantime, can you find the journal?"

"If you promise to go home and rest, I'll see what I can do. Okay?"

"Stop worrying. I'm fine."

"It's just that...the accident."

The smile disappeared from Indira's face as she focused on his intent. "What aren't you telling me?"

"I'm not sure it was an accident."

"What do you mean?"

"I've looked at the photos from the scene. There were no skid marks."

No skid marks?

"As in you think somebody hit us deliberately?"

Jason hesitated. "It's possible. We don't know anything for sure."

Turning away from the railing, Indira climbed the second set of stairs. She reached the platform and swept her gaze across the crowd. There was nothing menacing about the group of commuters gathered impatiently behind the yellow line. They were just regular people going about their everyday lives. No one was looking her way. She was invisible among the crowd. Still,

Jason's warning had raised a note of alarm. Unsettled, she hung back, awaiting the next train.

She'd feel better once she was at home. In her space. Safe.

"Shit," Jason muttered as a call came in. "I've got to go. Text me when you get home?"

"Sure."

"Promise?"

He really was worried. It was sort of sweet.

"First thing," she said.

The rumble of the SkyTrain approaching drowned out Jason's response. The brakes squealed and the train thundered to a halt. Indira hung up. Shoving her cell phone into her pocket, she boarded the last car.

60

WITH EVERY STEP FROM THE SKYTRAIN STATION TO THE CONDO
building, the throbbing inside Indira's skull grew. She shuffled
through the lobby like a zombie and headed for the elevator,
craving the dark quiet of the apartment. While she'd never admit
this to Jason, she was glad Hazel was with him. She had neither
the strength nor the energy to manage another walk today. The
physical exertion of getting home from the hospital on top of the
injuries she'd sustained during the crash had drained her reserves.

Indira fished her keys out of her pocket and cut through the
lobby toward the elevators. A few hours of sleep might give her a
fighting chance of being conscious when Jason arrived. Her heart
lifted at the idea of seeing him again. She didn't know whether the
attraction between them could withstand the toll her complicated
family dynamics would have on any relationship, but Jason
seemed like the kind of guy who wouldn't be intimidated by the
likes of her father.

The bright elevator lights intensified her headache. Indira shut
her eyes. The doors closed and her stomach lurched as the car

moved swiftly up the shaft. The elevator came to a stop, and Indira exited onto the sixth floor. The building manager, Mrs. Ying, was coming down the hall. Catching sight of Indira, she smiled.

"Oh, you poor dear. I heard about your accident. How are you feeling?"

"Just a little stiff and sore, Mrs. Ying. I'm okay."

"Thank goodness. When the policeman came for your dog, I was so worried. He certainly was a handsome one."

Mrs. Ying fanned her face in a comical display that left Indira grinning. The inference was clear. Jason was hot. It was a fact. Mrs. Ying's curious expression slid her way.

"Come to think of it, I didn't know police did things like that. Pick up dogs and such."

Indira's shoulder hitched in a shrug. "He's a friend."

But Mrs. Ying wasn't so easily fooled. "A boyfriend?"

"No. Maybe."

Mrs. Ying looked pleased by the news. "I wish my daughter could meet someone like that. So handsome. And a police officer. Maybe he has a friend. Oh, by the way, your cousin stopped by."

"My cousin?"

"Or maybe it was your auntie. Anyway, she wanted to pick up a change of clothes, for when you left the hospital."

"When was that?"

"Not long. Maybe fifteen minutes ago."

Mrs. Ying's glance strayed to the dried blood on Indira's torn jacket. The terrible thought that it might be Sabina's blood struck Indira, and she felt sick. She longed for a nap, but she would shower first.

Other than Jason, she hadn't asked anyone to stop by her apartment, but then, that was just the kind of thing her family would do. Not wanting her family to worry if they showed up at the hospital to find her gone, she resolved to send a text letting them know that she was home.

"Thanks, Mrs. Ying."

Indira slid the key into the lock and opened the door. A jab of pain shot down her back as she removed her jacket. She tossed it on a nearby chair and shot a longing glance toward her bedroom door, where her soft bed beckoned, but headed down the short hallway toward the bathroom instead. The warm water would soothe her aching muscles and make for a better sleep.

Water hissed from the showerhead. Steam fogged the mirror as Indira scrubbed the film from her teeth. She bent over the sink to spit out the foam when a noise from the bedroom sent a chill racing up her spine.

Was her cousin or auntie still here?

"Hello?" she called.

Her heart thudded like a sledgehammer inside her chest as Indira eased quietly down the hall. The bedroom door sat partially closed, obscuring her view of the room. She paused, holding her breath, not making a sound, straining for any indication that something wasn't right. Indira angled her body and peered through the narrow gap. The blinds were closed, engulfing the room in shadows.

Cold fear prickled in the pit of Indira's gut. She wished Hazel was here. Or Jason. With the flat of her trembling hand, she pushed the door open and scanned the room. Nothing looked out of place. It felt as if the room was looking back at her, wondering if its long-term resident had taken one too many hits to the head and had somehow gone insane.

Indira let out a nervous laugh. *Seriously.* The thump had probably come from next door. Nothing to worry about. Jason's paranoia about the accident had rubbed off on her. Exiting the bedroom, she traversed down the hallway toward the bathroom.

Halfway down the hall, a shadow flickered in the mirror above the accent table, and Indira's heart stopped. Adrenaline scorched through her veins like battery acid.

Danger.

A figure darted from the bedroom and rushed toward her. Indira gasped. *A black hoodie. A mask.* And then the assailant slammed into her.

Knocked off balance, Indira pitched forward and crashed into the accent table. A blistering pain lit up her side as the corner of the table impaled her ribs. Her skull cracked into the mirror and sent it sailing toward the floor.

The mirror shattered. Glass flew everywhere. Instinctively, Indira lunged for the fleeing assailant. She wrapped her arms around the figure's legs and held on tight. The intruder stumbled, arms flailing in a desperate attempt to regain their balance. A heel popped up and cracked into Indira's jaw.

Stars of pain danced behind Indira's eyes, causing another searing dose of battery acid to fire. Her vision dimmed and she lost her grip. Lurching forward, the intruder fell and slammed into the floor. Indira heard a shrill cry. The suspect lay spread-eagle, sprawled amid the silver shards of glass strewn across the floor. Crimson blood seeped through the hoodie, pooling beneath the assailant's side.

Her chest heaving, her head throbbing, Indira struggled to her knees and crawled toward the figure.

The assailant grunted and started to move. Indira made a grab for the hoodie. Clenching the soft fabric in her fist, she yanked the figure closer. Using her weight to pin the suspect down, Indira ripped the mask free. The world shifted on its moorings as the intruder's face came into focus.

That face. She knew that face.

Dark eyes burned bright as coals as they bored into hers.

"What the hell...?" Indira gasped. "Rani?"

61

THE SOUND OF HER NAME JARRED SOMETHING LOOSE IN RANI.

"Where is it?" she gasped.

"What?"

"The journal!"

Indira rolled onto her knees and Rani sat up. She tore a silver shard of mirror from her side and dropped it to the floor. Her trembling hands pressed against the wound, staunching the flow of blood.

Indira raised her palms. "It's not here. I don't have it."

Rani hissed. Indira recoiled from the fear and fury that blazed in Rani's eyes, and she knew in that moment that she was seeing a side of Rani she never imagined existed. She had thought Rani benign, submissive, but she was wrong. Dead wrong. The woman sitting less than a meter away was a far different creature. Desperate. Capable of violence.

Rani lurched to her feet and staggered for the door. Head booming, numb with shock, Indira let her go. In the seconds that ticked by, Indira's pulse slowed.

She half-crawled, half-limped into the kitchen to retrieve her phone. Her hands shook as she called Jason.

"I expected you to be asleep by now."

The warmth of his greeting caused the dam to crack, and tears streamed down Indira's face. She was sobbing too hard to speak, overwrought by a barrage of emotions, too powerful to ignore. Horrified by how easily her safety had been breached. Relieved that Rani was gone. Terrified by the realization of what might have happened to her.

"Rani..." she managed between gasps.

"Calm down. Are you okay? I can't understand what you're saying."

"I got home and—" She broke off. Her breath hitched with a sob. "And Rani was here."

Indira sank to the ground, her back pressed against the cupboards as she forced herself to focus.

"It was Rani. She was in my apartment. She has Amar's phone. When I saw the data, I wondered, but I never thought she was crazy. Homicidal."

"Stop. Back up. Rani was at your place?"

"Yes, she lied about being a relative and talked the building manager into letting her inside. She was here looking for the journal I stole. Did you find it? The journal?"

"Not yet."

"You've got to find it, Jason. I saw Rani's cell phone data. She was stalking Mallory. She was inside Mallory's house. I was going to tell you, but..."

But then the accident happened and messed up her memory. Until just now, she had forgotten all about the data that had sent her to Rani's house.

"Wait. Are you saying that Rani was inside Mallory's house the night she was killed?" Jason asked, stunned.

"No, eleven days before. She may have gone there intending to kill Mallory but lost her nerve, or...I don't know. All I can say for sure is that she was stalking Mallory. She's crazy, Jason. I think she killed Mallory and brought Amar's phone with her to frame him."

She heard the long exhale of Jason's breath as the impact of her words sank in. "Where is she now?"

"Gone."

"We have to find her," Jason said.

"And the journal. It may have evidence that could help Amar."

Hope cut deep. Indira held her breath, awaiting Jason's response.

"Dammit, I shouldn't have let you go home alone. We need to get you somewhere safe. I'm on my way."

The vehemence of his words betrayed the depth of his feelings, and an unexpected rush of warmth flooded through her. She tipped her aching head back and rested it against the cupboards.

"No. Get the journal. I'm okay."

"Are you really okay?"

A jagged laugh escaped her. "I won't lie. I've had better days. Considering I got attacked by a homicidal freak, I escaped relatively unscathed."

Her joking tone eased the tension she sensed on the other end of the line.

"I'll put a BOLO out on Rani. She won't get far. Call 911. Report the break-in. Wait there until the officers arrive."

"Okay."

"Indira—"

The sudden urgency in his voice made her heart skip a beat. She waited for him to continue, but instead, she heard him sigh.

"Promise me that once you give your statement, you'll get a ride to your parents' house."

"Yes, sir, officer sir."

She snapped off a mocking salute that he couldn't see.

"What, no argument?"

"I'm too tired to argue."

"Now that's something I'd need to see to believe."

Indira emitted a gentle laugh.

"I'll drop by your parents' place later to check up on you."

"You don't have to."

"Like hell I don't," Jason growled.

Indira hung up and waited for the police to arrive.

62

THE PROPERTY OFFICE ON GLEN DRIVE STORED ALL PUBLIC PROPERTY obtained by police, including vehicles and evidence. Jason handed the request to the officer on duty. Keying in the report number, the older man frowned.

"Hasn't been fully processed yet. Might need another day."

"I don't have another day. I need it now."

"You know how many wrecks we get daily? Old people afraid to merge. Assholes who run red lights. Teenagers driving Audis who have no business getting behind the wheel. And that's not the half of it."

Jason's expression darkened. He fixed the guy behind the desk with a hard look. Based on the tuft of unruly white hair and expanding midsection, Jason figured the guy was a short-timer, counting the days to retirement.

"We have a murder suspect in custody. If she walks because you were too busy to rattle some cages, we'll both have a lot of explaining to do."

The officer's mouth pursed as if he'd tasted something foul. "Fine. Fine. But it could take a while."

"I'll wait."

"Yeah."

The officer picked up the phone and Jason stepped away from the desk to check his messages. He wasted no time relaying the good news to Indira.

JASON: Patrol located Rani. They're bringing her in now.
INDIRA: Do you have the journal?
JASON: Working on it.

Jason was banking on the hope that when they logged the contents of Sabina's car, the journal was still in there. For all he knew, it could have been thrown from the car during the crash. Whatever was in it was damning enough for Rani to risk breaking into Indira's apartment.

As bad as things had turned out, they could have been so much worse if Rani had been armed. If he'd obeyed his instincts, there was no way he would have let Indira go home alone. Instead, he'd gotten lucky. As far as strategies went, luck was a lousy one. What if Indira had gotten hurt? He couldn't afford to be so careless next time.

JASON: Do you have your computer with you? It might be useful to compare Rani's movements with the entries from her journal.
INDIRA: No laptop. At my parents' place. Dylan has access. Maybe he could get what you need.
JASON: I'll ask him.
INDIRA: Let me know what happens with Rani.
JASON: Of course. Get some rest!

He smiled at Indira's response. A saluting emoji. Jason pocketed his phone and paced the hallway. It took the better part of an hour, but finally the news came. They'd found a small, green hardcover book that matched the description Indira had given of Rani's journal. The property clerk handed it across the desk.

"This it?"

Jason grinned. "I think so. Thanks, man."

The officer grunted in response and nudged the evidence log across the desk for Jason to sign.

On his way to the elevator, he examined the journal. The smudges of blood smeared across the green cover caused his stomach to twist. Tucking the book under his arm, he pushed the elevator button. The car arrived and he climbed onboard, anxious to get back to the station where Rani was being questioned.

Jason exited the building. On his way to the cruiser, he dialed Dylan's number.

"What's up? Is Indira okay?" Dylan asked.

"Hello to you too, and yes, she's fine."

"Good. Sorry." Dylan's laugh sounded hollow. "When I saw your number, I thought..."

Jason knew that Dylan was worried, the same way he knew that Dylan's feelings for Indira weren't entirely platonic. At some point, they would need to have that discussion, but not today.

"I have a favor to ask," Jason said.

"Sure. Shoot."

"Apparently, Indira's voodoo magic software has surfaced some geodata from Rani's cell phone that proves she went to Mallory's house."

"No shit?"

"That's what she says. Anyway, I could use your help. Would you be able to access the data and let me know what you find?"

"Sure, but why can't she?"

Jason climbed into the squad car and slammed the door

closed. He tossed the journal onto the seat beside him and cranked the engine to life.

"She's at her parents' place and doesn't have access. So, what do you say? Can you hook a brother up?"

"So does this mean you believe us now?"

Jason let the question hang as he exited the parking lot and pulled onto the street.

"I hear the data doesn't lie."

Dylan chuckled. "I'll let you know what I find."

Traffic moved like sludge through the clogged arteries of the downtown core. The trip from the property office to the station took twice as long as it should have, and Jason was glad to get back to the station so he could skim through the book.

Seated at his desk, he began to look through it. It didn't take long to find the pen and ink drawing of Mallory. He kept reading until he reached one journal entry that stopped him cold. He closed the book.

Jason found Detective Bradford standing outside an interrogation room, studying Rani on the video monitor.

"How's it going in there?" he asked.

"She's almost catatonic. Hasn't uttered more than a word or two since she arrived. Hard to believe the same timid woman we interviewed only a few days ago was capable of attacking anyone."

"According to this," Jason held up the journal, "her mother's a piece of work. Abuse a kid long enough, the rage builds up until, one day, the kid snaps."

Bradford gave him a grim nod and Jason handed over the book.

"What's this?" Bradford asked.

"Her journal. The whole reason why she broke into Ms. Saraf's condo. Check out the page I marked. Maybe it will get her talking."

Bradford thumbed to the page in question. When he landed on the highlighted passage, his eyes widened in surprise.

"Damned fine work, Black."

Bradford returned to the interrogation room, leaving Jason to watch on the monitor. Rani's expression remained blank as Bradford took a seat across from her. He placed the journal on the desk. Within seconds, her expression changed. A flicker of recognition lit her eyes as her gaze locked on the green cover.

"I'm going to ask you again, Ms. Khatri, what were you doing in Indira Saraf's apartment?"

Rani's jaw worked, but she said nothing. She never looked up, never moved her gaze away from the green book.

"Do you deny breaking into her apartment?"

Nothing. Bradford waited. A full thirty seconds passed.

"Do you recognize this?" he asked, holding up the journal, as if she needed another reminder of its presence. Rani flinched.

"Where did you get it?"

Ignoring Rani's question, Bradford forged ahead. "Do you deny it's yours?"

"It was stolen from my house."

"So it is yours?"

She crossed her arms and looked away, refusing to answer. Bradford opened the book and skimmed through the pages. He paused and appeared to be reading something before lifting his gaze once more to Rani's face.

"When we spoke last week, you denied knowing anything about your fiancé's affair with Mallory Riggins, but that's not true, is it? You knew he was involved with her. You knew where she worked. In fact, you went to her place on several occasions, didn't you?"

Bradford read a few short excerpts from the journal, but Rani appeared not to listen. Sweat glistened on her forehead, and she looked as if she might be sick.

"How long can you keep up this façade, Rani? We know you've been lying. Your journal proves it. You were involved in Mallory's murder. Was killing Mallory Amar's idea or yours?"

Tears spilled down Rani's cheeks. She shook her head, refusing to speak—to deny the accusation.

"Did you force Amar to kill her?" Bradford drilled.

Rani pitched forward, pinning her elbows on the table. She buried her face in her hands.

"Amar..." Rani stopped, choking on a sob. "Amar had nothing to do with it."

The implication of Rani's admission rocked Jason. He leaned closer to the monitor, not wanting to miss a single word as Bradford continued to press.

"But you wanted her dead, didn't you?"

Rani gave her head a violent shake. "No."

"She was sleeping with your fiancé. You hated her. It's all in here, Rani."

Rani sniffed and wiped her eyes. Jason watched as the struggle to contain her emotions played out across her thin face. The silence in the room deepened. Rani refused to look up.

"No one would blame you for hating her. You went to her place that night to confront them both, and things got out of control."

"No."

"She was the reason Amar broke up with you. You almost killed yourself to get him back."

Rani dropped her face into her hands. Her shoulders shook from the force of her sobs.

Bradford leaned forward, his voice soft.

"It's okay, Rani. Just tell me what happened, and this could all be over."

"He...was mine. She...she didn't deserve...him. She...she had to...die."

63

From the kitchen, Indira heard her mother carrying on a conversation with another woman in the living room. Having just woken up from a nap, she hadn't realized they had visitors. Her phone pinged. She checked the text.

JASON: Rani's confessed. I'll call you when we're done.

The sense of relief Indira felt was almost euphoric. Her body felt buoyant, as if the weight of dread she'd been carrying around in the days and weeks since Amar's arrest had been suddenly lifted and she could breathe again.

It was over. Really over. Amar would be released and soon he'd be home again.

Excited to share the news with her mother, Indira rushed into the living room. The scent of cardamom and chai filled the air. Her mother was pouring tea and serving sweets. The sight of Falguni perched regally on the couch stopped her cold.

"Indira!" her mother cried in surprise. "I didn't know you were home."

"I got here a few hours ago. I was taking a nap. I hope you don't mind."

"Are you feeling all right?" Concern filled her mother's voice, but Indira brushed it aside.

"I'm okay. We can talk about it later."

Indira turned her puzzled gaze on Falguni, trying to figure out what the hell she was doing in her parents' home. She should be at the police station, or on the phone, frantically searching for a lawyer to represent her daughter. Instead, she was here. Was it possible that she didn't know about Rani's arrest?

Deeply unsettled by the presence of their unwanted guest, she fired Jason off a text.

INDIRA: Falguni's here.

"Put the phone away," her mother scolded. "We have guests."

Reluctantly, she complied. "Did you stop by to discuss wedding plans? Where's Rani?"

Though Indira's tone was casual, she caught Falguni's subtle wince. "Rani is visiting friends. She dropped me off so I could visit with your mother."

The lie deepened Indira's suspicions. Falguni reached for her cup of tea. Only then did Indira notice the brace on her wrist, the abrasion over her eye.

"You look as if you've been in an accident, Falguni. What happened?"

Falguni's fingertips grazed the rugged scab on her lined forehead. "A clumsy accident. A fall outside the house. Nothing more."

Falguni's cold eyes settled on Indira and she boldly met the woman's gaze.

"Where did you say your car was?"

"Rani has it."

"Did Mom mention that my friend, the wedding planner, and I were on the way home from your house when we were broadsided by another car? A hit and run."

"How lucky for you that you were not more seriously hurt."

Indira flashed a thin smile. "Lucky. Yes. My friend wasn't so fortunate. She's still in the hospital."

"You have a friend who is a wedding planner?" her mother asked. "How did I not know this?"

"I'll ask her over for tea someday. You'll like her."

"I hope that means—"

Indira cut her mother off mid-sentence. "It doesn't mean anything, Mom. She's my friend and she happens to be a wedding planner."

"What does she say about your obvious disdain for marriage?"

Ignoring her mother's question, Indira held Falguni's gaze.

"Rani and I were quite surprised by your unexpected visit. I was wondering if you were able to find my daughter's journal."

"Me? No. Never saw it. Losing something so personal must be very upsetting, though. I hope Rani recovers it soon."

Falguni's glacial stare made Indira's skin crawl. Oblivious to the menacing undercurrents of the conversation, Indira's mother gestured toward the table.

"Indira, pour yourself some tea and try some of the sweets. Falguni, you do make the best Ghewar. I must get the recipe from you."

"Of course," Falguni acquiesced with a nod.

Her mother adored the sweet cakes soaked in syrup, but Indira had never been fond of them. She found them disgustingly sweet, but there was no polite way to refuse. Transferring a small portion onto a dessert plate, she poured herself a cup of tea and settled in a nearby chair.

"Did I ever tell you about my sister?" Falguni asked Indira's mother.

"You never mentioned. Older or younger?"

"Younger. Her name was Rasha. She was beautiful."

Indira's mother smiled. "Oh yes, I have no doubt. One needs only to look at Rani to know that beauty runs in your family."

Her mother didn't seem to notice Falguni flinch at the remark, but Indira understood. She knew what it felt like to have your appearance constantly critiqued. Falguni was plain. Homely even. For a mother like Falguni, Rani's looks must be an extraordinary point of pride.

"My sister was lovely. She was so beautiful, in fact, that she caught the eye of a young doctor."

"Oh, did she marry a doctor like you?"

The bitterness of Falguni's laugh caused the hairs on Indira's neck to rise.

"She and the doctor *were* married. They had a child. A year after their daughter was born, Rasha died."

Falguni paused and gestured toward Indira's plate, where the Ghewar sat untouched.

"You do not like them?" she asked.

"I suffered a mild concussion in the car accident, and the doctor says that too much sugar will aggravate my symptoms."

"It's just cake, Indira."

Avoiding her mother's reproachful look, Indira took a polite nibble. Just as she feared, it was cloyingly sweet. She set the plate on the table. It was a miracle that consuming a full serving of the stuff hadn't sent her mother into insulin shock.

"Your sister was so young," Indira's mother clucked, full of sympathy. "What happened?"

Falguni's gaze remained on the teacup in her hand. She smiled politely. "My sister was poisoned."

"Poisoned?"

Indira's voice cracked on the word.

64

HALF AN HOUR AFTER SHIFT CHANGE, THE LOCKER ROOM HAD cleared out. Jason shed his uniform and pulled on a pair of jeans. Hell of a long day, but at least it had ended well. He could hardly wait to see Indira, to see the relief in her eyes when he shared the details of Rani's confession.

Pulling his shirt over his head, Jason heard his phone ring. *Dylan.*

"Hey, man, what's up?"

"I've been working on the community algorithm Indira designed, and I found something."

"We know about Rani. She's been arrested. She's being booked now."

The pause on the other end of the line was so long that Jason checked the connection, thinking the call must have dropped.

"You still there?"

"Did Indira explain what the community algorithm does?" Dylan asked.

"It creates a network of links between people and their contacts."

Jason had no doubt the technical explanation was far more complicated. He figured that both Indira and Dylan could go on at length about how it worked and what it meant, but he didn't need that kind of detail.

He slung his bag over his shoulder and left the locker room. Navigating through the maze of cubicles, he passed the detective's bullpen. Bradford gave him a thumbs-up.

"Good work today," the detective said.

"Thanks," Jason answered and continued toward the door.

"You're essentially right. Indira loaded all of Mallory, Amar, and Rani's contacts into the community algorithm to show relationships. Once I got it working, I took the results of the algorithm and fed them into the marketing application to see if there was anyone in the vicinity of Mallory's house around the time she was killed."

"So? We already know that Amar's phone pinged near Mallory's apartment at the time of the murder. Thanks to Rani's confession, we also know that she had Amar's phone and—"

Spying Carla coming toward him, Jason broke off. He abruptly changed course, cutting through the break room to avoid another lengthy and pointless conversation. With the phone still pressed against his ear, he headed for the exit. Jason passed through the station doors, into the underground garage where his car was parked. Static buzzed over the line as the concrete structure deadened some of the signal.

"God," Dylan snapped. "Would you just shut up and listen? Someone else's phone also pinged outside Mallory's house that night."

"Rani's? No," Jason said. "Indira's data showed that Rani's phone was at home."

"That's right. Rani's phone wasn't there but Falguni Khatri's was."

The mention of the name caused Jason's heart to lurch.

Falguni Khatri.

Rani's mother.

"Oh, fuck," he said.

Indira had sent him a text saying that Falguni was at her parents' place, which meant that Indira and her mother were at home alone with a murderer.

65

INDIRA'S MOTHER GASPED. "YOUR SISTER WAS POISONED?"

Falguni's expression darkened. She leaned forward in her chair, her gaze fixed with an intensity that turned Indira's blood to ice.

"The doctor was meant for me, you understand. *I was the healer.* My parents had arranged the match, but then, he met my sister."

The glacial tone in Falguni's voice caused Indira's hands to shake. Her phone buzzed, but she ignored it, unable to tear her eyes away from Falguni's jagged smile.

"Bah. Men. You know what they're like. How easily their heads are turned by a pretty face. My sister was spoiled. Because of her beauty, she got everything she wanted while I—I was expected to make do with her castoffs."

Falguni sat back in her chair, her proud chin held aloft as she stared coldly down her nose at Indira's mother, who looked stricken with shock. Several heartbeats of silence passed. Indira's mind raced.

"Wait? So Rani's not your daughter?"

Falguni turned her frigid gaze on Indira. Her eyes burned as bright as coals.

"She *is* my family. She has *my* blood. From the time she was a baby, I am the only mother Rani has ever known. You understand how it is," Falguni said. Her sharp gaze cut past Indira and settled on her mother. "There is a bond between mother and daughter that can never be broken. From the time they are born, you care for them, cook for them, fix their hair. You raise them to know the things a woman should know. You want the best for them—a good home, a good family, a good marriage."

"A marriage to someone like Amar," Indira said, pointedly. "Your sister stole your husband and so you killed her."

Ignoring Indira's accusation, Falguni continued as if no interruption had occurred.

"When your child hurts, you hurt. When they cry, you cry. Someday, if you ever have a child of your own, you will understand. Everybody wants a boy. A son. But boys are spoiled. They want to control everything and do nothing. But a daughter...a daughter is *everything*."

Fear clawed its way up Indira's throat. She rose from the sofa, positioning herself between her mother and this woman who she now believed was capable of murder. She wanted Falguni out of this room. Out of this house. Out of their lives.

"You need to go."

Falguni uncoiled from her seat like a cobra ready to strike.

"Yes. You're right. I do need to leave. It seems that, thanks to you, *my daughter* is sitting in a police station."

"A police station? What do you mean? Indira, what is she talking about?"

"Your daughter stole something from my house, and now she's going to pay," Falguni hissed.

"I don't understand."

Indira ignored her mother's distress, keeping her eyes pinned on Falguni.

"Rani's exactly where she belongs. She murdered Mallory Riggins and framed my brother for the crime. Then, she offered him a way out—an alibi. But she's not going to get away with what she's done. The police know everything. She confessed, and now she's going to pay for what she did."

Falguni's face convulsed into a mask of pure hatred. Pure evil. The venom in her gaze nearly stopped Indira's heart.

"I sacrificed my life for my daughter. Family means sacrifice. Family means everything. A daughter needs her mother to care for her, to guide her, to help her become the woman she was meant to be. This is a concept you clearly do not understand. But one day, when your mother is gone, you will know I spoke the truth." Falguni's poisonous gaze drilled into Indira. "Without a mother, a daughter is nothing."

Falguni's chilling words hung in the air, brimming with hate. Shaking with rage, Indira advanced toward Falguni and jabbed her finger toward the door.

"Get out. Get out of our house and don't ever come back here. I don't want you or your daughter anywhere near my family again."

"Indira!"

Her mother's cry barely registered. Her whole being was focused on her enemy and her need to drive this menace from their lives. A reptilian smile flickered across Falguni's thin mouth.

Indira's phone rang.

Pulling it from her pocket, she stole a glance at the screen. *Jason.* Jason was calling.

When she craned her head back toward Falguni, the old woman was gone.

66

INDIRA'S HANDS SHOOK UNCONTROLLABLY. SHE PRESSED THE PHONE to her ear.

"It was Falguni," Jason said.

"She was here. She just left."

"Falguni killed Mallory. It wasn't Rani."

Indira's head swam as she tried to absorb what Jason had said.

"Wait. No. Rani confessed."

"She lied to protect her mother."

Her mother? Indira closed her eyes and let out a groan. It made so much sense. Rani wasn't strong enough to kill anyone, but Falguni... Darkness lived inside that woman. She was the very personification of what it meant to be evil.

Indira craned her head toward the window, hoping to catch a glimpse of her, but Falguni was nowhere in sight.

"She's gone," Indira said.

Indira heard a noise. A groan. She whirled around to see her mother doubled over on the floor. A jolt of panic surged through her.

"Mom!" *No.*

"What's wrong?" Jason yelled into the phone.

"It's my mom. She's..." Sweat glistened on her mother's face as she convulsed in pain. "Oh my god, I think...I think she's been poisoned."

A buzz of terror filled Indira's head as she lurched forward and fell to her knees.

"Is she breathing?" Jason asked.

"Yes. I think so. She's unconscious."

"Call 911. Tell them that she's been poisoned with oleander."

"What?"

"Oleander. Yellow oleander."

"What. How do you know that?"

He wasn't here. He couldn't possibly know.

"Indira! Hang up. Call 911. I'm on my way."

Jason's command snapped her out of her stupor, and she hung up. The 911 operator answered the call. Indira choked on a sob as the whole story came pouring out.

"What did she take?"

"Oleander. In the sweets. I—"

Indira broke off. Crouched over her mother's body, tears streamed down her face.

"Mom. Mom!"

"Stay calm. You're doing great. An ambulance is on its way. It should be there soon."

Indira barely heard her. She wished that her father was here. *Amar.* She didn't know what to do. How to save her. The woman who had given her life. Bandaged her cuts. Dried her tears. Taught her to cook. To read. To sing.

Every thoughtless word she had said, every stubborn thought, flooded through Indira's mind, as she stared helplessly down into her mother's face. A hundred arguments. A thousand regrets. The times she had talked back. All of them. She wished she could take all of them back.

But she was too late. There was no way Indira could save her.

"My mother...she's not breathing..."

"Do you know CPR?"

"What? Yes."

"Start compressions. Now. Do you hear me?'

"Yes," Indira croaked.

She folded one hand over the other and pressed her palms into her mother's chest. The next few minutes were a blur. Sweat dripped off her forehead as she counted. Paused. Listened for breath.

In the distance, she heard the far-off wail of a siren. The crash of the door opening. Thundering footsteps entered the room.

"What did she take?"

"Oleander," Indira said, crying. Gasping.

And then somehow, inexplicably, Jason was there. He tore her away from her mother's side as the EMTs went to work.

67

INDIRA LEANED AGAINST JASON IN THE HOSPITAL'S WAITING ROOM, drawing from his strength, his warmth. Her eyes burned from all the tears she'd shed. She felt exhausted. Hollowed out.

"How did you know, about the oleander, I mean?" Indira asked him.

Jason planted a soft kiss on her hair.

"It was in Rani's journal. Her mother poisoned her tea, just enough to make her sick."

It was unthinkable. Monstrous.

"How could she do that? Why?"

"Maybe she thought she could guilt Amar into resuming the engagement," Jason said.

Just like Katie Lord. Katie had engineered her own kidnapping to get her fiancé back. Falguni claimed to be a healer. She'd baked the oleander into the cake she'd fed to her mother. If Indira had eaten the Ghewar, they'd both be dead right now.

"Thank you," she whispered, leaning her head onto his chest, grateful for his quick thinking, for the steadfast solidness that she'd come to rely on over the past few weeks.

"If not for you and your kleptomaniac tendencies, we might never have known."

A tremulous smile touched Indira's lips.

The hospital doors opened. Indira straightened when she caught sight her father's ashen face. He burst through the door, head swiveling in every direction until his gaze locked on hers. Indira rose and sprinted toward him.

"Your mother—"

"She's going to be okay. Dad, she's going to be okay."

"Oh!" His eyes filled with unshed tears. "Oh, thank god."

He pulled back. His gaze fixed on Jason.

"Who's this?"

Indira blushed all the way to her toes.

"This is...Jason. He's my..." A dozen words flashed through Indira's mind as her father waited for her to respond. "He's my boyfriend."

68

Amar awoke before first light. A man of faith might spend the waiting hours praying, thanking god for this unexpected reversal of fortune, that even after hearing the details from his lawyer, Simon, he could not quite believe. Tentacles of desperation and betrayal clawed their way into his heart, leaving behind wounds that would never heal.

He hadn't killed Mallory, but he wasn't innocent either. His inability to speak the truth, his actions, his lies, had caused the people he loved unimaginable pain. Because of him, Mallory was dead. Falguni had determined that he would marry her daughter, and once her mind was made up, nothing could have deterred her from her course. The ensuing tragedy was a weight he would carry with him always.

His family had suffered. Falguni had almost succeeded in killing his mother. His father's business had been decimated. The cost of Amar's defense left their savings drained, and his sister had risked her safety and her job to prove his innocence.

The combined weight of it bowed his shoulders. He sat

hunched on his bunk as the sound of the alarm roused the sleeping inmates. Like clockwork, the rattle of carts bearing breakfast trays filled the pods, along with the voices of prisoners, the guards. Another day, but unlike the many days that had preceded it, this one was different.

Amar rose slowly from the bunk, taking stock of his cell, knowing that this was the last time he would see it. His cellmate, Michael, dangled his legs over the top bunk and gazed down at Amar. A brief smile crinkled the corners of his watery blue eyes set deeply into his weathered face.

"I hear you're sprung, Professor."

Amar's voice was husky with the weight of all he felt. Fear. Apprehension. Hope.

"Yes."

"You got what most of us don't get—a second chance. Don't fuck it up."

"I won't."

Amar stumbled through the morning's activities as if in a trance, half sick with fear that he would wake up and find that this was all a dream. But then the guards came, and a tremor passed through him. For the first time, Amar allowed himself to believe that this was really happening.

Too many nights he'd lain awake on his cot, terrified that this day might never come. He remembered the night he arrived, how they'd dressed him in a smock and placed him on suicide watch. They need not have worried about the first night of his incarceration. The real danger would have come years later, after a false conviction, when all the appeals had run out. The death of hope. It would have been in those dark nights when the thoughts of ending his own life would have grown too powerful to ignore.

The guard escorted Amar through the byzantine maze of hallways in silence. The rituals of the discharge process unfolded without event. He signed for his personal effects, was handed back a manila envelope and a stack of clothes. *His clothes.* Alone, he undressed.

He slid the wool dress pants up his legs and buttoned the waist. Even with the belt buckled to the smallest notch, the pants still gaped around his waist. The cashmere sweater he slid over his head felt impossibly soft. A whisper. A ghost of his former life.

Once dressed, Amar was led down another hallway to a set of doors, and this was where the guards left him. Morning light shone through the windows, penetrating the layer of grime left by the days, weeks, months of rain. Amar straightened his shoulders and emerged out into the day.

The first lungful of air smelled new—like fresh rain and grass. *Life.* The brightness of the morning blinded him, but soon, he saw a familiar shape take form. She was standing in front of a dark car. Her figure, in silhouette, looked slight.

She stood with her hands clasped beneath her chin, bouncing on the balls of her feet. Their eyes met and she burst forward, sprinting toward him. Amar held out his arms and caught her mid-air.

She felt small, and strong, crying and laughing all at once. Amar's heart cracked open with the intensity of what he felt. Pain. Joy. Love.

"Indira," he breathed.

69

AMAR TREMBLED AS SHE HELD HIM. HER ARMS TIGHTENED AROUND his shoulders as if she couldn't quite believe he was real. She had almost lost him, and now she felt as if she never wanted to let go. His body shook, and her gut twisted with a deep pang of sorrow as she realized that he was crying too. The realization came as somewhat of a shock. Since they were little kids, she had never once seen her brother cry.

"It's going to be okay," she whispered. "You're free."

She felt the bones of his shoulders, more prominent than they had been just weeks ago, relax their grip. Her feet touched the ground. Amar pulled back. He averted his gaze, as if ashamed of his tears.

"Come. Our parents are waiting."

Amar followed her to the car and climbed into the back seat. Her eyes locked with Jason's. He stood by the driver's side, waiting patiently. No words passed between them. His smile said everything that needed to be said.

Indira buckled into the passenger's seat and Jason pulled onto the road. There were a million things she wanted to say to her brother, but Indira held back, sensing Amar needed time to process. Finally, once they reached the highway and were heading southwest toward White Rock, he spoke.

"Simon said, if not for you, they never would have figured out what really happened."

Indira's eyes welled. She shot Jason a sideways glance and reached for his hand. He laced his strong fingers with hers as she cleared her throat.

"It was a group effort," she said.

"But I know you. You wouldn't let this thing go until you found out the truth. I owe my life to you, Indira."

"The data doesn't lie," Jason murmured with a crooked smile.

"I'm afraid I drove everyone crazy."

"She does that, you know," Amar said, addressing Jason for the first time. "Fair warning. My sister's relentless."

Jason's grin turned into a soft chuckle. "I'm starting to get that about her. Yeah."

"Have they located Falguni?"

Indira's smile faded. "Not yet. The police are watching the airports, bus stations, train stations, but..."

She raised an upturned palm in a shrug.

"We'll find her," Jason said.

Amar shook his head. "You won't. Falguni is many things, but dumb is not among them. She probably took the first flight out of the country."

Though Jason remained hopeful, privately, Indira suspected the same thing. Falguni had come to her mother's house with a plan, and that plan would have included a way out.

"I still can't forgive Rani," Indira said, her gaze hardening as she stared out at the road unfurling ahead. "She knew that Falguni was planning to kill Mallory, and she did nothing to stop it. And when you were arrested..."

Indira shook her head, her heart as cold and heavy as a stone in her chest. Between the two of them, they had almost destroyed her family.

"Rani's not to blame. Years of living with that woman broke her down. Falguni controlled her every deed, every thought. The poor girl didn't stand a chance."

"You've forgiven her?"

Amar nodded. "In her own way, she tried to save me. The only one I can't forgive is myself."

Amar's words hit Indira with the force of a physical blow. Her whole body rebelled at the idea that her brother blamed himself. But now wasn't the time to challenge him. He needed time to think, time to heal.

"You didn't kill Mallory," Jason said. "Falguni did."

"No, but my lies lit the fuse."

Amar lapsed into silence. Indira sank back into her seat. For weeks, she had seen this as the end of the ordeal, but now she realized that this was only the beginning. She would be there for Amar; she would be strong, make sure he had the support he needed to put his life together again and still give him space.

She could do that.

Half an hour later, they arrived at her parents' house. She cast a fretful glance at the driveway, half expecting to see it crammed with cars. Aunties, uncles, cousins. The whole family gathered to welcome Amar home. But to her relief, the only car in the driveway belonged to her parents. Indira breathed out a sigh.

As she exited the car, her heart ached at the sight of her parents, standing on the path with their arms wrapped around each other, as if combining their strength to withstand the coming storm. Her mother was crying. Amar emerged from the car slowly.

Indira hung back as he walked down the path toward them. Jason rounded the car and stood by her side, looking on while her parents and her brother embraced.

"This is good," he said.

Indira swallowed the lump of emotion in her throat and wiped her eyes.

"Thank you." She gazed up into his dark eyes and was rewarded with a smile that made her pulse quicken. "I mean it."

"You did all the hard work."

"Since when did you become so modest?"

She elbowed his ribs good-naturedly. He caught it and pulled her into a hug. Amar released his parents and the three broke apart. Her father started up the path with a grave look. Indira tensed. Jason's arms fell away.

Her father stepped forward and pulled her toward him. The rare display of physical affection took Indira by surprise, but as the seconds passed, she allowed herself to relax into him, grateful that her family was back together. Releasing his hold, her father blinked back tears.

"Come inside. Your mother has been up since dawn, cooking."

"Of course she has."

Indira shot Jason a fleeting look and advanced toward the house, but her father didn't follow.

"You too, Jason. Join us. Please."

Indira gaped at her father in shock. Jason shook his head.

"Next time. Today's a day for family," he said, meeting Indira's gaze. "I'll call you later."

"You'd better. Go home and walk my dog," she called after him.

Jason snapped off a mock salute. "Yes, ma'am."

EPILOGUE

It was a Friday night, a few days after Amar's release, and the first time Indira had left her parents' place since Amar had been released from jail. Jason had driven all the way to White Rock to pick her up. The dreaded meeting between the parents, although a little awkward at first, hadn't been so bad. Amar was still quieter than she would like, but she began to see glimmers of his old self break through as Jason engaged him in conversation.

"I think my father likes you," Indira said.

"You sound surprised."

"Well, it's just that...they're pretty traditional, you know."

Jason glanced over at her. A flicker of amusement lit his dark eyes. "Huh, I didn't notice. Wait until you meet my family."

Jason's statement sounded ominous, and Indira wondered if they would like her. None of her past relationships had been serious enough to worry much about what his family thought. She was surprised and a little dismayed to realize how much she cared.

"Do you really have three sisters?"

Jason chuckled. "Would I lie about that?"

"Do you think they'll mind that I'm...?"

"Short? Opinionated? Stubborn?"

Indira shook her head. "Not white."

Jason parked the car a few blocks away and killed the engine. The streetlamps overhead illuminated the interior of the car as Indira met his gaze.

"I mentioned that I was adopted, didn't I?"

Indira nodded, wondering what that had to do with anything.

"My sisters were adopted too. I never said they were white. You assumed."

"Oh," Indira said, surprised and intrigued by the revelation.

She swooped toward him. Tipping her head onto his shoulder, she held up her phone and took a quick selfie of the two of them. Clicking on the photo, she attached it to a text message and hit send.

"Who was that for?" Jason asked.

"My mom."

They exited the car and walked through the busy streets toward the Yaletown Brewery. Suddenly, she felt as nervous as a girl on her first date. Together, they walked inside. Indira reached for Jason's hand. She liked the feel of his calloused palm, the way his strong fingers wrapped around hers.

"You okay?" he asked.

"Yeah," she said. "How'd he sound?"

"Dylan?" Jason asked, raising his voice to be heard.

"Yeah. Who else?"

"Just the Girl" by the Click Five blasted through the speakers as they bypassed the hostess. Indira scanned the crowd, looking for him.

"He's fine. Why wouldn't he be?"

"It's just that..."

Because when this whole crazy nightmare began, they kind of had a thing. But that was stupid. True to form, Jason picked up on her train of thought. It was scary how well he read her sometimes.

"You thought he might be heartbroken?"

She shot him an indignant look and swatted his arm, not wanting him to know just how on the nose he was.

"No, I just thought...that maybe it would be awkward. That's all."

"His ego might be a little bruised, but he's fine," Jason assured her.

Dylan was sitting in a booth in the corner, but much to Indira's surprise, he wasn't alone. Sabina was sitting with him.

Indira's heart leapt at the sight of her friend, and she rushed over to greet her. Sabina's arm jutted out at an odd angle because of the cast. One side of her hair was shaved short, the red arc of the wound beneath still visible along the curve of her skull. The two exchanged a gentle hug.

With a laugh, Indira skimmed a palm along the stubble on the side of her own head. "Look at that. We're twins."

Sabina flashed a grin. "Who would have thought it? Indira the fashion trendsetter."

Indira settled in the booth across from Sabina, unable to tear her gaze away from the bruising still visible on Sabina's face.

"When did you get out? Why didn't you call me?"

"You needed time with Amar. How is he?"

Indira hesitated. "He's okay. It's going to take time for him to adjust. He says he's going to work with my dad. I think he feels guilty for what he put my parents through. What about you?"

Sabina gave a brittle laugh. "I won't be doing hot yoga any time soon, but the doctor says I will be fine."

"Good. Good. I'm so glad. I never would have brought you to Falguni's house had I known what she was capable of doing."

"No big. I never much liked that car anyway."

A burst of laughter rippled through the group, releasing any tension that remained. Indira's gaze drifted across the table toward Dylan.

"And you. How can I thank you? Jason told me what you did. You found the missing link to Falguni."

Dylan smiled and took a sip from his pint glass, which was filled with an amber ale.

"Technically, you found the link. The data doesn't lie. The community algorithm you designed revealed the truth. You were so focused on Rani that you didn't see it."

"Confirmation bias," Jason said. "It's human to bend a situation to fit your needs, especially when you're emotionally involved."

"Yeah." Indira released a sigh. "Thank you."

Sabina shook her head. "I can't believe Falguni murdered Mallory. I almost feel bad for Rani."

"She was trying to push Rani to do it, but Rani just didn't have it in her," Jason said. "The stuff we found in her journal...years of psychological abuse. Sad."

A waiter stopped by the table, and they ordered drinks. The ins and outs of the case were discussed until they'd exhausted all conversation. And when Jason's hand rested on Indira's thigh, it felt natural. For a brief second, Dylan's blue eyes met Indira's and then he reached for Sabina's hand.

A look of understanding dawned across her face, erasing all lingering traces of guilt. Sabina smiled shyly, looking happier than Indira had ever seen her.

"So, when are you coming back to work?" Dylan asked. "Preet's been asking if you're planning to take the architect's role she talked to you about."

"You mean the one in San Jose?" Sabina asked.

Indira nodded. Jason's hand began to slide away from her thigh, but Indira's grip tightened, holding it in place.

"I'm not taking it. There's no way I can leave my family now."

"I figured you'd say that, so I convinced Preet that there's no reason why the role can't reside in Vancouver. You could take the job and stay."

Indira was touched that he'd done all that for her. It made what she had to say harder.

"Thank you, Dylan. Really. But..."

"But?"

"But I'm not coming back," she said in a rush, anxious to get it out.

Dylan's eyes rounded in surprise. Sabina looked equally shocked.

"There's an opening for a crime analyst at the station," Jason said, interrupting the silence. "Indira's decided to apply."

Sabina shook her head. "So you're going to strap on a cape and become a crime fighter?"

Indira laughed. "Nothing so dramatic as that, but yeah."

"Hang on, weren't you the one on the warpath because we were stomping all over an individual's right to privacy?" Dylan's eyebrows arched as he waited for Indira's reply.

It was true. She had believed they had no right to gather the kind of information they did, but without it, her brother would have been convicted of a crime he didn't commit. Indira had wrestled long and hard with the ramifications of what she'd done. In the end, she realized that there were no easy answers.

"We're going to use that incredible brain of hers to lock up more bad guys," Jason said, interrupting her thoughts.

Indira squeezed his arm. "Not exactly. I'm going to use this incredible brain of mine to make sure that no innocent person is ever locked up for a crime they didn't commit. Not on my watch."

Jason's smile widened.

"Fair enough. The point is, we make a pretty good team."

THE END

I SINCERELY HOPE you enjoyed reading *The Perfect Brother*. If you did, please leave a review. Reviews are one of the primary ways new readers find my work. If you're interested in reading more of my stories, you can find a full list of my books on the "Also By" page. If you like your stories a little more on the gritty side, check out my Holt Foundation series. If you're looking for something a little lighter and enjoy small-town crime thrillers, you'll love the award-winning Lacey James Series.

AFTERWORD

Dear Reader,

Thank you for reading *The Perfect Brother*. It's been over twenty years since I lived in Vancouver, BC and writing this book brought back so many memories of my time there. The apartment where Mallory lived bore more than a passing resemblance to the tiny apartment where my husband and I lived when we first moved to the area, right down to the barking Chow upstairs, who may actually have been named JoJo. Like Indira, I too worked at a tech company in Yaletown right across the street from the Yaletown Brewery. I spent my weeks working on technical projects for some of the biggest software vendors, and Friday nights drinking wine with my co-workers as the work week came to a close. Good times.

Writing this book has been a journey, and many of my ideas about the story evolved over time. Likewise, data privacy laws continue to evolve, and many of the loopholes that Indira exploits during the course of her investigation may have already or could soon be closed, but the idea that big data is the life's blood for artificial intelligence and predictive analysis are most definitely not science fiction. It's there in the ads you see on your phone and your online experiences every day and will only continue to expand its reach.

I want to take a moment to thank some of the people that helped me along the way. My editor, Mark Cooper, who stuck with me through several iterations of the story, helping me get the character arcs right. My copyeditor, Audrey, who is a master at the dance of commas. My friend, Ken, who works in big tech, and planted the seeds for this story one night over a bottle of wine in Cannon Beach, Oregon. If ever there was a place for inspiration, Cannon Beach is pretty much it. My tireless beta readers— Michele, Misty, and Eva who read several drafts and provided their encouragement and insights. Writing about characters who come from a different cultural background than mine was a risk, but my beta readers loved the family scenes and if anything, were anxious to learn more.

Thanks to my good friend Varsha who I collaborated with during the editing phase and who provided insights into the cultural aspects of the story. One of the reasons why I chose to write the story from this perspective was the appreciation and admiration I have for the sense of family demonstrated by some of my friends who come from cultural backgrounds different from mine. I admire the relationships they have with their families— not only their closeness, but their sense of loyalty and duty. I can only hope that I got the details right.

A special thanks goes to my friend, Cara. I first met Cara when I was attending a Citizen's Police Academy hosted by the department she works for, and she was such a big help in ensuring that the details of Indira's digital endeavors rang true. She, along with Tim, a detective in the same department, and Paige were all pivotal in answering my procedural questions.

And last but not least, a big thank you to my husband who is not only great at providing honest feedback, but never complains when I spend my weekends glued to my laptop working on a story. I wouldn't be able to do any of this without his support.

One of the things I love most about writing fiction is being able to envision life from a different perspective. I enjoy the process of crawling inside my characters minds and discovering what makes them tick. Both Indira and Amar were fascinating characters to write about.

Wishing you and yours all the best!

ABOUT THE AUTHOR

Chris Patchell is an award-winning USA Today Bestselling Author who started writing to curb the homicidal tendencies she experienced during her daily Seattle commute. She writes gripping suspense thrillers with romantic elements set in the Pacific Northwest and believes good fiction combines a magical mix of complex characters, compelling plots, and well-crafted stories.

Over the years, she has written numerous popular books and series, including bestsellers *Deadly Lies*, *In the Dark*, and her most recent collection of small-town crime novellas, the *Lacey James Series*. Along the way, her writing has won several awards, including a 2022 Next Generation Indie Book Award, an Indie-Reader Discovery Award, and a Pacific Northwest Literary Award.

To learn more about Chris and her work, sign up for her newsletter on her author website, or follow her on social media.

Facebook | Twitter | Instagram

ALSO BY CHRIS PATCHELL

THE JILL SHANNON MURDER SERIES

Deadly Lies

Vow Of Silence

THE HOLT FOUNDATION SERIES

Justice for All

In The Dark

Dark Harvest

THE LACEY JAMES SERIES

Find Her

Save Her

Tell Her

Hide Her

STANDALONES

Deception Bay

The Perfect Brother